PINO
D1374141

WEAK WITH LONGING

"Andrea?" Her fingertips grazed his cheek, outlined his lips, moved to his chin and lingered there. "Dear bear." Her smile was tremulous.

"I am no bear," he said, his voice husky with repressed desire. "That was no bear hug. I am a man. At the moment, an overeager man who feels himself growing weaker with every breath he takes."

"Valeria has warned me that you are not yet fully recovered," she said. She glanced toward the bed. "Do you want to lie down?"

"There is nothing in this world I want more than to lie down there," he said. "But only with you."

"Oh." Her silver eyes grew large and round and Andrea saw comprehension flood into her gaze. "Oh," she said again, with new understanding.

"Andrea, I am sorry. I did not mean to—yes, I did. I wanted you to kiss me. But I did not want to embarrass you."

"I wanted to kiss you, too," he said, charmed by her innocent honesty. "But it would not be wise to do it again, and certainly, it would be unwise to do it here, in my bedchamber, while I am unclothed."

Other *Love Spell* and *Leisure* books by Flora Speer:

LADY LURE
FOR LOVE AND HONOR
LOVE JUST IN TIME
VENUS RISING
A LOVE BEYOND TIME
NO OTHER FOOL
A TIME TO LOVE AGAIN
DESTINY'S LOVERS
BY HONOR BOUND

FLORA SPEER

LOVE SPELL NEW YORK CITY

LOVE SPELL®

September 1996

Published by

Dorchester Publishing Co., Inc.
276 Fifth Avenue
New York, NY 10001

Printed in the United States of America.

Rose
Red

Prologue

"They have gone," said Niccolò Stregone in answer to the question just posed to him. "They have fled away and disappeared, no doubt with the aid of the ever-faithful Bartolomeo. You need not worry about them any longer."

"No?" Marco Guidi cast a dark and marveling look upon his associate, wondering how the man could be so unconcerned that three of their most important intended victims had escaped.

Niccolò Stregone was unusually short, a wiry man with a long, pointed chin and lank black hair. Seeing him against the background of the ducal reception room, with its overturned furniture, slashed and torn draperies, bloody stains on floor and walls, with the last of the contorted bodies being dragged away by the men-at-arms, Marco Guidi decided that Stregone looked perfectly at home in the midst of the hellish scene. The red glare of the fires outside the palace, which shone through the long windows and flickered over Stregone's angular, swarthy features, only added to the infernal effect. Marco Guidi almost expected to see horns sprouting from Stregone's forehead.

In a time when most people were known by their baptismal names, and those who had reason to do so boasted freely of their family names, this man preferred to be known by the name he had given to himself. Stregone. *Wizard.* Marco Guidi thought *evil dwarf* might be a more accurate appellation. No one knew the true name of Stregone's family, or the name of the place where he had been born. Still, for all the mystery surrounding Stregone, not to mention the distaste he aroused in the hearts of honest folk, he had proven to be both useful and thorough in fulfilling the most dangerous or delicate assignments. It was astonishing that he had failed in an important aspect of this particular plan.

"Why didn't you kill them, too?" Marco Guidi demanded, annoyed and secretly fearful because his expressed wishes had not been carried out to the final detail.

"I have been occupied with far more important concerns than mere women and children. As you well know, it is largely thanks to me that this particular eagle will not fly again," Stregone said.

With deliberate care he wiped the bloody blade of his dagger on a tattered shred of green velvet curtain. The velvet was embroidered in golden thread with a design of eagles with outspread wings. Stregone made certain that at least one pair of golden wings was tarnished with red, then took an extra moment to be sure the ornate hilt of his dagger was clean. Satisfied, he sheathed the weapon. Finally, he looked around, his thin lips twisting in distaste.

"This room is a mess. You will want new draperies

at the windows and new furniture.''

''It would appear that you and the men you led were more vigorous than I anticipated. Or was it that you met more opposition than you expected?''

Marco Guidi turned his attention from the ruined reception room to what was happening in the piazza. Outside the tall windows the night was loud with the cries of those who had opposed the deposition of the Farisi family and the ascent of the Guidi. The noise would soon be silenced by resignation, for what had happened in the ducal palace on this autumn evening was an event common enough in the city-states of Italy during the mid-fifteenth century. A little money distributed here, a touch of clever treachery there, an accomplished assassin who knew exactly when and how to strike—that was all it took to effect a change of rulers. In another hour, after his men had finished securing the city, Marco Guidi would be proclaimed the new duke of Monteferro.

Unfortunately, the new duke owed Niccolò Stregone a debt for this day's work. Marco Guidi hated Stregone, but the little man, demon that he was, knew too many secrets and had too many powerful contacts to be eliminated as easily as the late duke. Truly, Girolamo Farisi had been a political innocent to trust a creature like Stregone. Or to trust Marco Guidi.

''You have accomplished all that you said you would do.'' Marco Guidi could not bring himself actually to touch Stregone or to clasp his hand in thanks, but he did summon up a false smile. ''However, I am not sure that what we have done here will be enough.''

''Indeed?'' said Stregone. ''Why not, when we have been so successful? Your position is secure. I have seen to it.''

''True enough,'' said Marco Guidi. He uttered a dissatisfied sigh that appeared to contradict his own words and then went on to explain. "Being Duke of Monteferro is all very well, but as you are aware, I have a large family to care for. Some of my relatives are remarkably greedy."

"Greedy, my lord?" Stregone never smiled. He drew back his lips instead, in an unpleasant grimace. His small, oddly delicate fingers stroked the gold-and-enamel hilt of his dagger, lingering on the green stone set at the top. "I know a permanent cure for greed."

"No, that will not do. Not for blood relatives." Marco Guidi shut his lips on the comment that Stregone should have known as much. For an instant he allowed his dislike of Stregone to show, before he quickly covered his uneasy emotions with another oily smile. "Eventually, to pacify certain of my relatives, I am going to require greater resources than even wealthy Monteferro has to offer. Not immediately, you understand, but in time. To that end I have conceived a plan that I am certain you will appreciate, for it will provide you with remarkable opportunities to exercise your talents. And to become wealthy, if you wish."

Stregone said nothing to this speech. He simply watched with unwavering black eyes as Marco Guidi moved to the windows to look northeastward, as if it were possible to see through the darkness, across the wide plain that stretched from the walls of Monteferro to the boundary of the next city-state. A wise man never turned his back toward Niccolò Stregone, and Marco Guidi did not do so now. With a skill born of long acquaintance with Stregone, he appeared to be leading the little man toward the window to show him the possibilities that lay in the broad vista beyond the palace—and in the future.

"Suppose," said Marco Guidi, using his smoothest,

most persuasive voice, "that you were to fear for your life if you remain in Monteferro and, thus fearing, you were to flee the city to seek sanctuary at another court. At this very wealthy, nearby court, you would no doubt be welcomed for your well-known devotion to the late Duke of Monteferro, as well as for your diplomatic abilities and your wisdom as a councilor, qualities which that same late, much lamented duke frequently praised." He paused, eyebrows raised in a silent question, watching his companion's reaction.

"I am listening." Stregone's dark eyes were unfathomable. "Do go on."

"There may be some suspicion of you at first, but no matter. Given nothing to feed upon, all suspicions pass in time, and acceptance will banish wariness. We can afford to be patient until you establish yourself. It will take years before we are ready to strike. When the time is right, you will be in a perfect position to act. As you acted here, today, after years of patience."

"What am I to do for pleasure while I am waiting?" asked Stregone.

"You will earn a great deal of money, from me as well as from your new employer, who is famous for his generosity. Buy whatever pleasures you like. Just be discreet, as you have always been. And hide the bodies afterward."

"This idea of yours holds a certain appeal," said Stregone, "especially considering how disliked I am in Monteferro. It might be advantageous for me to absent myself from the city as quickly as possible."

"I was certain you would recognize the virtue in my plan," Marco Guidi said. "As usual, we are in perfect agreement."

"If I am to flee in desperate haste, fearing for my life," said Stregone, waving one hand in an airy gesture that mocked the words he spoke, "then I had best be off without further delay."

"As you wish. Once you have established yourself, you will be contacted by my agents. You will know them by the gold ducats and florins they deliver to you. It will be wiser not to use coins minted here in Monteferro, to avoid even the hint of a connection between us."

"I understand. Well, then, *arrivederci.*" Stregone disappeared from the reception room as if by magic, though Marco Guidi knew it was not by magic at all, but only the effect of the quick, unexpected way in which the little man habitually moved.

"You are mistaken, Stregone," Marco Guidi murmured after his accomplice had gone, "sadly mistaken, if you think because she has no male family members left to avenge her, Eleonora Farisi is finished. You should have killed her, and her children, while you had the chance. We may both live to regret that you did not, for I am certain if ever she discovers the right weapon for her purpose, *la duchessa* Eleonora will bring down retribution upon us without mercy for the deeds we have committed this day."

Chapter One

"I have two daughters, one a flower as pure and white as the new-fallen snow and the other a rose as red and sweet as the fires of passion."
Eleonora, Duchess of Monteferro.

"Rosalinda, where have you been? If you are late to the table this evening, Mother will be greatly annoyed with you. Luca has come with news."

Rosalinda had slowed her horse to a walk when she saw her sister waiting for her, and now Bianca caught at the animal's bridle, bringing the horse to a halt at the stableyard entrance.

The late afternoon sun glistened on Rosalinda's dark hair, setting errant curls aflame with reddish light. Before going out to ride, she had pulled the thick mass into a single long braid that hung down her back in the Milanese fashion but, as always, her hair would no more be confined than would the girl's bright spirit.

"Mother is always annoyed with me," Rosalinda scoffed. "And Luca never reveals his most interesting news to us. Only Mother, and sometimes Valeria and Bartolomeo, hear what he has to tell. They all keep secrets from us as if we were still small children." She swung a shapely leg over her horse's back and jumped to the ground as effortlessly as any man, landing in a graceful swirl of brown wool skirt.

"Must you ride astride?" Bianca asked. "It is most unbecoming for a lady to allow her legs to be seen in public."

"Public?" Rosalinda gave a short bark of laughter, the sound making Bianca grimace with disapproval. "We live so well hidden here at Villa Serenita that no one from outside our lands ever sees me, and the men-at-arms are used to me and think nothing of the way I choose to ride. I never go into the village, Bianca," she added, seeing her sister's concerned expression. "Please don't be afraid for me." She put an arm around Bianca, hugging her.

"How can I help but be frightened? I know, as you do not, what will happen to all of us if our enemies should discover that we are still alive." A worried look crossed Bianca's delicate features. Her soft blue eyes were shadowed by memory. Even the gold of her hair appeared momentarily dimmed. "You are too young to remember what life was like while Father was still alive, or to know just how much we lost on that awful day. I cannot ever forget, no matter how hard I try.

"When I close my eyes, I can relive those dreadful scenes as if they were happening again." Bianca moaned softly and buried her face in Rosalinda's shoulder. She went on, speaking in disjointed sentences as if she could only see the past in bits and pieces, "The shouts—terrified people running to and fro—men in armor storming through the ducal palace. The blood—dear God in heaven, all the blood! And Father lying so still. Then Bartolomeo picking me up and carrying me away from Father's reception chamber. Valeria weeping while she tried to pack a few clothes for us. Bartolomeo shouting at her to hurry. Mother frightened. I never saw her anything but happy before Father was killed. I think she has been frightened ever since that day. I know I have been afraid."

Rosalinda hugged Bianca more tightly, hoping thus to reassure her that the terror of her early childhood was long ago and far away. Physically, the sisters were not at all alike. With her soft blond beauty and gentle manner, Bianca, at age twenty-one, resembled their mother. Two years younger than Bianca, Rosalinda was very like their father in appearance, having inherited his dark, lustrous curls and his flashing gray eyes. Bartolomeo, who had been their father's best friend, claimed that Rosalinda was also similar to him in character, brave and daring like Girolamo Farisi, the late Duke of Monteferro.

Rosalinda believed the comparison was inaccurate. She could not only deny her impetuous nature, least of all to herself, but the closest she could come to bravery was to ride her horse into the mountains whenever she had the chance, in defiance of her mother's wishes that she should always stay close to the villa.

"Despite what you and Mother think, I do pay heed to what she says when she admonishes me."

Rosalinda looked over her sister's shoulder to the mountains she loved to roam. The first frosts had come and gone, their icy touch changing the leaves of the trees and the thick undergrowth that grew upon the lower elevations to soft shades of red and gold, or to rusty browns. Where shadows fell upon them, the bare gray rocks of the soaring mountaintops turned a misty shade of purple. Some of the nearer peaks displayed a faint white hint of early snow. Above the mountains and the protected valley where the villa stood, the northern Italian sky stretched deep blue and clear, with only a few fluffy clouds. But the wind was chill. For warmth Rosalinda was wearing a short jacket cut like a man's doublet over her brown wool dress.

"There will not be many more days like this one. Winter is coming. You of all people, Bianca, know how I hate to be confined by the ice and snow. Will you begrudge me a final taste of freedom while it is still possible?"

"Of course not, my dearest," Bianca responded, touching Rosalinda's cheek in a loving gesture. "But please do take care. You ought to ride with a groom and a man-at-arms."

"The men-at-arms who are not standing guard are all busy helping with the last of the harvest. Bartolomeo cannot spare anyone to attend on my pleasure. Besides, I prefer to ride alone. I love it up there in the wild mountains. I feel free, as I never can be here at the villa. Alone, I can be quiet and watch the birds and the animals without frightening them away. Today I saw an eagle and a bear. Mother would have liked the eagle."

"An eagle is not likely to threaten you, but a bear?" Bianca cried, her eyes widening with a new fear. "Oh, Rosalinda, you should not have told me. Now I will be more worried about you each time you go out. Bears can be dangerous."

"Not that bear," Rosalinda declared. "I am sure the bear I saw was afraid of me, because he stood up on his hind legs and ran off into the trees as soon as I rode around the curve in the path. I am late because I wasn't sure of what I had seen and I spent time looking for him. It was a strange place for a bear to be at this time of year. He should have been down here in the valley, fishing in the streams or searching for honey to fill his belly before he goes to sleep for the winter."

"If a bear comes to the valley, I trust the men-at-arms will kill him," Bianca said. "Then we shall have a bear rug to lay before the fire in Mother's sitting room."

"If that were to happen," Rosalinda responded, "I would feel sorry for the poor bear and never look at the rug we made of him. Meanwhile you, dear sister, would probably sit upon his unmoving back each evening and roast chestnuts in the fire."

"You are teasing me. But I am not quite the coward you think I am," Bianca snapped. Putting on her best big-sister manner, she continued, "I am older and have seen more of the treacherous world than you. Therefore, I know when to be cautious. Bears *are* dangerous. Some men are even more so. Never forget that, Rosalinda.

"Now, you have wasted enough time. Take care of your horse as quickly as you can," Bianca instructed. "I will see to it that you have a pitcher of hot water in your room for washing. Try not to be late. I will tell Mother that you have come home safely and will be down in time for the evening meal."

A short time later, with her horse settled for the night, Rosalinda hastened through the garden toward the rear entrance of the villa. It was the quickest way from the stable to her room on the upper floor, and it was also her favorite way to enter the house. She loved the scented air in the garden. Each time she walked along the gravel paths, she wondered what her grandfather, who by all accounts had been a rough fighting man, would think of what his daughter had made from the area just beyond the rear terrace of his house in the mountains.

Well concealed in an untraveled area where the higher reaches of mere foothills began to rise into the soaring heights of the Alps, Villa Serenita had been built by Rosalinda's grandfather, Mariano Ricci, a famous and highly successful condottiere. Fully aware of the perils to which a mercenary commander like himself was exposed during the constant warfare and political intrigues taking place amongst Venice, Milan, Genoa, and the other city-states of Italy, Mariano had decided it would be wise to maintain a safe, carefully hidden retreat in case his way of earning a living should turn even more dangerous than usual. But throughout his long life, Mariano's fortunes had never faltered. He had died in bed at the age of seventy, rich and full of honors, though somewhat concerned over the future of his only child, Eleonora, whom he had married off to his last employer, Girolamo Farisi, the Duke of Monteferro. Through his clever banker, Mariano was able to make secret arrangements to leave Villa Serenita to Eleonora.

Mariano's worry about his daughter was well founded. Five years after Mariano's death, the Duke of Monteferro was assassinated by a political rival who brought in his own army of mercenaries to take over the small but wealthy city-state. Knowing her children were certain to be murdered as well, since they could be considered the only legitimate heirs to Monteferro lands, the quick-thinking Eleonora gathered up her daughters and a few belongings and made a hasty escape from the city. With her husband's majordomo and close friend, Bartolomeo, his wife, Valeria, and a dozen men-at-arms who remained loyal to the murdered duke's family, Eleonora sought sanctuary at Villa Serenita. There, known only as *La vedova,* the widow, to the few inhabitants of the small and isolated nearby village, she and her daughters embarked upon a reclusive life.

During the ensuing fifteen years, Eleonora had found her only relief from constant worry for the safety of her daughters in the creation of a garden on the sheltered southern side of the villa. There, it was warm enough for a plum tree to grow, along with an apricot tree, and other tender plants. A low wall of the same pale yellow stone used for the house and outbuildings enclosed the garden, and within it Eleonora planted lilies, lavender, thyme, rosemary, and other useful herbs, including a few Florentine iris near a small pool.

In tribute to the daughters she loved more than life itself, Eleonora added two rosebushes to her garden, planting them on either side of the steps leading down from the terrace at the back of the house. One rosebush bore pure white flowers, while the blossoms of the other were bright crimson. The bushes bloomed most profusely during the long, warm days of June, though occasionally one or the other would send out a few late-season flowers, as if to bid a sweet farewell to summer's fleeting warmth.

Rosalinda hastened through this garden, pausing for only an instant to breathe in the air that was scented by her mother's herbs. As she brushed past the rosebushes, she noticed one red blossom. Quickly she plucked it, deciding she would wear it in her hair that evening.

Like Bianca, the white roses Eleonora had planted in her name were dainty and delicate, and they breathed forth a pure, sweet scent. But the red roses planted in Rosalinda's name unfurled many more petals to each bloom and their fragrance was rich and mysterious, beguiling Rosalinda's senses when she inhaled it, making her wish for something more than the placid life she lived at Villa Serenita.

She did not know exactly what it was that she wanted, only that she longed for someone to speak to her and to touch her in a new way, a way in which no one had ever spoken to her or touched her before. With her nose buried in the soft red petals, Rosalinda dreamed of laughter and music, and of falling stars blazing across the velvet night sky. She imagined warm masculine lips gently touching hers, in the way in which she had once observed Lorenzo, one of the men-at-arms, kissing his wife. After a long moment Rosalinda gave a wistful little sigh, went into the villa, and ran up the stairs to her room.

Luca Nardi was the older brother of that same Valeria who was Bartolomeo's wife and Eleonora's dearest friend and constant companion. The House of Nardi had long served as bankers to the family of the late Duke of Monteferro and, thanks to Luca's honesty and cleverness, a fair portion of the duke's wealth had been saved from confiscation after the assassination. Thus, Eleonora was not destitute and she was able to provide for the people who had escaped into the mountains with her.

At first the men-at-arms had thought of themselves only as warriors, but as time passed, they had been compelled to learn additional skills. A few of them had become expert hunters who made valuable contributions to the villa larders. Other men-at-arms were skilled carpenters, while some tended the livestock. All of them worked in the fields when necessary. They still took their turns at sentry duty and regularly attended weapons practice, joined now by their sons. For, by the good offices of Luca Nardi, the families of many of the men had been spirited out of Monteferro to join their husbands and fathers in the safety of Villa Serenita. There, some of the younger men had married the teenaged daughters of others and, within a few years, a self-sufficient community was established under Eleonora's rule, with Bartolomeo as her second in command in charge of defenses and masculine concerns.

Over the years Luca Nardi made periodic visits to Villa Serenita, always bringing with him a single, trusted servant and two pack horses loaded with supplies that were not locally available. Eleonora and her daughters regarded Luca as an old friend and always made him welcome.

On this first evening of Luca's latest visit, Rosalinda arrived in her mother's sitting room slightly out of breath, just as Luca was beginning to distribute the personal goods he had brought at the request of household members.

Eleonora's cool look stopped her tardy daughter just inside the door. Rosalinda noted that Bianca was already there, standing beside their mother, quiet and composed as a lady should be, in a blue silk gown. Valeria, in dark red brocade, and Bartolomeo, in a deeper red doublet and brown hose, both looked happy to see Valeria's brother again. Eleonora wore gray and silver brocade, with her still-lustrous gold hair piled high beneath a sheer silver scarf. All of the ladies' gowns were similar in style, with low necklines, long sleeves, high waists, and flaring skirts. Even Luca, who as a newly arrived traveler might be forgiven a crumpled appearance, was freshly bathed and clothed in his dignified dark blue banker's robe that reached below his knees, with matching hose and shoes.

Seeing how elegantly attired the rest of that company was, Rosalinda felt sadly disheveled in her hastily donned russet silk gown. Her face was still damp from washing it, her hair was smoothed back with her hands instead of being properly brushed and rebraided, and the red rose she had plucked from the garden was tucked loosely behind one ear. She tried to straighten her skirt but caught her mother's stern eye and immediately stilled her fluttering fingers, folding her hands at her waist as a lady should.

Upon a wall of the sitting room, a portrait of Girolamo Farisi hung. Candlelight reflecting on the surface of this painting suggested a gleam of humor in the eyes of the late Duke of Monteferro. Regarding her father's likeness, Rosalinda wished she could remember him, but she could not. She had been only three years old, little more than a baby, when he was killed, and so she was forced to depend upon the portrait and the recollections of others. She wondered if, like her, he had always been so preoccupied with more interesting matters that he was frequently late for meals. And if he was, had his wife recalled him to recognition of his social duties with the same look that had just put Rosalinda in her place?

"As always, I wish I could bring more," Luca said, handing Eleonora a package containing a book for her library. He then presented fabric for a new gown to Valeria and a thick sheaf of parchment to Bartolomeo, who used it to keep the estate records and for the writing he did late at night. "But if I were to lead a train of packhorses or carts loaded with goods to the villa, we would attract notice. I will do nothing to draw unwanted attention to this area. Even after so many years have passed, there are still people in Monteferro who fervently wish you and your daughters dead, Madonna Eleonora. Many folk believe that you *are* dead, that you were all killed along with the duke and your bodies hidden to prevent a public uprising at the outrageous murder of innocent babies.

"Your best hope of safety continues to lie in that mistaken belief. Thus, two or three times a year, I pretend to make a retreat to a monastery built high in these mountains. In fact, I do stop at that monastery for a few days both before and after I come here, in case anyone should enquire too closely as to my whereabouts. Thanks to you, madonna, I now have a reputation as a deeply religious man," Luca ended on a chuckle.

"As long as I live, I shall always be grateful to you, Luca, for your faithful honesty toward my family," Eleonora responded. "Wherever I am, there you are welcome."

"As always, it is a great joy to see you again, madonna. And no small pleasure to reassure myself of my sister's continued good health." These formal curtesies completed, Luca embraced Valeria and also Bartolomeo, who in his exile from Monteferro was serving Eleonora as majordomo as well as supervisor of the estate surrounding the villa.

The evening meal was more lively than usual with Luca there. He regaled those around the table with the latest gossip of the world beyond the mountains.

"Genoa and the Holy Roman Emperor have allied against the power of Venice," Luca said. "Sienna and Florence are at odds again. The Sforza duke of Milan rules his city with an iron fist and holds out against all challengers. By next month or next year, or even next week, these alliances will change again as friends become enemies and enemies, friends. These dukes and princes cannot be trusted, as you know to your great sorrow, Madonna Eleonora. *Gesù,* what a time in which to live! I fear this constant warfare born of greed and treachery will never end. It's bad for business, you know. Bankers are forced to make loans to the rulers of these battling states so they can wage their foolish wars. The loans are seldom repaid. And then the bankers suffer.

"But enough of such depressing subjects," Luca went on with a smile. "As to more cheerful news, the Duke of Ferrara is to marry the famously beautiful daughter of King Ferrante of Naples."

Rosalinda sat with her back straight, as she had been taught to do, and she smiled and spoke when she was expected to respond to some question or remark directed at her, but she had little interest in gossip about people she did not know. She did know her mother well, however, and Rosalinda was aware that beneath the superficial talk there was an unspoken conversation going on at the table. She could guess why it was so. Eleonora was protecting her daughters. *Again.*

"Good night, my dears." At last Eleonora rose from the table, the others rising with her as a mark of courtesy. She looked first at Bianca and then at Rosalinda. "It is time for you to be in bed."

At once the dutiful Bianca kissed her mother's cheek and said good night to the other adults. Rosalinda followed suit, though somewhat reluctantly. She was sure the most interesting part of the evening was about to unfold and, as usual, she and her sister would miss it. As she mounted the staircase behind Bianca, Rosalinda glanced back to see her mother leading Luca, Bartolomeo, and Valeria across the hall toward her private sitting room.

"Always, they have secrets," Rosalinda muttered.

"You don't want to know their secrets," Bianca told her.

"Oh, yes, I do." Rosalinda paused outside her sister's bedroom door. "They think we are still children, but we aren't anymore. Were we not living in this strange exile, both of us would have been married years ago. We would be mothers by now and no one would treat us as if we were ignorant babies. Don't you want to be treated like a grown woman, Bianca? Or do you want to continue to live like an untouched nun for the rest of your life?"

"Of course I want to marry. I can remember how happy Mother and Father were together, always laughing, always touching hands. I remember the beautiful warmth that emanated from them and enfolded you and me in their love. I want the same kind of affection for myself. I want it for you, too, Rosalinda."

"In that case, let us make a solemn vow," Rosalinda suggested. "Let us swear that we will marry only for love."

"For love alone." At once, Bianca nodded her agreement with this sentiment. "I do solemnly swear to you, Rosalinda, that I will marry only if I can be assured of enjoying the kind of love our parents knew."

"And so do I most solemnly swear the same." Rosalinda put out her hand and Bianca clasped it. They stood there in the upper hall, smiling at each other, until Rosalinda spoke again. "Let us hope the loving men who ask for our hands will also be brave and handsome."

"How I wish it could be so," Bianca said with a little laugh. "But the truth is, in our situation we are not likely to meet any suitable men who would dare to offer for us. The vow we just made is meaningless, however much we wish our dreams could come true."

"I think we ought to take steps to change our situation," Rosalinda declared, "and work to make those dreams into reality."

"No!" Bianca's face went white, her eyes were wide with fear. "You must promise me you will do nothing foolish. Rosalinda. You simply do not understand how an impulsive act on your part might be the end of us, and of Mother. I could not bear to see violence done again. You were not there on that dreadful day. You do not know how terrible it was. I want no blood spilled on my account.'' Bianca shuddered, covering her face with both hands.

''Hush, don't cry.'' Rosalinda's arms were around her sister's heaving shoulders. ''I won't cause trouble. I promise.''

It took a while, but eventually Rosalinda was able to convince Bianca to undress and go to bed. She sat beside Bianca, holding her hand until the troubled blue eyes closed and Bianca's breathing was quiet and even.

Upon leaving her sister's room to go to her own bedchamber, Rosalinda noticed the gleam of light coming from the lower floor. When she looked over the stair railing, she could see that the light came from her mother's sitting room, where the door was slightly open.

Feeling a bit unnerved by her sister's display of fear, Rosalinda moved down the stairs, heading toward the source of light and comfort, to the room where her mother was. No one was in the hall to stop her. The house was empty and silent. The few servants at Villa Serenita were the wives or the children of the loyal men-at-arms who had come north from Monteferro under Bartolomeo's command. At this late hour none of them were about. Save for the light around the edges of the sitting room door and the quiet murmur of voices from within, the villa slept.

Consumed by curiosity about what was being said behind that door, Rosalinda crept forward on tiptoe. When she was nearer, she could hear her mother speaking in a low, passionate voice.

''So,'' Eleonora said with barely contained pleasure, ''at last the man who plotted my husband's death has met a similar fate. Federigo Sotani, the Duke of Aullia, is dead. This is good news indeed, Luca. It would appear there is justice in the affairs of men, after all."

"Madonna, I know you have always believed that the Duke of Aullia arranged for your husband's assassination," came Luca's voice, "but I still find it difficult to accept that accusation."

"In truth," Bartolomeo put in, "from what you have said over the years on this matter, Luca, no one knows who backed Marco Guidi in his family's bloody rise to power in Monteferro. It might have been the Duke of Aullia, as you maintain, Madonna Eleonora. Or it might have been Venice. The Venetians have spies everywhere and, where profits from trade are involved, murderous intrigues are not beneath them. Or it could have been someone else, someone with a secret motive of his own."

"Do not overlook the most obvious conspirator," Luca said. "We now know that Niccolò Stregone was a secret advisor to Marco Guidi at the time he seized power in Monteferro."

"Ah, yes," said Valeria, "but we also know that Stregone fled across the border to neighboring Aullia soon after we escaped from Monteferro, a fact that indicates he quickly fell out with the Guidi and feared for his life."

"He then took service with the Duke of Aullia," Eleonora noted. "Which only proves the truth of my contention. The Duke of Aullia was in some way involved in the death of my husband, Marco Guidi was little more than the duke's puppet in that sad affair, and Stregone was the connection between Aullia and the Guidi family. Murderers and thieves always stick together for their own safety."

"And now the Duke of Aullia has been assassinated,'' Valeria said in a pensive tone. ''How interesting that Stregone should be in each city when its duke was killed.''

''Stregone.'' Eleonora repeated the name in a voice throbbing with hatred. ''That nasty dwarf is vicious, devious, and diabolically clever.''

''He is therefore a very dangerous man,'' Luca added, ''who would not stop at murder if the murder would benefit himself in any way. Which, madonna, is why I believe he was deeply involved with your husband's death, either in the planning or as the actual instrument of the murder.''

''I thank all the saints in heaven that I no longer have anything to do with any of these matters,'' Eleonora said. ''Where once I was entangled in the maneuverings of those power-hungry rulers, now I care more for my beloved children and my garden than I do for wealth and power. I find I sleep more securely here at Villa Serenita than I ever did at Monteferro.'' She broke off suddenly, turning her head to listen. ''Who is there, outside the door?''

''It's Rosalinda.'' She pushed open the door to step into the room. ''I wanted to talk to you, Mother. I am worried about Bianca.''

''It is much too late for you to be awake, child,'' Eleonora scolded.

''Indeed, it is late.'' Bartolomeo interrupted with a smile for Rosalinda. ''I am certain Luca must be tired after his long journey. Madonna Eleonora, with your kind permission, may we continue our discussion tomorrow?''

''Yes, you are right, old friend. You are all excused. Sleep well.'' Eleonora waited until her company had left before she held out a hand to Rosalinda. ''Come here, child, and tell me what is wrong with Bianca.''

Rosalinda did as instructed, pulling a stool near to the chair where her mother sat. Eleonora took her daughter's hands and held them while Rosalinda recounted how, twice in one day, Bianca had been overcome by her dreadful memories.

"Ah, the poor child," Eleonora murmured. "No matter how she tries, she cannot forget the terrible sights she beheld at too young an age."

"I think the distress she felt today was my fault," Rosalinda confessed. "Whenever I venture too far from the villa for her comfort, Bianca becomes frightened. Knowing that, today I made the further mistake of telling her I saw a bear." Rosalinda then told her mother, as she had not told Bianca, the entire story.

"The bear ran out of the trees right into the path of my horse," she said. "When I pulled hard on the reins, the bear ran off again, back into the forest. Only then did I notice that the path just ahead had crumbled away in a rockfall, so there was no longer a path there at all, but only a dangerous gap that opened into a deep ravine. It was almost as if the bear intended to warn me and, having done so, he then left the vicinity."

"How very peculiar," said Eleonora when she heard this tale.

"Even stranger was my horse's reaction," Rosalinda said. "It did not rear up in fright as you would expect a horse to do when it suddenly comes upon a bear. It simply stopped when I pulled on the reins and then stood there quietly until the bear was gone from sight."

"An angel must have been watching over you, keeping you from harm," Eleonora said. "Or perhaps it was your dear father's doing. You mentioned seeing an eagle." Eleonora's gaze moved from Rosalinda's face to the portrait of her husband. Girolamo Farisi had been painted with an eagle perched upon his wrist. He had insisted on the inclusion of his family emblem, though certain people at the court of Monteferro, criticizing the picture when it was finished, had whispered most unkindly of ambition that soared as high as an eagle.

"Oh, Mother, please," Rosalinda said, laughing at this notion, "do you imagine that in heaven Father has obtained the power to command the eagles as they fly?"

"I can think of no other explanation for what happened," said Eleonora with a sniff of offended dignity. "I trust you will have the good sense not to ride that way again."

"I think it's far more likely the bear was an angel in disguise," Rosalinda said gently. Well aware of her mother's undying devotion to the memory of Girolamo Farisi, Rosalinda hid her amusement at her parent's romantic notion as best she could. And she did not say she would not ride the dangerous path again. She was not going to make a promise she could not keep.

Luca stayed at Villa Serenita for two days more, resting from his long journey and holding private discussions with Eleonora and her faithful companions, Bartolomeo and Valeria. Rosalinda did not overhear anything they said on those occasions. She suspected her mother of taking extra care to be sure that Rosalinda, and especially Bianca, would not be privy to conversations that might cause them distress.

On the day after Luca departed, Rosalinda again went riding alone. At this time of year, each such excursion was precious to her, for the weather was growing steadily colder. Soon snow would make venturing into the mountains impossible. Rosalinda chose the route she had taken on the day when she had seen the bear. Just before she reached the curve in the path where the ground had fallen away, she dismounted and walked to the edge to contemplate the ravine below.

"I was right," she said aloud. "From the direction in which I was coming, I could not have seen the rockfall until I was on top of it. Until it was too late for me to stop. That bear saved my life. It's a good thing I told Bartolomeo about the break in the path, so he could warn the men-at-arms, though I don't think any of them is likely to come this way."

Clutching her horse's reins more firmly and still on foot, she led the animal from the dangerous spot. Soon the path widened again and Rosalinda remounted, springing onto the horse's back with ease. A little farther on she paused, listening intently and peering into the wilderness of gray rocks and almost leafless trees.

"I thought I heard something," she told the horse. "Whatever it was, it's gone now. Perhaps it was only the wind, or the sound of running water from a nearby stream."

A short distance farther down the path, she stopped for a third time.

"What was that I saw, moving through the trees? Could it be my friend the bear again? If only I knew where his cave is, I think I might take a pot of honey to him there, to thank him for what he did for me. Oh, how Bianca would shiver if I were to tell her about that idea!"

Seeing not the slightest trace of a bear, Rosalinda continued homeward without further incident. In fact, she saw few animals or birds. The small creatures were already burrowing in for the winter and most of the birds had flown south to warmer climes. Coming out of the hills and nearer to the villa, Rosalinda could see that the tilled fields across which she was riding were stripped of their harvest as humans, too, prepared for the long, cold months ahead. When she glanced back at the mountains she noticed a banner of icy-white cloud streaming across the sky, and she knew the snows would not be long in coming.

That evening, when Bianca asked where she had gone on her afternoon ride, Rosalinda took care not to mention the mountain path or the bear.

The wind howled around the mouth of the cave where Andrea had taken shelter. Leaves and dust blew into the cave, forcing him to move farther back into the damp interior. Even with the skin of the bear he had slain wrapped around him for covering, he was miserably cold, but he dared not light a fire for heat. Darkness would fall soon and then a fire might be seen.

He was terrified, not so much for himself as for the companions from whom he had become separated during the first hours of their desperate flight. He thought he had continued onward in the direction upon which they had all agreed. He had tried his best not to get lost while hiding from those who were pursuing him. He prayed he would meet his absent companions again at their designated rendezvous. But he was no longer certain they would be there. In the cruel world he had recently entered, he could not be certain of anything.

Cold and fear and hunger were taking their toll on him. And loneliness. Never before in his twenty-five years had he been completely alone. He found he did not like the feeling. But then, he had known in his soul that he would not. If the others were dead . . . He could scarcely bear to think of that possibility, but the thought came without bidding, and grimly he forced himself to complete it. If the others were dead, then he would be alone and only half a person for the rest of his life.

And that might not be for much longer. He knew he could not remain in the rude shelter of a cave, without food or adequate warmth, for many days more. If he wanted to survive, sooner or later he would have to descend to the valley, there to seek a place to stay for the winter.

Braving the wind, he stepped outside the cave entrance to look down and across the mountain slopes to where a villa sat in a wide, pleasant valley. It was no very grand dwelling, but Andrea did not care about grandeur. He had seen more than enough of the treachery that lurked in grand palaces.

The girl lived there, in the villa. Each time she rode to the mountains, she returned to that snug place. She was no great lady, but Andrea had seen—and heard—enough of great ladies, too. This girl had a fresh, innocent face, a sense of humor, and a generous heart. He knew as much from overhearing her whimsical comments to her horse. He wished she would find his cave and bring that pot of honey to him, along with a loaf of bread and a large skin of wine. A warm blanket would be appreciated, too, he thought, pulling the smelly bearskin more closely around his shivering form.

She would never find his cave. It was too high in the mountains and too well hidden, which was why he had chosen it. He would have to go to her. He would do it soon, once he was absolutely certain the others would not be coming to meet him. . . .

Chapter Two

Early each morning, the guards made their reports to Bartolomeo on their patrols of the estate during the previous day and night. Only rarely were there intruders on the private lands surrounding Villa Serenita, and those were always local folk who had wandered too far in search of brushwood for their fires. Occasionally, someone was caught poaching rabbits or fishing in the streams. By Eleonora's orders, any game or fish was confiscated from these miscreants before they were escorted to the boundary, there to be turned off her land with a stern warning never to trespass again unless they wished to receive severe punishment.

Actually, Eleonora did not want to punish anyone. She had seen enough violence for one lifetime, and she was pleased that no poacher, once warned, had ever been caught a second time. Thus, it was with open dismay that she listened on a frosty morning in late autumn to Bartolomeo's account of a disturbing incident.

"One of the men-at-arms has discovered signs that someone is living in the old gamekeeper's cottage," Bartolomeo said.

"I know that place," Rosalinda spoke up at once. She and Bianca were at the big, round table in the sitting room, working on their Latin lessons under their mother's direction. Ever ready for any distraction from boring declensions, Rosalinda had been listening to what Bartolomeo was saying. "Who would want to live there? The house is falling down. The last time I rode past it, the roof had collapsed."

"You are right." Bartolomeo sent a conspiratorial wink in her direction, as if he understood her impatience with her lessons and her eagerness to be out-of-doors on such a fine day. To Eleonora, Bartolomeo said, "There has been no gamekeeper here since the time of your father, and that cottage is no longer fit for habitation. I was planning to suggest to you that it be torn down next spring. Now I think we ought to do something about it sooner than that. The man-at-arms who spoke to me reported finding the remains of a cooking fire and the bones of small animals."

"This is a serious matter," Eleonora responded, frowning. "How could an unknown person be living on my land? I thought our guards were dependable."

Rosalinda could tell that her mother was deeply distressed and that she was trying to hide it from her daughters. Her effort was not succeeding. Bianca was positively white with fear. Seeing Bianca's pale face, Rosalinda tried to allay her sister's concern.

"Perhaps it was some lone traveler who only stopped for a night or two before continuing on his way," she suggested. "Bartolomeo, could your man tell if there was more than one person?"

"More important, did he actually see whoever is living there?'' Eleonora asked.

''He saw no one,'' Bartolomeo replied. ''Madonna, allow me to assure you that Lorenzo, who discovered the evidence, was puzzled to think how such a thing could happen when our sentries patrol the boundaries of your land so thoroughly. Acting as my deputy, Lorenzo ordered extra guards out before he even reported to me. If the intruder is still in this area, he will be found before the day is over.''

''I want that cottage pulled down at once,'' Eleonora commanded. ''I don't care how many men it takes. Level it. And if you do catch the person who has been living there, bind him and bring him to me. It must be a man. No woman would dare to live off the land in such a way.''

''I understand. The cottage will be gone before nightfall. With your permission, madonna, I will leave you now and give the order.''

''Wait a moment, Bartolomeo,'' Eleonora said as he headed for the door. ''I have another order for you. I am certain Bianca will have the good sense to remain at home after hearing this troubling news, but I am not so sure of my overly curious Rosalinda. Until this stranger on my lands has been caught, I specifically forbid Rosalinda to ride alone, or to ride out of sight of the villa, even in the company of a pair of men-at-arms.''

''As you wish, madonna.'' Bartolomeo bowed and left the sitting room.

''Mother, no!'' Rosalinda protested. ''I will go mad if I am forced to stay at home all day.''

''You will soon be forced to do so in any event,'' Eleonora responded, ''since you cannot ride in the ice and snow that will arrive before much longer.''

''Please,'' Rosalinda begged.

"I gave the order to Bartolomeo with your safety in mind, child. If you insist upon arguing with me, I will send you to your room."

"But, Mother—"

"Oh, Rosalinda, do be quiet," Bianca hissed across the table. "Can't you see how upset Mother is? Must you always add to her worries?"

"Why can't you and Mother understand that I feel like a prisoner here?" Rosalinda hissed back at her.

"You are not a prisoner!"

"I am! We all are!"

"You are not! *We* are not!"

"Girls, be silent," Eleonora interrupted the building dispute. "Return to your lessons. Rosalinda, you will decline the following Latin verbs . . ."

Rosalinda's heated protests had their desired effect of making an irritated Bianca forget her fears. However, Rosalinda's continued pleas that she be allowed to ride were useless against her mother's firm insistence that she must not venture out of sight of the villa. In any case, her arguments proved unnecessary, for that night a rainstorm broke over the valley and continued into the next day. When the sun reappeared, it was accompanied by cold and windy weather, which lasted for a mere two days before the snow began and the issue of Rosalinda's desire to ride was resolved by Nature. Soon both mountains and valley were buried under several feet of white, and the snow kept falling.

In the villa itself and in the outbuildings where the men-at-arms and their families lived, as well as in the other buildings where the livestock was sheltered, all was prepared for the winter, so humans and animals were as comfortable as they could expect to be.

For Eleonora and her daughters, the winter routine

was soon well established, with household duties in the mornings, lessons in the afternoons, and in the evenings, the quiet pleasures of games in which Bartolomeo and Valeria also joined, or of reading aloud from one of the books in Eleonora's library.

Bartolomeo reported the gamekeeper's cottage had been destroyed and no further signs of the mysterious intruder had been noticed. Rosalinda thought she was the only person who wondered from time to time whence that unknown person had come and where he had gone. She knew she was the only one at Villa Serenita who remembered a bear she had once encountered, who had done a good deed for her. She hoped the bear would find a snug cave in which to keep warm through his winter hibernation.

Andrea knew he was going to die. He had known his death was inevitable since the moment when he realized he was alone, that he had somehow lost the others in the darkness and confusion of that first, frantic night. Against all the claims of logic and good sense, he had struggled to keep hope alive in his breast, telling himself that he would see his missing companions again. But they had failed to appear at the agreed-upon meeting place. Their continued absence finally destroyed his fragile optimism. If it were in any way possible, he knew they would have met him. That they had not done so meant they were most likely dead.

Sunk in sorrow too deep for weeping, Andrea had left the meeting place and wandered back into the mountainous area where he had spent the recent autumn. By now, weeks later, even the loss of closest kin and dearest friend scarcely mattered, for Andrea was about to join them in death.

He was numb from the cold and so starved that when

he put his hands to his armpits to try to warm them, he could feel his bones jutting through the skin. Were he a less stubborn man, he would have just stopped where he was, dropped to the ground, and let the cold and the never-ending snow have him. Everything had been taken from him. His family and friends and all his worldly possessions were gone. Even the rude shelter he had found and used for a few days had been torn down to drive him away from it. And now his very life was to be claimed by Fortune's cruel whim.

"But if I die," he muttered, voicing his disjointed thoughts in a growl scarcely recognizable as issuing from a human throat, "then *they* have won—the liars, the traitors, the assassins. Vanni, where are you? What has happened to you? God in heaven, at least let me know what has befallen Vanni before I die! And Francesco, too. What a trial we have been to him. Dear God, I pray they are not in my condition—or worse, imprisoned and tortured. Though I shall die, if they by some unexplainable chance are still alive, then I pray that they are safe. And warm."

He stood in several feet of snow, weary unto death, swaying on feet he could no longer feel, with more snow piling up on his shoulders and his ragged beard with each moment that passed, his fortunes and his life force at their lowest ebb. The light he was trying to reach was barely discernable through the heavy crust of snowflakes that stuck to his eyelashes. Surely, he could never walk as far as that light.

Through the fog of failing consciousness, he remembered the girl. The memory of her had kept him from giving up even as his strength had waned and his hopes had faded. He had glimpsed her only a few times, when she rode into the mountains alone, but her energy and her exhilaration at being young and alive and free had communicated itself to him. Once he, too, had been that young, that enthusiastic.

With the girl's bright image in his confused mind, Andrea forced himself to lift one foot, to drag it forward through the obstructing weight of the snow, to place it in front of the other . . . and then, after an agonizing pause, to lift the other foot. *She* was there, where the light was. If he could but reach her, she would help him. That girl would give honey to a wild bear. She would not turn away a freezing man. If he found *her,* he would find himself again. And then he might learn Vanni's fate. . . .

" 'How dared you make your way to this high mountain? Do you not know that here man lives in bliss?' "

In her warm sitting room, Eleonora was reading aloud from Dante's *Purgatorio,* reciting in a low voice throbbing with emotion the words of Beatrice, the poet's lost love.

Valeria moved quietly, filling a Venetian glass globlet with wine and setting it on a table next to Eleonora. Nearby, Bartolomeo sprawled in his chair, entranced by the images evoked by Dante's beautiful language.

Bianca sat on a stool at her mother's knee, with her pet kitten curled up asleep in her lap. Behind her on a pedestal stood the cage that housed a pair of doves. Bianca had covered the cage for the night, but an occasional rustling hinted that the birds were not yet asleep.

Rosalinda was sitting closer to the window than the others. At the words of the poetical Beatrice, she glanced out the window in the direction of the mountains. It was an involuntary motion that lasted for only an instant, but her gaze caught on something on the terrace that should not have been there. A form hovered, its shape indistinct in the falling snow. Rosalinda went still, her vision sharpening.

Most definitely, something was moving on the other side of the glass. She did not think it was one of the men-at-arms. If one of them wanted to speak to Bartolomeo, he would knock on the door.

" '. . . on the spine of Italy the snow lies frozen hard,' " Eleonora continued her reading. " ' . . . in winter when the northeast tempests blow . . .' "

Rosalinda's thoughts were no longer on poetry. Instead, she concentrated on the darkness beyond the window, where a real tempest was blowing and where the form she had seen appeared to be moving closer to the glass. A hand—or was it a paw?—lifted in a despairing gesture. Rosalinda had the eerie feeling that the figure was motioning to her.

She was about to rouse Bartolomeo from his poetry-induced torpor and ask him to investigate when Bianca, ever alert to her sister's moods, transferred her attention from her mother to Rosalinda. At once Bianca followed the direction of Rosalinda's gaze toward the window. Bianca drew in a deep, gasping breath. Then she let out the breath in a blood-curdling scream that sent the kitten in her lap scrambling to get away from her and caused a furious flapping of wings from under the covering on the birdcage.

"A bear!" Bianca pointed a shaking finger. "There is a bear at the window!"

Bartolomeo leapt to his feet and rushed toward the window. Eleonora and Valeria were close behind him.

"Where is it?" Bartolomeo asked, peering through the glass. "I don't see anything."

"Something has been out there, though," Valeria

said. "The snow on the terrace is trampled."

While the others exchanged amazed remarks and tried to see through the window, which was rapidly becoming steamed with their breath, and while Bianca hung back as if she feared the bear she thought she had seen would leap through the glass to attack her, Rosalinda took action. She unbolted and flung open the door leading directly from the sitting room to the terrace. She stepped outside, into swirling snow and wind.

"Rosalinda, come back!" Bianca screamed.

Rosalinda paid no attention to her sister. Instead, she put out both hands toward the shape that stood frozen and staring into the light of the sitting room.

"Come," Rosalinda said in a quiet voice. "Come inside where it's warm. We won't hurt you."

"Rosalinda!" Bianca's voice rose to an hysterical shriek.

"Daughter, come back here at once," called Eleonora, sounding frightened but under control.

"Bartolomeo, help me," Rosalinda cried. "He's half frozen. I don't think he can walk alone."

"Bartolomeo, bring my daughter inside and shut the door," Eleonora ordered.

"You—" The voice of the creature on the terrace was a growl, as if he had not spoken for a long time. "You—will—help."

"Of course I'll help." Ignoring his size and his fearsome appearance, Rosalinda took him by the arm. Bartolomeo joined her on the snowy terrace and she gave him a firm command. "Take his other arm. He is having trouble walking. I think his feet must be frozen."

Together, supporting him on either side, Rosalinda and Bartolomeo got the stranger through the door.

"It *is* a bear!" Bianca screamed. "Rosalinda, you have brought a bear into the house!"

"Be silent or leave the room, Bianca," her mother ordered.

Indeed, the creature Rosalinda and Bartolomeo were leading to the fireplace did appear to be a bear standing on its hind legs. It was as tall as a bear, it had a bear's head, and two bear arms complete with long bear claws were crossed upon its chest. But just under the bear's open jaw, a snow-encrusted, heavily bearded human face could be seen. Further inspection showed that the bear's hind legs were missing. The fur that had once covered those legs was now wrapped about the lower legs and feet of a very real man, over what had been a pair of fine, red leather boots. These boots were badly scuffed and had holes in the toes, around which ice had congealed. A doublet so soiled and torn that its original color could not be discerned and a pair of ripped hose completed the man's remarkable costume.

Bartolomeo removed the snowy bearskin from the man's broad shoulders, while Rosalinda bade the stranger sit near the fire and warm himself.

"Give him Bianca's stool," Eleonora said, and at this direction from her mother, Rosalinda pulled the stool forward.

"Madonna," the man gasped. He was staring at Eleonora. He tried to bow to her but he was already swaying on his feet and when he moved, he nearly lost his balance. Rosalinda and Bartolomeo caught his arms, once again steadying him.

"Do not trouble yourself with formal courtesies just yet," Eleonora said. "Sit down on that stool. And, since you appear to be able to speak, tell me who you are."

"I—am—Andrea." The man transferred his burning gaze from Eleonora to Rosalinda. "I knew—you—would help."

"Certainly, we will help you," Rosalinda said to

him. "Do sit down as Mother advises."

"It was a command," he said, sitting.

"Yes, it was, wasn't it?" Rosalinda supressed a chuckle before she turned to practical matters. "Bartolomeo, I think we should remove his boots at once. His hands are as cold as ice, and his feet must be, too." She began to struggle with the bearskin thongs that held the fur wrappings around his ankles. Those same thongs, she now noticed, were also holding his ruined boots together.

"You won't be able to untie the thongs, Rosalinda. We'll have to cut them." Bartolomeo pulled his dagger out of the sheath at his belt and went to work on the thongs. "Valeria, bring us a basin and a pitcher of hot water."

"Warm water," Valeria corrected her husband. "Hot water will burn his frozen skin. I won't be long." She left the room.

"Did you come here alone?" Eleonora demanded. When Andrea did not answer she repeated the question, adding, "I mean to have an honest response from you, fellow."

Andrea winced. Rosalinda could not tell if it was from her mother's peremptory tone of voice or if the sudden release of his swollen feet from their wet, cold covering had elicited the response.

"Answer me," Eleonora commanded, "or I will have Bartolomeo cast you back into the snow without that evil-smelling skin and in your bare feet."

"From the way my feet are burning, madonna, putting them into snow would be a kindness," Andrea ground out between clenched teeth.

"I am sure they do burn." In contrast to her mother's nervous harshness, Rosalinda was sympathetic to Andrea's plight. "Whenever my fingers start to freeze in the cold, they hurt when they begin to warm again. But I am happy to see that none of your toes are blue. They are only white. One of the men-at-arms told me last winter that blue toes are a sure sign the frozen toes will later turn black and drop off, and perhaps the entire foot, too. I think you will be spared such a fate."

"You will not be spared my wrath if you do not answer my questions, fellow," Eleonora stated. "Do you come here alone, or are there others with you? If so, how many are there, and where are they?"

"Answer her, Andrea," Bartolomeo advised him in a kinder voice. "If you have companions who are lost in the storm, perhaps we can find and help them, too."

"I wish you could." Andrea's brown eyes glistened with sudden moisture. "There were three of us. I lost the others weeks, perhaps months, ago. I am not sure how long it has been. I think they must be dead by now," he ended on a choked sob.

"What were you doing, wandering for weeks or months in these mountains?" Eleonora asked.

"Madonna, I cannot—" Andrea's eyes closed and he slid from the stool. Bartolomeo caught his head just before it hit the floor.

"*Buffone,*" Eleonora muttered. "Has he really fainted, or is it a trick?"

"He is not a clown at all, Mother," Rosalinda protested. "From what he says, he may have suffered a great tragedy. Furthermore, I think he may be a person of some importance, for his clothes were once very fine."

"He could have stolen the clothes," Eleonora objected.

"His speech is that of an educated man," Bartolomeo noted.

"All the more dangerous for us," said Eleonora.

By this time Valeria had returned with the large pitcher of warm water and the basin Bartolomeo had requested, along with several linen towels. Together she and Rosalinda began to soak Andrea's ice-cold hands and feet.

"If we take off the rest of his wet garments, he will warm faster," Valeria said to her husband.

Bianca had remained silent during all of this. Now she drew closer, staring at Andrea in fascinated distaste, as if she feared he might jump up and seize her at any moment.

"He is ugly," Bianca said, noting the heavy beard and the long, unkempt hair. She wrinkled her dainty nose. "Now that he is warming up, he smells like an animal."

"That's partly because of the bearskin," Bartolomeo informed her. "It hasn't been properly cured."

"He is a young man," Valeria said. She was using Bartolomeo's dagger to slice through the filthy fabric of Andrea's doublet, making short work of both doublet and underclothes. "See, Bartolomeo, his throat is not wrinkled. And he is not a poor man. This dirty shirt beneath the doublet is fine linen."

Rosalinda was staring at the manly chest beneath the linen shirt. Andrea's skin was pale and smooth, with dark hair across his chest. His ribs stuck out in hard ridges and as Valeria pulled down his hose, Rosalinda could see how hollow his belly was, as if he had not eaten for a very long time. She also noticed how the hair on his chest trailed downward in a line. . . .

"Rosalinda, come away," Eleonora instructed. "It is not right for a young girl to undress a man."

But he is my bear. Rosalinda almost said the words aloud, but caught herself just before they left her tongue. For a reason she could not have explained save to say that all her instincts told her it was so, she was certain it was this man, covered with the bearskin, who had warned her away from a dangerous rockfall. She was also fairly sure he was the man who had been using the gamekeeper's cottage. So few strangers came to this part of the mountains that he must be the one.

"Rosalinda!" Eleonora repeated in growing exasperation.

"Would you find a blanket?" Valeria asked Rosalinda. "After I remove his clothes we can wrap him in it. Madonna Eleonora, we will need a bed for him. Perhaps Bianca could see to the preparation of a guest room while Rosalinda locates the blanket."

"Excellent suggestions." Eleonora nodded her approval of this means of removing her daughters from the vicinity of an unclothed man. "Do as Valeria asks, girls."

Rosalinda and Bianca went up the stairs together, both heading for the room where extra linens were kept.

"Make up the guest room on the south side, where we usually put Luca," Rosalinda said. "It is the warmest of the unused rooms. After I take the blanket to Valeria, I'll help you carry in wood to build a fire."

"I wonder who he is?" Away from the sight of the dirty, ragged man, Bianca had lost much of her fear of him.

"He will tell us when he is able." As she spoke, Rosalinda threw open the door to the linen room.

"You find this exciting, don't you?" Bianca sighed. "How I wish I were as bold as you. I acted very badly, didn't I? All that screaming and saying nasty things about a poor soul who is almost dead from the cold. Now Mother is annoyed with me."

"She never stays angry with either of us for very long." Rosalinda paused with a thick woolen blanket in her arms. "I think Mother was afraid, too, at first, only she has learned to hide her fears better than you do. For all we know, Andrea may be innocent of any evil intent. I cannot believe that everyone in the world wants to see us dead."

"I know you are right," Bianca said. "Are you angry with me?"

"Of course not. You are the dearest person in the world to me. I love you too much to be angry with you. Although," Rosalinda teased, "sometimes I am just a bit irritated, especially when you scream in my ear as you did a little while ago."

"Our lives will change with a sick man in the house," Bianca said.

"With Valeria's good care and plenty of food, he may not be sick for long." Rosalinda's gray eyes sparkled at the thought. "From the way the snow is falling, Andrea will not be able to leave very soon. This winter may not be as boring as I expected."

Upon returning to the sitting room, Rosalinda discovered Andrea still lying before the fire with his eyes closed. Eleonora and Bartolomeo were discussing how to deal with the unexpected guest.

"One man, alone and unarmed," Bartolomeo said, "cannot do much harm if we are careful. Not in this weather, which will allow no escape after an evil deed. And, certainly, he is harmless while in his present condition. I will watch him closely and if I think it necessary, I will set a guard on him."

"And when he leaves us, which he surely will do if he recovers," Eleonora said, "what then?"

"As he appears to be a gentleman, perhaps he will give his word of honor not to reveal where we are," Bartolomeo suggested.

"Have you forgotten how little honor means beyond the safety of these mountains?" Eleonora asked.

Unnoticed by her mother and Bartolomeo, Rosalinda went to Valeria, who had finished stripping Andrea of his wet clothes. The remnants of his linen shirt lay draped across his loins. The fire had been built into a roaring blaze to warm him. Rosalinda could tell that Valeria had bathed him, for a bowl of soap sat on the hearth, along with a second pitcher of steaming water.

Andrea had long, straight legs and his hands and feet were slender. On the little finger of his left hand he wore a plain ring with a single ruby deeply embedded in the gold band. The stone winked in the firelight when Valeria moved his arm. Andrea's fingernails were broken and not very clean in spite of Valeria's efforts with water and soap, but that was to be expected of a man who had been living in the mountains for weeks. His left arm bore three long, almost parallel red scars, evidently of recent origin and evidence to Rosalinda of a mauling by the bear whose skin Andrea had been wearing. Apparently, the bear had attacked him and that was why Andrea had killed it.

Rosalinda watched his broad chest rise and fall with each breath he took, and she noted how breathing seemed difficult for him. The painful thinness of what had once been a powerful male body roused a fresh stirring of sympathy in her heart.

"When he wakes, we should feed him some chicken broth," Rosalinda said, kneeling beside Andrea. Together she and Valeria unfolded the blanket and wrapped it around him.

"There are more claw marks on his back," Rosalinda went on, noticing a second trio of scars across Andrea's left shoulder. "How did he fight off the bear?"

"Bartolomeo found two daggers in his belt and took

them into safekeeping,'' Valeria answered. ''They are the only weapons he carried. A remarkable feat, to kill a bear with only a knife, but I think that must be what happened. Most of the discoloration on his clothes is from dried blood. I imagine some is Andrea's own and some came from the bear.

''Let us hope he does not develop lung fever. He is so emaciated that I do not think he could withstand the strain of a serious illness.'' Valeria sat back on her heels. ''I have done all I can for him here. I trust Bianca will think to heat bricks to warm his bed.''

Andrea appeared to be either semiconscious or half asleep from exhaustion. He was not much help to them when Bartolomeo, Rosalinda, and Valeria pulled him to his feet and, once standing, he was unable to walk. With a groan from the effort, Bartolomeo slung Andrea over one shoulder and headed for the stairs.

Chapter Three

''I will sit with him tonight,'' Rosalinda volunteered.

Andrea was sleeping in the bed Bianca had prepared for him, with heated bricks wrapped in cloths against his feet and plenty of blankets to cover him.

''No, you will not,'' Eleonora said.

''Though at present he is too weak to harm anyone, still, your mother is right,'' Valeria said to Rosalinda. ''It would be most improper for you to remain alone in a bedchamber with a man overnight. Bartolomeo and I will take turns sitting with Andrea. If Madonna Eleonora agrees, you may see him in the morning. Let us hope he will be well enough by then to provide answers to our questions about why he was wandering in the mountains and what brought him to the villa. In the meantime, he desperately needs uninterrupted sleep and warmth.''

Eleonora at once concurred with these remarks, and Rosalinda had to be content to know she would see

Andrea again within a few hours. She could not dispute Valeria's contention that the man needed sleep. There were dark shadows under his sunken eyes, and every sharp angle of the gaunt shape beneath the bedcovers proclaimed a weariness beyond anything Rosalinda could imagine.

Even in exhausted sleep, he drew her to him. Her fingers itched to stroke his pale cheeks above the dark beard. She longed to see his face clean-shaven. But, shaven or bearded, he was *her* bear, who had saved her from a dreadful plunge down a mountainside. By warning her of the rockfall, he had established a connection between them; by coming to the villa to seek shelter from the storm, he had allowed her to repay the debt she owed to him. In so doing he had bound them together by a second thread of circumstance.

In a way that Rosalinda was as yet too innocent to comprehend, Andrea was, in truth, *hers,* and the protectiveness she felt toward him would not be denied. But there was something more, an inherent masculinity apparent in his relaxed form, that called out to her, that touched a chord in Rosalinda's soul. It took her mother's firm hand on her shoulder and Bianca's grasp on her hand to make Rosalinda leave the guest chamber.

Bianca was eager to talk about the evening's events, so after the girls had said good night to their mother, she followed Rosalinda into her bedroom.

"Who can he be?" Bianca asked. "How did he survive in the mountains? Valeria says he is a young man."

"You are remarkably interested in him now," Rosalinda said, "considering how frightened of him you were at first."

"The only young men we ever see," Bianca responded, "are the sons of the men-at-arms and they are hardly suitable companions for us. It might be nice to have a young man of rank staying at the villa for a while. You have heard Mother's stories about the court at Monteferro, how elegant it was, how cultured and refined."

"Mother's stories are mostly warnings about intrigue and treachery." Rosalinda spoke more sharply than usual. She was feeling oddly irritated by Bianca's sudden interest in Andrea and by her dreamy tone of voice when she spoke of him.

"Not all of the stories are warnings," Bianca objected to her sister's statement. "Mother has taught us manners and proper bearing by recalling the more pleasant aspects of life at Monteferro." She sighed, looking wistful, and at once Rosalinda was contrite over her petty annoyance.

"I cannot remember anything about those days," Rosalinda said in a kinder tone, "but you can, and I know you still feel the loss. Bianca, do you wish our family could be restored to its former position at Monteferro? I know Mother does."

"It would be lovely." Bianca sighed again. "I remember Father holding me in his arms, showing me the view from high in the *castello* tower and telling me that all the farm land I could see beyond the city walls, the hills in the distance, and the crowded city streets just below us were my inheritance, and that I must cherish the land and love the people of Monteferro. Yes, I would like to return there to live, if we could do it safely. But all the menfolk in our family were killed in one day, so there is no Farisi male left to rule Monteferro."

"If you were to marry a strong man, who loved you enough to take the risk, and who had an army at his command—"

"It isn't very likely that I will ever marry," Bianca scoffed. "My dowry is a war, with only a slim chance of taking Monteferro back from the Guidi family who, according to Luca's reports, hold it with iron fists. What noble would want me on those terms? Even an ambitious condottiere would insist on a surer prize for his military efforts. And under such circumstances love, however strong and true, would count for very little."

"Circumstances can change," Rosalinda insisted. "There is always the possibility that ours will, too."

"I know, my dearest." Bianca embraced her sister, kissing her on the cheek. "You are always so good to me, even when I irritate you. Thank you for encouraging my dreams. And now, good night. I wonder if either of us will sleep after so much excitement."

To her own surprise, Rosalinda did fall asleep, instantly and deeply, upon climbing into her bed. But she awakened well before sunrise to the soft murmurings of voices in the corridor outside her room. When she opened the door, it was to see Valeria with candle in hand vanishing in the direction of the room she shared with Bartolomeo, while Bartolomeo was making his way toward the guest chamber where Andrea lay.

"The changing of the guard," Rosalinda whispered to herself. "Since Bartolomeo is always more lenient with me than either Valeria or Mother, he will not object when I join him. I am sure he heard me open the door, though I tried to be quiet. He will be expecting me."

She dressed quickly in the old russet wool gown she wore when doing her morning chores and pulled her hair into a single thick braid, tying the end with a bit of ribbon. A fast splash of water on her face and she was ready.

She found Andrea lying motionless in bed. Bartolomeo stood by the window, holding back the curtain to watch the sky lighten.

"It is still snowing hard," Bartolomeo said without turning around. "Come in, my dear. As you saw a short time ago, I have sent Valeria to sleep for a while, since she was awake all night. Our guest is sleeping."

"How still he is. How pale." Rosalinda drew near to the bed to look at Andrea.

"And how fortunate that he came to us when he did," Bartolomeo added. "He would not have lived through the night in this weather." He dropped the curtain and crossed the room to stand beside Rosalinda.

"Who can he be?" Rosalinda whispered. "What is the story that brought him here?"

"Judging by his clothing, by that ruby ring on his finger, and by the fine daggers he was carrying, I would guess he is the son of a nobleman," Bartolomeo said. "Or, perhaps, a rich merchant's son."

"Mother probably thinks he is a spy, sent to watch us."

"A poor spy, indeed, to allow himself to sink into this sad state."

"Mother will say his condition is a clever ruse to get into the villa and gain our sympathy."

"Your mother has tragic experience behind her suspicion of strangers and her strictness where you and Bianca are concerned," Bartolomeo said. "She is determined to keep her daughters alive and to find a way for you to regain your rightful heritage."

"It will be Bianca's heritage, not mine. She is the heiress to Monteferro," Rosalinda said. "For myself, I would rather live at Villa Serenita than at any court."

"You remind me of your father, who never wanted to be Duke of Monteferro. But like my dear friend Girolamo, when the call to duty comes, you will rise to answer it.''

Andrea interrupted Bartolomeo's comments, stirring with a moan. At once Rosalinda bent toward him. When he put up a trembling hand, she took it, finding it hot and dry.

''Where—where am I?'' he asked, in a weak, hoarse voice.

''You are safe at Villa Serenita,'' Rosalinda told him, giving his fingers an encouraging squeeze. She placed her free hand on his forehead. ''Bartolomeo, he is feverish.''

''He needs food,'' Bartolomeo said. ''Valeria left a pot of broth on the hearth to keep warm, and she also brought bread and wine for him.''

Bartolomeo ladled some broth into a bowl and Rosalinda began to feed it to Andrea. When he had finished the broth, she gave him pieces of the bread dipped in wine.

''Not too much,'' Bartolomeo cautioned, ''and not too quickly. He is half starved. Eating too fast will only make him ill.''

''That broth was so good,'' Andrea said. He moved restlessly, frowning and wincing. ''My feet are throbbing.''

''I'm not surprised,'' Bartolomeo told him. ''You have barely escaped a severe frostbite. Your feet will be red and swollen, and very sore, for some days to come. I advise you to remain in bed and not to try to walk until they are completely healed.

''Young man,'' Bartolomeo went on, ''if you have family whom you want notified that you are safe, we will be glad to send a messenger as soon as the snow clears enough to allow travel. You have only to tell us where the messenger should go and to whom he should take the good news that you are alive and recovering from your ordeal.''

Rosalinda stifled a gasp. Her mother would never let Bartolomeo send such a message, and Bartolomeo knew it. Bartolomeo seldom lied. That he had done so in front of her was surprising, but she thought she understood why he had done it. He wanted to learn as much as he could from Andrea, so he could relay what he discovered to Eleonora.

''You asked me similar questions last night,'' Andrea said to Bartolomeo. ''I told you then, as I tell you now, that I believe they are all dead. All of them,'' he repeated, turning his face away and swallowing hard as if fighting back tears.

A faint rustle of silk skirts made Rosalinda turn her own head. Her mother had come quietly into the room. Eleonora moved forward, apparently with the intention of taking up the interrogation Bartolomeo had begun.

''Where did you live before you took to wandering in the mountains, Signore Andrea?'' Eleonora asked with a certain threatening edge to her words.

''Madonna.'' Andrea met Eleonora's eyes squarely and spoke with every appearance of complete honesty. ''No person outside your household knows I have come here, nor could anyone have tracked me to this place. I will impose upon your hospitality only so long as I must in order to regain my health. I beg you to respect my privacy and not question me about my past or my family. And since I perceive that you are also bent upon maintaining your privacy from the world, I do solemnly swear upon my mother's soul—which I devoutly trust rests even now in heaven—upon my mother's soul, I say, and upon my own hope of a reunion with her in heaven one day, I do swear to you that I will never reveal the location of this villa, nor the name of anyone who lives here."

"Fine words," said Eleonora. "I am sure you mean them, too. But I have heard of tortures that could wring information out of an unwilling saint."

"Mother!" cried Rosalinda. "What kind of hospitality is this, to speak so to a guest, and a sick man at that?"

"I believe Signore Andrea knows whereof I speak," said Eleonora, her gaze still on the man in the bed.

"Yes, madonna, I do." Andrea's finely shaped mouth pulled into a bitter line; his brown eyes grew hard at some distant memory. "Very well, let me revise my oath. I will promise nothing beyond what flesh and bone can endure, but I assure you, madonna, that I have no desire to cause harm to those who have shown kindness to me when all the rest of the world has turned against me."

"That is better," Eleonora said. "An oath to do your best to honor my need for privacy I can accept and trust. Nor, honoring your own wish for privacy, will I ask at what court you have lived and there learned to make extravagant promises using poetic words." Eleonora paused, considering Andrea's serious face.

"You are welcome to stay with us for as long as you want," she said. To Rosalinda she added, "Come now, child. While you have been nursing Signore Andrea, Bianca has done your morning chores for you. It is past time for your lessons to begin."

Rosalinda was so shocked by Eleonora's words to Andrea that she could only rise in silent response to her mother's order. She could scarcely believe that Eleonora had just invited Andrea to remain at the villa. The only guests they ever had were Luca and his trusted servant. Any other travelers, lost or otherwise, were turned away by the men-at-arms and directed to the village, to seek shelter there. Eleonora must have her own reasons for her unexpected generosity to Andrea.

More secrets, Rosalinda thought, knowing the chances were good that she would never learn what those secrets were.

"Lessons?" Andrea said. "Lessons in what, may I ask?"

"In Latin." Rosalinda answered him with a grimace. "Also Greek, which I like just a little less than Latin. And lessons in history, which I do find very interesting."

"I can understand a young woman being trained in ancient languages," said Andrea, "perhaps even training in rhetoric. But history? What an odd subject for a woman to read."

"It is not odd at all," Eleonora said. "Only by understanding the past can we hope to improve upon it, or avoid repeating unfortunate mistakes."

"You are wise, madonna." Andrea's smile was sad. "I have known men who might have profited from your lessons, if only they had learned them in time."

Later that day Andrea developed a high fever. He lay tossing and muttering in bed, clearly unaware of where he was. They all took turns nursing him. When Rosalinda was with him, she listened to the sounds he made, trying to distinguish words, but nothing he said made any sense to her. Except for one phrase. Andrea clung to her hand and over and over again said the same thing.

"The girl. The girl."

"What girl?" she asked, fearing he might have a lover somewhere far away, where his real life was.

"Rosa-linda," he whispered. "Rosa-linda."

Overwhelmed by an unfamiliar tenderness, Rosalinda

lifted his hand to her cheek and held it there. The mystery that lay about Andrea like a heavy cloak, and the masculinity inherent in him despite his present physical debility, together beckoned to all that was feminine in Rosalinda. Andrea intrigued her, and tempted her to dream. . . .

"Not a usual name," he said suddenly, his liquid brown gaze fixed upon her face. He seemed rational and so, in an attempt to prevent his mind from drifting back into the shadowy realm of fever, she told him how she had come by her name.

"In fact, Rosalinda is Spanish," she told him. "I was tiny and red when I was born and my first baby hair was red, too. When my mother's old Aragonese nurse took me from the midwife's hands, I curled up into a little knot, at which the nurse cried out in her native tongue, '*¡Ay, qué rosa linda!*' which is to say, 'Oh, what a pretty rose!' My father was in the room, and when he heard the nurse's exclamation he declared it was the only name for me. That same day I was baptised Rosalinda Maria."

"A pretty story for a pretty girl," Andrea murmured. "You are like a rose, sweet and fragrant." On those last words, his voice drifted off.

"Andrea?" Rosalinda lifted his hand, which she was still holding, and pressed his fingers to her lips. "Don't give way to the fever. Try to keep your thoughts here, with me."

"Beautiful," he muttered again. "Gloriously free. Rosalinda!"

"Andrea, look at me," she begged. "Please look at me."

But his brief period of awareness of her presence had ended. Andrea was already slipping back into a state of semiconsciousness. Once more his breath became labored. He tossed and wept and cried out over and over for someone whose name Rosalinda could not understand because his voice was so choked and ragged. All she could do for him was put cloths wrung out in cool water on his brow and hold his hands when he thrashed about too wildly. She talked to him, but he did not seem to hear her.

"Just as I feared," Valeria said when she came to relieve Rosalinda. "There can be no doubt now that he has lung fever. Help me to pile the pillows behind him so we can raise him and ease his breathing."

"Will he live?" As she spoke, Rosalinda was following Valeria's directions, heaping pillows against the head of the bed. "We cannot let him die."

Valeria gave her a sharp look before lifting Andrea so he was almost sitting against the pillows.

"Please, Valeria, tell me the truth. Can you save him?"

"It is not up to me," Valeria said. "I will do everything I can to help him, but in the end, the recovery of any sick person is in the hands of the Lord."

"Only tell me what to do and I will do it."

"Begin by going below to join your mother and Bianca for the evening meal," Valeria said. "Don't object, Rosalinda, and be sure you eat well. If you want to be of help to Andrea, you must take care not to fall ill yourself. Surely, you can see the sense in that."

"I do." Rosalinda brushed Andrea's dark hair off his burning forehead. "I will return as soon as I have eaten."

"What you will do," Valeria said, "is stay with your mother and sister for a while, before you retire to bed and sleep the night through. If you do not, I will refuse to allow you back into this room tomorrow, when it is your turn to sit with him."

"You are a hard taskmaster, Valeria."

"And you are a stubborn, willful girl." Valeria's smile and the gentle caress she bestowed on Rosalinda's cheek took all the sting out of her words. "Because you are so stubborn, and because I love you so well, I want you to do as I say. You are looking pale, and Bianca tells me you have lost your appetite."

Knowing Valeria was right and that she was stern enough to keep anyone who disobeyed her away from the sickroom as threatened, Rosalinda tried to follow her orders. She changed her dress and went down to the evening meal. After the meal she sat in her mother's sitting room, playing with Bianca's kitten and talking with her mother and sister, but her thoughts, and her heart, were above, with the man lying ill in the guest room bed.

Andrea lay near death for three days and three nights. On the fourth morning, Rosalinda entered the sickroom at her usual time to find a weary Valeria spooning soup into him. It took only a glance to tell Rosalinda that Andrea's condition was much improved. Gratitude to heaven for sparing him, and to Valeria for her nursing care, overwhelmed Rosalinda, leaving her temporarily speechless.

"The fever broke during the night," Valeria said when she noticed Rosalinda. "He is still very weak, but I am sure now that he will live. Don't talk to him too much while you sit with him, Rosalinda. Let him rest, and please remember that someone who has been desperately ill—especially an active, vigorous man—is certain to suffer from downcast spirits until he recovers his full strength."

Having finished feeding Andrea the soup, Valeria left to seek her own bed and Rosalinda sat down in her place next to Andrea. He lay quietly, his eyes on her face.

"You do look much better today." Rosalinda smiled at him, expecting an answering smile. Instead, Andrea turned his head away from her.

"Andrea, you must not be discouraged. It will take a while for you to recover completely."

"What does it matter whether I am strong or weak?" he whispered. "I have lost everything. Family, friends, position, all are gone."

"That is what my mother might have said, years ago when we first came to this villa," Rosalinda told him. "But she never lost hope. Neither must you."

"Your mother had you and your sister," Andrea said. "Whatever the events that led her to seek refuge in these mountains, she still had loyal friends in Bartolomeo and Valeria. Whereas I am alone."

"No, you are not alone. I am here. So are the others, all of them, Bianca and Mother, Valeria and Bartolomeo. We are your new friends." Unable to prevent herself from seeking physical contact with him, Rosalinda put her hand over his. Andrea did not respond, but neither did he withdraw his hand from her touch.

Andrea was silent, as if he could not argue against her logic. After a while he asked, "Why does one man live while another, possibly a much better man, dies?"

"I do not know," Rosalinda said. "Andrea, it is clear to me that a great loss is weighing on your heart. If it would help you to talk about it, I will keep your confidence."

"I am sure you would," he responded. "But I cannot burden you with knowledge that might put you into danger. No, my dear Rosalinda, this matter I must keep to myself."

He said no more on the subject and Rosalinda had

the impression that he was trying hard to dismiss his sad thoughts and be cheerful. He was basically a strong and healthy young man. Now that he was relieved of the stress of trying to survive in the wild, now that he was sheltered and fed regularly and the fever was gone from him, his condition improved with astonishing speed.

Careful probing by Rosalinda of her mother and sister, and of Bartolomeo and Valeria, revealed that Andrea had not mentioned to anyone else the sorrow with which he was wrestling. The fact that he had spoken of it only to her made her feel even closer to him.

Not that he displayed an overt affection for her. He was the very soul of discretion. Any casual observer might have thought that he enjoyed the company of Valeria or Eleonora or Bianca as much as that of Rosalinda. Only rarely did Rosalinda intercept a soft glance from his brown eyes that hinted at a warmer feeling toward her than toward the other ladies. Always, with him or apart from him, in Rosalinda's own heart there resided a sense of connection to Andrea, as if their fates were woven together. He remained a fascinating enigma to her, but if they were given enough time, she was sure he would reveal the mystery that bound him to silence about his past.

While he was still at that stage in his recuperation during which he was restless without being able yet to get out of bed for any length of time, she read to him. Her discovery that he preferred Petrarch's sonnets to Dante's long, allegorical poetry suggested to her that their minds were well matched. She was even more convinced of this when he confided that he, too, had disliked learning Latin. She treasured the hours they spent alone together.

Then, to Rosalinda's surprise, Bianca began to join

her in Andrea's room with some frequency, saying she ought to take a turn at reading, too. Once, when Rosalinda had stayed behind in her mother's sitting room to find a particular book she wanted from the shelves there, she walked into Andrea's chamber to discover Bianca smoothing back his hair and offering a cup of wine to him. Later, Bianca offered an explanation.

"Andrea is a fascinating person, unlike any other man here at Villa Serenita," Bianca said. "I do believe he is even more clever than Bartolomeo. And you know how Mother values Bartolomeo's keen wits."

"I knew you would grow to like him if only you could forget your fear of strangers," Rosalinda answered. But a knot had formed in her stomach as she watched her sister bestow that gentle caress upon Andrea. She told herself it was foolish to be jealous. Bianca was merely being kind.

There came a day, almost two weeks after Andrea's arrival at the villa, when Bartolomeo decided the younger man was recovered enough to be shaved and to have his hair trimmed. Accordingly, Bartolomeo called in the man-at-arms who usually acted as barber for his fellows and for Bartolomeo. The ladies were banished from the guest room, several large buckets of hot water were carried in, and the door was shut upon the three men.

Two hours later Bartolomeo appeared in Eleonora's sitting room, where Rosalinda and Bianca were, as usual during the afternoon, engaged in their lessons.

"Well, Bartolomeo," said Eleonora, seeing him at the door, "you look uncommonly pleased with yourself."

"Madonna, I think you will be pleased, too," Bartolomeo said with a smile. "Will you allow me to escort you to Andrea's room? He would like to speak with you."

"May we go too?" Rosalinda spoke up at once.

"I believe he would be happy to see you," Bartolomeo said. Eleonora was already passing through the door, and behind her back Bartolomeo winked at Rosalinda. "Both of you may join us if you like."

The guestroom had been cleared of all traces of medicines and of the barbering and scrubbing that had taken place there. The bed was freshly made up, with the covers turned back as if to invite the occupant of the room to lie down and rest. But Andrea was no longer in the bed. Shaved, shorn, newly bathed and wearing clean, borrowed clothes, he was sitting in a chair by the window. At Eleonora's brisk entry, he rose to greet her.

The beard had made him look older than he was. Rosalinda thought he could not be much more than twenty-five. He was still lean after weeks of near-starvation and illness, but from his tall frame it was clear that he was a man of considerable strength. His black, curly hair was trimmed to his earlobes, and the absence of a beard revealed sharply carved features accented by his high-arched, Roman nose and a remarkably firm jaw.

To Rosalinda's eyes he was the most handsome man she had ever encountered and far better-looking than she had imagined before seeing his entire face.

"Oh, my." Upon entering the room behind her sister, Bianca came to a sudden halt, staring at the man wearing one of Bartolomeo's too-large doublets, and hose, both in a rich shade of dark red that made his skin look fascinatingly pale and his hair and eyes mysteriously dark.

"Madonna Eleonora," Andrea said, bowing to her, "I must thank you for all you and your household have done for me. I do hope and pray there will come a time when I am able to repay you, though nothing would be adequate payment for the kindness of saving my life.''

''As always, you use fine words.'' Eleonora motioned with one hand. ''Sit down, young man. I can see that you are trembling from some residual weakness.''

''I believe I will be stronger very soon, madonna.'' Nevertheless, Andrea did sit, waiting only until Eleonora had taken the chair Bartolomeo placed facing him.

''In that case, you may join us for meals whenever you feel well enough.'' Eleonora's eyes were sharp as she regarded her guest. ''I have promised to respect your wish for privacy about your past, and I will do so. However, I do have one question, born of a very natural curiosity. Now that your voice is stronger, and now that I am able to inspect your features without the barrier of that thick beard, I have the impression that you were born and raised north of Rome.'' Eleonora paused, looking at Andrea expectantly, but he let her wait for a long moment before he answered her.

''You have guessed truly, madonna, but I must beg you not to ask any further questions of me.''

''Nor will I. As I have already told you, Andrea, you are welcome to remain with us until you are completely healthy once more.''

''Again, madonna, I am eternally in your debt.''

''Perhaps you will repay that debt in part by contributing to our evenings,'' Eleonora said. ''Our life here is a quiet one. We read aloud or play games for entertainment.''

''I play a fair game of chess, madonna,'' Andrea offered.

''Bartolomeo is doubtless glad to hear that,'' Eleonora said with a glance in the direction of her faithful friend. "Valeria and I are much too easy for him to best."

"I find it difficult to believe that anyone might win over you, madonna." Andrea's voice was soft, holding an inflection the listening Rosalinda could not understand, save that it was there and it puzzled her.

"Do you play the lute or sing?" asked Bianca.

"I do, indeed, Madonna Bianca." Andrea smiled at her.

"Yes, I rather thought you would," Eleonora said. Her eyes on Andrea were shrewd. "We sometimes make up stories to entertain each other. Perhaps you will tell us new stories, about life in the world beyond these mountains."

Andrea went very still, looking back at her. Again he let Eleonora wait before he responded. Watching the two of them, Rosalinda thought they were playing a game of some kind, the rules of which were a mystery to her.

"I am fond of fanciful tales," Andrea said at last, "though I think it would be wise of me to listen to the stories you and your companions have to tell before I venture to recount one of my own. Thus, I will make no embarassing mistakes."

"You are a clever man, Signore Andrea." A faint smile curved Eleonora's lips. "Since Bartolomeo and I have work to do, we will leave you with my daughters to entertain you for an hour or two. I feel certain they will be delighted to avoid further lessons for this afternoon."

"Your appearance is much improved," Bianca said, taking the chair facing Andrea as soon as her mother had vacated it.

"I thank you for the compliment, Madonna Bianca," Andrea responded with great seriousness.

"What I meant to say," Bianca went on, blushing a little, "is that you looked so much like a bear when you first appeared on the terrace that you frightened all of us."

"I am sorry for that," Andrea said.

"Except for Rosalinda, of course. Nothing ever frightens her," Bianca said. "Tell us, please, why you were wearing that dreadful, smelly bearskin."

"For warmth, Bianca," Rosalinda said. She was feeling more than a bit exasperated with her sister. What was Bianca thinking of, asking silly questions and blushing and fluttering her eyelashes at Andrea? Since there were only two chairs in the room and Bianca had taken the second one—which, to be honest, Rosalinda reminded herself, was the prerogative of an older sister—Rosalinda pulled up a stool and sat on it. "Without the bearskin for warmth, Andrea would have frozen to death."

"Yes, I would. The skin also served as a disguise," Andrea told the sisters. "Which is why I left the bear's head attached to the fur."

"Why did you need a disguise?" Bianca asked.

"I have always heard that fierce bandits live in the mountains," Andrea replied. "I reasoned that even the most desperate outlaws would run away from a bear without looking too closely at it. I do believe the disguise worked well, for never did anyone threaten me while I wore it."

"But," Bianca persisted, "why were you roaming in the mountains in the first place?"

"Bianca, if you ply Andrea with so many questions, you will tire him and impede his recovery," Rosalinda protested. She could tell that Andrea did not want to answer Bianca's last question. He was letting her wait for his response, in the same way in which he had let their mother wait.

"In truth, though I do not like to admit it, I find I am tired," Andrea said at last. "Perhaps, if I were to rest for an hour or two, I might restore my energies enough to allow me to join you for the evening meal as your mother so kindly suggested."

"Will you play the lute for us?" Bianca asked.

"If not this evening, then I promise I will do so soon," Andrea said.

"We will leave you to rest." Rosalinda was on her feet with a hand under her sister's elbow, raising Bianca out of her chair. Bianca was not ready to go. Rosalinda had to exert a certain amount of pressure to make her stand up, and then had to keep her hand on Bianca's arm to draw her toward the door and push her through it.

As she went out of the room Rosalinda glanced back and caught Andrea's eye. He smiled at her, a warm, enticing smile that took her breath away and made her believe that he would like her to stay with him because he knew that, unlike Bianca, she would not ask questions he did not want to answer.

Chapter Four

''Why did you do that?'' Bianca demanded, pulling her arm out of Rosalinda's grasp. ''I might have extracted some information from Andrea if only you were not so protective of his health.''

''With you and Mother both interrogating him at every opportunity, someone has to protect him or he will have a relapse,'' Rosalinda snapped back at her. ''Did Mother tell you to question him, because she has promised not to do it?''

''Of course not.'' Bianca rubbed at her elbow. ''I thought I could be of help to her, that's all. I know she wants to learn more about him.''

''When Andrea is ready, he will tell us all we need to know about his life,'' Rosalinda said, hoping it was true. Relenting, she went on, ''Did I hurt your arm? I didn't mean to, but you would not stop talking and, my dearest, you did ask too many questions. It seemed to me the only way to silence you was to get you out of the room.''

''My arm is fine,'' Bianca admitted. ''Rosalinda, don't be angry with me. I was only trying to help Mother.''

''I know. Sometimes I talk too much, too. I am going to join Valeria in the kitchen. Would you like to come with me?''

''I think I will return to the sitting room and complete that Latin translation I was working on. Mother will be pleased if I get it just right.''

''I'm sure she will be. But I hope you know that Mother will love you, no matter what you do.''

''If I am very good,'' Bianca said, ''then she will have one less cause for worry. We should both try to be as good as we can.''

''I do try,'' said Rosalinda with a rueful twist to her mouth. ''For all my good intentions, I still annoy Mother far too often.''

''Then come to the sitting room with me now, and I will help you with your Latin,'' Bianca suggested. ''I know it would please Mother.''

''Perhaps there is something I can do to help Valeria instead. That will also please Mother when she hears of it.''

''And at the same time you will avoid that Latin lesson until later,'' Bianca teased.

''I would avoid it altogether if I could.''

Leaving her sister, Rosalinda headed for the kitchen, where Valeria supervised several of the wives and daughters of the men-at-arms, who did the cooking and the other kitchen chores. Rosalinda was not especially interested in cooking, though she did willingly help Valeria when it was her turn to do so, and she agreed with her mother that every lady ought to know what went on in the kitchen of her home. Rosalinda's consuming interest of the moment was Andrea. She thought Valeria might have a few answers for her about the actual state of his health.

On her way to the kitchen, Rosalinda passed the room that Bartolomeo used as his office. There he kept the account books for the estate, and in the late evenings after the ladies had retired, he worked upon the history of the Farisi dukes of Monteferro that he was writing. It was not at all unusual for Eleonora to be in the room with Bartolomeo, either discussing matters having to do with the estate or reading the most recently completed pages of the history.

Rosalinda paused at the open door, intending only to stick her head inside and tell her mother where she would be. What she heard kept her rooted to the spot where she stood. Her mother and Bartolomeo were talking about Andrea.

"There is no question in my mind that he is nobly born," Eleonora said. "Just think, Bartolomeo! What an opportunity presents itself in the person of that young man."

"I have no wish to contradict you," Bartolomeo told her, "but a nobleman who has been wandering alone in the mountains must have some tragic event in his past. It is my belief that Andrea has gone into exile, either because he was sent away from his home by his family as the result of a scandal, or he left by order of the authorities wherever he once lived, or perhaps he has fled to avoid imprisonment."

"All the better for us," Eleonora insisted. "Many fine and capable men are exiled because they disagree too vigorously with their governments or because they are fleeing rival family members. There is no disgrace in exile, which is a kinder fate than imprisonment or assassination.

"I believe that Andrea is the weapon for which I have been waiting all these years," Eleonora went on. "Heaven has sent him into my home and made him obligated to me for saving his life. Now I will use him as heaven must have intended me to do."

"Use him?" Bartolomeo repeated. "Eleonora, what are you planning?"

"If I place an army of mercenaries at Andrea's disposal and offer him a high office as reward for his efforts, he may be willing to help me regain control of Monteferro," Eleonora said. "Which, from what Luca told us during his last visit, will also mean taking over neighboring Aullia, since the Guidi family now controls both cities.

"Then, at last, I will force the Guidi into exile, as I was once forced to leave my home," Eleonora went on. "And I will imprison that miserable wretch of a dwarf, Niccolò Stregone, for the rest of his life! Since the Guidi have already conveniently killed the treacherous duke of Aullia for me, and doubtless the duke's entire family with him, we can forget about them. Perhaps I will grant the governorship of Aullia to Andrea. But only if he first shows skill in managing my army."

"Raising an army will cost you all the money you have deposited with the House of Nardi," Bartolomeo objected. "If you lose this gamble, you will have nothing left with which to make another attempt. And Andrea may not be willing to fall in with your plans."

"He will if I wait until the perfect moment to approach him. That young man has the necessary spirit," Eleonora said. "You have heard how he bandies words with me, how clever he is. And how careful to keep his own secrets."

"Those same secrets may defeat us before we begin," said Bartolomeo.

"Have you lost your courage, old friend?"

"No, but I do worry about your daughters, whom I love as if they were my own children. Knowing you, I am certain that you have thought of what will happen to them. If Andrea is all that you believe he is, then gratitude for his life or not, he will surely demand one of those girls in marriage in return for helping you."

"Let him but help me regain Monteferro for Bianca and her future children, and I will marry Andrea myself if he asks for me!" Eleonora declared with a laugh.

"Your late husband always said that you were far better than he at planning and intrigue." Bartolomeo's voice was tinged with admiration. "I do believe Girolamo was right about you."

"I have waited so long for Fortune to show me the way to regain what rightfully belongs to my daughters," Eleonora said. "Now that I see the way to do it, I will not be thwarted. Bartolomeo, dearest and most loyal of friends, the day will soon come when we will return to Monteferro in triumph!"

Rosalinda burst into Andrea's room without knocking. Startled, he spun around to face the door, one hand going to his waist, reaching in vain for the dagger Bartolomeo had taken away. More tired after his busy day with the barber and the ladies of the villa than he cared to admit, Andrea had divested himself of doublet, shirt, and shoes. Clad only in his borrowed hose, which he was about to remove, he took a surprised step backward when a delicious armful of a girl flung herself at him.

"Andrea." She clung to him, her soft cheek pressed against his bare chest. "Oh, take care! I am so afraid for you."

"What is it? Is there some danger?" He was instantly alert, silently cursing the absence of his only weapon. Still, he could not stop his arms from closing around Rosalinda or keep himself from breathing in the rose fragrance she wore. The effects of her closeness and the rose scent were immediate. The sudden flush of heat emanating from those portions of his body now in direct contact with her soft form told him that his recovery from starvation and illness was progressing remarkably well. "Rosalinda, what is this about? Do you need protection?"

"No. You do. But it's not an attack. It's my mother's plans for you."

Her arms were locked around his waist. He could feel her trembling. Her head fit perfectly into the angle between his shoulder and his neck. He dared to let his lips brush across a loose strand of curly hair.

She stayed where she was, clutching his waist, until she ceased to shake. Andrea thought she must be aware of his body's quickening eagerness. She was too close to him not to notice it.

With a deep, shuddering breath, she lifted her head and moved back a little. Her eyes were wide and soft, a luminous silver-gray, and they were bright with tears. Never had Andrea seen such beautiful eyes, or such thick, long eyelashes. He wanted to kiss each faintly shadowed eyelid. More than that, he ached to press his own mouth to her rosy-red, softly parted lips.

With one hand he stroked the lock of dark hair that had come loose from her braid, smoothing the silken strands of it, pulling the hair down the side of her cheek and under her chin. He had seen noblewomen wearing their long hair that way, drawn under the chin and up again on the other side, to twist the end of the lock into braids and pearl-encrusted ornaments. In Florence, Aullia, and Urbino it was the very latest style. Or it had been, during the previous summer. . . .

"Andrea?" Her voice was a faint whisper on his ear.

He saw the innocence and confusion on her face and knew she had never before experienced the emotions that must be unsettling her now. He tried to remember himself, where he was, and what was at stake, but all he could see, all he could think of, were Rosalinda's eyes, those silvery pools of light. And her mouth. Her lips were much too tempting to ignore. Slowly, he lowered his head and put his mouth upon those lips.

Sweetness beyond anything he had known or dreamed of in the past coursed through Andrea. Rosalinda's lips trembled beneath his. He could tell she did not know what to do, which meant no other man had claimed those perfect lips before him. Carefully, mindful of her innocence, he led her to a new awareness until she opened to him and let him taste the wet heat of her inner mouth. She tasted of cinnamon and rose petals.

Her arms wound around his neck, a motion that lifted her breasts, pushing their gentle curves hard against his chest. Andrea tightened his embrace, one arm across her shoulders, while the other arm moved lower, to pull her hips nearer, against the burning ache he was hard put to control. He could feel a slight shifting in her stance as she accommodated herself to the new sensations, to her first hint of what it meant to be a woman who was desired by a virile man.

She was as reluctant as he to end the kiss, but Andrea was fast approaching the limits of his control. He eased her away from him, while still keeping his arms around her so she would not feel deserted or unwanted. For he did want her. After his long abstinence, his body hungered not just for a woman, but for Rosalinda. Only

Rosalinda. He thought he would die from his compelling desire for her.

Andrea considered his half-naked state of undress, and eyed the inviting bed with its fresh linen sheets turned back, and he groaned. And for a moment, with a rough motion, he pulled her hard against himself once more, before he let her go.

"Andrea?" Her fingertips grazed his cheek, outlined his lips, moved to his chin and lingered there. "Dear bear." Her smile was tremulous.

"I am no bear," he said, his voice husky with repressed desire. "That was no bear hug. I am a man. At the moment, an overeager man who feels himself growing weaker with every breath he takes."

"Valeria has warned me that you are not yet fully recovered," she said. She glanced toward the bed. "Do you want to lie down?"

"There is nothing in this world I want more than to lie down there," he said. "But only with you."

"Oh." Her silver eyes grew large and round and Andrea saw comprehension flood into her gaze. "Oh," she said again, with new understanding.

"Andrea, I am sorry. I did not mean to—yes, I did. I wanted you to kiss me. But I did not want to embarrass you."

"I wanted to kiss you, too," he said, charmed by her innocent honesty. "But it would not be wise to do it again, and certainly, it would be unwise to do it here, in my bedchamber, while I am unclothed."

"I understand. I do. Mother has explained to Bianca and me—" She stopped, her face lowered, her hands fluttering among the folds of her skirt.

"Do you know how adorable you are?" Andrea asked. "Standing there in confusion, gnawing at your lower lip, with your cheeks bright red, you are irresistible.'' He took a step toward her, closing the distance he knew he ought to keep between them. ''I long to gnaw upon your lip as you are doing,'' he whispered.

''You do?''

Andrea watched the play of emotion across her blushing face as she considered that possibility. Her small, pointed tongue came out to lick across her lower lip.

Andrea's blood began to boil in his veins. He could endure no more temptation. It was not Rosalinda's fault. She did not know what she was doing to him. Andrea flung away from her to the window. He put both hands on the sill, holding on tight to prevent himself from reaching for Rosalinda, from drawing her back into his arms. He cleared his throat loudly and took several deep breaths. When he was calmer, he turned again to face her.

She stood where he had left her, but he could tell that she, too, had used the interval to calm herself. Her hands were folded, one over the other, at the high waistline of her dress in the typical noblewoman's pose he had seen countless times before, in other places. Her cheeks were still rosy pink, but she was no longer blushing. He noted that a certain softness lingered in her eyes.

''So formal,'' he murmured.

''I thought formality was what you wanted, Andrea.''

''Formality would be best,'' he said. ''It will help to keep me from violating you.''

''If you did it, it would not be a violation.'' Her voice was quiet and perfectly controlled, yet her eyes were glowing.

''When you came rushing through that door,'' he said, keeping his distance from her, trying to think about something other than the surprising sweetness of Rosalinda in his arms, ''you were greatly disturbed by something your mother said or did. Why did you come to warn me, Rosalinda?"

"I heard Mother and Bartolomeo talking." She stopped rather abruptly and began to chew on her lower lip again.

"What did they say that frightened you enough to send you flying to my room and into my arms for protection?"

"I was frightened for you, not for myself," she said.

"Why?"

Rosalinda stared at him. Her first thought had been to warn him of her mother's plan to place him at the head of a mercenary army and send him to take back Monteferro. On such a quest, Andrea might well be killed. And while she knew from listening to Bartolomeo's tales that men craved the opportunity to perform feats of great valor, she thought Andrea had suffered enough. There was a terrible sadness in him. During the worst days of his illness, he had spoken as if he believed he ought to be dead along with the family and friends he had lost. Sent into battle, he might well seek death. She could not let that happen to him.

And yet, telling him in advance of her mother's scheme was, in a way, a betrayal of her mother. And of Bianca. Her beloved sister longed to return to Monteferro. Bianca was the rightful heiress of that city-state. She deserved high honor and respect, and a brilliant marriage to a man who would love and appreciate her and, for her sake, keep Monteferro—and Bianca—safe and happy.

"Rosalinda?"

Andrea was standing very close to her. She could feel his warmth. Rosalinda caught her breath, afraid he would kiss her again and make her feel all those wonderful, forbidden urgings of her youthful body. At the same time, she was afraid he would not kiss her, for she longed to have his lips on hers. She thought about his mouth and the plunging heat of his tongue, and her heart began to pound harder. Still, her mother's training exerted a strong influence over her, forcing duty to do battle against romantic longing.

"I don't know what to say," she faltered.

"Say what you came to tell me."

"I really should not. Mother would be furious with me if she knew I was here, or that I overhead what she said."

He looked hard at her for a moment, and she saw something change in his face, as if a sheer veil had been drawn across his features to hide his deepest thoughts from her. The notion came to her that he did not entirely trust her. She was not used to dissimulation or to any kind of intrigue. At Villa Serenita there was no need for either. But Andrea had not grown up at Villa Serenita, and she saw in him now the difference between them because of their separate upbringings. And then he smiled at her and was her Andrea, her dear bear, once again.

"Rosalinda." His mouth drew nearer; his fingers caught in her hair to hold her face close to his. Rosalinda held her breath as Andrea's lips quickly brushed across hers. While she stood entranced, his hand slid out of her hair, across her cheek, and down along her neck to her shoulder. With his eyes holding hers, he let his hand move lower, until it covered her breast. He pressed gently, holding the high, firm roundness against his palm. His thumb and one finger moved across her nipple.

Deep inside Rosalinda a flame leapt up, burning brightly. She could not move, she could not even breathe, but she was sure Andrea could see in her eyes that she was on fire with an unnameable need. He took his hand away from her breast and rested it on her shoulder again, but that did not stop the flame inside her.

"Tell me what your mother said that so upset you." He spoke softly, but his words were a command.

A flash of intuition told Rosalinda that this was the sort of thing nobles did in great palaces. They played games of power and desire. She had heard her mother speak with disgust of such practices, but until this hour she had not guessed how seductive the game could be.

Valiantly, Rosalinda fought against her desire to have Andrea put his hand on her breast again. She wanted his other hand on her other breast at the same time. She wanted him to pull her into his arms and hold her so tightly that she melted into him until they were one.

Through the mist of mounting emotion, Rosalinda sensed that she must not give way to the carnal lure Andrea was offering. What was happening was her own fault. She had begun it by rushing into his room and by not leaving the instant she discovered that he was undressed. The urge to reveal to him all that her mother had said to Bartolomeo had been a foolish one. Frantically, Rosalinda sought for a way to warn Andrea and keep him safe, while not betraying her mother or harming Bianca's future prospects. Then she saw the path she must take between her two desires.

"My mother told Bartolomeo that she has decided how she will require you to repay her kindness and her hospitality," Rosalinda said, keeping her eyes wide open and on Andrea's face. "She will soon seek a great favor from you. She is a deep thinker, Andrea. There are many levels to every sentence she speaks and every action she takes. Think long and carefully before you decide whether or not to agree to do what she asks of you.''

''Is that all?'' he said when she fell silent.

''I beg you not to tell her what I have just revealed. She will be angry with me if she learns I have repeated portions of a sentence that I overheard because I was where I should not have been.'' It was an evasion, but it was the best Rosalinda could do with her wits spinning from Andrea's seductive attentions.

''She will not learn of our conversation from me,'' Andrea said.

''Thank you.'' Rosalinda stepped away from him. ''I ought to go. I should not have stayed as long as I did.''

''You are right. But I cannot regret that you came to see me,'' he said. ''Nor that I kissed you.''

Rosalinda feared her knees would give way. She longed for Andrea to kiss her again and to touch her. And he knew what she was feeling. She could see that he knew.

''Go now,'' he said in a harsh whisper. ''For if you stay any longer, if I so much as brush against you with the tip of one finger, I will keep you here until I have ruined both of us. Please, Rosalinda, leave me.''

Rosalinda fled from him, running to her own room, thanking heaven and all the saints that she met no one on the way.

She had gone to his chamber as an innocent girl, fond of him and fearing for his safety. She left his room with a new awareness of her own womanly urges, yet unable to fulfill them. Rosalinda ached to feel Andrea's arms around her once again. She burned for his touch. And she wept for a loss of innocence and trust that she did not fully understand.

She left behind her a man as confused and unhappy as she was. For a few weeks, Andrea had lived in a state of pure friendship with Rosalinda, until his improved health had allowed him to feel desire again. He was not ashamed of kissing her, for he alone would bear the burden of containing his longing to have more than just a kiss or two from her. What shamed him was the cold-hearted way he had used her to learn what he wanted to know about her mother's plans for him.

His weeks in the mountains had been a cleansing experience and, later, he had been almost glad to be sick unto death, for mountains and illness both had required of him only physical strength and his natural, determined reaction when faced with a challenge.

But now he had leapt back into a dishonest, treacherous world, and he had dragged Rosalinda with him by tempting her with sexual desire. And, having recognized Eleonora as a woman born to that world outside the mountains and familiar with its dangerous rules, Andrea wondered if either he or Rosalinda would ever be safe again.

Chapter Five

Another week passed, during which Andrea grew healthier by the day. After Bartolomeo suggested it would improve his strength if he began a regular program of sword practice with some of the men-at-arms, Andrea began to work out in the muddy practice yard, or, when the snow prevented that, in the cleared space in one of the barns that the men used as a substitute practice area.

It was a pleasure to return to manly pursuits, and Andrea found that the vigorous exercise relieved some of the tensions he was feeling. He was soon on excellent terms with Lorenzo, who acted as captain of the men-at-arms under Bartolomeo's command. As for Bartolomeo, despite the lines on his face and the streaks of silver in his black hair, he remained hard of muscle and sharp of eye. Bartolomeo practiced regularly with sword and dagger, frequently besting the younger men, who all respected him. So did Andrea respect Bartolomeo, for his loyalty to Eleonora and her daughters, as well as for his skill with weapons, and the two of them developed a cautious friendship.

Honor, as well as his position as a guest at the villa, required that Andrea stay away from Rosalinda and not compromise her by giving in to the desire he felt for her. Therefore, he was forced to keep his emotions under a tight rein. He was also on constant guard lest Eleonora spring her plan on him, requesting of him the favor Rosalinda had spoken of with such fear. So far, Eleonora had kept her own council—and, possibly, Bartolomeo's council, too, for Andrea did not believe that Bartolomeo's suggestion that he begin working with weapons was made purely out of concern for his health.

On the second day after he was permitted to take up a sword, which he borrowed for practice and returned immediately afterward, Andrea asked Bartolomeo for his two daggers back. Since they were at that moment in the practice yard, Bartolomeo promised to return the daggers later, saying they had been put away for safekeeping. However, the week passed and the daggers were not yet returned. Andrea was cautious about pressing the issue, lest Bartolomeo imagine he had some evil intent.

Andrea chided himself for his suspicious thoughts, while at the same time sensing that they were far from foolish. On the surface, Villa Serenita was a pleasant place, its tranquility maintained for the sake of Bianca and Rosalinda. Beneath that placid surface, plans were being formulated. Andrea knew it was so. He had grown up in a similar atmosphere, and he recognized it.

Each evening Andrea joined the ladies and Bartolomeo in Eleonora's sitting room. There they discussed the girls' lessons, and Andrea chuckled to himself at Rosalinda's impatience with Latin verbs. He played chess with Bartolomeo and found the man a formidable opponent. When Bianca or Rosalinda asked him, Andrea played the lute and sang for them. He was careful never to give any indication of preferring Rosalinda over Bianca.

As the holy season of Christmas drew near, the snows continued, piling up around the villa and its outbuildings, forcing postponement of any thought of leaving. For Andrea did want to leave. If he did not go soon, he was afraid his ever-present desire for Rosalinda would lead him into an indiscretion that would only hurt her. He had nothing to offer her—or more accurately, to offer her mother—in return for a more honorable connection with the woman he wanted. To acquire the wealth and position he would need in order to make an honest offer for Rosalinda, he would have to return to the world outside the mountains.

Moreover, Andrea had made a solemn, silent vow that he would discover what had happened to his lost companions. With each day that passed, with every bit of new strength he could feel in his rapidly recovering body, he grew more eager for action. All he required was a few days of clear weather—and a suitable excuse for going.

"I cannot stay in this sitting room, at this table, a moment longer!" Rosalinda, too, was growing restless from forced inactivity. Ignoring Bianca's scowl, Rosalinda looked up from her slate to gaze through the window with longing.

"You cannot ride when the snow is so deep," Bianca protested. "Please, Rosalinda, pay attention to your lesson. If Mother comes in and discovers you are not working, she will be annoyed."

"The sun is shining and here comes Andrea from his

sword practice,'' Rosalinda said. ''Let us at least walk along the terrace, or to the stable and back. The path is well broken by now, with the men tramping out there every day. I can't think Mother would object to that.''

''Well, perhaps, just for a short time.'' Bianca sent a thoughtful look toward the tall, muscular figure now making its way to the terrace steps. Even wearing a worn and patched green doublet that Bartolomeo had contributed as suitable only for sword practice, Andrea in restored health was a sight to catch the eye of any woman.

''I'll get our cloaks.'' Rosalinda was gone from the room before Bianca could change her mind.

Bianca put down her quill and stoppered the ink bottle. By the time she stood at the terrace door, Rosalinda was back with their outer garments.

''I told Valeria where we would be. Mother is closeted with Bartolomeo in his office.'' Rosalinda pulled open the door just as Andrea arrived on the terrace. ''Come with us, Andrea. We are going to take a bit of exercise.''

''Oh!'' Bianca cried out when she slipped on the ice underlying the latest fall of snow. Andrea caught her, steadying her, and she grabbed at his arm. ''Andrea, I can't walk alone. I will have to hold on to you.''

''Pah!'' laughed Rosalinda. ''Where's your courage, Bianca? Take advantage of the ice and slide on it, as I do.'' On those words, she gave herself a push with one foot and went skidding across the terrace, stopping only when she reached one of the large urns at the top of the steps and flung her arms around it.

''I am sure I could never do anything so dangerous,'' Bianca said. ''Rosalinda, you will break your neck.''

''Not I!'' Rosalinda took a few running steps before launching herself into another slide, this time back across the terrace toward the house. She stopped just short of the sitting room door. Bending, she scooped up a handful of snow. "Bianca, Andrea, arm yourselves!"

"That is a declaration of war!" Andrea's eyes were sparkling. "Madonna Bianca, I must ask you to release my arm so I can defend myself. Will you fight on my side or with your sister?"

"Fight? I—I'm not sure." Bianca took her hand from Andrea's arm and stood unsteadily on the slippery terrace. With a loud whoop, Rosalinda let a loose handful of snow fly toward her sister. It glanced off Bianca's cheek, the gentle impact shattering both the makeshift missile and Bianca's primness.

"You can't do that to me and escape retribution!" Bianca yelled. In an instant, her own scoop of snow was in her hand and she threw it at Rosalinda.

For the next few minutes, a barrage of snowballs went back and forth between the sisters, with Andrea caught in the middle, fighting two opponents. Before long all three combatants were covered with snow. Then Andrea lost his footing on a patch of ice. His arms flailing wildly, he fell backward into a snowdrift. At once the laughing girls joined forces to bombard him with chunks of white.

"I surrender!" He was laughing so hard that he could not get up. "But I fear I am sorely wounded. Gentle victors, help me to stand."

Rosalinda took one of his hands and Bianca the other. Together they exerted all their strength to lift Andrea. At exactly the right moment, he gave a jerk on each arm and the girls went flying face first into the snowbank, Rosalinda on one side of him and Bianca on the other. Dragging themselves free of the snowbank, the three of them sprawled on the terrace, howling with laughter. Even Bianca was wiping tears from her cheeks, leaning her back against the urn plinth, for once unafraid and unconcerned about decorum.

From the sitting room door Eleonora watched them, with Bartolomeo close behind her. Eleonora's gaze went from the rosy-cheeked Rosalinda, who was laughing uproariously, to the paler Bianca, trying to catch her breath between giggles, to Andrea, brushing snow off his knees before he gallantly offered a hand to help Bianca.

"Take care, Andrea, that your hands and feet do not freeze again," Eleonora said mildly, before leaving the doorway with Bartolomeo following in her wake.

That evening, after the ladies had retired for the night, Andrea went to Bartolomeo's office.

"I would like my daggers back now," he said, being careful to keep any hint of threat or impatience out of his voice.

"They are put away, under lock." Bartolomeo looked up from the manuscript on which he was working.

"I will wait while you get them."

Bartolomeo looked at him for a while longer, then took up a ring of keys and went to a heavy wooden chest that stood in one corner of the room. There he paused.

"You do not really need a dagger while you are here," Bartolomeo said.

"You wear one," Andrea said in the same quiet tone of voice. "Like any man, I feel undressed without my knife. Those daggers are among my few belongings."

Another long look passed between the two men until Bartolomeo nodded and opened the lid of the chest. Drawing out the daggers, he handed them to Andrea.

"I notice they are almost identical. Why do you have

two of them?'' Bartolomeo asked.

''This one is mine.'' Andrea slid the knife with the red enamel-and-gold hilt into his belt. He kept the other knife in his hand, looking down at its blue enamel-and-gold hilt. ''This belonged to my brother.''

''How did you come by it?''

''I found it,'' Andrea answered shortly. Bartolomeo said nothing to break the silence that followed the abrupt words. Finally, taking a deep breath, Andrea explained. ''My brother would never have given it up without a struggle. Finding it covered with blood, in a place where I knew he had recently been because I was following him and trying to catch up with him, I took it as evidence that he must be dead. I have kept it, as I know he would want me to do, until I can plunge it into the heart of his murderer.''

''Then you are bent on revenge.''

''Wouldn't you be, too, under the same circumstances?''

''You have not told me what those circumstances are.'' Bartolomeo paused, as if considering a serious decision, then asked, ''Will you take a glass of wine with me? My throat grows dry after an hour or so of writing.''

''What are you writing?'' At a wave of the older man's hand, Andrea pulled the second chair in the room up to the desk.

''A history of the dukes of Monteferro.'' Bartolomeo handed a parchment page across the desk to Andrea. ''You may read it if you like.''

''The Farisi dukes of Monteferro,'' Andrea amended Bartolomeo's remark. His eyes on the other man, Andrea took the page but did not look at it at once. Bartolomeo nodded his comprehension of the meaning behind Andrea's alteration of his statement.

"I have seen you looking at the portrait in the sitting room." Bartolomeo sat back in his chair, a goblet of wine in his hand. "The painting is a fine likeness. You have recognized my old friend, Girolamo Farisi."

"If I did not recognize his face, I should have known him by the eagle that accompanies him in that picture. All of Italy remembers the Farisi eagle, and how that symbol once represented an honest ruler. Having recognized the late duke, it was but a small step further for me to identify the ladies of Villa Serenita. You need have no fear for them on my account, Bartolomeo. After everything the duchess Eleonora and her daughters have done for me, I would give up my life before I allowed any harm to come to them. I will never tell anyone where they are hiding."

"It is my hope, and also the hope of Madonna Eleonora, that you will do more than keep the secret of their whereabouts. Read the page I gave you."

Andrea lowered his eyes to the parchment and began to read. A minute or two later, he clenched his jaw and he could tell by the warmth in his cheeks that his face was flushing with anger.

"Stregone," he said through gritted teeth.

"What do you know of Niccolò Stregone?" Bartolomeo asked.

"He is an evil person, who has caused the deaths of many who are far better men than he."

"I agree with you. While Madonna Eleonora is convinced that the late Duke of Aullia was responsible for the assassination of her husband, I believe Stregone, acting on behalf of the Guidi family, was behind the deed. I also think Stregone created a situation at the court of Monteferro before the assassination occurred that led Madonna Eleonora to look toward Aullia to discover the instigator of murder."

Andrea sat very still, absorbing what Bartolomeo had just said, accepting some of it, rejecting part. And aware all the time of Bartolomeo's searching eyes on him.

"Is something wrong?" Bartolomeo asked when Andrea kept silent too long.

"Why are you telling me this?" Andrea put the parchment page down on the desk.

"Perhaps to see what your reaction will be."

"Then I trust my reaction pleases you." Deliberately, Andrea drawled the words as he sat back in his chair, trying to appear relaxed. He was sure there was more to Bartolomeo's revelations than mere interest in his reaction to them. When Bartolomeo slid a goblet of wine across the desk to him, Andrea raised it to his lips and pretended to swallow, but he did not drink. He wanted to keep his wits clear. Beyond the natural effects of wine, he had known men—and women, too—who would think nothing of putting certain herbs into the drinks they offered. He did not class Bartolomeo in that devious group, but it usually paid a man to be careful. He was still alive because he had been careful at the right time. While Vanni . . .

"Tell me about your brother," Bartolomeo said. "When did he die?"

"In the autumn. He was with a dear friend of ours, a man we trusted."

"Do you think this friend caused your brother's death?"

"Never. More likely, he died defending my brother." Andrea looked straight into Bartolomeo's eyes. "You will understand that I prefer not to talk about this."

"I beg your pardon. I assure you, I do not ask these painful questions without forethought."

"Then why are you asking them?"

"For several reasons. I have learned to know you

fairly well during your stay with us. I judge you to be an honest man, though, clearly, you have your own secrets. It is no crime; most men prefer to keep parts of their lives to themselves.'' Bartolomeo paused to take another sip of wine, then said, ''Allow me to ask just one more question. Have you experience in leading men into battle?''

''I am no condottiere,'' Andrea said.

''I did not think you were. But you are a daring and courageous man. Your survival under terrible conditions proves as much. If, in addition to courage and daring, you have the necessary military experience, then I may have an offer to make to you.''

''You?'' asked Andrea. ''Or the duchess Eleonora?''

''Since such matters are best discussed between men, I am acting on her behalf. I am also, I do confess, acting before she might have done. However, when you spoke of your brother's death, the moment seemed propitious, for it occurred to me that you might be able to combine repayment of Madonna Eleonora's hospitality with your search for your brother's killer. If, of course, you are interested in what I propose.''

''Suppose you tell me what this offer is,'' Andrea said bluntly. ''Then I will tell you whether I am interested in it.''

''The duchess Eleonora has long hoped for an opportunity to restore the Farisi family to Monteferro,'' Bartolomeo said. ''She has the funds to hire a mercenary army, but has never dared to trust a condottiere to lead such an army, fearing the condottiere would only use her money to put himself in power.''

''That is often the way of things,'' Andrea observed dryly.

''Therefore, she has waited for an honest man to appear. The duchess Eleonora believes you may be that man. I agree with her."

"You want me to conquer Monteferro for you?" Andrea repeated.

"And see to the disposition of the Guidi family," Bartolomeo added. "All of them, every last child, every ancient grandmother, must go into permanent exile, with no hope of ever returning."

"To accomplish that particular feat, it will be necessary to prove the Guidi guilty of a terrible treachery," Andrea said, "and, probably, to kill any male member of the family who is capable of bearing arms, or who will be capable in the future."

"It might be simpler to see that they are all left bankrupt," Bartolomeo suggested.

"Now, that is an interesting idea, and one far more to my liking than the thought of shedding the blood of an entire family." Andrea smiled. "Tell me, Bartolomeo, what is the duchess Eleonora offering me in return for this great favor she expects of me?"

"Great favor?" Bartolomeo repeated. With a dry chuckle, he said, "It is only thanks to the efforts of Madonna Eleonora's household that you are still alive."

"If I accept this offer, I will be putting my life in danger once more," Andrea countered Bartolomeo's remarks with the negotiating skill he had been taught in what now seemed like another lifetime. "Any condottiere would expect some reward for winning a city."

"Two cities," said Bartolomeo. "You will have to conquer Aullia, too, for the Guidi control it as well as Monteferro. Marco Guidi's younger brother is the new ruler of Aullia."

"Is he, indeed? Well, in that case, my reward should be all the greater," Andrea responded. "How, may I ask, do you imagine the accomplishment of this enormous task will help me in the discovery of my brother's murderer? The conquest of two city-states can only present a distraction from my primary quest."

"A man as clever as yourself should have no difficulty at all in achieving everything he desires," Bartolomeo said in a smooth tone that made his companion look sharply at him. "Once you hold both cities securely, the duchess Eleonora is prepared to offer you a position of responsibility in Aullia."

"Really?" Andrea's smile made Bartolomeo frown. "Is that the best for which I can hope? Is there to be no daughter's hand in marriage? It is the usual reward for a successful condottiere. Especially when there is no son to inherit."

"Madonna Bianca is the legitimate heiress to Monteferro," Bartolomeo said. "She will be expected to make a grand marriage of state."

"To consolidate her family's power." Andrea nodded and smiled again.

"Naturally." Bartolomeo was looking a bit annoyed by the course the discussion was taking. "Of course, Madonna Rosalinda, as the younger daughter, would have a bit more freedom in her choice of husband."

"*Her* choice of husband?"

"The duchess Eleonora would want her younger child to marry well."

"To a man in a position of responsibility in Aullia?" Andrea suggested.

"That is a possibility." Bartolomeo spoke with diplomatic blandness, revealing nothing, yet hinting at much.

"It had better be a certainty, or the duchess Eleonora will have to look elsewhere for someone to lead her army," Andrea said.

"We can discuss the matter with the duchess Eleonora," Bartolomeo offered.

"Tell me," said Andrea, "if, after our little talk this evening, I decide to say no to this offer, will I leave Villa Serenita alive?"

"If you refuse the offer," said Bartolomeo smoothly, "there will be no need for you to leave the villa at all."

"I thought so." Andrea rose. "You may tell the duchess that I will consider the proposition most seriously. I will give her my answer on Christmas Day. In the meantime, she may want to consider with equal seriousness my requirement that the hand of Madonna Rosalinda be added to the reward she is offering. A good night's rest to you, Bartolomeo."

Andrea was out of the room and well on his way to his own chamber before he released his breath in a low whistle. While he knew full well that it was the way marriage negotiations were usually conducted, he did not like the idea of bargaining over Rosalinda as if she were no more than a piece of property to be disposed of at her mother's whim. Rosalinda was far more than that. Still, the offer just made to him presented an honorable way to win the woman he so desired.

Furthermore, as the head of an army responsible only to him, he would have the means to discover what had happened to Vanni.

"Tell me truly, Bianca, when have you ever had so much fun?" Rosalinda wrapped her arms around her knees. She was sitting on Bianca's bed, while Bianca sat before her mirror brushing her long, golden hair. "Dearest sister, I have never heard you laugh so hard before."

"It was pleasant." Bianca put down her hairbrush and began to rub a rose-scented oil into fingers that were slightly chapped from her unaccustomed outdoor exercise.

"Pleasant?" Rosalinda cried, laughing at her. "You had a wonderful time. You know you did. You really ought to leave your studies and your household chores more often and ride with me. Or take a long walk. Just get out of the house and enjoy yourself."

"Perhaps," Bianca said, "when the snow melts, when spring comes."

"No, now," Rosalinda insisted. "Now, when the cold air will put roses in your cheeks."

"And chilblains in my hands and feet." Bianca sent a teasing look toward her sister. "Do you want me to act as chaperone for you and Andrea? Is that why you are suddenly so concerned with how much exercise I get?"

"I don't need a chaperone. I haven't seen Andrea alone for more than a week."

"And that troubles you?"

"I thought he liked me."

"I am sure he does, my dearest. So far as I can see, he likes all of us." Bianca grew still, the oil shining on her clasped hands. "What are you saying, Rosalinda? Has he made improper advances to you?"

"I don't think so. That is, I didn't mind."

"What did he do?" Bianca asked, her eyes going wide.

"He kissed me, and he put his hand on my breast. Just for a moment, you understand. Then he told me to leave him at once."

"An order which indicates that he has a strong sense of honor." Bianca got onto the bed next to Rosalinda and curled her legs up, sitting so she was facing her sister. Her next words were an intimate whisper. "What was it like, to have a man's mouth on yours?"

"I was overwhelmed," Rosalinda said. "But I liked it. If Andrea had not sent me away, I am sure I could have stayed there in his room all afternoon, letting him do whatever else he wanted."

"Oh, my." Bianca moistened her lips. "And when he touched you? Did it hurt?"

"It burned," Rosalinda said. "But not exactly where his hand was. I felt as if a fire had started somewhere deep inside me. Now, every time I see him, the fire flames up anew. I think of what he did, and I want him to do it again. But I never see him alone anymore, and when we are together he will scarcely look at me." Rosalinda put her head down on her knees.

"From what I have seen of Andrea, he treats you as he treats me," Bianca said, "and as he treates Mother or Valeria. I think he is trying to behave honorably toward you. He can hardly kiss you on the mouth or touch your breast in the presence of others."

"Do you really think that's it?" Rosalinda turned her head to look at Bianca.

"Probably. Of course, you have more experience in these matters than I have." Bianca's soft voice was tinged with regret. "No man has ever kissed me."

"That's true. I have wondered every day since it happened just what Andrea meant by those caresses and by what he said to me that afternoon." Rosalinda buried her face in her knees again, so the request she made was somewhat muffled. "Please, Bianca, don't tell anyone about this."

"Haven't I always kept your little secrets?" Reaching out to her sister, Bianca smoothed down Rosalinda's springy curls. "Though this is not such a small secret. Rosalinda, you must not fall in love with Andrea. He will not stay at Villa Serenita beyond the spring thaw, if he stays that long, and we cannot leave here. You know why it is so. Do not torment yourself by longing for what you cannot have. And, please, I beg you, my dearest, do not allow your affection for Andrea to lead you to grant him liberties that will only cause you greater regret when he does leave."

Chapter Six

There was no priest at Villa Serenita. Nevertheless, late on Christmas Eve the entire household, along with the men-at-arms and their families, gathered in the large reception room that was almost never used. The room had been cleaned on the previous day and decorated with fresh, fragrant greenery brought in from the forest. New candles had been placed in the chandeliers and in all the wall sconces for this occasion, and their flames illuminated the gilt trim and the frescoes on the walls and the high ceiling. Beginning a little before midnight, Eleonora read the appropriate Christmas passages from her missal and then added a few prayers of her own.

From his position between Bartolomeo and Rosalinda, Andrea watched Eleonora. He imagined that she must be wishing she could include among her prayers a mention of the enterprise upon which she wanted to send Andrea. She had not spoken to him about it at all, and neither had Bartolomeo said anything more on the subject after their late-night talk. Andrea believed those two accomplished schemers were simply leaving him alone to make his own decision, because they were already certain what that decision would be.

The entire population of Villa Serenita had been fasting since early morning. Once the Christmas prayer service was ended, the white-clothed tables that had been pushed against the walls of the reception room were pulled to the center of the room and platters of food were carried in by willing kitchen workers, for it was by now well past midnight and the pre-Christmas fast was over.

Poached whole fish, roasted chickens, and joints of meat were set in places of honor, while truffles uprooted from the forest added their pungent, earthy aroma to the other inviting smells. Nuts and preserved fruits from the summer harvest, fresh apples and pears, roasted chestnuts pureed and blended with whipped heavy cream and eggs to make a sweet pudding, dried figs and dates brought to the villa on Luca's last visit, and sweet bread made with raisins all crowded the tables. Large pitchers of wine completed the feast prepared to celebrate the holy day.

Andrea was invited to sit next to Eleonora. It was an honor he could not refuse, though he would have preferred a place between Rosalinda and Bianca.

"Well, Signore Andrea." Eleonora looked at him over the rim of her jeweled, golden wine goblet. "Here it is, Christmas Day."

"So it is, madonna." Andrea tried his best to sound noncommital while his heart was beating as hard as if he were about to go into battle. Which, in a way, he was. "I wish you all the blessings of this holy season."

"Do not trifle with me, Andrea." Eleonora's blue eyes were hard and her mouth was pulled into the firm line it assumed when she wanted her daughters to do something to which they objected.

"I would not dream of trifling, madonna. Let us say instead that, when I think of all you have done for me, I am overcome with gratitude. And with astonishment."

"Indeed?" Eleonora's finely plucked eyebrows rose. Her eyes were sparkling now, a sign to Andrea that she was relishing their exchange.

There were men and women, bred in the courts of the Italian city-states, who found the manipulation of others and the bargaining for power and position a far more exciting game than any sport. Andrea recognized Eleonora as one of those souls. He marveled that she had remained quiescent for fifteen long years, though he knew why she had stayed hidden at Villa Serenita. It was for her daughters' sake. Now, for the sake of those daughters, for the chance of winning back their heritage, Eleonora was willing to risk her entire fortune. And, perhaps, all of their lives.

"Why should you be astonished by me?" Eleonora asked.

"Because you are willing to place your trust in a man who is, in all save the most basic essentials, a complete stranger to you."

"It is those basic essentials that matter beyond all else. Do not mistake me for a fool, Signore Andrea. I am an excellent judge of men. If my late husband had only listened to my opinions about certain of his advisors, not to mention some of his allies in neighboring states, then he might well still be ruling Monteferro, and I would have no need of your services."

"But you do need me," Andrea said. "And thus, you trust me."

"As far as I would trust any man who has much to

gain by promising future deeds of valor,'' Eleonora said.

''I will not betray you.'' He met her glittering blue eyes. ''In this world there are but two things I want. You hold one of them in your possession. If I betray you, or if I cause harm to you in any way, then I will lose my heart's desire. For all that you have lost in your life, still you are a fortunate woman, madonna. Your daughters love you, and neither of them would willingly give herself to a man who had hurt her mother.''

''There are men who would not scruple to take an unwilling woman,'' Eleonora said.

''I am not one of them. If you trust me in nothing else, Madonna Eleonora, believe me in this. The woman I make my own must come to me freely, under no compulsion, because *I* am *her* heart's desire.''

''I do believe you, for in this you are like my beloved Girolamo.''

For a moment Eleonora's eyes softened with memory and her lips curved into a tender smile that made her look years younger. But only for a moment. She returned at once to the business at hand, and her smile disappeared. ''Am I to assume, then, that you accept the offer Bartolomeo has made to you on my behalf?''

''I shall do all that you require of me,'' he said. ''And more, if I can.''

''Good.'' She did not seem to hear the hidden message in his simple words, but went on with her planning. ''We will meet later today to discuss the details. For privacy, I suggest Bartolomeo's office. Do you by any chance know Luca Nardi?''

''The banker?'' Andrea shook his head. ''I have only heard of him.''

''You will be dealing with him about the money you

will require. Signore Andrea, I have a new request to make of you."

"Which is?"

"For their own safety, I do not want my daughters to know about our enterprise until it is completed and Monteferro has been secured."

"There we are in complete agreement, madonna."

"Then I wish you not only a blessed holy season, Signore Andrea," Eleonora said, lifting her wine goblet, "but a most successful year to come."

The time for giving gifts was not on Christmas, which was a solemn, if joyous, holy day. Rather, the Feast of the Epiphany, the day of the three kings who had traveled to Bethlehem bearing gifts to the Christ Child, was the traditional time for generous folk to emulate those most famous gift-givers by doing the same for family and close friends.

On the morning of January 6, Eleonora once more stood in the large reception room to read from her missal to the assembled company and to say a few prayers. Afterward, she and her daughters handed out the gifts that had been piled on the tables. There were special sweetmeats or toys for the younger children, trinkets for the older ones, and for the grownups, presents that could not be made at the villa or lengths of fabric for new clothes.

"How did your mother acquire all of these gifts?" Andrea asked Rosalinda as the last of the children were led from the room by their parents.

"Luca brings them." Rosalinda's smile tugged at Andrea's heart. Too soon he would have to leave her, and she might think he was deserting her. Indeed, after the last few weeks of care on his part not to show any open preference for her over her sister, Rosalinda might imagine he had no special interest in her at all.

"Luca?" he asked, to keep her by his side while she explained who Luca was.

"He is Valeria's brother. He comes to visit us two or three times a year and when he comes, he brings pack animals loaded with whatever we need."

"Luca Nardi is Valeria's brother?" Andrea exclaimed, not hiding his surprise. "I did not know that. No one told me." He wondered what else Eleonora and Bartolomeo had not told him.

"How do you know Luca's family name?" Rosalinda asked. "I didn't mention it."

"Bartolomeo said something about him," Andrea answered, making up a hasty excuse. "For some reason, I didn't connect him with Valeria."

"You will meet him the next time he comes here. I think you will like Luca."

Andrea said nothing to that. He knew he was going to have to tell Rosalinda he was leaving the villa, but for days he had postponed the moment. They had settled into a routine in which either Valeria or Eleonora always seemed to be present when Andrea and Rosalinda were together, and he was doing his best to treat her as if she were a sister or a dear friend. But he could not deny to himself the passion he felt for Rosalinda, and all too often he saw her puzzled gaze on him, as if she were trying to reason out in her own mind why he was no longer playing the part of the eager would-be lover.

With the men-at-arms and their families gone to their own quarters, Eleonora and her companions retired to the sitting room. There a more private gift-giving ceremony took place. Most of the presents exchanged were small items, made by hand, but the sisters received gifts of some value.

"Mother," Bianca exclaimed, "these are your pearl earrings."

"I have more than enough jewelry," Eleonora said, "and you are old enough now to wear such jewels. Rosalinda, this bracelet is for you. It was my mother's."

"There is a ruby set in it. How beautiful. Oh, Mother, thank you." Rosalinda embraced her mother.

"Perhaps you ought to give Andrea his gift," Eleonora suggested.

"I hope you like it," Rosalinda told him. She picked up a neatly folded pile of bright blue cloth and held it out to him. "Valeria said wool would be warmer than silk and much more sturdy. Bianca and I made the doublet, and Valeria made the hose, because Mother said unmarried girls ought not to sew such an intimate garment for a man."

"I do hope it fits well," Bianca added in her soft voice.

"I am sure it will." Andrea held up the doublet, measuring it against his chest and arms. "Dear ladies, I do not know how to thank you for this."

"Signore Andrea will be doubly glad of his gift," Eleonora said. "Since he will be leaving us in a few days, he will require new clothes."

"Leaving?" Bianca whispered, looking stricken.

"No, you can't go," Rosalinda cried.

"You knew he could not stay here forever," Eleonora said. "Young men have interests of their own to pursue, in the world beyond these mountains."

"Andrea, please don't go," Rosalinda begged, with tears in her eyes.

"I will return one day." Silently, Andrea cursed Eleonora for being so blunt, until he saw the look on her face as she regarded her younger daughter. Rosalinda moved to the window, where she stood with her back to the room. By the rigidity of her shoulders Andrea suspected she was trying hard not to cry. Eleonora gave him an abrupt little nod, and he understood that she had taken on the unpleasant task of telling the girls so he would not have to do it.

"We will miss your pleasant company," Bianca said to him.

"As I will miss yours, Madonna Bianca." He took her hand to bow over it and Bianca leaned close to him.

"Go to her. Talk to her," Bianca said under her breath, and Andrea obeyed.

"Rosalinda." When he tried to take her hand as he had taken her sister's, she pulled it out of his grasp. "You must know that your mother is right. I cannot stay here forever."

"Of course not. Your life is elsewhere," she said in a small, lost voice. "Go, then. I do not care."

"I swear to you, I will return, and sooner than you think." He sought for a way to cheer her up without revealing too much. "When the snow melts so you can ride in the mountains again, remember the bear you once met on a dangerous path and know that he will never forget you."

"I wish I had not met that bear, and that you had never come here," she said, still in that broken little voice, so unlike her usual tones. "Before I knew you, I was at least reasonably contented."

"Would you rather I had died in the mountains?"

"No." She turned upon him the full force of gray eyes swimming with tears. "I am glad you did not die. But I wish with all my heart that you would not go away."

Andrea had never in his life wanted anything more than he wanted at that moment to take Rosalinda into his arms, to kiss and comfort her, to reassure her of his deep affection, to make her understand why he must go and that he would certainly return to her as soon as he could. But there were other people in the room, and Rosalinda and Bianca must be kept in ignorance of the plan their mother had set in motion. Andrea sent a helpless glance in Eleonora's direction. She reacted at once.

"Rosalinda," said her mother in a bracing way, "stop being silly. You will make Andrea regret that he knows you."

"I could never regret that, Madonna." Andrea could tell by the way Eleonora was looking at him that she was wondering if he would break his word by revealing to Rosalinda any part of their plans.

"I have obligations," he said, trying to put both mother and daughter at ease. "I cannot discuss them with you, Rosalinda, but as soon as those obligations are discharged, I intend to keep my promise to return."

"Come," Eleonora said. "It is time for us to eat. I have given the kitchen staff the afternoon free so they can join their families. If they are to finish their work in time, we must take our midday meal early."

Rosalinda went to the dining room reluctantly and, once there, she ate little. However, after the meal she appeared to recover a little and for an hour or so she sat at the table in the sitting room, playing a board game with Bianca.

"You have not spoken to Andrea at all since you learned he is leaving us," Bianca observed in a quiet voice.

"I do not care what Andrea does," came the whispered response from across the round table.

"If you regret this sulkiness after he has left, it will be too late for you to apologize," Bianca pointed out with perfect logic.

"He could have told me before today what he was

planning to do. He could have been honest with me. Instead, he has avoided me for weeks. I thought it was because he—well, you know why I thought he was keeping his distance from me," Rosalinda said. "Now it seems he was not gallantly restraining his passion at all. He was hiding his secret plans."

"If a handsome man were as obviously interested in me as Andrea is in you," Bianca said, "you would not find me seeking flimsy excuses to quarrel with him. I would be thinking about ways to make him eager to return to me at the first opportunity."

"What if he cannot return? What if he does not want to return?" Rosalinda bit down hard on her trembling lower lip. If Andrea left and she never saw him again, she feared her heart would break in two. Perhaps it had already broken, for there was a constant hard pain in her chest and she could not swallow past the lump in her throat.

"You knew that Andrea would leave at some time," Bianca said.

"I thought the time would not come until the winter was over and all the snow had melted from the mountain passes," Rosalinda whispered.

"I know you well, dear sister." Bianca's hand rested on Rosalinda's. "You dared to dream that when Andrea left, he would take you with him."

"I should have known it was only a foolish girl's misplaced hope." Rosalinda's low voice was choked with tears. "Mother will never permit either you or me to leave Villa Serenita. And while Andrea may be fond of me, he does not care enough to defy Mother."

"Few people ever do dare to defy Mother," Bianca murmured.

"What shall I do?" Rosalinda asked.

"I cannot tell you *how* to do it. You have more experience of private meetings with lovers than I.'' There was the faintest tinge of envy in Bianca's whispered words. ''But if I were in your place, I would send my lover away knowing exactly what my feelings for him were.''

''Come, girls.'' Eleonora broke into this quiet discussion. ''You must have finished that game by now, and whispering in front of others is rude, as you very well know. Andrea has agreed to play the lute if the two of you will sing.''

''Yes, Mother.'' At once Bianca rose from the table. ''We will be glad to sing, won't we, Rosalinda?''

After that there was nothing Rosalinda could do but assent to her mother's request. If she refused, she would appear to be sulking as Bianca had accused her of doing.

The rest of that festival day, which should have been a happy one, passed all too slowly for Rosalinda—and at the same time, all too quickly. While she ached to escape to the privacy of her own room, which she knew her mother would not permit until bedtime, Rosalinda was sadly aware that every hour brought Andrea's departure closer.

Even with Bianca's whispered words of support it was agony for Rosalinda to stay in the sitting room after she finished singing, to play yet another childish game as if it were a year ago at the same time, as if no changes had occurred since then in her life or her emotions.

At last the short, midwinter day did draw to a close and the first stars of evening began to sparkle in a cloudless sky.

''It seems the storms are over for a while.'' Bartolomeo turned from the window to look from Eleonora to Andrea, who was reading aloud from a book of Petrarch's sonnets. "A determined man might well make his way out of the mountains and down to the Lombard plain before the snows begin again."

"I have been watching the skies, and I think the same thing," Andrea responded, closing the book of poetry. "I have no baggage to pack so, Madonna Eleonora, if you will lend to me that sturdy riding horse you promised, I will be on my way early tomorrow."

Rosalinda stopped breathing, and beneath the table where she sat with Bianca, she clenched her hands into tight fists. How could Andrea say so lightly that he would be gone on the morrow and out of her life forever? She did not believe he would return. There was something in the way he looked at her mother and at Bartolomeo that frightened Rosalinda. She watched her mother and Bartolomeo exchange glances. *Significant glances.* Something more was happening than Andrea's departure. Rosalinda was sure of it.

"Since you have all agreed that the weather is clear," she said, leaping to her feet so quickly that she almost upset the table and the game board, "I am going to walk on the terrace for half an hour."

"It is bitterly cold," Bianca objected. "You will freeze."

"I cannot stay inside another moment," Rosalinda exclaimed.

"Shall I go with you?" Bianca asked, rising to join her.

"No." From somewhere in her aching heart Rosalinda dredged up a tearful smile for her sister. "I know you hate the cold, and I am poor company, I fear."

"Wear your cloak," Eleonora said in an absent-minded way, as if she were thinking of something else entirely. "And don't forget your gloves."

Out on the terrace, the cold almost took Rosalinda's

breath away. She welcomed the scorching sensation in her lungs when she drew in a mouthful of the icy air. She paced along the terrace and down the steps to the well-trodden path leading toward the stable.

"Who goes there?" A man-at-arms challenged her, and Rosalinda knew she would have to get control over her emotions so she could answer him.

"Giuseppe, it's only me," she said. "I want some exercise."

"Be careful and don't slip," Giuseppe warned. Like all the men-at-arms, he was too familiar with Rosalinda's vigorous habits to expect her to remain indoors, however cold it might be. With a brisk, "Good evening, madonna," he continued on his rounds.

Rosalinda reached the stable, intending to go inside to see her horse. While Bianca loved doves and kittens and puppies while they were small, Rosalinda had always preferred full-grown dogs and horses. On this unhappy night she thought she might find a little comfort in stroking her horse's silky coat and rubbing its soft nose. But when she pulled the small side door open a crack, Rosalinda heard voices within. A man and a woman were murmuring and laughing, their voices low and tender. Quickly, before they noticed her, Rosalinda closed the door again. She would not disturb lovers. Let someone else be happy, if she could not. Having no place else to go, she headed back to the villa.

"Rosalinda." A cloaked shape moved toward her on the path.

"Andrea?" Rosalinda stood still, waiting for him.

"I told your mother I would find you and see you safe inside before you are completely chilled."

"I don't care if I freeze to death," she informed him with a childlike petulance she immediately regretted.

She stood facing him in the starlight, while their

breaths formed misty clouds around them. Andrea made an impatient movement. Rosalinda caught his ungloved hands and held on tight, to keep him with her for a little while, at least.

"Why are you going away so suddenly?" she asked. "Tell me, please. I must know. Perhaps, if I can put a reason to what you are doing, then I might be able to bear your absence.

"Forgive me," she said when he did not respond. "I know I should not speak this way. Mother would scold me if she could hear. Perhaps I am only a silly girl, who read too much into a few kisses and a single caress. Andrea, if our embrace that day in your room meant nothing to you, then tell me so right now. Do not leave me wondering what it meant to you."

"You are unlike any other woman I have known," he said, pulling her hands to his chest and holding them there. "No other lady would speak so directly."

"I am neither mild-mannered nor dignified enough to be considered a true lady." Her breath caught on a choked-back sob. This was not the way Bianca, who *was* a true lady, would have handled the situation. Rosalinda was far more straightforward than her sister. "Answer my questions, Andrea. What am I to you?"

"You are all the world, and more," he said. "You are my heart, the blood that flows in my every vein. You are the air I breathe. You are the very breath of freedom, of sunshine, of warmth and goodness, of innocence in a wicked time."

"If that is so, why are you leaving me?"

"Because I must."

"But why?"

"The reason is a secret," he said.

"What secret? Andrea, are you leaving here to return to another woman? Are you betrothed? Is your wedding day set? Is that why you are so eager to go?''

''There is no other woman than you to whom my heart is pledged,'' he said. ''That has been so since the first moment I saw you riding among the mountains as if those peaks and valleys belonged to you alone.''

He fell silent and Rosalinda waited, sensing that there was more he wanted to say. Finally, he asked, ''Can you keep a secret?''

''Tell me anything you want,'' she said. ''I will not repeat a word of it, not even to Bianca.''

''I hear someone in the barn. Let us walk, so no one can overhear us.'' He drew her along the path and into the garden, until they stood in an open space. ''Rosalinda, give me your word of honor that you will never reveal what I am about to say.''

''You trust the word of a mere woman?''

''I trust your word. Swear to me, Rosalinda, knowing that my life—and yours—may depend on keeping your word.''

''I do swear that I will repeat to no other person what you say to me now,'' she said solemnly.

He put his arm around her, drawing her close, so they stood as one figure. Rosalinda's head rested on his shoulder while Andrea spoke softly into her ear.

''I have nothing in this world to call my own, except my dagger,'' he said. ''Even my brother has been taken from me.''

''I did not know you have a brother.''

''He is dead.'' Andrea's voice was bleak. ''The two of us were with a dear friend. I became separated from the others. Later, while I searched for them, I discovered a blood-encrusted dagger on the path. It was my brother's dagger. I think he fought for his life, and was killed. When the murderer took his body away or concealed it, the dagger was left behind. I searched, but could find no other sign of brother or friend, either alive or dead."

"Oh, Andrea, I am so sorry." Rosalinda could not bear to think of what she would feel should Bianca be taken from her by violence.

"I vowed on that bloody dagger to seek out and punish my brother's killer," Andrea went on. "As I said, I have nothing—no property, no funds, not even a horse of my own."

"Why should that be?" Rosalinda asked. "You are plainly a nobleman." She was going to ask about other family members who might be willing to help him when Andrea interrupted her thoughts.

"Why it is so is unimportant to this story," he said. "Rosalinda, do be quiet and listen. We may not have much time before your mother sends someone to look for us."

"I won't interrupt again."

"Your mother has asked me to carry a letter for her, to Luca Nardi in Monteferro. In return for this favor, which she says is an important one, Madonna Eleonora will ask Signore Nardi to grant a loan to me. With that money to live upon and to use as payment for information, I will be able to search out my brother's murderer. I am hoping that Signore Nardi will also provide recent news on the whereabouts of certain people whom I suspect of complicity in the deed, news that will make my search for the actual killer easier.

"You must understand, Rosalinda, that until this final obligation to my brother is fulfilled, I cannot give myself to any other purpose."

"I do understand," she said. "But why must the search for your brother's killer be a secret?"

"For reasons of her own, your mother does not want it known that she is helping me. Both she and Bartolomeo insisted that I should swear an oath of secrecy before they made any offer of aid to me."

"I know why they did that," Rosalinda said. "It was to keep the secret of where we are living. Mother is afraid that someone who means harm to us, perhaps an agent of the Duke of Aullia, whom she believes is the source of all our troubles, will discover our whereabouts."

"The Duke of Aullia is dead," Andrea said in a harsh voice.

"Yes, I know. Luca told us last autumn that he was assassinated. But I think Mother fears that someone attached to him, perhaps even the notorious Niccolò Stregone, will still want our lives." She stopped because Andrea's arms had tightened around her.

"Bartolomeo did mention Stregone." Andrea's voice was harsher than before. "And it was shortly thereafter in our conversation that he said I must never discuss the location of Villa Serenita or the names of its inhabitants."

"I understand now why you must go and why you have been so secretive," Rosalinda said. "I wish you well and I will pray constantly for your safety. But, oh, Andrea, I will miss you every day."

"No more than I will miss you. I will come back as soon as I can. I do not want to give you false hope of my return," he went on, "but it may be that Luca Nardi will have a response to your mother's message and will ask me to bring it to her before I set out on my own quest."

"Then, you might return in just a few weeks?" Rosalinda's voice held all the joy she felt at that prospect.

"I can make no promises on the matter," Andrea said. "It will depend on Signore Nardi."

"I know, but it is a hope. Thank you for telling me all of this. Thank you for trusting me."

"There is much more I wish I could say," he told her. "Words too deep for utterance now, when I am pledged to another purpose. But if I am successful—"

"*When* you are successful," she corrected.

"When I am successful," he repeated, "then I will have a declaration for you to hear that I cannot voice tonight. And a question, which I will want you to answer only after careful thought. It would not be honorable of me to say more at this time."

Rosalinda's heart was so full that she could make no response except to put her arms around him and hold him tight. When she lifted her face to his, Andrea's mouth at once found hers. It was a chaste kiss at first, a sealing of Rosalinda's promise of silence on the subject of his secrets, and Andrea's promise of a nearer, more profound relationship between them when the time was right for it.

Then Rosalinda sighed and pressed herself more closely against him, her lips opening to him without warning. Andrea's tongue plunged into her mouth, seeking out the velvet heat of her tongue and stroking it. His hands found their way beneath the edges of her long cloak, to catch her hips and pull them firmly forward. Through the silk of her best gown, Rosalinda felt for the second time in her life the eager, thrusting hardness of a fully aroused man. The heat she had known only once before flared again, more powerfully this time, making her weak with longing. She gasped against Andrea's mouth and then went soft in his hands, letting him mold her body as he wanted.

Her breasts were crushed against his doublet, her arms encircled his waist, and she held on to Andrea as if she were drowning and he were her lifeline. She threw back her head so he could kiss her throat. The motion pushed her breasts harder into his chest. Andrea's hand slipped to her thigh, lifting one of her legs, pulling her closer still. She realized with a shiver of pleasure that his palm was on the bare flesh of her thigh, that the edge of her skirt was up around her hips. She felt the cold night air on her skin, but it did nothing to cool the growing fire inside her.

She was intensely aware of Andrea's hardness pressing against her aching heat, and of Andrea's fingers slipping between their bodies to touch her where she was just beginning to notice an unusual moistness. Something marvelous was about to happen, something earthshaking. All it would require was for Andrea's hand to move a little higher, to slide a little deeper into the liquid warmth inside her. Rosalinda could feel her body tensing, waiting. . . .

The terrace door opened and Eleonora stepped out.

Beneath the cover of Rosalinda's cloak Andrea withdrew his hand and smoothed down her dress. He kept his other hand at her waist, supporting her, for Rosalinda was trembling so uncontrollably after his passionate onslaught upon her senses that she could not stand unaided.

"Thank your mother," Andrea whispered, kissing her cheek on a breath of husky laughter. "Without Madonna Eleonora for chaperone, I might have taken you in the snow.

"If ever you doubt my affection," he went on in a voice only slightly calmer than before, "think of this evening and of that time in my chamber when we first embraced and know that I want you with all that is in me. So long as I live, I will never stop wanting you."

And when the time is right, he vowed silently, *I swear I will tell my entire strange story to you, Rosalinda, my dear.*

"When you leave here tomorrow, you will be riding

into danger,'' she said, clinging to him for a moment longer.

''Just being alive is dangerous,'' Andrea replied, thinking of the tasks that lay ahead of him over the next few months. He had not told Eleonora all of his reasons for accepting her proposal, and he was not fool enough to believe that Eleonora had told him everything, either. There were bound to be unpleasant surprises in store for him. But Rosalinda had just shown him how great the rewards would be if only he could win them.

Chapter Seven

"It appears that you are growing up at last, Roslinda, my dear," Eleonora said. "Valeria tells me you are spending more time with her each day, learning how to manage a household."

"I am happy if you are pleased, Mother." Rosalinda could not tell her parent that she had asked Valeria for extra chores so she would not have time to brood about Andrea.

A few days after he had left the villa, the winter storms had begun again. Rosalinda hoped that Andrea had reached one of the cities on the plain and found shelter before he was overtaken by the snow. Lacking any news of him, she could only pray for his safety. She grew quieter during those days, her usual bright eagerness becoming subdued as she kept Andrea's secrets and waited for his return. However, there was one question she could not resist asking of her mother.

"Do you know when Luca will come to visit us

again? Valeria said she wasn't sure of the date.''

''It will not be until the snow melts.'' Eleonora frowned. ''Why are you so eager to see Luca?''

''He promised to bring me a new book.''

''Are you so bored that you want to sit still and read?'' Eleonora placed a hand on her daughter's forehead, then put one finger under her chin, lifting her face and making Rosalinda look directly into her eyes. ''You don't appear to have a fever. Is there something you want to tell me, Rosalinda?''

''You already know everything I have to tell, Mother,'' Rosalinda snapped with a bit of her old spirit. She pulled her chin from her mother's grasp. ''You are quite right. I am bored. I want to go riding.''

''Not in this weather. Have patience, my dear. Spring will come soon enough.''

''But not soon enough for me,'' Rosalinda muttered.

Bianca was a bit more sympathetic. But then, Bianca knew more about Rosalinda's true state of mind than their mother did.

''Some days I think I will go mad.'' Rosalinda paced back and forth in Bianca's bedchamber. ''Why doesn't Andrea come? He said he might.''

''*Might* is not the same as *will,*'' Bianca noted.

''Or Luca.'' Rosalinda turned when she reached the window and began prowling back to the bed where Bianca sat. ''If Luca comes, he may have a letter for me from Andrea. Or, at least, a message of some kind.''

''Do sit down,'' Bianca said. ''If you go on this way much longer, you will make yourself ill. You are growing thinner by the day.''

''I can't sit. I can't eat, nor can I sleep. Where can Andrea be? Is he safe? Why hasn't he returned?''

''Rosalinda, he has *left.*'' Bianca was beginning to be irritated. She spoke slowly, as if trying to impress an unwelcome fact upon a child who did not want to hear it. "Andrea is gone. Very likely he will not return for a long time, if at all. Why should you think otherwise? And why would Luca know anything about Andrea?"

Rosalinda stopped her nervous pacing, telling herself she should have been more careful. In her worry and frustration, she had said too much. Now she would have to make an explanation without betraying her promise to Andrea.

"Please don't tell Mother." Rosalinda sat down beside her sister. "I suggested to Andrea that he could leave a letter for me with Luca, so Luca could deliver it the next time he visits us."

"Luca Nardi has more important things to do than carry love letters to silly girls," Bianca scolded, sounding remarkably like her mother. "Can't you see how dangerous it could be, if a note to you were intercepted?"

"Luca is always careful," Rosalinda said.

"What are we to do with you?" Bianca cried. "You have never fully appreciated how careful we must be to stay hidden. I really ought to tell Mother about this proposed correspondence between you and Andrea."

"No! Don't," Rosalinda begged. "Bianca, if there were someone you loved and you were longing to hear from him, you would have done the same."

"*I* would have sense enough to be more cautious," Bianca said with her nose in the air.

"Would you really?" Rosalinda asked. "Or would you forget caution in the name of love?"

"If Mother could hear you, she would forbid you ever again to read Petrarch, for it must be from his sonnets that you are getting these dangerous ideas." Bianca's delicate features were set in hard lines. "Since there is no man who loves me, we will never know if I would forget caution, will we?''

''You're jealous,'' Rosalinda said, the realization dawning only slowly. ''You wish there were someone to love you, too. Oh, Bianca, I do hope you have not fallen in love with Andrea.''

''Of course I have not. While I will admit that he is a handsome and charming young man, so far as we know he has no wealth or title and no prospects. Therefore, he is most unsuitable for any relationship except that of casual friend. I do rather think, Rosalinda, that you are not as deeply in love with him as you imagine. I suspect Andrea may be attractive to you because, except for the sons of the men-at-arms, he is the only young man you have ever met.''

''He is also the only young man *you* have ever met. You *are* jealous.''

''*I*,'' said Bianca, as if to close the subject, ''am the heiress to Monteferro. Unruly passions are beneath my dignity.''

This statement did not have its desired quelling effect on Rosalinda's accusations. The words were scarcely out of Bianca's mouth before Rosalinda gave a hoot of disbelieving laughter and rolled over on the bed, holding her sides.

''Just wait,'' Rosalinda said, trying her best to subdue her first bout of real laughter since Andrea's departure, ''wait until you meet a man who moves your heart as Andrea moves mine. Then we will see how unruly your emotions can be.

''But let me warn you to take care, dear sister,'' Rosalinda went on, completely sober now. ''Do not let that man be Andrea. For if you were to love the man I love, that would be the one thing that could end the affection that has lain between us all of our lives.''

* * *

Andrea did return, at the end of March, but he came in such secrecy and haste and he left again so quickly that Rosalinda almost missed seeing him. She was on her way to the kitchen to help Valeria when she heard his voice, followed by Bartolomeo's deeper, more mature tones. The two were in Bartolomeo's office, with the heavy door not quite closed.

Rosalinda paused, wanting to break in upon them but knowing it would be far more polite to wait until their discussion was over. She had learned a few hard lessons in self-control over the past three months and so she reined in her impatience and stood quietly by the office door.

"Madonna Eleonora will be pleased with what you have accomplished," Bartolomeo said. "She will want to speak with you herself. You may stay the night in one of the rooms on the upper floor where no one will see you. I will carry food and water to you myself."

"Perhaps that arrangement would be best." Andrea paused. "How does Rosalinda fare?"

"I think she misses you," Bartolomeo answered. "Andrea, let me emphasize that I am housing you in an attic room because it will be best if no one but Madonna Eleonora and I knows you are here. That way, we will have to answer no awkward questions. You know how inquisitive Rosalinda can be. And how persistent."

"I suppose you are right, but I was looking forward to seeing her again." Andrea's sigh was loud enough for Rosalinda to hear it out in the corridor where she stood listening. "I ought to leave before daylight tomorrow. When shall I speak to Madonna Eleonora?"

"I will take you to the room now and see you settled," Bartolomeo said. "Then I will tell Madonna

Eleonora in private that you are here. As soon as she can leave her daily chores without causing comment, she will join you. A signal will prevent you from opening the door to some wandering servant. Either she or I will knock twice and pause, then knock twice more."

"Very well."

Hearing the scrape of a chair from within the room, Rosalinda ducked around a corner and into a window niche. She heard Andrea and Bartolomeo walking quickly along the corridor in the opposite direction from where she stood, toward the narrow stairs that led upward to the topmost floors. The rooms up there were servants' quarters, but they were not used at present, except for storage. For security reasons, the men-at-arms and their families all lived in the outbuildings. At night, after Bartolomeo locked the doors, only Eleonora, her daughters, Valeria, and Bartolomeo were left in the house.

On this night, Andrea would also sleep in the villa. Rosalinda could not imagine what business he had with her mother that would prevent him from seeing her, too, but she was not going to let anything stop her from spending at least a few minutes with the man she loved.

It was all she could do to hide her excitement from the others, especially from Bianca, who was always aware of her moods. She managed it by the simple strategy of keeping silent. It did occur to Rosalinda that, without wanting to, she was learning the ways of courtiers and of intrigue as Eleonora had described those skills to her daughters out of her own youthful experience. There was much to be said for the patience and silence that Eleonora recommended, though Rosalinda did regret the loss of freedom involved in thinking carefully before she spoke and in waiting patiently for something to happen when she much preferred to take immediate action to make things happen. She told herself a private visit with Andrea would be worth her efforts during the day.

At last the ladies and Bartolomeo retired for the night and the villa was silent. Rosalinda waited a bit longer, just to be sure everyone was asleep. When she thought it was safe, she wrapped a heavy shawl around her shoulders over her linen nightgown and took up a lighted candle.

Walking in her bare feet for quietness, she made her way along the corridor, tiptoeing past the suite of rooms used by Eleonora and the smaller suite where Bartolomeo and Valeria slept. At the end of the corridor, the door to the servants' stairs swung open on well-oiled hinges. Rosalinda stepped onto the landing, pulling the door partly shut behind her but leaving it unlatched for a quieter exit.

In front of her, the stairs led down into the darkness of the lower level of the house. To her right they proceeded upward. Gathering the skirt of her nightgown in one hand so she would not trip on it, and holding the candle high in the other hand, Rosalinda began to climb.

There was no door at the top. The steps simply opened out onto a hall. Rosalinda knew this uppermost floor of the villa well, for she and Bianca had often played there when they were children, and periodically Eleonora decided the rooms must be cleaned and her daughters must help. Rosalinda looked along the floor of the hall, seeking a sign of candlelight showing through a crack at the bottom of one of the doors leading to servants' bedrooms. She found what she sought beneath the third door on her left. Going to it, she rapped twice, waited a moment, and rapped twice more, giving the signal to open as she had heard Bartolomeo describe it to Andrea.

She heard a sound from within, as though someone was startled at being disturbed so late at night. Then, very quietly, the latch was drawn back and the door opened.

Poised to defend himself, Andrea was holding his dagger with the red-and-gold hilt. He wore only his linen shirt, and his hair was in such disorder that Rosalinda decided he must have pulled the shirt over his head in haste before opening the door. The candle in her hand threw light upon his cheekbones and his high-bridged nose. He looked freshly shaven and he was so sharp-eyed that Rosalinda knew he had not been asleep. He stared at her as if he could not believe she was standing before him.

Rosalinda took advantage of his surprise to push past him and into the room. He peered into the hall behind her. Apparently satisfied that no one else was with her, Andrea turned back to find her firmly planted in the middle of the room. Her candle sat beside his on a small table next to the bed, the twin flames sending flickering light and shadow across the whitewashed walls. Andrea laid his dagger on the table, ready to his grasp should he need it. Rosalinda caught her breath at the silent implication that he believed danger lurked even here, in his spartan room.

Then his eyes met hers. They gazed at each other in silence until Rosalinda spoke, forgetting the caution she had learned since first meeting him, forgetting everything save her love for this man, and her anger at him.

"Why am I not supposed to know you are at Villa Serenita?" she demanded in a harsh whisper. "You promised to return to see me, yet now that you have come back, you keep your presence a secret from me."

"Rosalinda." He lifted one hand as if to touch her cheek. Before he made contact with her skin, he pulled his hand back, clenching it into a fist at his side. "Surely you know what you risk by coming here to me, at so late an hour, wearing only your nightgown?"

"And a warm shawl." She pulled it more closely about her shoulders. Her bare feet on the wooden floor were cold. She told herself that was why she was trembling.

"You must leave at once," Andrea said. "If anyone heard you prowling about and followed you, your reputation will be in ruins before morning."

"No one followed me. Even if someone had, there is no person in this house who would spread gossip about me." She glared at him, fully aware that he could see how she was shaking. But it was all from anger now. Furious at his chilly reception when she had expected a warm embrace and words of affection, she spoke with her own calculated coldness, each word falling separate and distinct into the space that separated them.

"Do not attempt to change the subject, Andrea. If I had not accidentally heard your voice this afternoon, I would never have known about your secretive visit."

"You were eavesdropping," he accused her. "How else could you know the signaling knock Bartolomeo suggested?"

"Not eavesdropping. Waiting for you. As I have been waiting for almost three months. Waiting for you to tell Bartolomeo that you intended to see and speak to me, no matter what he said. But it seems that you will speak to him, and to my mother, but not to me. Why, Andrea?"

"You don't understand," he protested.

"That is what I have just said. Explain to me what I do not understand."

"I cannot." His mouth was hard, closing tightly on the clipped words.

"You do not trust me. You think I am a foolish girl who will tell everything she knows to anyone who asks a question of her."

"It's not that I don't trust you," he insisted. "It's because I have sworn an oath not to speak to you or Bianca about what I am doing."

"You told me that what you were doing was seeking your brother's killer." Rosalinda halted on an indrawn breath, because one of his words had just rung a warning bell in her mind. "An oath, you say? And it is intended to protect Bianca and me? Then it must have been sworn to my mother."

"I owe her a great favor," he said, "in return for taking me into her house and saving my life."

"It was I who brought you inside," she reminded him. "Everyone else thought you were a wild beast. The others would have left you to die outside, in the cold. I think the favor you spoke of is owed to me. You may repay it by speaking honestly."

"I haven't forgotten what you did, Rosalinda. But even for you, I cannot break my word to the Duchess Eleonora."

"The duchess? Oh, Andrea, what have you discovered and what have you promised to do?" She sank down on his hard, narrow bed. "Shall I tell you what I think?"

"Please, let it go. Don't say anything more." He went to the single window and rested his hand on the latched shutter as if he would fling it wide to gulp the fresh outside air.

"Better not open that," Rosalinda warned. "Someone might see the candlelight and wonder who is in the servants' quarters."

Andrea could not have missed the blatant sarcasm in her words. With a muttered curse that expressed deep frustration, he left the window to kneel before her.

"Go now," he commanded. "For your own good, return to your bed and say nothing about my presence here."

"You know who we are," she said, refusing to respond to his order. "You have seen my father's portrait in the sitting room. You have recognized my mother as the Duchess Eleonora. I am amazed that you were allowed to leave Villa Serenita alive."

"Your mother had—" He stopped.

"Yes, she had extracted your oath of silence. Furthermore, she had a mission for you. That is why you were sent with a letter to Luca Nardi. You see, I am not a complete fool. I can reason as well as anyone else in this house." Rosalinda's mouth twisted with her disdain for all secretive intrigues. She could not bear to think of Andrea caught up in a plot that would put his life in danger, and the idea that he was keeping secrets from her was even more distressing.

"Why don't you tell me the truth, Andrea?" She watched his face as she spoke, seeking confirmation of all she knew to be fact and, in addition, what she so far had only guessed at. She did not miss the way he quickly hid his feelings behind a bland expression.

"Everyone who knows her knows my mother's dearest dream," Rosalinda said. "That dream is to take back Monteferro from those Guidi upstarts, then to marry Bianca to a strong man who will hold the city with Bianca as his duchess. Are you to be that man, Andrea? Are you to be the next Duke of Monteferro, with my sister for your wife?" she demanded, her voice rising out of control.

"No! Be silent." Andrea clapped a hand over her mouth, cutting off her too-loud words. Rosalinda struggled, but there was no real contest. Andrea was far stronger than she. The most she could do was pull him down until he sat awkwardly beside her, his left arm across her shoulders, his right hand still on her mouth.

"Will you be quiet and let me explain before you rouse the entire house?" he demanded.

Rosalinda was tempted to bite the side of his hand, but he was looking at her so beseechingly that she did not have the heart. She nodded her agreement instead and Andrea took his hand away.

"I remain bound by the promise of secrecy I made to your mother," he began. "So I will say only that you have guessed a part of the truth."

"My mother has set you the task of taking back Monteferro for her. The message you carried to Luca Nardi was her order to Luca, telling him to give you the money you will need to raise an army, and also to give you any information he may have that will help you succeed." Rosalinda's heart was aching as she worked out the details of the scheme. "I suppose Mother has also promised you shall have Bianca as your wife, so that after you conquer Monteferro you can hold it legitimately in Bianca's name."

They were sitting side by side, their faces turned toward each other, their noses almost touching while they hissed and snarled their claims and accusations, trying to keep their voices low yet unable to do so because they were both fighting emotions that threatened to break through and overpower them.

"I don't want Monteferro," Andrea growled. "Nor do I want Bianca. What do I have to do to make you believe me?"

"I am not sure I can be convinced," she told him. "In fact, I am beginning to believe that everything you said to me on your last night here was a lie."

"I do not tell lies." Andrea's face flushed at the insult and he spoke through gritted teeth. "Especially not to you."

They were so close, with their shoulders and thighs touching. Rosalinda was aware of his warmth. He had not stopped to pull on his hose before he answered her knock, so his legs and feet were bare beneath his shirt. He moved as if to rise from the side of the bed, and his foot brushed against Rosalinda's ankle.

She caught the front of his shirt in her fist, holding it so he could not pull away from her without tearing it. He paused with one knee on the bed and his other foot on the floor. Something told Rosalinda that if she let him go now, he would be forever lost to her. They were both so angry—she at the truth of the secret she had inadvertently uncovered, and he that she had dared to seek him out and then to challenge him—that a desperate act was required to salvage the sweeter emotions that had risen between them during the early winter. An ancient, atavistic female knowledge woke in Rosalinda's heart, telling her what she must do, spurring her next actions.

"Exactly what are your feelings for me, Andrea?"

"I have told you—" he began.

"Don't tell me," she interrupted. "Show me."

"I warn you—"

"Don't warn me. *Show me,*" she said again. While she continued to hold tightly to his shirt, she lifted her other hand to brush his hair off his forehead. She let her fingertips trail down the side of his face. He shuddered in response to her touch.

"If I dare the slightest part of what I want to do," he whispered, "if I indulge in the least kiss or caress, then we will be lost, for I have not ceased to think of you since the day I went away. And I tell you now, Rosalinda, those thoughts were far from pure."

"If you do not kiss me, then I will be forced to kiss you." With a delicate touch she outlined his mouth and when she was done, she inserted her little finger between his lips. His reaction was a groan that rose from deep in his chest. Rosalinda saw a flame leap in his eyes until his usual soft brown gaze changed into a blaze that scorched her—and that aroused in her an answering fire. She ran her tongue across her lips and watched his mouth part in response to what she did. Yet still he clung to his control.

"Let go of my shirt," he whispered.

"You will have to pry my fingers off, one by one," she told him. Nearly overcome by the potent combination of mystery and tough maleness that Andrea represented, Rosalinda let herself fall backward until her head rested on his pillow.

"You are innocent. You cannot know what you are doing," he said.

"I know that I want you to kiss me, and to put your arms around me. How can I be completely innocent after the way you kissed me and touched me in the garden on that last, cold night? I want you to touch me that way again."

"This is too much for any man to bear," he groaned. "If I do not kiss you, I will die."

"I do not want you to die, Andrea. Surely, you know that by now." Rosalinda had never before heard her own voice sounding so low and seductive. She feared that she, too, would die if Andrea did not kiss her without further delay. She did not fully understand why he should hesitate when he admitted he wanted to kiss her and when she was afire to be in his arms. She tugged a little harder on his shirt, and he came down on top of her.

His mouth was gentle on hers, sweet and tender, just

as she remembered. A delicious warmth began to spread through her body. She soon realized that this was partly caused by Andrea's own body heat. Her nightgown was twisted up around her knees, so her bare legs were tangled with his, but more than that, her insistent pulling at his thigh-length shirt had lifted its hem up to his waist. Her linen nightgown offered only the flimsiest of barriers between Andrea's torso and hers. And she was begining to understand that there was a great deal more to his torso than she had previously appreciated. A large part of Andrea was extremely hard and it was pushing against her in a most determined way.

At the same time that she became aware of his hardness, Andrea moved his mouth on hers and his tongue flicked over her lips in a hint that she should open them. In response, Rosalinda parted her lips a little. Emboldened by this sign of encouragement, Andrea gathered her closer and let his tongue surge into her mouth. Rosalinda felt as if her entire body was opening to him, for her thighs parted even as her lips did. She was being swept away by a tide of longing, by a desire to go on lying in his arms while he continued to kiss her. She could lie in his arms forever and not grow tired of it.

Andrea's tongue stroked against hers, inflaming her senses, while between her thighs he also stroked against her, only the fabric of her nightgown separating his flesh from hers. Between her bosom and his broad chest, her hand was still clenched on his shirt. When she was trembling and writhing against him, consumed by the new longings he was arousing in her, Andrea broke off the kiss to raise himself on his elbows. He smiled to see her fist at his chest. Gently he unwound her fingers from the linen and kissed each fingertip, slowly, one by one.

When he lifted the upper part of his body, the lower

portion of him pressed more closely against the increasingly sensitive area between Rosalinda's thighs. She sighed and pushed back.

"My sweet, innocent girl," Andrea whispered, "do you know where this is leading?"

"Yes." She felt as though her body was about to dissolve into his. "Don't stop. I'll die if you stop."

"So will I, though I know well enough that I ought to stop." With a swift motion he tore off his shirt.

Rosalinda laid both of her palms flat against his chest. He gave her only a moment to touch the firm muscles, to let her fingertips find and circle his nipples. She whimpered when he pulled away from her, but it was only to remove her nightgown. He pushed it and her shawl to the foot of the bed, leaving Rosalinda naked to his eyes. She was not at all ashamed. She let him look at her, taking pleasure in his open delight, murmuring softly when his hands enclosed her breasts, moaning low in her throat when he kissed them. Slowly his fingers moved across her body, caressing shoulders and breasts, abdomen and hips, thighs and knees.

"Lift your hips, my darling," he instructed, and she obeyed.

"Andrea, what are you doing with your shirt?"

"You will understand soon enough." He tucked the linen beneath her hips, then separated her thighs and knelt there, between them. His hands stroked upward in the way she remembered from the night in the garden. The part of her that longed for his touch felt the pressure of his fingers. She closed her eyes, savoring the moment, aware of her own moisture and heat and knowing that this time the wonderful thing they had almost achieved on their last encounter would happen without interruption.

Then Andrea removed his fingers. Startled and disappointed, wanting him to continue that delicious pressure, Rosalinda glanced downward. For the first time she saw clearly the hard part of Andrea that had been pressing against her thigh. She watched in fascination as Andrea moved forward, pushing himself into her. The stiff portion of his flesh began to disappear between her thighs. She was aware of it stretching her body. She tore her gaze away to look into Andrea's eyes, to see the joyous wonder there. And the question still lurking.

"Yes," she said, answering that unspoken question. To emphasize her assent, she wrapped her arms around him and pulled him closer.

She did what she could to help him, pushing herself hard against his masculine intrusion, opening herself to him, body and heart together. Then, with a cry of pleasure, he plunged deeply and they were one.

He began to kiss her again—long, slow kisses, with his tongue and that other, harder, part of him moving in and out of her in a matching rhythm, until Rosalinda was drawn out of herself to become part of Andrea, as he was part of her.

He dragged his mouth from hers, gasping for air. Rosalinda did not mind the end of their kiss, for she was gasping, too, clutching at Andrea's shoulders, while her hips moved of their own accord and the rhythm of their joining quickened. Suddenly, she was flying somewhere in the heavens, while still inside her own, familiar skin. Andrea's mouth covered hers again, this time to stop her wild cry of release and to smother his shout of triumph that came an instant later.

It took Rosalinda a while to return to herself, to become a person separate from Andrea once more. She sensed that he was as reluctant to remove himself from her as she was to have him go. Yet she knew, even when at last they lay side by side, that they would never really be separate again. Not after being so close that their souls as well as their bodies had touched.

"As close as two people can be," she whispered.

"As close as my own heart," he said. "I hope you never regret what we have done."

"How could I? What happened between us was too beautiful to regret."

"I hope I have succeeded in convincing you that I do not want your sister," he murmured, kissing her ear lobe. "The only woman I want is you."

"Andrea?" They were still lying so close together on the narrow bed that she only had to move her head a fraction of an inch to look into his eyes. "You told me before you went away that your purpose in leaving was to discover your brother's killer."

"It was true then, as it is now."

"But what of my mother's plan to regain Monteferro?"

"Her plan fits perfectly with what I want do," Andrea said.

"I don't see how." Rosalinda leaned on one elbow, looking down at him. Andrea put his hands behind his head and stretched out his long, muscular legs, crossing them at the ankles. Now that he was healthy again and completely recovered from his ordeal in the mountains, he was lean and tough and, to her eyes, incredibly handsome. Rosalinda loved him with all of her heart. She prayed that she would not have to choose between Andrea and her mother.

"It will not be enough to conquer just Monteferro," Andrea explained. "The Guidi control Aullia, too."

"The city-state that borders Monteferro," Rosalinda noted. "It is said to be beautiful, though I have never seen it. Have you ever been there?"

"In my youth." Andrea dismissed the question with

a smile and went on to the important issue. "In order to secure Monteferro, it will be necessary for me to take Aullia, too."

"This scheme of my mother's seems more dangerous the more I hear of it." Rosalinda shivered.

At once Andrea sat up to snatch her shawl from the foot of the bed and drape it around her shoulders. He held the edges together over her bosom while he kissed her with a tenderness that made Rosalinda think he understood her fears.

"Any danger is worth the risk if, at the end of it, I win my heart's desire," he told her. "Rosalinda, I would lay the world at your feet if I could. Lacking power over the entire world, I will lay Aullia at your feet."

"Aullia?" she breathed.

"I will have you, and Aullia, and my brother's death avenged," he said.

She stared at him wordlessly, trying to comprehend all that he was promising, and failing to do so. Perhaps seeing her confusion, Andrea pulled the ring off his little finger. The ruby shone as red as blood in the candlelight. He slipped it onto Rosalinda's hand.

"This is my pledge," he said. "When I return to Villa Serenita the next time, we will lie together like this again. Every night we are apart, I will think of you and what we have done in this room, and I will hope that you are also thinking of me and remembering."

"I cannot wear it. Someone will notice and remember it was yours." Rosalinda looked at the ring on her finger, wanting to keep it there and knowing she could not. "I know. I'll tie a bit of ribbon around it and pin it to my underdress each day. I will wear it over my heart in the daytime, and on my finger at night, when I am alone."

"And you will wait for me to return?"

"Till the end of the world, if I must. Though I do beg you to come sooner, for I will ache during every moment we are apart to be in your embrace once more."

"I want to love you again," he whispered, his lips against her shoulder. "I would love you all night long if I could, but if we are discovered, your mother will be very angry with both of us. I do not mind for myself, but I do not want to leave you in an unpleasant situation."

"Andrea, how soon must you leave?"

"Well before dawn. Bartolomeo will come for me. I want you out of here and into your own room again before he stirs."

"I know you are right, though I don't want to go." Rosalinda reached for her nightgown. As she moved, she looked down.

"Andrea, there is blood on your shirt. My blood." She looked at him, sudden tears trembling in her eyes. "That's why you put it under me. It was for my sake, so no one would see the blood on the sheet and guess that we have been together. But now your shirt is bloody."

"I will wear it proudly," he said. "That pure blood is your gift to me, a gift I will treasure for the rest of my life."

"Do you think there is time for one more gift-giving?" she asked. She knew that when he left the villa he was going into certain danger. They might not meet again for a long time. Or they might never meet again. Her heart constricted painfully on that thought. Loving him, she wanted to give herself to him once more before they parted. She tried to speak lightly, so he would not guess how frightened she was for his sake. "I can see that you do want me again, and I want you so much that I do not believe it will take us very long this time.''

''I knew you were a passionate woman the first time I saw you riding that horse of yours.'' Andrea pulled her down beside him and, to her great delight, he put his mouth and his hands on her again.

Chapter Eight

Bianca awakened suddenly, sitting up with her hands over her mouth to hold back a cry of alarm. Her room was cold and the quilt had slipped away while she thrashed about in her sleep. Even as the dream faded from her mind, she tried to call it back so she could piece together the remnants of her too-familiar nightmare. Her thoughts grappled with the impression that this time there had been something different about the dream, something she ought to remember because one particular image had been so vivid.

The same dream had tormented her since she was five years old. It always began with a sense of doom for, after so many years, she knew what was going to happen and knew there was nothing she could do to prevent the horror.

Once again she was a child and back in Monteferro. She had run away from her nurse and was playing a game of hide-and-seek, peeping into every room she came to as she explored the ducal palace, and hoping the nurse would not find her. She knew she was being naughty and knew both her mother and the nurse would be annoyed with her, but she was having so much fun that she didn't care a bit what punishment they decreed when they finally located her.

Having reached the great reception room, she tiptoed inside. It was the most beautiful room in the palace and certainly the most resplendent room Bianca had ever seen. There were tall marble pillars and wonderful paintings in golden frames on the walls. The long windows that lined one wall were draped in a rich shade of green velvet that had the Farisi eagle embroidered in gold. Bianca's father was sitting in his chair of state, relaxing for a few moments between audiences. Half a dozen of his trusted guards stood about the room. At the scuffing sound of Bianca's soft slippers on the polished floor, her father turned his head toward her.

"What are you doing here, little one?" he asked. It was said that Girolamo Farisi's smile could charm the birds from the air to sit on his shoulder. Certainly, his smile charmed his daughter. "Come and give your father a kiss."

Bianca ran forward and he swept her up in his strong arms, depositing her on his lap. His clothes were very fine, all red velvet and soft fur trimming, with a heavy gold chain hanging down across his chest. Bianca cuddled against him, enjoying the softness of his clothes while knowing the man himself was strong and indestructible. To Bianca at age five, her father was as constant as the stars she saw each clear night when she lifted the curtains over the window in her room. After kissing him, she rubbed her little cheek against his, feeling the faint stubble on his otherwise smooth skin. Aware of the rumbling beginning deep in his throat,

Bianca sighed with happiness and awaited the affectionate laughter she so loved to hear.

But she never did hear her father's laughter. His arms tightened around Bianca until they began to hurt her. Then he stood her on her feet, pushing her behind his chair with a rough gesture very different from his usual treatment of her.

"Go away, Bianca," he said in a voice he had never used to her before. "Run to your nurse. Find your mother. Do as I tell you. Go!"

Bianca stumbled, catching at the back of his chair. She knew she had been naughty, but she did not understand why her father should welcome her and lift her onto his lap and hug her, and then suddenly change his mind and send her away as if he was angry. Because his order made no sense to her child's mind, she did not obey it. Instead, she scurried across the room and ducked behind one of the green velvet curtains. Thus, she was present to hear the shouts, the clash of weapons, and her father's roar of rage.

"Traitor! Villain!" Girolamo Farisi shouted at someone Bianca could not see. "To think I trusted you!"

Always in her dream, as on the day when it had actually happened, Bianca began to cry at this point. Always she looked down to see a trickle of red seeping beneath the edge of the green curtain and oozing toward her toes. Bianca twitched aside the curtain. One of her father's guards lay upon his back at her feet. He was staring up at her with wide, open eyes, but she did not think he could really see her because he did not smile as he usually did for her. His right arm was flung out, with his sword lying beside his hand.

Elsewhere in the room men were sticking swords and daggers into each other. Bianca's father was using his dagger, holding off another man who also had a dagger.

Bianca did not think they were playing a game because her father looked so angry.

Bianca knew she ought to pick up the fallen guard's sword and go to help her father. She reached down to the sword, but it was so heavy she could not lift it. She tried again and got both of her hands around the hilt, but the sword slipped out of her small fingers to make a loud clattering noise when it landed on the floor. Afraid someone would see her and stick a dagger into her, Bianca jumped back behind the curtain.

Gradually, the shouts and screams moved off into the distance. Bianca could still hear the noise, but it sounded farther and farther away. Save for a few groans, all was silent when she finally dared to step out from her velvet hiding place for a second time. She found the once lovely room in a state of terrifying disarray. Her father's chair was tipped onto its side and many of the curtains had been slashed or pulled down from their poles. The gold-embroidered green velvet hung in long strips that trailed across the polished floor. In places the green was stained with a red that was still wet. In addition to the guard lying near her, there were several other men on the floor, all of them unmoving.

Bianca saw that her father was on the floor, too. He was lying very still, with a dagger buried up to its hilt in his chest. After wiping her wet cheeks and runny nose on her sleeve, Bianca went to him, walking through rivers of blood, tripping over unmoving arms and legs, ignoring the last moans of the one guard left alive. Those moans trailed off into silence as Bianca crossed the room.

"Father?" With her eyes now dry and burning, Bianca sank to her knees, not noticing the sticky wetness that seeped through her skirts. "Father, please speak to me."

Bianca laid her head on her father's shoulder, hoping for some response from him. There was none, and when she opened her eyes wide, all she could see was the gold hilt of the dagger that had ended his life. She stayed where she was for a long time, unable to move, her dress soaked in her father's blood, the only creature alive in a room filled with death.

"Merciful God in heaven!" Bartolomeo's voice penetrated Bianca's languor. "I could not believe the terrible news, but now I see it's true."

"The child was here." The second speaker was a guard whom Bianca knew. "Bartolomeo, she is so still. Is she dead, too? Or have her wits fled at the awful sights she has beheld in this room?"

"Dead or alive, she comes with us." Bartolomeo swooped down on Bianca, gathering up her small form, cradling her against his shoulder.

"The duke is dead," said the guard, bending over the red-robed form.

"I can see as much, Lorenzo." Bartolomeo's voice cracked, as if he wanted to cry, but couldn't. "Come along. We have no choice but to leave him. There isn't much time before those bloodthirsty mercenaries return. They only left the room because they thought everyone here was dead. We have to get Madonna Eleonora and her children to safety. It is what Girolamo would tell us to do if he could still speak to us."

Only when Bartolomeo started to carry her out of the reception room did Bianca stir.

"Father!" Bianca stretched out her arms toward her unmoving parent. "I'm sorry. I tried to help, but the sword was too heavy."

"Thank God she's alive," Lorenzo said. "But keep her quiet or we won't get out of the city."

"Bianca," Bartolomeo said with quiet authority,

"you are too small to lift a sword. You could not help your father, but you can help your mother by being a good girl. You must be very quiet, and very good, and do without question everything you are told to do. Can you understand me?"

"Yes," Bianca whispered. "I promise I will be good."

"I know you will. Your mother will be depending on you in the days ahead."

The last image of Bianca's dream was always the same, of Bartolomeo carrying her out of the reception room, while she looked over his shoulder at her laughing, active father lying so still, with a gold-hilted dagger in his chest. Her small arms stretched out to him as she wailed her apology and her grief—but silently, as Bartolomeo had ordered. For she knew, with the absolute certainty only a child's heart can hold, that her father's death was her fault. If she had not been naughty and run away from her nurse, if she had not interrupted him, and most of all, if only she had been brave enough and strong enough to pick up the sword of that fallen guard and join the fray, she might have saved him. If not for naughty little Bianca, her father might have lived.

The grown-up Bianca understood in her mind that this was a child's fantasy, that nothing could have saved Girolamo Farisi from the well-armed men who were determined to kill him for their own advantage. But deep inside her heart, in the place where all grown-ups remain children forever, Bianca recognized her own guilt. The only way she could make reparation for her naughtiness on that terrible day was by obeying Bartolomeo's orders, by being a good girl, a quiet girl, a girl who caused no trouble to anyone, for the rest of her life, and by never, ever again giving her mother cause to worry about her or be annoyed with her.

* * *

Bianca sat shivering in her cold bedroom while the last, clinging tendrils of her nightmare dissolved. What was it about this night's dream that was different? Was it really different, or was it just that something she had seen in it had struck a new chord in her memory? Was such a thing possible after so many years, after countless repetitions of the same scenes?

"I cannot stay here," Bianca whispered. "Not in this room. I have to talk to someone else. I need to touch another person."

She could not wake her mother. For years Bianca had hidden the fact of her repetitive dream from Eleonora, afraid the revelation would disturb her mother and make her unhappy. Bianca knew her mother was living with entirely too much unhappiness.

Nor could she go to Bartolomeo or Valeria. Both of those loyal friends got such sad looks on their faces whenever the assassination of Girolamo Farisi was mentioned or even hinted at.

There was only one person to whom Bianca could unburden herself. Rosalinda knew about the dreams. There had been many a night when Bianca had crept into Rosalinda's bed, to huddle there against her sister's warmth, to cry as quietly as she could while Rosalinda stroked her hair and whispered to her that it was only a nightmare and all would be well again as soon as the sun rose.

Bianca slipped out of bed. She did not bother with either a candle or a shawl, for it was only a few steps along the corridor to Rosalinda's bedchamber. She stepped into the dark, silent corridor and, keeping one hand on the wall, made her way to her sister's room. Rosalinda was not there.

"Where can she be?" Bianca drew back the window

curtains to make certain. Moonlight spilled into the room, revealing the only sign of Rosalinda to be the tumbled bedclothes, tossed aside as if she had left the room in haste. The candle that was kept by her bed was gone. Obviously, something was amiss. Her own troubles forgotten in concern for her sister, Bianca headed for her mother's room, in case Rosalinda had gone there.

Then she saw a glimmer of light farther down the corridor. Thinking that Rosalinda might have gone to Bartolomeo because she had heard a threatening noise that Bartolomeo ought to investigate, Bianca moved toward the light. She soon realized that it did not come from Bartolomeo's rooms, but from the open door to the servants' stairs. What could Rosalinda be doing in the unused servants' quarters, in the dead of night?

Bianca paused on the landing, looking up toward the light, which she now saw was cast by a single candle held in her sister's hand. Rosalinda was not alone. She was with a man, a man whose bare legs and feet extended below the shirt that was his only garment. The candlelight flickered on the man's face and Bianca recognized Andrea. But Andrea ought to be miles away from Villa Serenita.

Immobilized by shock, Bianca stared at the pair as Rosalinda tilted her face upward and Andrea kissed her on the mouth. The kiss went on and on and Bianca, watching, felt a peculiar warmth gathering inside herself, a sensation that made her yearn for someone to kiss her as thoroughly as Rosalinda was being kissed. Only when Rosalinda and Andrea drew apart to gaze tenderly into each other's eyes did Bianca recover her own good sense.

They must not see her. She retreated along the corridor, moving as quickly as she could in the dark. She heard the faint click of the latch on the door to the stairs, and then Rosalinda's hurried, quiet footsteps. Bianca had reached Rosalinda's room and she slipped inside, to press herself against the wall behind the open door.

Light from the candle Rosalinda carried revealed her sad, tear-streaked face. Not seeing Bianca standing in the shadows, Rosalinda pushed her bedroom door shut and went to set the candlestick on the bedside table.

"Would you care to explain to me what you have been doing abovestairs with Andrea?" Bianca kept her voice to a whisper but still Rosalinda jerked, gasped, and spun around to face her.

"What are you doing here?" Rosalinda's eyes were huge and dark with pain, and full of tears.

"I had the dream again and came looking for you, but you weren't here so I searched for you. I saw you kissing Andrea, and he wearing naught but his shirt. I think you are the one who owes an explanation."

"I love him," Rosalinda said.

"That is no excuse for visiting a man in your nightgown, while he is all but undressed. What will Mother say?"

"Mother knows he is here, and so does Bartolomeo. Bianca, please don't tell anyone you saw Andrea and me together."

"Mother knows he is here?" Bianca repeated.

"He is leaving in just an hour or so, and heaven alone knows when he will be able to return. I had to see him. I had to hear him say he has not forgotten me."

"Andrea comes and goes in secret, only Mother and Bartolomeo knowing of his movements? Dear God, what are they planning?"

Into Bianca's mind a picture flashed, of a dagger stabbing Andrea in the chest, as a dagger had once stabbed Girolamo Farisi. The image lasted only an instant, before Bianca blocked it out, unable to accept the possibility that someone else she knew might meet a similar, bloody fate. Immediately, the terrible picture was replaced by blind fury. "Do you realize how angry Mother will be when she learns of your visit to a man whose presence here she wants kept secret?"

"She won't know unless you tell her," Rosalinda said.

The two sisters stared at each other for a long moment before Bianca nodded once and turned away, determined to regain her self-control. She took a long, deep breath. It did little to calm the anger that filled her heart and her mind. A fair portion of that anger was directed at herself; only part was against her sister.

"Bianca," Rosalinda said softly, "I do love him. He has promised to return to me."

"If he lives long enough to return."

"Don't say that!" Rosalinda cried.

"Hush, you foolish girl, or you'll wake the others." Bianca stepped nearer. Her words might have been dipped in acid before they left her lips, so unerringly did they sear the close ties between the sisters, burning and hurting both of them. "How can you be so thoughtless, so careless of Mother's feelings? While I—I have tried so hard to be good and never to cause any trouble or to worry Mother. I do everything she asks of me. I never complain. And for all my efforts—" Bianca broke off, choking back bitter sobs.

"Mother loves both of us." Rosalinda's arms went around Bianca's shoulders, holding fast even when Bianca tried to pull away. "Dearest sister, you cannot think that Mother loves me more than you. If it sometimes seems that way, it may be because I do get into trouble and worry her, while you do not, so I require more of her attention than you do. Mother knows she can always depend on you.''

''Dependable, quiet, good little Bianca! Unnoticeable Bianca! Invisible Bianca!'' With that, Bianca tore herself out of her sister's arms and left Rosalinda's room, where she could not bear to stay a moment longer.

Chapter Nine

"Well?" Niccolò Stregone glared at the man standing before him. "Where did he go?"

"Signore, forgive me." The man's teeth chattered in fear, though he was far larger and physically more powerful than his master. "These mountain trails—I am a man of the city, signore. I lost my way and lost the person I was following."

"Lost him?" Niccolò Stregone repeated, as if he could not believe what he was hearing. *"Lost him?"*

"I beg you, forgive me, signore."

"Imbecille! Cretino! Incompetente—!" Stregone's hand rested on his dagger. He would have liked nothing better than to slit the throat of the man who was now kneeling before him. But they were presently housed in a monastery, in a pitiful little cell with none of the luxuries to which Stregone was accustomed. He detested everything about the monastery and could not understand why Luca Nardi should make a habit of visiting

it two or three times a year.

Unless, of course, there was some reason other than the state of his soul that brought Luca Nardi to such a desolate location. Since Nardi himself was far too valuable to the Guidi rulers of Monteferro to be dragged to the *castello* and interrogated under torture, as Stregone wanted to question the head of the House of Nardi to obtain all his secrets, then another way must be found.

Stregone had set his spies to watch Luca Nardi day and night, to discover all they could about his opinions, habits, and activities both social and political. Having learned enough interesting details to make him even more curious about Nardi, Stregone had then directed a supposedly trustworthy spy to trail the mysterious young man who had recently paid several clandestine visits to Nardi's house. From the description furnished by his people, Stregone thought he knew who the young man was. He considered the matter important enough to prompt him to leave Monteferro and venture into the mountains on the heels of his own spy—who had now most ineptly lost the young man.

"Signore?"

The wretched spy looked up at him, a situation Niccolò Stregone found entirely pleasing. It was always a delight to force others to their knees—or onto their bellies or backs—so he could look down on them. Being of abnormally short stature himself, Stregone cherished a deep resentment against big, strong, handsome men.

"Signore," the spy said, his voice quavering in fear, "shall I return to the place where I lost the man I was tracking, and try to find him again?"

"Of course not, you fool. He is long gone from that location by now. No, I want you to carry a message for me."

"A message, signore?"

"Yes, a message, you dolt. What kind of a spy are you, that you cannot understand a simple statement? Don't worry, you won't have to remember what I want to say. I will write it down and you will deliver it only into the hands of Marco Guidi himself."

Stregone found parchment and quill on the small table in the room. Quickly, he wrote the message. When he was finished he folded and sealed it, wishing he could be present when Marco Guidi read it, so he could see the smile on the face of that most bloodthirsty nobleman. The river that ran through Monteferro was deep and swift in early springtime. Dumped into that river, a man's body would be carried out to sea before he was missed, and no one would be the wiser about his fate.

The spy who remained on his knees, looking distinctly relieved to be sent away from the mountains and the presence of Niccolò Stregone, would never make another stupid mistake like the one he had made this day. Only at his journey's end would he realize that the message he carried to Marco Guidi contained in its postscript his own death warrant.

"Before you go," Stregone said, handing the sealed parchment to the spy, "I want you to tell me exactly where you tracked that young man you were following. Give me every detail you can remember about the last place you saw him and the direction you believe he was taking."

"Are you going to track him yourself, signore?" asked the spy.

"Indeed, I am. I could not possibly do a worse job than you have done, could I?" Stregone said. "Besides, I have other business to conduct while I am in this area. I can kill two birds as easily as one." Stregone smiled at his own words.

Seeing him smile, the spy shuddered.

Chapter Ten

As the spring weather grew warmer, relations between Bianca and Rosalinda grew steadily cooler. No matter how often Bianca might hint that she would listen without indulging in any further criticism and would keep her sister's confidences, Rosalinda steadfastly refused to reveal the entire story of what had happened on the night when she had met Andrea in the servants' quarters. Bianca had some idea of what had occurred, but she did not like to think about it, for every time she did, she became aware of disturbing emotions of her own that she would prefer not to feel. All too often during those lengthening days, while she watched the earth turn green with the promise of fresh growth and eventual fruitfulness, Bianca found herself hard pressed to maintain her quiet, polite demeanor.

Always before when she was upset she had been able to talk to her mother. That source of comfort was no longer available to her, for Eleonora was increasingly distracted and, on occasion, short-tempered. Bianca was sure the change in her mother had something to do with the secret plans that involved Andrea. Again, as with Rosalinda, Bianca could draw no information out of this other beloved relative. Never had Bianca been so lonely; never had her desire to be a good and perfect daughter and sister seemed so unattainable. She did not know how much longer she could contain her anger or that other, unidentifiable, emotion that sometimes threatened to choke her.

"I am going riding," Rosalinda announced one sunny afternoon. "Mother, you cannot object. Bianca and I have finished our lessons and our household chores for today. The snow has melted except in the highest passes, and I promise I will not go near them. I will stay in the valley and the lower hills."

"I wish you would remain at home," Eleonora said.

"If I do, I am certain to get into trouble," Rosalinda said, only half joking. "I am so bored that I hardly know what to do with myself."

"Then take one of the men-at-arms with you. I do not like you to ride alone."

"No, I don't want a man along." Rosalinda paused, regarding her sister with a speculative gleam in her eyes. "However, I would enjoy Bianca's company. Tell her to go with me, Mother. You know if we are together, I won't venture into rough territory."

"Why not?" Bianca snapped. "Is it because you think I am a coward?"

"Perhaps it's because I think you have better sense than I," Rosalinda responded.

"If you stay off the higher, dangerous paths that still have ice on them," Eleonora said, "and if Bianca goes along, then I will agree that you may ride for an hour or two. Rosalinda, I am glad to see you are trying to repair the ill feeling between you and your sister. I never did understand why you have been at odds during these past weeks, but I beg you to be friends again as you once were."

"Well, Bianca?" Rosalinda challenged. "Are you willing to make an effort, too? Will you ride with me?"

"If you promise to obey the rules Mother has set down," Bianca said, "then I will ride with you for an hour."

It was hardly the warmth that Eleonora wanted to see restored between her daughters, but she appeared to think it was a start. She sent them off with a smile and only one warning to be sure to dress carefully, since the spring winds could turn chill at any moment.

"Where shall we go?" Bianca asked when the two young women were mounted and riding out of the stable yard.

"I would like to race into the hills and beyond," Rosalinda said with a laugh. "But I have promised to be good. Let us ride along the meadow to the river, and then just into the foothills. Some of the early flowers should be blooming. You would like to see them, wouldn't you?"

"Of course."

Bianca's politeness was so artificial that Rosalinda made a face and caught at the reins of her sister's horse, pulling it close to hers.

"I wish we could be friends again," Rosalinda said. "I miss you, Bianca."

"So do I miss you," Bianca responded. "But you have gone to a place where I cannot follow. You live with secrets you will not divulge, and with hopes that I can only imagine."

"I have changed, that's true. But I still love you, Bianca. You are my best friend."

"I thought that was Andrea." Bianca could not keep the bitterness out of her voice.

"Don't separate yourself from me this way," Rosalinda cried. "Yes, I need Andrea, but I need you, too. You and I were so close that we always knew each other's heart."

"I have not stopped loving you, Rosalinda. It's only that I am bewildered by your actions. I feel lost, and very much alone. I can confide in no one."

"It could be different between us. We quarreled from time to time when we were children, but we always made up and became friends again."

"We are no longer children." Bianca wanted to return to the loving affinity she had once enjoyed with her sister, but she could not. She was not sure why this was so. It was not entirely because of the changes wrought by Rosalinda's close relationship with Andrea. Something had also changed in Bianca's heart.

"Can we at least agree to try to be friends again?" Rosalinda asked. "If Mother sees us making the effort, I know she will be happier."

"We can try," Bianca said. She sighed, feeling infinitely sad, and glanced across the spring-green meadow to where an ancient bridge spanned the river in two very solid, pale stone arches. The Romans had built the bridge and the stone-paved road that marched in a northwestward direction straight across the valley. Centuries ago, Roman armies had tramped along that road on their way to conquer the barbarian tribes of the north, but on this spring day the valley was entirely peaceful. The river sparkled in the sunshine, blue as the sky it reflected, cold as the mountain snows that fed it.

On the other side of the river the foothills rose, robed in lacy shades of early green. Behind these more delicate trees were the darker, sturdier evergreens of the deep forest and, higher still, the bare gray rocks of the mountain peaks, most of them cloaked in white. In the clear sky an eagle soared, gliding lazily on the wind currents. The beauty of the landscape and the sight of that single bird caught at Bianca's heart as never before, holding her spellbound, making her ache with a peculiar dissatisfaction and a longing for she knew not what. She heard her sister's voice as if from a great distance.

"Since we are to be friends again, could we also agree to race as far as the bridge?" Rosalinda was grinning at Bianca as if all of their differences had been put behind them.

"I can see that you won't be stopped no matter what I say, and I know you have tried to be patient with all the winter days when you were kept indoors." Bianca could not admit to her own, more recent, restlessness. She could, however, issue a teasing challenge that would result in the physical action she suddenly craved. "In fact, dear sister, you are so weak from sitting at lessons all winter that I do believe I could win a race against you."

"Never!" Rosalinda laughed aloud at the very idea of Bianca winning over her. "Count to three, and we're off!"

"One, two, three!" Bianca dug her heels into her horse's sides and headed for the bridge. Rosalinda was right beside her. Together they galloped across the field, Rosalinda laughing and shouting that she would surely win, Bianca quiet and concentrating on handling her horse. Neck and neck they raced across the bridge and pulled up together on the other side.

"A tie!" Rosalinda brushed several locks of loosened hair out of her eyes. "Bianca, my dear, that's the best race you have ever run."

"I am glad we both won." Bianca reached over to

catch yet another lock of her sister's hair, to tuck it behind her ear in a once-familiar gesture. "You should have let me braid it for you."

"I was in too much of a hurry to leave the house to think about my hair." Rosalinda wriggled her shoulders, took a few deep breaths of the earthy spring air, and let her gaze rest with longing on the mountain heights. As if making a difficult decision, she said, "No, I promised Mother I would stay in the valley or the lower foothills. Bianca, shall I show you a place I know, where tiny flowers bloom?"

"We could pick some to take home to Mother," Bianca said. "Which way do we go?"

"Wait." Rosalinda put out a hand, signaling silence. "Listen. Do you hear someone calling?"

"It's probably only the water rushing under the bridge," Bianca said.

"There it is again." Leaving the bridge, Rosalinda began to ride along the side of the river.

Over the course of centuries, the river had cut a channel almost six feet deep through the meadow. Because the river was fed by melting snow and therefore was highest in the spring season, the small, sandy or stony beaches that edged the bottom of this channel during the rest of the year were presently submerged, with the water reaching almost to meadow height. Here and there a few large boulders reared above the swift current, and foam eddied and surged around these wet rocks. On the flat top of one of the rocks, a figure was hopping up and down and waving frantically.

"Is that a child?" Bianca asked, following her sister along the side of the river. "How did he ever get out there without being swept away?"

"We can ask him after we rescue him," Rosalinda responded.

"How are we to do that?" Bianca demanded. Regarding the short figure on the rock, she suggested, "I could try to calm him while you ride home as fast as you can and fetch Bartolomeo and one of the men-at-arms. Tell them to bring a rope and they can throw it to him and pull him through the water to land."

"I don't think we have time to bring more help. He doesn't look to me as if he will calm down until he is safe on dry land," Rosalinda objected. "If that child does not stop hopping around out there, he is going to slip and fall into the river. Then he will surely drown."

"We can't let that happen." Bianca squinted against the sun's glare on the water. "Who is he? I don't think he belongs to any of the men-at-arms. Could he be from the village on the other side of the mountain pass? If so, what is he doing this far from home?"

"Those are more questions we can ask once he's safe."

Without further comment or speculation on how the child had gotten where he was, Rosalinda dismounted. To Bianca's astonishment, she began to strip off the doublet she wore for riding and then the wool dress beneath the jacket.

"Rosalinda, I hope you aren't planning to go into the water?" Bianca was on the ground, too, now, pulling off her cloak to free her arms for action. "It must be freezing in there."

"That boy will freeze if we don't help him." Rosalinda was down to her shift and was kicking off her boots as she spoke.

"How are we going to do this?" Bianca asked.

"I am going to reach across the water to catch hold of that foolish boy. While I do, you, my dear, are going to keep me from falling into the river by holding on as tightly as you can to both of our horses' reins with one hand. With your other hand, you are going to hold on to me.''

''Am I?'' A thrill of fear sliced through Bianca. From the brief explanation, she understood what Rosalinda was planning and she knew that all of them—she, her sister, the boy on the rock, and perhaps the horses as well—could fall into the river and be swept downstream in the swift current. They might all drown in that icy, choking coldness.

Recalling another day fifteen years in the past, when she had not been strong enough to help someone who needed her, Bianca resolved not to fail at this opportunity to prove she was not a coward. She grasped the reins Rosalinda put into her hands, winding them several times around her left arm to secure them. She wrapped the fingers of her right hand around Rosalinda's left wrist, while Rosalinda held her wrist in the same manner. With Bianca's feet planted at the very edge of the precipitous slope into the river, Rosalinda stepped toward the rock, stretching across the water with her free right hand toward the short figure that watched them, yet never ceased to dance to and fro from one side of the rock on which it stood to the other.

''Take my hand,'' Rosalinda shouted above the sound of the rushing water. ''Hurry! I can't hold on much longer. Stop that bouncing around and grab my hand!''

Bianca could not hear exactly what the person on the rock said. A few syllables drifted to her ears, startling her with their vehemence. Surely, the person they were trying so hard to help could not be cursing them? Then she was distracted by a new danger. She was so close to the edge that she was about to lose her footing.

''I'm slipping,'' she yelled to the person on the rock.

"For heaven's sake, we are trying to help you! Do as my sister says."

She could not tell whether he heard her or not, but he did grasp Rosalinda's outstretched hand. Bianca pulled on the reins. The horses stepped away from the edge and Bianca, Rosalinda, and the small person at the end of this chain of rescue slowly moved out of the water, up the slope, and onto solid footing in the grass.

Rosalinda dropped to her knees and Bianca at once took up her discarded cloak, using it to cover her shaking sister.

"Don't you have anything to cover me?" the person they had just saved asked in a complaining voice. "I warn you, I expect something better than that old cloth."

Infuriated by his complete lack of gratitude, Bianca spun around to confront him. He was dripping wet, his black hair was hanging in lank strands over his forehead, and his dark eyes were blazing with anger. Bianca saw that he was not a child at all, but a man so short that he barely reached to her shoulder. She guessed that he was in his mid-fifties. Every line of his wiry body radiated an imperious rage.

"How dare you handle me so roughly, you peasants?" the little man demanded. "Don't you know a gentleman when you meet one?"

"What we knew about you," Bianca said, bending toward him with her fists planted on her hips, "was that you were about to be swept off that rock and carried away down the river. We just saved your life, but if I had known how rude you were going to be, I might well have let you drown."

"Ignorant peasants," the man said, attempting to brush the water off his clothes.

"That won't work," Bianca told him. "You need to

take off your clothes and wring them out thoroughly, then spread them on the grass in the sun to dry."

"I didn't ask for your advice, you stupid laundress," the little man snarled at her.

"No, you didn't, but I am going to give you more unsolicited advice," said Bianca. "You are trespassing on private land. If the owner discovers you are here, it will go hard with you. I insist that you leave at once."

"All I wanted was a drink of water," he said, glaring at her.

"Then you should have walked downriver to a calmer spot," Bianca said.

"Walk? Not I. Walking is for servants and farmers."

"Indeed?" Bianca's nose was high in the air. Her diminutive opponent did not appear to notice. "Get off these lands and don't come back."

"I am going, you impudent wench. Count yourself lucky that I do not toss you onto the ground and use you as a man uses a female."

"I count myself the most fortunate woman in the world to escape your embrace," Bianca shot back at him.

"What are you laughing at, wench?" the little man exclaimed, turning his attention to Rosalinda, who was still sitting on the ground, covered with Bianca's cloak.

"I was wondering what you were planning to do with me while you were trying to force my sister to the ground," Rosalinda said in her most impudent manner.

The man looked from Rosalinda's glowing face and water-soaked braid to Bianca's paler, more angry expression. He shrugged his shoulders as if the two young women were of no importance. But he did offer an explanation, of sorts.

"I am here because I am searching for someone," he

said. "A dark-haired young man, a stranger in these hills. Do you know him?"

"The only strange man we have seen in many a year is you," Bianca told him. She wondered if he realized just how ridiculous he was, how rude and impolite. Even now, he did not thank the very people who had saved his life but, instead, addressed them in a manner that constituted a grave insult to anyone of gentle birth.

"I know that few people come this way so, if he did, you must know of it. Are you sure you haven't seen anyone new lurking about?" He looked from Bianca to Rosalinda, who merely shook her head, saying nothing. "You had better be telling the truth. If you are not, I will discover your lie, and I will see you punished for it." With those contemptuous words, he strode off in the direction of some nearby trees.

Never taking her eyes off the man in case he had attendants hidden in those trees, Bianca moved closer to her still shivering sister. A few moments later, the little man rode out of the trees upon a black stallion so huge it made him look like a young child on its back. Without another glance at the two who had rescued him and still without uttering a single word of thanks, he cantered across the meadow to the bridge.

"See that you never return here!" Bianca shouted after him.

He did not answer her, but rode over the bridge and along the Roman road that led across the valley and into the mountains.

"And learn some manners if you want to get on in the world!" Rosalinda added to her sister's remarks. She got up to stand next to Bianca and, as the little man disappeared into the distance, she began to laugh.

"No wonder he thought we were peasants," Rosalinda said. "Just look at you, Bianca. Your skirts are wet, your hair is all undone, and with your fists on your hips like that, you could easily be mistaken for one of the laundresses back at the villa."

"Could I?" Bianca turned from contemplation of the spot where she had last seen the little man to glance at her sister. Her mouth curved in amusement. "And there you are, Rosalinda, wearing only a wet shift. What could our ungrateful friend have thought of you?"

"I am sure he found my demeanor as shocking as yours." Rosalinda's eyes gleamed with humor. "It has been a long time since I've seen you so angry."

"Shocking or not, I haven't felt so wonderful in months," Bianca said and burst into laughter along with her sister.

"Damnable wenches, both of them," Niccolò Stregone muttered to himself. "It was the sight of those stupid females riding across the fields that made me drop my bag into the water. I saw it down there, between the rock and the river's edge, and might have dragged it up again if those two hadn't come along. But the water pulled the bag open and everything inside spilled out. Now there was no way for me to recover it. All that lovely gold lost, and a beautiful ruby ring, too. So this long journey was made for nothing, unless I can locate that foolish boy before I must leave. But why the devil would I come to this part of Italy? There is nothing here but mountains and isolated villages.

"What do you want, you cursed bird?" This last sentence was shouted at an eagle that had swooped out of the sky toward him. Pulling his dagger from its sheath, Stregone waved his arms as if to strike at the bird. But apparently a mere human was beneath its notice, for the eagle flew straight on to the river. There it dove to the water to snare a fish in its talons, after which the eagle flew away again, heading back toward the mountains with its next meal held in a firm grasp.

"Control yourself, Stregone," the little man said to himself. "You are wet and cold and upset at losing part of your hard-earned treasure, and so you are imagining threats where none exist. Those two girls were no more than peasants, and that bird didn't even notice you. All it wanted was its dinner. Soon enough, you will be eating your dinner, too, and wearing dry clothes."

Stregone sheathed his dagger again. Sparing a single backward glance for his rescuers, he noted that they were riding in the opposite direction from the route he was taking. Then a stand of trees blocked the girls from view, and Stregone put them out of his thoughts.

"Are you sure that is everything?" Bartolomeo asked. Frowning deeply, he looked from Rosalinda to Bianca.

The three of them were standing in the stable yard, where Bianca had espied Bartolomeo as soon as they rode in from their encounter with the odd little man. They had not gone to look for early wildflowers after all, but had ridden home immediately after Rosalinda had pulled on her clothes.

"Bartolomeo, we have told you every detail of the man's appearance and every word he spoke. We have repeated the story twice," Bianca said, exasperated by his continued questioning. "Now, let us go, please, so Rosalinda can get into a hot bath before she catches a serious chill."

"You were both very brave to attempt such a rescue," Bartolomeo said with his eyes on Bianca as if he were trying to convince her of the truth of his words. "I do have a request to make of you. Do not disturb your mother with this tale. You said the man rode away from the estate and toward the mountains. I will inform the guards about this incident and they will take extra care to see that he does not set foot upon these lands."

"You are right, Bartolomeo," Rosalinda agreed before Bianca could voice her opinion. "Let Mother hear of this afternoon's adventure and she will keep Bianca and me inside the house for at least a month. I, for one, could not tolerate the confinement."

"Bartolomeo, if you are certain there is no danger," said Bianca somewhat more reluctantly, "then I suppose we needn't upset Mother, or Valeria, either."

But Bianca could see that Bartolomeo was upset by the tale she and Rosalinda had told. She thought he must have said something to Valeria after all, because over the next few days, under the guise of cleaning out the dust of a long winter, Valeria found so many tasks to keep both Rosalinda and Bianca busy that neither sister had an opportunity to go riding, or even to venture beyond the garden.

"You know what she is doing," Rosalinda muttered to Bianca one morning in the dining room, as they each polished a chair with a mixture of beeswax and oil, rubbing the wood with soft cloths until it shone.

"Of course I know," Bianca responded. "I am not as stupid as that nasty little man believed. Bartolomeo wants to be absolutely certain the man has gone before we are allowed out again, but he doesn't want you to be annoyed by our confinement or me to be frightened, so he has convinced Valeria to keep us occupied."

"They won't keep me indoors for long," said Rosalinda with an impish smile.

"Do be careful." Bianca put her hand over Rosalinda's fingers, and Rosalinda gave her sister a quick kiss on the cheek in response.

And Eleonora, standing in the doorway with Valeria, smiled and nodded and went away pleased to see her daughters on warmer terms again.

The next day Rosalinda went riding alone. She did ask Bianca to go along, but Bianca had some work to finish for Valeria. An hour or so later, with her tasks done, Bianca gave in to a new bout of restlessness and went in search of her sister. Believing Rosalinda would go first to the bridge, Bianca rode in that direction. The river was slightly lower than before, as Bianca could see by the level of the water rushing past the rock from which they had rescued the strange little man. There was no sign of Rosalinda, but perhaps she had gone into the woods in search of the flowers she had spoken of, to pick some for their mother.

While she looked around for some trace of her sister, a delightful idea occurred to Bianca. If there were areas in the forest where enough sunlight filtered through the foliage to allow flowers to bloom, then berries might also be growing wild in the woodland soil. Just the thought of the delicate, tiny strawberries that Rosalinda sometimes carried home from her excursions made Bianca's mouth water.

A short distance beyond the bridge, Bianca noticed a narrow stream that fed into the river. There seemed to be a path beside it. Dismounting, she tied her horse's reins to a sapling so it could feed on the grass at the edge of the wood while she was gone. Then, knowing she could not become lost so long as she followed the stream, Bianca ventured into the leafy shade. Dead brown leaves carpeted the soil and crackled pleasantly when she stepped on them; the little stream bubbled and gurgled cheerfully, and here and there flowering plants did poke their fragile heads up into patches of sunlight, just as Rosalinda had described.

Some distance into the woods, Bianca came to a spot where her explorations were halted by a solid rock wall that extended well above her head. The rock was not bare. Bushes grew in a few crevices, vines drifted downward from trees to underbrush, and from the top of the gray rock a waterfall tumbled down the sheer face into a mossy pool. Venturing to the very edge of the pool, Bianca put out her hands to catch some of the falling water and carry it to her lips. It was sweet and pure, and very cold.

"No wonder Rosalinda likes to explore. I never knew this lovely spot was here. How pleasant it must be on a hot summer day." Thinking she heard her sister's voice, Bianca went still, listening. At first all she heard over the sound of the waterfall was the rustling of leaves as a breeze blew by and the songs of the birds that flew among the trees. Then, very distinctly, she heard someone whistling.

Rosalinda sometimes whistled. Always, when they heard her, their mother or Valeria reminded Rosalinda how improper it was for a lady to make such a noise. Bianca smiled at the notion of her sister whistling in the woods, where no one would hear or criticize her. The merry tune was coming from just above Bianca's head. How like her sister to find a way to climb up over those sheer rocks so she could stand atop a waterfall and whistle!

"Rosalinda," Bianca called, stepping back from the pool to look upward. "Come out, my dear. If you do not scold me for following you and discovering at least one of your secrets, I promise to tell no one how well you have taught yourself to whistle."

The whistler broke off in mid-note.

"Come down, come down," Bianca called, laughing now at the thought of Rosalinda's discomfiture at being found out. "I shall not punish you. Word of honor."

"I do admire an honorable lady." A tall, masculine shape moved into view on the rocks above the waterfall.

"Andrea?" Bianca whispered. The man who perched precariously above her looked like Andrea and sounded like Andrea, but she could not be certain that was who he was. At first she thought sunlight and leafy shade were playing tricks with her eyesight. There was only one way to identify him and that was by seeing him face to face at closer range. In a louder voice, Bianca called, "Come down from there at once before you fall."

"At your command, madonna." Catching a tree limb, he swung downward to land lightly on his feet no more than a few inches away from her. The tree branch swung back up again when he released it, showering bits of greenery over both of them. He reached out to pluck a leaf from Bianca's hair. "Here I am, madonna, as you wish. Now that you have me, what do you plan to do with me?"

"Do? Why are you here?" Shaken by the vital male presence confronting her, Bianca took a step backward. She slipped on the moss. Quick as lightning, Andrea's arm was around her waist, pulling her away from the pool, drawing her firmly against his hard, very manly body.

His clothes, which Bianca did not recognize, were worn and soiled, and his dark beard had grown back again, though it was neatly trimmed. She wondered if he was traveling in disguise. Then she noticed the gold ring on his left little finger and she knew he was not. Still, his unexpected presence puzzled her. She could not think why he had not presented himself at the villa, to make his report to her mother.

"Why am I here?" he repeated her question. "I do

believe the angels sent me here to find you, madonna."

"I'm sure you mean you wanted to find Rosalinda. That is why you are here, isn't it? For an assignation with my sister." It was the only explanation that made sense to Bianca.

"Since your sister obviously is not here, perhaps you will allow me an assignation with you instead."

His smile really was charming. Andrea had never smiled at Bianca in that way but, seeing him now, she could understand why Rosalinda found him irresistible. Bianca knew she ought to be ashamed of herself for permitting him to continue his embrace, but it was lovely to be held so closely, to gaze into his liquid brown eyes, to see the smile that made her smile back at him.

"That's better," he said, seeing her smile. "You were altogether too serious before, when you ordered me to join you down here."

"Of course I was serious. I was afraid you would slip and fall off those rocks."

"If I were injured, would you care?"

"Yes, I would. You know I would. Didn't I—" Bianca could not go on. His mouth was much too close to hers. She could not think about what she wanted to say. She could only stare at his beautiful lips.

"Didn't you what, madonna?" he murmured.

"Why are you calling me madonna, as if we were strangers?" she asked. "You know my name is Bianca."

"Bianca." The word was a caress on his lips. "You are well named, Bianca, with hair like silver sunlight and eyes the color of the sky over the mountains."

"You should not say such things to me."

"Why not, when they are true?"

"This is wrong. I must not allow it." But she could

not stop what was happening. His arms were tightening around her and, heaven help her, she did not want him to release her. Not yet. Not until he had kissed her. No man had ever kissed Bianca. She knew Andrea would, in just a moment more. Her lips parted on the thought. His mouth brushed across hers.

"Oh." The single word was a soft whisper of sound on Bianca's lips, granting free consent to whatever he would do next. Then his mouth slanted across hers with firm assurance and Bianca was lost. Her hands fluttered briefly over his shoulders and then went still. Her heart stopped, and the breath halted in her lungs. The world pitched crazily around her, and Bianca was swept into a new place where wild emotion reigned. All that mattered was this man's arms around her, his mouth on hers, and the hardness of his muscular frame. He was supporting her, he was her lifeline, and she recognized that he was the very reason for her existence.

His fingertips were on her cheeks, on her throat, then on her breasts, caressing, squeezing gently. When his thumb rubbed across her nipple, Bianca pulled away.

"I—I cannot," she stuttered. "I should not have allowed so much."

"Bianca." His hand cupped her cheek, and Bianca turned her face into his palm. "Lovely Bianca. You have never been kissed before today, have you?"

"Could you tell? Did I do it badly?"

"You did it sweetly," he told her. "As sweetly as any innocent girl could ever return a kiss."

"It was wrong. I ought to be ashamed."

"And are you?" he asked.

"No," she whispered. "And my very lack of shame makes me ashamed. I mean—" She bit her lip in confusion, until he put a finger on that lip and rubbed it with a softly sensual touch.

"I know what you mean, sweet Bianca. You are a lady of noble birth, that's plain to see, and I have presumed too much. The fault is entirely mine."

"I think I should take half the responsibility for what we have done."

"If that is your pleasure, sweet Bianca." He seemed amused by what she had said.

"Pleasure?" Bianca whispered, looking hard at him. His smile was warmer than she remembered, but now she noticed a difference about his eyes. He seemed more cynical, a bit more calculating, and somehow more daring than the Andrea she remembered from their winter evenings together. Perhaps a change in him was to be expected. Her mother had sent him out on a secret mission that Bianca was certain had been dangerous and, judging by his next words, might still be dangerous.

"Sweet Bianca," he said, "I want you to promise you will tell no one that you have seen me. It is vitally important that no one knows I am here."

"I promise," she said at once. "But An—" He stopped her with a finger on her lips.

"Not another word," he said. "I saw you come here to the waterfall. Now I want you to return by the same path. Do not look back. Do not ask why. Just go, believing that I send you away for your safety and not because I want you to leave me. You are the sweetest lady I have ever met. Do not forget me, Bianca. Go, now. Go."

She trembled at those last few words of his which, unknown to him, dredged up terrible memories for her. She stared at him, wanting to stay with him, yet knowing that this time she must obey. He took her by the shoulders and turned her around, pushing her gently along the path he wanted her to take. Wracked by memory, Bianca took a deep, sobbing breath.

"Ah, don't cry, sweet lady. We will meet again, I promise you." Still holding her by the shoulders, he drew her back to rest against his chest. His mouth lingered on the nape of her neck, before his tongue traced a warm, moist path down to the neckline of her dress. Then he steadied her, stepped away from her, and gave her a gentle shove between her shoulder blades.

"Go." His voice was so soft it sounded like the murmur of the spring breeze.

Bianca walked along the stream until it curved around a huge, mossy boulder. Only then did she look back.

He was gone. She wondered if he had been a dream, a man formed out of her own fevered imagining, to provide the tenderness, the soft laughter, the warm desire that she so desperately needed. Not until she touched her lips and recalled the pressure of his arms as if he were still holding her, was she convinced that he was real. Then cold reality struck her and she wished with all her heart that he *were* the product of her imagination. For, whatever he might be to her, he was the man her sister loved.

Chapter Eleven

In that household where secrets and half-truths had burgeoned in recent months like the new leaves on the trees, at last Bianca had a secret of her own, and she hugged it to her heart. Andrea, who last winter had had eyes only for Rosalinda, was interested in *her*—in pale, quiet, almost invisible Bianca.

Well aware of her high birth and of the lost inheritance of Monteferro that ought, by right, to be hers, Bianca understood that she had allowed Andrea too many liberties with her person and that she would be foolish beyond belief to permit him more than he had already enjoyed. Still, she took a perverse pleasure in the knowledge that Rosalinda was not the only girl capable of attracting the romantic attentions of a handsome man.

Throughout the rest of that day and the evening that followed, Bianca existed in a state of terrified anticipation, jumping nervously at every sound, expecting

Andrea to stride boldly into the villa. When he came, would he look first at Rosalinda and smile his beautiful smile at her, or would his eyes seek out Bianca before her sister?

Such thoughts finally produced the guilt Bianca had not felt during her encounter with Andrea. She was certain that Rosalinda, who was honorable to her very bones, would never have done what Bianca had done. Rosalinda would rather die than ever embrace or taste the lips of the man her sister loved.

Bianca felt like weeping, not only for shame, but for the unworthy jealousy of her sister that had prompted her shameful actions in the first place. But had it all been the result of jealousy? Hadn't Andrea encouraged Bianca's response to him? Did that mean he was not as fond of Rosalinda as Bianca had thought? Or did it mean he was not the honorable man she had believed him to be? Consumed by this inner debate, Bianca kept her distance from Rosalinda and rebuffed every overture her sister made.

"Bianca, you are remarkably distracted this evening," Eleonora said, frowning at her. Bianca could almost feel in her own heart her mother's disappointment at seeing the returning warmth between her daughters ended so quickly.

"I am tired." It was a lame excuse and Bianca knew it, but in her present state of mind she could think of nothing clever to say.

"Perhaps it is my fault." Valeria offered her own excuse. "I have kept Bianca occupied for long hours every day recently."

"I trust you are not unwell?" Bartolomeo was watching her closely. Bianca was sure he was wondering if her encounter with the strange man whom she and Rosalinda had rescued might have stirred old, unhappy memories.

"I am in perfect health, thank you, Bartolomeo." Wanting to prevent any further questioning, Bianca went on, "Nor have my cleaning chores tired me. I think the sudden advent of warmer weather has produced this lassitude. In fact, I am so sleepy that, if you will excuse me, Mother, I will seek my bed."

"If it is what you wish, then go to bed," Eleonora responded. "However, if a good night's sleep does not refresh you, Valeria and I will prepare a tonic for you to take."

"Thank you, Mother. Good night." Bianca had to grit her teeth to keep herself from declaring that she was a grown woman, with her own needs and wants, and not a child to be fussed over or fed tonics whenever she lapsed into a bad mood.

It did not take long for Bianca to realize that retreating to her bedroom was the wrong thing to do. With no one else present to take her mind off the tormenting subject, all she could think of was Andrea. She went over every word he had said to her, every touch, every kiss. She could even recall the funny little tune he had been whistling when first she saw him perched above the waterfall. Remembering Andrea's embrace, Bianca ached, as if a hollow place inside her must be filled or she would go mad with longing.

She drew back the curtains, opened the shutters, and leaned out of her window to see the stars and the faint gleam of white on the mountaintops. There was no moon. The night was still and dark, save for the dim starlight.

As if in response to the quietness, still more questions crowded her mind, giving her no peace. Why had Andrea returned to the mountains? What drew him there?

Why did he not come to the villa? What would happen if he did?

Bianca wished there were someone to whom she could talk, but Rosalinda, the one person in whom she had always before been able to confide, was also the one person who must never learn what wicked Bianca had done with her sister's lover.

"I am surprised at you, Bianca," her mother said. "Whence comes this sudden lack of interest in your household duties? It is usually Rosalinda who forsakes Valeria and me when we require her presence."

"Oh, let her go and I will stay to help you," Rosalinda said. "My stomach is upset from eating too much freshly baked bread and I am out of sorts today. I don't feel like riding. Go on, Bianca. Enjoy the fine weather." Rosalinda kissed her sister and patted her shoulder, sending her off to the stable with a smile that only made Bianca feel more guilty than she already did.

Guilty or not, Bianca intended to ride for the third day in a row. On the previous day she had waited beside the waterfall for several hours, but Andrea had not appeared. Perhaps he would be there today. Bianca had smuggled food out of the kitchen, along with a small skin of wine. The old cloak she rolled up and strapped to her saddle would serve as a cloth on which to spread the *al fresco* meal she planned to serve to Andrea.

To her delight, when she reached the woodland glade, she found him walking atop the rocks just beside the spot where the waterfall spilled over the edge. While watching him for a few moments before making her presence known, Bianca had the impression that he was searching for something up there.

"Hello," she called, and he stopped what he was doing to look down at her.

"I was hoping you would be here today," he shouted over the noise of the waterfall.

"If you would care to come down," she called back, "I have bread and cheese and some good wine I am willing to share with you."

"You really ought to climb up here," he responded. "The view is quite remarkable."

"I could not possibly climb so high," Bianca protested.

"If you wanted to, sweet Bianca, I believe you could ascend as high as the stars." Grabbing a tree branch, he swung down to her in the same way he had done at their first meeting. "Of course, the view from this height has its own advantages." He smiled at her, looking directly into her eyes, and Bianca smiled back at him.

"Are you hungry?" she asked, making a motion with one hand to indicate the packets of food wrapped in napkins that she had piled by the pool.

"Sweet Bianca, I am ravenous."

From the way he said it, she did not think he was talking about the food. With her heart pounding, Bianca tore her gaze from his to pick up her cloak. He helped her to spread it on the ground and then to set out the light meal she had brought. She was a little surprised to see that he ate as if he really was hungry, as if he had not eaten for some time. While he lounged on one elbow on her cloak, she knelt to slice the loaf of bread.

"I have never tasted cheese like this before," he said, reaching to take the knife out of her hand so he could cut off another piece from the wedge.

"Don't be silly," Bianca said. "Of course you have."

"Have I?" He went very still, his eyes on her face.

"Last winter." Bianca retrieved the knife from his

unresisting fingers and went on slicing the bread. "Don't you remember? You were surprised to learn that we make it ourselves. Or, rather, that Valeria makes it. She is the one who knows how."

"Actually," he said with a slight tremor in his voice, "my memory of last winter is more than a bit hazy. I was unwell for a long time."

"I know that, and I am not at all surprised if the early months are lost to you."

"The early months," he repeated, as if he was unsure of her meaning.

"What I don't understand is why, after your terrible experience, you wanted to come back to the mountains and why, having returned to this area, you did not go directly to the villa. Surely you know you would be welcome there. Why *are* you hiding in the hills again?"

"I am searching for an evil dwarf, who has bewitched me, stolen my treasure, and killed the one person who shared my heart," he said in an odd, joking manner.

"A dwarf has bewitched you?" She stared at him, unsure whether he was teasing her or not. For an instant the image of a little man capering on a rock in the midst of a swiftly flowing river popped into her mind, only to disappear when she thought about his other claims. "What treasure? Who has been killed?"

"I would like a bit more wine, if you please."

Behind his enchanting smile, he was looking at her as if he was trying to learn everything there was to know about her without asking any questions, as if he feared the questions he wanted to ask would prove to be the very ones she would not answer. Wondering if his peculiar remarks were meant to prod her into an ill-considered response, and feeling very much as if she had stumbled into the wrong time and place, Bianca handed him the wineskin. His fingers covered hers on the neck of the skin. He lifted it to his lips, drank, and then stoppered the skin with its wooden plug, all with his hand still over hers.

Then the wineskin was gone and he was kissing her fingers. Bianca sighed at the touch of his warm mouth on her skin. The next thing she knew, she was lying on her cloak with Andrea stretched out beside her. Searching for something to say, she spoke the first words that drifted into her mind.

"Have you eaten enough?" She heard him chuckle, low in his throat.

"After the cheese and bread and olives," he said, "after the wine and the raisins from last year's grapes, it is time for the sweet. *Dolce* Bianca, the sweet is you."

She did not close her eyes when he kissed her. She kept them open so she could see his dark curls at close range, see his smooth skin and his thick, black eyelashes.

The neckline of her dress was too high for him to slide it down and put his hands on her breasts. The neck of her chemise was higher still, adding another layer of protection. But nothing could stop the heat of his palms through those layers of fabric, or the instantaneous reaction of Bianca's flesh. Her breasts hardened and tightened, the stiff nipples rubbing against the linen of her chemise in a way that heightened her awareness of what he was doing and of her own growing excitement. Warmth began to build far inside her, like embers glowing in the very depths of her body. Then she did close her eyes, to blot out all distractions to her rising emotions.

She longed to cry out his name, to beg him to tear off her dress so he could put his hands on her skin. Before she could utter a word, his mouth was devouring hers again, his tongue was plunging into her, and Bianca was burning with a wild desire. The empty place inside her screamed to be filled, by this man and no other.

With his mouth still on hers his hands roved over her, moving ever downward toward the hem of her gown. Slowly, he drew up her skirt, his fingers tracing patterns of desire on her legs at every inch of the way. When he reached the place between her thighs, Bianca's moan of erotic discovery was caught in his mouth. As was her cry when he slid one finger inside her a little way, slid it out, and slowly slid it in again.

Bianca was melting, dying happily as he caressed her. She opened her eyes again to see his free hand at his codpiece. She had never seen a man's private parts before, but she would, in just a moment more. He would release the part of himself that strained so boldly against the fabric and he would plunge it into her. She shuddered in anticipation, scarcely able to hide her eagerness for him to fill her. She had been waiting for him all of her life, and only when this man took full possession of her would she be complete.

He went still, frowning a little. Perhaps some slight change in her expression had given him pause, or perhaps his sudden hesitation was because his probing finger had slipped deeper into her overheated warmth to reach a spot where the intrusion began to be slightly painful. He withdrew his hand, then pressed into her again. Bianca winced.

"You are a virgin," he said.

"I don't care. Don't stop. Oh, please, I want you to do this." She was not sure he heard her frantic plea, for her face was pressed into his doublet as he gathered her close against him.

"I have never yet despoiled a virgin." His whisper was harsh in her ear. "I will not start now, not with a girl as sweet and innocent as you."

''Please, please.'' Bianca began to cry. ''I'll die. I know I will.''

''Hush, sweet Bianca. You won't die of the longing for love, that I can promise you. Look at me, Bianca.''

When she obeyed him and lifted her face from his shoulder to meet his eyes, he kissed her hard. Again his hand stroked between her thighs, not entering now, not filling the empty part of her, but still a pleasant sensation. The stroking continued. Bianca caught her breath, quivering, and he pressed a bit more firmly, touching an exquisitely sensitive spot that Bianca had not known existed. She dissolved into sweet, pulsating bliss. He kept his hand where it was until her body was at peace once more.

''But you?'' she whispered when she could speak again. ''What of you?''

''I will survive. I have lived through worse discomfort.'' He smiled at her, that warm, enticing smile that made all the ills of the world seem to disappear. ''I rather enjoyed watching you take your first pleasure as a woman without the distraction of seeking my own release. It was a new experience for me.''

''I want you to have your release. I want *everything,* every experience you can show me,'' she said, not caring that his words were an admission that he had been with other women.

''One day, I promise you, my sweet Bianca, I will give you the *everything* you so desire. We will enjoy it together.'' His smile warmed her again. ''For now, I must beg your pardon. I know it is ungallant of me to desert you so quickly, but I think I will feel calmer for a splash or two of cold water.''

He left her arms to kneel by the pool. Sensing that he would leave her soon, Bianca straightened her gown and then began to collect the leftover food. She would give it to him. She knew he had been hungry earlier. He could eat it later that night, or the following day.

She did not see the man come out of the trees. He moved silently, his booted feet not crackling a single leaf. He was almost upon her before she noticed him and froze. Her gasp made Andrea turn around, his face dripping, to ask what was wrong.

"My lord," said the man to Andrea, "you should not be here. You know you should not."

"Francesco, what took you so long? I have been waiting two days for you to reappear and I nearly starved in the meantime."

"I see you were not waiting alone." Francesco turned his cool gaze on Bianca. He was a tall, big-boned man, with reddish blond hair, clean-shaven, with an old scar on his jaw. The way he stood, poised for immediate action with one hand close to his sword, together with the way he assessed Bianca, told her he was a soldier before Andrea's introduction confirmed the fact.

"Madonna Bianca, may I present my dearest—indeed, my only—friend and my personal condottiere, Francesco Bastiani?"

"Signore." Bianca gave her hand into Francesco Bastiani's grasp. He bowed over it with a grace that spoke of intimate acquaintance with courtly life.

"Madonna Bianca," he murmured. "I did not expect to discover a gentlewoman in this desolate place."

"I live in retirement," she explained.

"A great loss to the world."

"Thank you for the compliment, signore." Bianca did not know what to make of this man. She looked to Andrea, who showed no sign of embarrassment at being found in a deserted spot, alone with a young woman. Bianca blushed to think of what Francesco Bastiani would have seen had he appeared just a short time earlier.

"My lord, we must go at once," the condottiere said to Andrea, a note of caution in his tone.

"I understand," Andrea replied. "Fare you well, Madonna Bianca."

"Here." She thrust the food into his hands. "In case you have nothing to eat later. You were so hungry when we first met today."

"So I was. Thank you for your thoughtfulness." Once more his smile suggested an interest in something other than food. He bent to kiss her on each cheek, murmuring to her as he did, "I will return the day after tomorrow."

"Yes." By the sparkle in his eyes, she knew he had heard her whispered response.

"Madonna." Francesco Bastiani nodded to her before walking off through the woods with Andrea at his side.

Bianca gazed after them, her thoughts in turmoil. It was clear to her that Andrea was a more important man than she, or anyone else at Villa Serenita, had guessed. Francesco Bastiani had addressed him as "my lord," and though insistent that they must leave at once, he had been respectful.

A delightful idea seized her. It was just possible that Andrea would prove to be important enough for her to marry him. If he had wealth and fighting men, as his designation of Bastiani as his condottiere indicated, then he might be willing to help Bianca regain her lost patrimony. The idea would certainly appeal to her mother.

And Andrea did appeal to Bianca. She had enjoyed his every caress, had relished the way he made her feel emotions she knew were most improper for an unwed young woman. If they were married, he could do the same and more with her, whenever he liked. He could do that *everything* they both had wanted so much, yet had denied themselves. The fact that he had stopped upon discovering her virginity proved he was an honorable man. Alone though she was, the memory of what he had done instead of possessing her as a man takes a woman made Bianca's face flame and made her press her hands to her hot cheeks. Before she set off on the path leading out of the woods, Bianca dipped her hand into the cold pool and splashed the cooling wetness to her face as her would-be lover had done.

She was more than halfway across the meadow, heading back to the villa, before her selfish dreams came crashing down like a castle built of playing cards, and the guilt set in. She and Andrea could never be happy together. Their marriage, or even the suggestion that they might marry, would break Rosalinda's heart.

Worse, Bianca was sure that Rosalinda and Andrea had lain together and had done many of the same things that Bianca and Andrea had done. Perhaps they had done more. This was undoubtedly the secret Rosalinda was keeping, for it explained her presence in the servants' quarters on the night when Andrea was secretly there, and it also explained why the two of them had been all but undressed when Bianca had seen them together.

Grief for what could not be, jealousy, her life-long love for her sister, and her new-found passion for Andrea—all these emotions collided in Bianca's heart, reducing her to bitter tears. Bianca Farisi was the most treacherous of sisters, the most unworthy of daughters, a worthless, cowardly, scandalously lascivious female.

There was only one way for her to redeem herself and that was by allowing her own heart to be broken instead of her sister's.

Bianca could easily arrange matters so the right man and woman would be joined. On the day after tomorrow, when Andrea planned to meet her by the waterfall again, Bianca would take Rosalinda with her. Once the lovers had met, Bianca would give them her blessing, and then she would leave them alone together.

After that, the matter would be up to the Duchess Eleonora, who had the right to choose her daughters' husbands. If Andrea proved to be the nobleman that Bianca suspected he was, and if he had succeeded in carrying out his mysterious mission to Eleonora's satisfaction, then there could be no impediment to Rosalinda's marriage to him.

Though Bianca might come near to dying of unhappiness to see the man she wanted married to her own sister, still she would have the comfort of knowing she had done what was right. In time, wed to Rosalinda, Andrea would forget his brief interlude with Bianca and all would be as it should be.

As she thought about this future, Bianca discovered within her heart an aura of peace, almost of happiness. She now began to understand, as she had never understood before, the strength her mother derived from always doing her duty. Bianca knew Eleonora had loved her husband, yet as soon as he was dead, she had taken command of her remaining family and had never ceased to consider the welfare of her daughters and of the friends and retainers who were dependent upon her. With Eleonora's example before her, Bianca believed she, like her mother, could attain the serenity that came from obeying a higher duty than the demands of earthly passion.

She reached the villa in a state of emotional and spiritual exultation.

Chapter Twelve

"It's just a little farther. I know you are going to like this spot." Bianca brushed aside the overgrown leaves of a tall bush, holding the branches back until Rosalinda passed by. "I feel quite proud of my discovery."

"This is most unlike you." Rosalinda waved a hand at a swarm of tiny insects buzzing around her face. "What has come over you, Bianca? I have always been the sister who explores, the one who rides too far on dangerous paths." Rosalinda's voice trailed off as the two of them left the undergrowth and stepped into an open area.

"Here we are." Bianca moved toward the waterfall and the pool. "What do you think of my special place?"

"It's very nice," Rosalinda said, looking around.

"Is that all you have to say? I think it is a beautiful spot."

"Who is that up there on the rocks?" Rosalinda tilted

her head back, squinting to see better.

"Where?" Bianca's heart missed a beat or two. This was the moment for which she had longed for two days, since her parting from Andrea. The moment of her redemption, which she both dreaded and embraced, was at hand. She looked upward, following the line of Rosalinda's pointing finger, expecting to see Andrea reaching for the tree branch he used to swing down to her.

"That isn't—" At first Bianca did not recognize the wiry figure prowling along the edge of the rocks from which the water fell. She knew only that it was not Andrea she saw.

"What do you think you're doing up there?" Rosalinda cupped her hands and shouted the question. "We warned you the last time we discovered you trespassing."

The figure jerked, spinning around. A few stones sprayed out from beneath his feet to bounce off the edge and splash into the pool below the waterfall.

"We told you before, these are private lands," Rosalinda yelled. "Be gone, you rogue, or I'll call the guards."

"Stupid wench! You can't tell me what to do." As if to prove his claim, the figure on the rocks took a determined step without looking where he was putting his feet. He misjudged his distance and slipped off the edge. For a few breathless moments he hung by his fingertips, legs dangling into the emptiness below. "Help me!" he cried.

"We can't help him," Bianca said. "It will take us too long to climb up there. Even if we could reach him, he will probably fall before then."

"Your own actions got you into this fix," Rosalinda shouted at the wriggling, gasping figure. "Now you will have to pull yourself up, or else jump into the water and hope you land without breaking any bones."

"You are no help to me at all!" the dangling figure screamed.

"That is just what I have been saying," Rosalinda retorted. "The choice is yours."

"I can't—yeow!" His fingers slipped too far on the moist rocks and the weight of his body did the rest. The man plunged straight down into the pool at the foot of the waterfall.

"Where is he?" Bianca cried, rushing to the pool. "Rosalinda, I can't see him. I had no idea the water was so deep."

"I have him." Rosalinda had thrown herself flat on the moss and had plunged her arms into the pool up to her shoulders so she could search through the foaming water with both hands. After a moment she caught a wrist and started pulling on it. Bianca knelt beside her and together they dragged the man out of the pool and laid him on the ground.

"He isn't breathing," Bianca said. "Did he drown so quickly?"

"Help me roll him over," Rosalinda ordered.

They rolled him face down and Rosalinda pushed on his back until he spat out water and drew a gasping breath. A minute or two later he sat up, glaring at the sisters as if he wished he could strike them dead.

"Little man, wet rocks will be the death of you," Rosalinda said.

"Get away from me, you sluts!" He wiped his face with his hands, pushed the wet hair out of his eyes, and looked more closely at the sisters. "Oh, it's you two again. I should have known it would be."

"This is the second time my sister and I have saved your life," Bianca told him. "A word of thanks would seem to be in order."

"Laundresses! Crude peasants! You almost broke my back just now with your rough handling."

"How would you like to take another dip in the pool?" Rosalinda asked, reaching toward him.

"Don't touch me!" He scrambled to his feet.

"Rosalinda." Bianca caught her sister's arm. "Come away. Don't ask why, just do as I tell you. *Now.*"

"What?" Rosalinda stared at her sister. Bianca tugged harder on her arm. Her eyes still on Bianca's serious face, Rosalinda allowed herself to be drawn away from the little man and into the undergrowth.

"What is it?" Rosalinda whispered.

"Hush. Someone is coming. We can't be sure if it's a friend of that man, or one of our own men-at-arms on patrol, but it's better to be cautious. I do not like that little man."

"Over here." Rosalinda moved between a tall boulder and a thick clump of bushes. "If we are quiet, they won't see us here. If it is one of our people, I want to tell him how rude that nasty little fellow has been to us. Then let the men-at-arms decide what to do with him."

" 'Little fellow,' " Bianca repeated under her breath. *"Evil dwarf."*

"What did you say?" Rosalinda looked at her in surprise. "No, he's not that small, just very short. And very nasty."

"To a tall man, he would seem like a dwarf," Bianca responded. "And I think he is more than nasty. I think he is dangerous."

"Shh." Rosalinda went tense and still. Carefully separating the leaves with one finger, she peered through the concealing bush to watch the area around the pool. Bianca looked over her shoulder.

Two men clad in woolen doublets and hose and

armed with swords and daggers walked into the clearing. They stopped short when they beheld the wet, bedraggled figure standing there.

"Oh, signore," cried one of the newcomers, "what has happened to you?"

"I knelt down to take a drink of water, you stupid servants," said the wet man, "and two peasant wenches sneaked up behind me and pushed me into the pool."

"A pity, signore," said the first servant, who appeared to be fighting back laughter.

"A disgrace to your dignity, signore," said the second servant in a more sober way.

"Have you by chance noticed two silly, giggling girls running away from here?"

"No, signore," said the first servant, "but I assure you, if we had, we would have made fine sport of them. After offering them to you first, of course."

"*Imbecille!* Be silent! I do not know which of you is worse! Unquestionably, you are the most incompetent servants I have ever been forced to endure! Be glad you are not in Monteferro, for if I had other men at hand to assist me, I would order both of you gutted! Now," the nasty little man went on a bit more calmly, "have you discovered any trace of that young upstart and his companion?"

"No, signore," the first servant replied. "Were you able to find a track in this area? You did say you thought it a likely place, with water and berries near by."

"If he ever was here, he is gone now," said the little man.

"Signore, I think we ought to search deeper in the forest," said the second servant. "If I were trying to escape someone who was hunting me, that is where I would go."

"Would you?" The little man cocked his head to one side, studying the speaker. He nodded his approval. "You may be right. The remains of the campfire I discovered were in the hills above this area."

"There may be caves in the mountains, where they could hide," the servant said.

"I am sure both of them would prefer a house and hot food," the little man responded. "But if they know how close we are, they just might take to the hills."

"There is a villa some distance down the valley." The first armed servant spoke up as if he did not want his companion to take all the credit for serious thought. "We tried to approach it but were stopped by a guard. When we asked in the village, we were told that an eccentric, elderly widow lives there, who won't allow anyone on her lands. If we couldn't get through the guard, then neither could our young lordling and his friend."

"Hmm." The little man appeared to be considering the possibilities. "All right, we will search in the hills first. Perhaps we can drive them into the lowlands, where it will be easier to capture them. Or to put an end to them. If we are unsuccessful in the hills, then I will decide on a way for us to penetrate the defenses around that villa, so we can search there."

The three men moved off together, disappearing into the undergrowth. Rosalinda and Bianca stayed where they were until well after the sound of voices had faded. When they dared to move again, it was to put their arms around each other, to cling together until their fear had subsided enough to allow them to make rational decisions.

This was more difficult for Bianca to do than for Rosalinda. Bianca was certain that the "young lordling" and his friend for whom the nasty little man and his servants were searching were Andrea and Francesco Bastiani. But how could she reveal her suspicions to Rosalinda without admitting that she had met Andrea in this very place and had not told her sister of it? And what was she to make of that mention of Monteferro?

"We must go home at once and tell Mother and Bartolomeo what we have seen and heard," Rosalinda said as they hurried out of the woods.

"Yes, I know you are right," Bianca agreed. "That dreadful little person and his henchmen can only mean danger for all of us."

"Here are the horses. We are fortunate that those men did not discover them." Rosalinda untied the reins and helped Bianca to mount from a nearby rock before she leapt onto her own horse's back. She studied Bianca, wondering what lay behind the unnaturally placid expression on her sister's pale face. She did not think Bianca had brought her to the forest and the waterfall just to show her a lovely woodland glade. There had been some other purpose behind today's excursion.

"We should hurry," Bianca said.

"We should also be careful," Rosalinda warned. "We don't want to be discovered and captured by those three men."

The took the quickest, most open route to the bridge. Once they were over the river and out on the wide meadow, Rosalinda felt safer, for she thought it more likely that anyone intending harm to them would be noticed by the men-at-arms that Bartolomeo kept posted as sentries around the boundary.

As they rode, Rosalinda pondered the mystery of what Bianca could be hiding from her. And she could not escape the recognition that her own once carefree days were ended, at least for a time. When Eleonora heard the news her daughters had to tell, she would insist that they remain at home, where she could be sure they would be safe.

"Stregone. That is who Rosalinda has described. Niccolò Stregone." In Bartolomeo's office, Eleonora pressed a trembling hand over her heart. Her face was ashen, her eyes dark pools of memory and fear. "After all these years, he has discovered where we are hiding."

"Mother, I do not think those men have any idea that we are living nearby," Rosalinda said. "They are looking for a young nobleman and his companion. The only mention they made of the villa was to say that folk in the village told them an elderly widow lives here."

"Please, dear God." Eleonora clasped her hands together in prayer. "Let them believe I am a hundred years old and that I live here alone."

"Mother," Rosalinda went on, fixing her parent with a sharp eye, "could this man they are tracking be Andrea? Perhaps he is traveling with a servant or a friend. But if so, why didn't he come directly to the villa? Why should he hide in the mountains again?"

"It may well be Andrea," Bartolomeo put in before Eleonora could answer. "Let us imagine that he was returning here, but along the way he discovered that he was being followed by that murderous Niccolò Stregone and his henchmen. Andrea would not want to lead them to us. Instead, he would attempt to throw Stregone off the trail by wandering through the mountains for a while and perhaps even going elsewhere until Stregone gives up."

"Stregone never gives up." Eleonora appeared more worried than ever by this possible explanation for the near presence of an enemy. "Bianca, Rosalinda, leave us. I wish to speak with Bartolomeo alone."

"Mother, we may be able to help you," Rosalinda protested.

"I said, go!" Eleonora's blue eyes flashed fire. "And you are not to leave the villa without my permission."

Recognizing there was nothing they could do to change their mother's mind, Bianca and Rosalinda obeyed. But by unspoken agreement between the sisters, Bianca did not close the heavy door very tightly and the two of them stood in silence outside Bartolomeo's office to listen to what was said within.

"I will have the guards search these lands inch by inch," Bartolomeo promised.

"What good will a search do if Stregone has discovered what we are planning?" Eleonora asked.

"Dear friend, we cannot be sure he knows." Bartolomeo spoke as if to calm her fears.

"I am sure," Eleonora said. "Why else would Stregone leave Monteferro—he who loves the city and hates all green and growing things? We have had reports that Stregone, or his masters, the Guidi, are having Luca's home in Monteferro watched. No doubt they investigate every person who enters or leaves that house, and their spies follow any associate of Luca who leaves the city.

"You know I speak the truth, Bartolomeo. You remember as well as I do the net of surveillance and intrigue the Guidis wove about my husband, slowly gaining control of those who lived or worked at the palazzo, so that when they were ready to strike there were few left to come to my Girolamo's aid. They probably used the same method to overthrow the Duke of Aullia, and now they are weaving their net around Luca, the wealthiest banker in Monteferro, who holds their loans. It would be to their benefit to bring Luca down and confiscate his wealth. What better way than to prove that Luca is involved in a plot to restore the Farisi family to power?

"I do not care what happened to the Duke of Aullia when his false friends, the Guidi, turned on him, but I do care about Luca, who has been honest in his dealings with me. I do not want to see Luca destroyed for my sake." Eleonora went on with a sigh, "I had such hopes of regaining Monteferro for Bianca. Bartolomeo, we thought we could trust Andrea because the prize we offered him was so great, but what if he is one of Stregone's spies?"

"If that is the case, why is Stregone seeking to capture him?" Bartolomeo asked.

"Perhaps Andrea has been working for both sides and Stregone has uncovered his perfidy. *Gesù!*" Eleonora cried. "I came to Villa Serenita seeking safety for my daughters and respite for myself from the plotting and intrigue and untrustworthiness of those I knew in Monteferro. Now I can feel myself becoming caught up in all of that again and I dread it. Most of all, I fear for my girls. Yet I swore on my dear Girolamo's soul that I would restore his family to its rightful position. What are we to do, Bartolomeo?" she ended on a most uncharacteristic sob.

"What you are to do," said Bartolomeo, "is, first, drink this glass of wine and try to calm yourself. Next, remember that every person on this estate is devoted to you. Each of the men-at-arms has good cause to hate Niccolò Stregone and the Guidi family. None of us will desert you or your daughters. And, finally, know that I will see to it that no one intrudes upon these lands who should not be here."

"If Andrea is true to our cause," Eleonora said, "then we must do what we can to protect him from Stregone. I cannot bear to think of the torture Stregone would inflict on Andrea to make him tell all he knows about our plans."

"Andrea knew the risks he was taking," Bartolomeo said. "We discussed them before he left. However, I do have two young men, both sons of one of the men-at-arms who came here with us. These boys love the mountains and are skilled at hunting there, and they also have experience in climbing at great heights. I will give them special instructions and send them out to look for Andrea. If he is hiding in the mountains, they will find him and bring him to the villa. Then we will hear what Andrea has to say about Stregone and whether he knows the man or not."

"My daughters and I would not have survived so long without you, Bartolomeo." Eleonora sounded weary and close to tears.

"Just this once, allow me to give an order to you," Bartolomeo said. "I am going to tell Valeria to make a soothing tisane for you, and I order you to drink it, so that you will sleep well tonight. Without it, I am sure you will lie awake worrying until dawn."

"Dear old friend, that sounds more like good advice than an order," Eleonora said.

"It is advice you should follow."

"I will. I promise. Thank you, Bartolomeo, for your loyalty to me, to my husband's memory, to my girls. You and Valeria." Eleonora's voice choked.

"Go now and rest," Bartolomeo said. "I have instructions to give to the men."

At this point Rosalinda and Bianca gave up eavesdropping in favor of fleeing as quietly as they could, away from Bartolomeo's office to their own rooms.

The conversation she had overheard left Bianca confused. None of the facts as she knew them from her own experience or from listening to her mother explained why Andrea had not come to the villa. At no time during her meetings with him had he acted as if he were fleeing or trying to hide. Even the condottiere with him, though cautious, had not been overly concerned. Andrea had said he was searching for a dwarf. Bianca believed he meant Niccolò Stregone. Having encountered Stregone twice without knowing who he was, she could understand why her mother feared the man. There was something intrinsically evil about him. She found herself wondering what would happen when Andrea and Stregone finally did meet.

In the days that followed, Bianca's old fear of violence rose up again to terrify her, to make her so dizzy that she came near to fainting several times a day. She could not eat or sleep and had great difficulty in keeping her mind on the simplest household tasks.

A week passed with no word of Andrea, or of Niccolò Stregone, and Bianca thought she would go mad from the strain. No matter the danger to her, she had to see Andrea again. With a single-minded ruthlessness that would have surprised her sister and dismayed her mother, Bianca concocted a plan.

Her monthly flux was due to begin in a day or so. Using it as an excuse to claim she had a headache and a cramping in her abdomen, Bianca accepted a cup of hot herbal brew from Valeria and retired to her bedchamber, asking that no one bother her, so she could drink Valeria's medicine and sleep until nightfall.

Once in her bedroom, she tossed the contents of the cup out the window. Next, she wrote a letter to Andrea, folded and sealed it. She might not need it, but she wanted to be prepared. Then, being fairly sure she knew where everyone in the villa was on a warm, early summer afternoon, she made her way to the stable and saddled her horse. Only a stableboy saw her, and he did not dispute her right to go riding if she wanted.

She knew where all the men-at-arms were posted, so she was able to avoid them as she took a roundabout route to the spot in the woods that she knew best. If she did not find Andrea there, and if he did not appear before it was time for her to return home, she would leave the letter for him, safely weighted under a rock, in the very place where they had lain together. She was sure that if he should spend even a few moments in their special place, he would look for some trace of her there and he would find the letter.

Chapter Thirteen

Rosalinda was by nature too healthy and active to tolerate for long the round of indoor chores that Eleonora had imposed to keep her daughters within the villa after the appearance of Niccolò Stregone. Sewing, fine embroidery, counting linens, or supervising the cleaning of unused guest rooms could not distract Rosalinda from thoughts of Andrea. She longed to hear his voice, to gaze into his soft brown eyes. Most of all, she wanted his arms around her again.

Deprived of Andrea's company, and of the freedom that might have given physical release to her growing impatience with her mother's restrictions, she grew ever more irritable. After a week of confinement during some of the best weather of the season, she had had enough. One afternoon, while her mother and Valeria were occupied in the kitchen, Rosalinda crept out of the house and headed for the stable.

"Are you going out, too, Madonna Rosalinda?"

asked the stableboy. "Madonna Bianca left over an hour ago."

Hiding her surprise at this news, Rosalinda saddled her horse and headed for the place in the woods where she had last seen Niccolò Stregone. Though she did not know it at the time, she chose the same route Bianca had taken and thus she also avoided the guards. Rosalinda was certain she would find Bianca in the little clearing by the waterfall and she thought she knew why.

Bianca was hoping to discover some trace of Stregone, or of the two men for whom Stregone was searching because, like her sister, Bianca was sure one of those men was Andrea. It was very unlike Bianca to defy their mother's orders to remain at the villa, but then, Bianca had been acting strangely since well before the day when she had taken Rosalinda into the wood to show her the waterfall.

Rosalinda found Bianca's horse tethered to the same sapling they had used for the purpose during their last visit to the forest. Dismounting, Rosalinda secured her own horse before setting out on the overgrown path to the waterfall. Not wanting to frighten Bianca, she moved as quietly as she could. When she stepped into the clearing, the couple standing beside the pool did not hear her. Rosalinda stopped dead, her jaw dropping in astonishment.

Bianca was wrapped in the embrace of a dark-haired man who was kissing her with unabashed enthusiasm. The man's hands roved down Bianca's spine to catch her hips and pull her closer. Rosalinda remembered how it felt to be held like that, with the beloved man's hardness pushing against her feminine softness.

Though she knew Bianca ought not to be meeting a man alone and unchaperoned, and she did wonder how Bianca had managed to discover any suitable man while she was living the sheltered existence they had shared for years; still, in those first moments, Rosalinda was happy for her sister. But as she watched them she was struck by something tantalizingly familiar in those broad shoulders and that dark, curly hair. An icy finger of doubt touched Rosalinda's heart.

"Bianca?" Rosalinda moved nearer as the embracing couple began to separate. The man lifted his head, smiling a little at Bianca, before he turned to see who had spoken. He displayed not the least bit of embarrassment at being caught in so intimate a posture with an innocent young woman. But was Bianca still innocent? It would seem she was not.

Rosalinda stood rooted to one spot, frozen where she was by a double betrayal so heart-wrenching she thought she would die from the pain of it. It was all she could do to force one accusing word past her lips.

"Andrea!"

"Madonna?" His smile turned to an expression of perplexity. Then, incredibly, he smiled at her as if he were entirely blameless of any wrongdoing. "I do not know you, but I think you must be my Bianca's sister."

"Not know me? Your Bianca? You villain!" Sheer, flaming rage broke the spell holding Rosalinda. She took a menacing step forward. "How can you speak so to me after our last meeting?"

"You called me Andrea," the young man said. The strangest expression now appeared on his face, as if he had been offered a hope in which he dared not believe just yet.

"Rosalinda," Bianca cried, "you don't understand."

"Indeed, I do not," Rosalinda said. She was close enough to touch the pair. She stared at the man before her, at his curly black hair and his warm brown eyes, at the neatly trimmed beard that covered his lower face, and at his mouth. There was something wrong with his mouth. The corners quirked upward, as if he laughed often and easily, and there was more than a hint of sensuality in his full lower lip. She did not remember that line of Andrea's lip. Andrea's mouth was firm and serious because, although there was wonderful humor in him, he was at heart a serious person. Those were not the same lips that had blazed a trail of blistering passion across her body. Looking at his mouth, she knew the truth.

"You are not Andrea," Rosalinda said.

"What?" Bianca cried. "Rosalinda, what are you saying? Of course it is Andrea. Look at his ring."

"Did you embrace him because you thought he was Andrea?" Rosalinda did not bother to look at her sister. Her eyes were still on the man she knew, and yet did not know. "You should have looked more closely, Bianca. The ring on this man's finger is set with a sapphire, but Andrea's ring is set with a ruby. Moreover, Andrea gave his ring to me before he left after his visit in March. I have it now, pinned over my heart as proof, if I needed proof, that this person truly is another man.

"Where is Andrea?" Rosalinda demanded of the man who looked so much like her love. "What have you done with him?"

"Do you mean he is alive?" The young man's face was lit with a joy that could not be counterfeited. "He must be alive, for you spoke just now of seeing him in March. Only tell me where he is and let me go to him!"

"He is your brother, isn't he?" Rosalinda said. "You and he are twins. Andrea neglected to mention that detail when he spoke of you, but then, he was careful never to provide any information about his family or the life he lived before he arrived at Villa Serenita. Always, he deflected my questions." Rosalinda paused, wondering if Andrea had been able to deflect her mother's inevitable questions, or Bartolomeo's.

"Twins?" Bianca gasped, apparently wrestling with this novel concept. "Andrea has a brother? You are not Andrea, after all?"

"Are you disappointed, sister?" In Rosalinda's voice was all the pain and anger she felt. The man standing before her had not betrayed her, but Bianca had. She returned her attention to the man. "You have not told me your name. From my sister's reaction, I suspect she does not know it, either."

He sent a fleeting, intimate smile Bianca's way before grasping Rosalinda's arms. Holding her tightly, he said, "My previous caution seems unnecessary now, since you and your sister are obviously not my enemies. I am Giovanni, but I am called Vanni. Is my brother alive? Is he well? You must tell me. I have been searching for some trace of him for months."

"Not searching so intently that you could not take time to dally with my sister," Rosalinda snapped. Seeing his chagrined expression, she took pity on him. "When last I was with Andrea, he was both alive and well, but I have not seen him or had any word of him since he left our villa in late March."

She watched disappointment cloud Vanni's handsome face. How could Bianca have thought he was Andrea? Born identical twins, their differing characters and spirits had marked their features in such a way that Rosalinda had no difficulty telling them apart. She rather liked Vanni, responding to him in a positive way because he was outwardly so similar to Andrea, but she knew she could never love him. Andrea was and always would be her only love.

"What is your family name?" she asked him.

"Andrea did not tell you? Then I think I should follow his cautious example and not do so, either. Not without his permission, since he is the elder by an hour,'' Vanni said with a charming smile.

''More secrets.'' Rosalinda scowled at him. She couldn't help it. She did not like the lack of trust implied in holding back such a basic fact, and she began to wonder anew why Andrea had never told her anything about his family except that he had a brother. ''Andrea thinks you are dead. He has your dagger. He discovered it, dripping with blood, where he thought to find you, and so he assumed the blood was yours.''

''So that's what happened to it,'' Vanni said. ''I lost it in a fight.''

''With Niccolò Stregone?'' Rosalinda asked.

''Yes.'' Vanni went still, his eyes dark with anger and a flash of some other emotion. ''Do you know that devil?''

''We have met him on two occasions. My mother knows him far better than Bianca or I do. If Stregone is your enemy, you must speak to Mother about him.'' Rosalinda hesitated for a moment before she continued, and she spoke with caution, not telling Vanni all she knew. ''My mother sent Andrea on a mission of some kind. I believe it had something to do with Stregone. Did you know Stregone was recently in this area, looking for a young man and his companion?''

''I was afraid of that.'' Vanni's open face was a study in conflicting feelings. His natural buoyancy and his great relief at learning his brother was alive warred with anger and a determination that sat upon him as if he found it difficult to maintain such a serious emotion.

Rosalinda was about to ask him if he was still traveling with the companion Stregone had mentioned when her question was answered before it could be spoken. A tall, large-boned man stumbled into the clearing, limping on a bloody leg and clutching a sword in one hand.

"Francesco!" Vanni ran to support him. "Is there danger? Have you been in a fight?"

"No. I heard voices raised in anger and thought I should arrive prepared." Francesco looked from Bianca to Rosalinda. In a wry tone he said, "You do have a tendency to attract lovely women, my lord. May I assume these two ladies are not planning to attack you and, therefore, it is safe for me to put up my sword?"

"You will remember Madonna Bianca," Vanni said with a graceful flourish of one hand in Bianca's direction. He extended the motion toward Rosalinda. "This is her younger sister. Madonna Rosalinda, this is my companion, the great condottiere, Francesco Bastiani."

"What happened to your leg?" Rosalinda asked.

"I slipped on some loose stones and fell a hundred feet or so down a rocky slope," Francesco Bastiani replied. "As you can see, Madonna Rosalinda, my clothes are torn and I am sure I will be sore tomorrow from the bruises, but I was fortunate enough to roll most of the way downhill, so I am not badly injured."

"You mean, you were quick enough, and clever enough, to think of rolling down the hill to save yourself," Rosalinda said.

"A man does learn a few tricks in a busy life like mine." The condottiere's grin was a flash of even, white teeth in his dusty face.

Rosalinda grinned back at him. There was an open, honest quality in him that touched a responsive chord in her own straightforward heart. Looking at Francesco Bastiani, she made a quick decision, which was made easier by her certainty that her mother would approve of what she was about to do.

"Have you been living in the forest?" she asked.

"We have, madonna." Beneath the grime, Francesco's face was pale, and Rosalinda saw the lines of strain and fatigue around his eyes.

"You cannot stay here any longer, not with Stregone searching for you," Rosalinda said. "Gentlemen, you are to go to Villa Serenita with us. If you have no horses, you may ride with me, Signore Francesco, and Vanni may ride with Bianca. I feel certain she will not object to that arrangement."

"You are more than generous, madonna," Francesco said, "but our presence at your villa could place you and your parents in danger."

"My father is dead."

"My condolences." Francesco bowed, his face solemn. "All the more reason why Vanni and I should not intrude on three ladies who are living alone."

"We have guards to protect us from creatures like Niccolò Stregone," Rosalinda told him. "Signore Francesco, I want you to meet my mother and our friend, Bartolomeo. I think the three of you will have much to discuss. We will be happy to provide you with a bath and clean clothing, and Valeria will tend to your injuries. The guards all say she is better than a doctor."

"You would seem to have an interesting household, Madonna Rosalinda. However, I still question whether Vanni and I should inflict ourselves on you."

"Question all you want, Francesco," said Vanni. "For myself, I intend to accept Rosalinda's invitation. I am weary of sleeping on the ground and of trying to catch fish for dinner. Besides, I think Bianca will be pleased by my presence, won't you, my dear?"

"I will be happy to know you are safe with us," Bianca said at once.

Noting the shadow in her sister's eyes, Rosalinda thought it was caused by guilt, and well deserved guilt at that. She would have a few choice words for Bianca once they were in private.

It was difficult for Francesco to mount Rosalinda's horse. She could tell his leg injury was painful, but he made no complaint. Once Rosalinda was in the saddle, he placed his good foot on hers, accepted the hand she offered and, gritting his teeth so tightly that Rosalinda could hear them grinding together, he swung himself upward on the third attempt.

"It is fortunate that you ride astride, Madonna Rosalinda," he said once he was seated behind her with his arm around her waist.

She thought he was a splendid man. She judged his age as somewhere near her mother's and she thought he had courage equal to Eleonora's. Rosalinda knew Bartolomeo would recognize Francesco Bastiani's toughness and courage at once, and she rather thought her mother would, too. Sparing not a thought as to whether Vanni was safely mounted behind Bianca, Rosalinda kicked her horse's sides and headed for home by the same route she had traveled earlier. Francesco said nothing throughout the ride. Rosalinda believed he was silent because he was in pain and was conserving his strength.

Miraculously, they were not stopped by the guards, though Rosalinda had a story prepared to explain why she and Bianca were bringing two unknown men home with them. How she was going to explain her absence from the villa to her mother she had not decided.

The two horses arrived in the stableyard at the same time, and when the stableboy ran out to take the reins, Rosalinda was ready with the explanation she had concocted.

"Signore Andrea has returned with a friend," she said to the stableboy. "Unfortunately, they had an accident along the way, and their horses had to be destroyed. Give this gentleman a hand to dismount.'' She waited, holding her horse steady, until Francesco was on the ground, before she leapt lightly down.

''Come along, Bianca, Andrea,'' Rosalinda called. ''Mother will be eager to see Andrea again.'' Without waiting for a response from the others, she took Francesco's arm on the side of his injured leg in such a way that he could lean on her without appearing to do so.

''We will go through the garden,'' she said to him. ''It is the quickest path into the house.''

''As you wish, Madonna Rosalinda,'' Francesco said. The skin around his eyes was white, his face was paler than before, and his reddish blond hair was damp with perspiration, but he went with her as readily as if he were not in great pain.

Eleonora was in the garden, cutting lavender flowers for drying. As she cut, she laid the long stems into a flat basket slung over her arm. The bracing fragrance of the lavender mingled with the scents from her other herbs, making the garden a delightful place to be on that early evening. The sun was sinking toward the mountains, casting long, purple shadows over the land, and the air was soft and warm, with a slight breeze to blow away the last of the midday heat. Above the villa, a lone eagle soared on the wind in wide, easy curves.

Eleonora was wearing a large-brimmed hat to keep the sun off her face, and she had an apron wrapped about her oldest dress, which happened to be a blue that had faded to the same shade as her eyes. Hearing footsteps on the gravel path, she turned to face those who had come to join her.

''What is this?'' Eleonora demanded. ''I thought both of you girls were inside, resting.

''Andrea, you have returned sooner than I expected.

It's good to see you again.'' Eleonora took a step nearer to the group just entering the garden, then halted, clutching the cutting knife in fingers gone white at the knuckles. She held the knife like a weapon, pointing it directly at Vanni. ''You are not Andrea. What have you foolish girls done? Who are these people you have brought to our home?''

''Madonna.'' Vanni swept her a low bow. ''As you can see by my appearance, I am Andrea's twin brother. I come here, at the invitation of your daughter, Rosalinda, to ask if you know where I can find my brother, whom I have believed dead since last summer. Having just learned that he is alive, I am eager to see Andrea again.''

''I am sure you are.'' Eleonora's speculative gaze swept from Vanni's smiling face to Francesco's more somber one. ''And you, signore? Are you also looking for a lost brother?''

''Mother,'' Rosalinda began a protest against the sarcasm in Eleonora's voice, but Francesco cut her off.

''Madonna Rosalinda has suggested that you and I might have much to discuss on the subject of Niccolò Stregone,'' Francesco said.

''That murdering intriguer.'' Eleonora's lip curled in disdain at the name of Stregone. ''That false, faithless dwarf.''

''Just so, madonna. It would seem that you and I have something in common. As for my brother, I know where he is and do not need to search for him. Thanks to Stregone, he is dead and buried, as is my sister. I will not sicken you by recounting what Stregone did to them before killing them.'' Francesco's pale face was grim. He swayed a little, then pulled himself upright.

''You are injured,'' Eleonora cried. ''Come inside at once. Bianca, run and find Valeria. Tell her we will need her healing skills and describe this man's injuries to her. Then search out Bartolomeo and bring him to me."

"Come with me, Vanni." Bianca took his hand.

"Vanni will remain here," Eleonora said. "I want to talk to him."

"By your leave, madonna," Vanni said, "I would much prefer to go with Bianca. You will get more sense out of Francesco than out of me, anyway. Anything you wish to ask me after you have spoken to him, I will be glad to tell you."

Eleonora stared after the hastily departing pair. Then she looked at Francesco, who bestowed one of his open, cheerful grins on her.

"Vanni is neither as shallow nor as light-witted as he sometimes appears to be," Francesco said, looking into Eleonora's eyes. "Humor and frivolity are but masks to him, disguises that have served well in the past to keep him out of danger. Beneath the masks he wears, Vanni is as intelligent as Andrea."

"I understand." Eleonora nodded. Taking his other arm, she and Rosalinda led Francesco toward the terrace and the door to the sitting room.

"What lovely flowers." Francesco looked around. "Have you made this garden yourself, Madonna—?" He quirked a reddish-blond brow at her, waiting.

"Eleonora," she supplied. "Yes, for the most part the garden is of my making. Watch this step now, it is higher than it looks."

"I do like roses." It was the season for them, and Eleonora's two bushes were in full bloom. Francesco paused to smell first the red rose at one side of the steps leading to the terrace and then the white rose on the other side. "A beautiful fragrance, a wonderful setting, with the foothills and the mountains for background, a garden nurtured with care and with thought for the placement of each plant grown here—Madonna Eleonora, you do honor to Nature to assist her in this way.''

''Gardening has been my sole pleasure for many years,'' Eleonora said. ''As for the roses, I planted them in honor of my two daughters, the red one for Rosalinda and the white for Bianca.''

''Remarkable as your garden is, and lovely and intelligent as the daughters whom you have also nurtured are,'' Francesco said, ''it seems a pity that tilling the soil should be the only pleasure for a woman such as you.''

''I perceive, signore,'' said Eleonora, ''that you have spent enough time at some court to allow you to polish your manners to a fine lustre. It is only fair to warn you that I am immune to courtly blandishments.''

''Then you are even more unusual than I first thought you to be, madonna, for I have never before known a lady to turn away an honest compliment.''

''Allow me to suggest to you, signore, that you ought to save your strength to get you up these steps and into the house. A condottiere ought always to conserve his strength for the battles that inevitably lie ahead.''

There was a note in Eleonora's voice that made Rosalinda look at her in surprise. Never had she heard her mother combine an order with barely repressed humor. Eleonora Farisi seldom said anything humorous. It occurred to Rosalinda that her mother might have spoken in the same tone to a courtier who paid her too obvious compliments, back in the days when Rosalinda's father had still been alive. Then she heard Francesco Bastiani's appreciative chuckle and knew she had missed something in their seemingly inconsequential remarks.

Rosalinda did not have time to think about this remarkable conversation. Having reached the top of the steps and limped onto the terrace, Francesco stopped to take a deep breath. Suddenly, without warning, he crumpled to the stones.

"Why is it," Eleonora said, going to her knees beside him, "that men think they must always appear strong when they are with women, whereas any woman with two eyes and a heart knows when a man is sick or injured? Signore, you must remain on these stones until help arrives, for you are too big for Rosalinda and me to lift you."

Francesco quickly regained consciousness. Pushing himself up on his elbows, he sent a rueful glance toward Eleonora.

"I apologize for this inconvenience," he said.

"It seems to me the inconvenience is yours, signore," Eleonora responded. She was still on her knees next to him, and now she sat back on the stones, looking down at her unexpected guest. As if to reassure him there was no threat in her next words, she placed one hand on his shoulder.

"You are Bastiani, aren't you? The famous condottiere who was once in service to the late Duke of Aullia."

"At *your* service, now, madonna," he said. "Or I will be, as soon as I can stand on my own two feet again."

The appearance of Bartolomeo and Vanni distracted Rosalinda from the remarkable sight of her usually dignified mother sitting upon the terrace paving stones, looking deep into the gray-blue eyes of Francesco Bastiani, while her slender hand rested on the shoulder of his soiled green doublet.

"Bianca told me what happened," Bartolomeo said. He reached to help Francesco. "She and Valeria are collecting what they will need to treat him. Signore, can you stand?''

''I will be happy to try,'' Francesco said.

With Bartolomeo and Vanni to lend masculine muscle to the effort, Francesco was soon on his feet, though leaning heavily on the men supporting him. They got him through the door and into the sitting room. There Francesco halted his forward progress, with his eyes on the portrait of Girolamo Farisi.

''Valeria wants him taken to one of the guest rooms,'' Bartolomeo said to Eleonora. ''She can treat his injuries there and settle him to rest without moving him again.''

''That makes sense.'' Eleonora turned her attention from Bartolomeo to the immobile Francesco. Noticing that he was staring at the far wall, she raised her voice a notch. ''Signore, can you walk with Bartolomeo's help, or shall we carry you?''

''I always prefer to walk, madonna.'' Francesco tore his gaze from the portrait he had been studying to stare at Eleonora.

''Then come along,'' she said. ''The sooner Valeria tends your wounds, the sooner you will begin to recover.''

''More than ever, madonna, I am at your service.'' Francesco's tone was heavy with unspoken meaning. His eyes remained locked with Eleonora's. ''In every way, I assure you.''

Rosalinda stood gaping at the procession making its way out of the sitting room and across the wide hall to the staircase. Eleonora led the way, followed by the three men, with Francesco making wry comments that seemed to Rosalinda to hold many meanings at once. She was about to follow them, to see if she could help to prepare the guest room, or perhaps to assist Valeria, when Bianca appeared in the hall, her hands full of linen bandages.

"Come in here before you go upstairs," Rosalinda said, motioning toward the sitting room.

"I really ought to take these to Valeria," Bianca objected.

"She won't need the bandages until after she has cleaned and treated Francesco's wounds."

"I suppose we ought to have it out and be done with it." Bianca followed her sister into the sitting room.

"Do you really imagine it will be done with so quickly?" Rosalinda demanded, closing the door. She waited no longer before attacking her sister. "You know I love Andrea. I told you so on several occasions. You also know how worried I have been about him. Yet when you saw a man who looked just like Andrea, instead of coming to me and telling me about it, you began to flirt with him."

"But it wasn't Andrea," Bianca cried.

"A fact of which you were blissfully unaware," Rosalinda reminded her.

"You don't understand how I felt," Bianca insisted.

"Then explain yourself so that I can understand." Rosalinda folded her arms over her chest and waited.

"I did know how much you care for Andrea. I watched you together last winter, and I wished someone would look at me as Andrea looked at you. Once, I saw him embrace and kiss you, and my heart ached because no one had ever kissed me in that way. I wanted a young man to want me, to care about me. But it wasn't really Andrea whom I wanted to kiss me. I just wanted *someone*."

"You were jealous," Rosalinda said.

"Yes, I suppose I was, though I could not admit it then, not even to myself. When you accused me of jealousy, I denied it and made excuses."

"And you were spiteful," Rosalinda said, "as your actions prove."

"No!" Bianca protested. "Never! This was not deliberate spitefulness on my part. I first met Vanni quite innocently and by accident. At once, *he* began flirting with *me.* Out of a yearning I did not understand then, I responded to him. Rosalinda, I could not help myself. I was drawn to him as a bee is drawn to a flower."

"A pretty conceit, sister," Rosalinda said, making her voice as cold as she could. "Tell me, did you lie with him?"

"No!" The hand not holding the bandages flew to Bianca's blushing cheek. "Well, not exactly."

"Really?" Rosalinda's eyes flashed. "Either you did or you did not, Bianca. Which was it?"

"We did lie down together on my cloak," Bianca said, "and he put his hands on me and kissed me many times. It was lovely. But he did not—he said when it was over that I am still a virgin."

"How kind of him. How thoughtful." The look Rosalinda gave her sister was as scathing as her tone of voice. "And you consented to all of this with a man whom you believed was your sister's lover?"

"I was sorry afterward." Bianca caught at Rosalinda's sleeve. "Please believe me. I was so filled with guilt, so ashamed. I knew there was only one way I could make up to you for my betrayal and that was by taking you with me the next time I was to meet Andrea. When the three of us were together, I was planning to confess what I had done and to beg you for forgiveness and promise that I would never touch or kiss or even think about Andrea again. Then I was going to leave the two of you alone, to settle things between you.

"But when we got to the waterfall, he wasn't there,"

Bianca went on. "Stregone was there instead. Rosalinda, I went to the wood today to try to find Andrea and bring him here to see you. I had to do something to make up for my misdeeds. I am so sorry, so very sorry, that I hurt you. Always, you have been the dearest person in the world to me."

"Until you found a lover," Rosalinda said.

"I do wonder now if I saw something in Vanni that is different from Andrea, if my heart knew they are not the same, just as you recognized at once that Vanni is not his brother, and if that is why I found it so easy to love him."

"You may believe that if you wish," Rosalinda said. "For myself, I do not credit a word of it. I think you wanted Vanni because you thought he was Andrea."

"I don't know anymore." Tears ran down Bianca's cheeks. "All I know is, I love Vanni. In loving him, I have hurt you, perhaps to the point that we cannot regain the affection and trust there once was between us. And I have failed Mother. I have tried all my life to be a good daughter, and a good sister, but by my own actions I have proven that I am neither."

"Oh, yes—Mother. I almost forgot." Rosalinda held her head between her hands, trying to think clearly, trying to stop the confusion that filled all her thoughts. "Go away, Bianca. I can't talk about this any more right now."

"Please forgive me," Bianca pleaded.

"I need time to think. You have no idea how shocking this day has been to me." Rosalinda took a shaky breath and went on, as if trying to solve a puzzle by thinking it through out loud. "First, I discover you in Andrea's arms, then I find it isn't Andrea at all, but his twin, a twin he never told me he had. And then there is Mother's strange behavior. I have never seen Mother look at a man the way she looks at Francesco. It's as if they are speaking a language I cannot understand."

"I didn't hear them speaking in a strange tongue," Bianca said.

"No, of course not," Rosalinda responded. "All you think about is Bianca."

"That's not true." Again Bianca dissolved into tears. "I have been thinking about you for days, about how I could arrange for your happiness, no matter how unhappy it might make me. I love you, Rosalinda. And I love Vanni, not Andrea."

"If you wipe your eyes and your nose on those bandages one more time," Rosalinda broke into her sister's remarks, "you will make them so wet and dirty that Valeria won't be able to use them."

"I—I didn't realize what I was doing." Bianca regarded the bandages as if she had never seen them before.

"That's just the trouble." Rosalinda's voice was quieter now. "And to think I have always been considered the impulsive sister. Take the bandages to Valeria. Stay with your Vanni. Leave me alone to think about what has happened. At the moment, Andrea's whereabouts, and his safety, are far more important to me than your remorse, whether real or feigned."

Bianca met Rosalinda's eyes. She opened her lips as if she wanted to say something more, but apparently she thought better of it and left the room instead.

Rosalinda felt as if the world was whirling past her too quickly for her to comprehend all the events taking place. Andrea's arrival in a snowstorm, her love for him that grew steadily over the winter, the sight of Bianca and Vanni in each other's arms, and now her mother and Francesco looking at each other as if they understood truths still unspoken, histories not yet explained—

all of this confused and frightened Rosalinda.

Francesco was going to be drawn into her mother's plans. So was Vanni. Rosalinda was sure of it, just as she was sure there was much more to Eleonora's schemes than either of her daughters knew. The quiet world Eleonora had created at Villa Serenita was changing, partly at her own instigation, and nothing would ever be the same again.

Chapter Fourteen

Rosalinda did not feel well. It was true that she sometimes pleaded illness when there was something her mother required of her that she did not want to do, but in fact she was almost always in the best of health. However, on the morning after the arrival of Francesco and Vanni, Rosalinda's stomach was definitely queasy. Under her mother's watchful eye, she ate a bit of bread and cheese. Then she excused herself from the table, saying she wanted to check on a minor problem with one leg of the horse she had ridden on the previous afternoon.

It was the only excuse she could think of that would quickly get her out of the villa and into the fresh air, where she was sure she would feel better. Taking deep breaths as she crossed the terrace and the garden, Rosalinda felt her stomach begin to settle. Certain that she would soon be back to normal, she continued to take deep breaths while making her way along the path to the stable.

But she had forgotten about the smells surrounding the stable. Drawing near, she took another long breath and gagged. Knowing she had only a moment or two to get out of sight, she rushed around the side of the stable to an overgrown area at the back of the building. There, behind a bush, she lost the entire contents of her stomach.

It was a few minutes later when she realized she was not alone. Someone else was also being sick in the bushes. Too weak and still too queasy to move, Rosalinda could do nothing but stay where she was until the other person revealed herself. It was Ginevra, the wife of one of the men-at-arms. Rosalinda knew the young woman fairly well because she often helped in the villa kitchen when Rosalinda was also there.

"You are sick, too," Ginevra said. "I heard you. Madonna Rosalinda, shall I call for help?"

"Thank you, but no," Rosalinda said. "I do feel better now. I must have eaten something that disagreed with me."

"You are known for your hearty appetite," Ginevra said, smiling though her face was pale and damp, and she looked decidedly unwell.

"Is there anything I can do to help you?" Rosalinda asked.

"Only time will help me," Ginevra said. "I know what's wrong. I am with child again."

"What do you mean?" Rosalinda asked. "You already have two small children."

"And a third on the way." Ginevra patted her abdomen. "It's a bit too soon after the last one, but I can't say I am truly unhappy about it. Giuseppe is delighted."

"Are you saying that being with child makes a

woman sick?" Rosalinda asked.

"Every morning for weeks and weeks," Ginevra replied. However, she did not look especially distressed to be ill. Instead, she looked pleased with herself.

"I did not know this," Rosalinda exclaimed. "Mother told Bianca and me how babies are made, but she never mentioned an illness connected with carrying a child."

"I suppose she didn't want you to know. She may have thought knowing would frighten you." Ginevra patted Rosalinda's arm in a reassuring way. "The sickness only lasts for a short time, at the beginning. Then, if the babe is well planted in the woman's womb, the sickness stops and a wonderful time begins. I never feel so well as in the middle months of a pregnancy. Oh, dear, perhaps I shouldn't have said anything. I'm not sure Madonna Eleonora would want you to know so much while you are still a girl."

"I won't tell her that I know," Rosalinda said. "Ginevra, thank you for explaining this to me. Now, if I ever marry and develop this illness, I will know I'm not sick, and I won't be frightened. I will be able to tell my husband what is happening and when I do, I hope he will be as happy as Giuseppe is."

"Childbearing is something you won't have to think about for some time yet," Ginevra said, patting Rosalinda's arm again in a friendly way. "You know that your stomach upset was caused by tainted food. Is anyone else sick?"

"No, just me, and I don't think the cause was bad food. I think I just ate too much. As you said, my appetite is a bit too hearty at times. And then, truth to tell, Ginevra, I did drink a little too much wine."

"Ah," said Ginevra, shaking her head wisely, "too much wine will do it."

"Please don't tell anyone I was sick," Rosalinda begged. "Especially not my mother or Valeria. I would be horribly embarrassed to have anyone know I was out here behind the stable, vomiting like one of the men-at-arms after a long party. You can trust me not to drink so much another time."

"I understand. We all drink too much wine now and then. If you are sure you don't need help, I'll go back to work. I am feeling quite recovered. Take note of how quickly my sickness has passed, Rosalinda, and remember it when your time comes."

After Ginevra had left her, Rosalinda leaned against the stable wall, overcome by an attack of sudden giddiness. Was it possible that, like Ginevra, she was with child?

"Oh, yes," Rosalinda said to herself, "it's possible." This was not the first time she had felt sick in the morning. It was just the first time she had actually *been* sick. Then there was her monthly flux, which hadn't come upon her since just before Andrea was at the villa at the very end of March. She had thought little of it since she was sometimes irregular. Could it be true that she was carrying Andrea's child?

The first thing she must do, she decided after a few moments of thought, was to be absolutely certain she was with child. Only time would prove whether she was or not. She recalled her mother saying that by the end of the third month, a woman could be certain, which meant she should be sure in another three or four weeks. Then, once she was sure, she would decide what to do. Andrea might return before then.

The thought of having Andrea's child made Rosalinda smile. At the same time, she was afraid. Andrea had never actually said that he loved her. She did not doubt that he had wanted her and his words at their last meeting had indicated that he foresaw a future with her, but circumstances could change. Andrea was in danger while on his mission for Eleonora, and Eleonora herself had plans that would surely alter the course of her daughters' lives. Uncertainty loomed for the future, adding to Rosalinda's concern.

"There is no reason to be upset right now," she told herself. "First, I must be sure that what I suspect is actually true. Then, true or not, I will go on from there."

Her hand stole to her abdomen, as if touch alone could give her the answers she sought. Beneath her fingers a new life might be growing. Despite her fears, a tender smile curved Rosalinda's lips.

After Valeria had finished her ministrations to his injured leg, Francesco slept through the night and for most of the following day. Vanni, as exhausted as his friend after months of wandering through the mountains, also slept late. It was almost evening again before the two men entered the sitting room to find Rosalinda and Bianca sitting at the round table, working separately on the lessons Eleonora had set for them that day.

"Vanni!" Bianca leapt to her feet, hurrying to Vanni as if she would throw herself into his arms. Restraining herself, she stopped when she was just a foot away from him and smiled into his eyes instead. "Are you quite recovered from your ordeal?"

"I believe I am, sweet Bianca."

"Would you like to see the garden?" Bianca was all smiles and fluttering eyelashes, ignoring the cautionary glances Rosalinda sent in her direction, ignoring, too, the way Francesco was once again staring at the portrait of Girolamo Farisi.

"You will far outshine any flower there," Vanni responded to Bianca's suggestion, "but a walk alone with you will fulfill my fondest hopes for this day."

Bianca placed her hand in the crook of Vanni's elbow and went with him through the open door and down the steps from the terrace. He paused to pluck a blossom from the white rosebush and present it to her.

"Here is the symbol of my love for you," he said. "A love which, for the present, must remain as chaste and pure as this spotless flower and your tender heart, my sweet Bianca."

"I am not so pure," she whispered, "as you very well know, Vanni."

"And now your cheeks are blushing red as this other bush. Shall I pluck a second rose to match your flawless cheeks?"

"No. The red rose is Rosalinda's bush. Vanni, I cannot stop thinking of you and of what we did together."

"Nor can I stop thinking of you, sweet Bianca. But I am a guest in your mother's house. I cannot take unfair advantage of my place here and do all I would like to do. For the present you and I must feast on memories instead of on kisses. Perhaps it's just as well. I do not think I could hold you as I did beside the waterfall, and restrain myself so well a second time. When next I take you into my arms, I will have all of you, every drop of sweetness you have to offer."

"Will there be a next time?" she asked, somewhat breathless after listening to his passionate declaration.

"Ah, the future." Vanni spread his arms wide, as if to embrace the garden, the mountains, and the very sky itself. "Andrea is still alive, which means I will not be forced to take his place. What a relief that is."

"You love your brother," Bianca murmured.

"As much as you love your sister. No, more than

that, because Andrea and I are identical twins. There is no closer relationship."

"Not even with the woman you love?"

"Love for a woman is a different thing," he said. "Andrea is the other half of *me.* When I feared he was dead, I was half dead myself. But I cannot hold Andrea in my arms all night and kiss him as I want to hold and kiss you, or touch him in the way I once touched you. I assure you, Bianca, he would take a dagger to me if I tried," Vanni ended on a laugh.

"Then you do care for me?" Bianca whispered.

"With all my heart," he said. "Never doubt it. I always knew that when the time came for me to love it would be swift and sure, and so it was."

Inside the sitting room, Rosalinda watched the two standing beside the white rose bush. Only when they began to walk down one of the side paths did she turn her attention to Francesco, who was still standing before her father's portrait.

"Vanni will do no harm to your sister," Francesco said as if he could read her thoughts, though he appeared to be fascinated by the painting and did not take his gaze from it when he spoke. Then, very softly, he added, "A fine man, your father."

"I am not concerned about Vanni," Rosalinda said. "I am worried about Andrea."

"Am I correct in believing your mother sent him to perform a task for her?"

"Yes, but you will have to ask her about it. I know only the few details Andrea told me. Actually, his reason for accepting my mother's commission was because he hoped it would enable him to find Vanni's murderer." Rosalinda's glance sharpened with sudden interest. "What did you mean when you said my father was a fine man? Did you know him?"

"I met him a few times, when I was a young condottiere sent to him with messages from the Duke of Aullia."

"Federigo Sotani."

"Don't say his name with such scorn." Francesco's voice was quiet and sad. "Like your father, he was a decent man and an honest ruler. There are too few of his kind in Italy these days."

"When did you leave Federigo Sotani's service?" Rosalinda asked.

"On the day he died," came the answer.

"Ah, there you are, Signore Francesco." Eleonora came rustling into the room in a gown of deep blue-green silk that set off her pale hair and blue eyes to perfection. "I trust your leg is healing?"

"Thanks to your kindness," he said. "Vanni and I can never hope to repay you for your generosity to two strangers."

"I am certain I will think of a way for you to express your gratitude," Eleonora told him.

"If you expect more from me than words of thanks," Francesco said quietly, "then, Madonna Eleonora, you must reveal your family name."

Rosalinda stared at him. He knew her family name, as his remarks to her proved. Why, then, did he want to hear it from her mother's lips?

"Such a revelation might prove dangerous to you and Vanni as well as to me and my daughters," Eleonora said.

"If you prefer to remain unrecognized by those who come to your home, madonna, then you ought not to leave that portrait hanging on your sitting room wall," Francesco said with a gesture toward the painting.

"In fifteen years, no one has come here whom I did not invite," said Eleonora.

"Until now." Still Francesco spoke in that same quiet voice, laden with hints of knowledge and humor.

"Until last winter," Eleonora corrected him, "when Andrea appeared in the middle of a snowstorm, looking like a giant bear, all covered with ice. He terrified us."

"Andrea always did appreciate the value of a grand entrance," Francesco said. He took a deep breath and went on, "And so, with a brave and intelligent—and no doubt a very grateful—young man at hand, you sent him forth to raise an army of condottieri and use it to take back Monteferro for you. Don't look so surprised at my accurate guess, Madonna Eleonora. It's what I would have done in your place. We are much alike, you and I. Both honest souls, forced to deal each day with deceit and intrigue. I would wager there were moments when you hated it as much as I always did."

"I would wager that you dealt with it very well, indeed, signore." Eleonora's voice was sharp.

"And I have heard that you did, too," Francesco said. "So well, in fact, that when disaster struck, you and your children were able to disappear, leaving all who knew you to wonder where you had gone. Especially those who wanted you and your daughters dead. I learned a valuable lesson from your example, Madonna Eleonora, and recently put that lesson into practice, though I do confess I am too straightforward a man to remain devious for more than an hour or two at a time."

"Sometimes, an hour is long enough," Eleonora said. "For myself, I always despised the manipulations and the lack of trust that inevitably accompanies such activities amongst courtiers and their rulers."

"And yet, you have not refrained from those same activities," Francesco noted quietly. "You are manipulating Andrea even now."

"Is Andrea also skilled in deceit?" Eleonora asked.

"When necessary, he will resort to it. But if Andrea has given you his word, he will not cheat or betray you, madonna. You may depend upon him." Francesco glanced toward the portrait. "Girolamo Farisi has been dead for more than fifteen years."

"I think of him every day," Eleonora said in a wistful voice. "I will never forget him."

"Nor should you. But you were a young woman when he was killed. Even after all these years, you are still a young woman."

"I do not regret what I have done by hiding here," she said. "Should the safety of my daughters require it, I would disappear again and stay hidden with them for another fifteen years."

"Let us hope that will never happen. A mother so loving deserves an end to hiding. And a fair reward for her devotion."

"You will understand, signore, that I can think of nothing for myself until my final duty to Girolamo is accomplished, until Monteferro is restored to the Farisi, and Bianca is its duchess."

"I honor your loyalty, Madonna Eleonora. But when your duty is finished, then what will you do?"

"Until yesterday, I had not thought beyond the day when Bianca will ride into Monteferro in triumph." Eleonora's face was lifted so she could look directly into Francesco's eyes, and he was gazing back at her with an intensity that Rosalinda could feel across the room.

"Perhaps you ought to consider the possibilities that will open to you on that happy day," Francesco said softly.

"Perhaps I should," Eleonora said.

Rosalinda knew they did not notice when she left the

sitting room for the terrace. She had not understood half of what Francesco and her mother were saying, but she was absolutely certain that they understood each other perfectly.

A crescent moon was rising over the mountains. Rosalinda picked a bloom from the red rose bush and stood alone in the silvery twilight, inhaling the flower's sweet perfume and thinking of Andrea. Behind her, in the sitting room, Francesco and her mother talked on, using hints and obscure references to convey what they wanted to say. At the other end of the garden, Bianca and Vanni walked. Rosalinda could just make out their figures in the shadowy evening light.

"And I am alone," she said to the red rose in her hand. "Where is Andrea? Why doesn't he come to me? Is it because he cannot come? Or because he does not want to?"

In a clearing beside a lake set in the foothills north of Monteferro, Andrea was meeting with the captains of the army of mercenaries he had raised.

"Some of you were formerly in service to my family," he said, "and some in service to the Farisi family."

"We are all of us ready to follow you," said Domenico Ricci, one of the captains. "Just tell us where we are to go and who we are to fight."

This bold sentiment was immediately seconded by all of Domenico Ricci's companions.

"There are still a few captains coming to join us with their men," Andrea said. "At dawn we are going to move up into the mountains, to wait for them where we won't be discovered before we are strong enough to make our assault."

"Where is that assault to be?" asked Domenico Ricci.

"On Monteferro," Andrea said. "And after that, on Aullia."

"Two nice prizes," said Domenico, nodding his approval. Several of the others whistled at the thought of the riches the two cities held. All of the captains looked happy.

"What will you be doing while we wait?" asked Domenico, who seemed to be the spokesman for his fellow captains.

"I shall renew the search for my brother. I received information earlier today that suggests he may still be alive and hiding in the mountains."

"Now, there's a fine hope for you," said Domenico with a broad grin.

"I heard more." Andrea decided to give them all of his news. It could only lift their spirits higher and keep them waiting in good order until he returned. "There is a rumor that Vanni is with Francesco Bastiani."

"Bastiani?" The captains had been talking among themselves, but at the mention of that magical name among condottieri they were all eager anticipation.

"That's the kind of good news we need to keep our men loyal," said one of them. "No offense to you, my lord, and we all know what a fine leader and brave man you are, but Bastiani has years of experience on you. If he joins us, we can't lose."

"It's my hope, too," Andrea said. "All I have to do is find him. If he lives, I will bring him back with me. And bring my brother, too."

And, he thought, but did not speak his other hope aloud, *if this new search takes me near enough to Villa Serenita, I may be able to steal a day or two with Rosalinda before I have to go into battle.*

Chapter Fifteen

Once again Rosalinda rode out alone, this time after obtaining her mother's permission. For the last week, normal routine at the villa had been in disarray. Lessons for the sisters had been suspended. Bianca and Vanni were spending their afternoons whispering together in the sitting room or the garden, while Eleonora, Francesco, and Bartolomeo regularly disappeared into Bartolomeo's office for long discussions. When her mother somewhat distractedly agreed that Rosalinda might ride and when, moreover, she put no limits on where Rosalinda was to go or when she was to return, Eleonora's daughter knew there were new schemes being hatched behind that closed office door.

The men-at-arms assigned to sentry duty were taking double watches to patrol the boundaries of the land. Perhaps this arrangement gave Eleonora the impression that her daughter would be safe. But with Rosalinda's knowledge of the various pathways and tracks gained from years of riding in the hills, she had no difficulty in eluding the sentries and escaping into the higher mountains. Rosalinda did not worry about Niccolò Stregone finding her. She did not think he would push so far in his search for Francesco and Vanni, and she was sure she knew the mountain paths better than Stregone did.

She made her way along the familiar path to the old rockfall. No attempt had been made to repair the path, and during the spring thaw more rocks and earth had fallen away, leaving a wide gap. Rosalinda turned aside, taking another route, urging her horse even higher.

She knew exactly what she was seeking and, with an unerring sense of direction, she found it. In a wide gap between two mountains, a narrow path wound, with steep meadows on either side of the path. At the edge of the meadows, clumps of fir trees grew. During these summer days, which were the longest of the year, the meadow was abloom with delicate wildflowers. Yellow and blue petals fluttered in the gentle breeze beside other blossoms of orange or white or several shades of pink. This was one of Rosalinda's favorite spots.

She drew a happy breath and prepared to dismount, intending to sit for a time among the flowers while she sorted out recent events. Her plans were abruptly changed when she saw that she was not alone in the meadow. A single rider spurred his horse along the path. By his large size, the man was not Niccolò Stregone, nor was he wearing clothing like that of anyone who lived at Villa Serenita. He was obviously a stranger to the area. Fearing the rider might choose the way that led to the rockfall and the dangerous gap, for that path was the quickest route to the next populated valley, Rosalinda remained on her horse and began to ride toward him, to warn him.

He saw her coming and slowed his pace. Then, with a joyous shout, he increased his speed and rode straight for her. Before she realized what he was going to do, before she had time to react, Rosalinda was snatched out of her saddle and pulled onto the other horse. Strong arms enclosed her, and a firm mouth fastened itself over hers.

"Andrea!" She could barely breathe, so tightly did he hold her.

"I knew it was you. No other woman in these mountains rides astride."

She could not get close enough to him. She clasped her hands behind his neck, pressed her breasts against his chest, and tried to wriggle herself into a nearer position, but it was a useless attempt.

"We should both get down before you frighten the horses into bolting and we have to limp home after being thrown," Andrea cautioned. He slid Rosalinda off his mount and onto her feet. An instant later he was standing beside her. "This is a good place to talk privately, unless someone comes along the path."

Rosalinda did not think talk was what he had in mind, not when his fingers lightly traced the side of her face, not with his hand tangling into the long braid at the back of her neck to move her face nearer to his so he could kiss her forehead.

"We could sit in the shade of those trees over there," she suggested demurely.

"So we could." He caught the reins of both horses in one hand, put an arm across Rosalinda's shoulders, and walked with her to the spot she had indicated. He looked around, nodding his approval of her selection. "I have so much to tell you."

"I have a lot to tell you, too. And many questions to ask." While Andrea secured the horses, Rosalinda moved out of the sunshine into deep shade. She was trying to decide what to ask him first, and whether to reveal to him her belief that she was with child, when Andrea forestalled any remarks she might have made. He came toward her with his arms open, inviting her to enter his embrace. The loneliness of recent months receded, and all the questions crowding her mind suddenly seemed unimportant. She went to him gladly, lifting her face for his kiss.

Andrea's mouth seared across hers, his tongue forcing her lips apart. Rosalinda made no protest at this treatment; she only held him tighter. He could not stop kissing her. He covered her face, her throat, her hands with kisses, and after he had kissed and nibbled on each finger, he pulled her sleeves higher so he could press his lips to her wrists and elbows as well.

"Rosalinda, it has been too long since last I saw you. During all that time, I have not so much as looked at another woman, and now I want you so badly that I cannot think of anything but you."

She caught his face between her hands to look at him, to recall each beloved feature and realize that she had forgotten nothing about this man during his absence. He was a bit thinner than he had been in March, his muscles were harder, and there was a new, steely air of assurance about him, but basically he was the same. Her Andrea. Her love.

She pulled at the fastenings of his doublet, loosening the garment and pushing it off his shoulders. She pulled up his linen shirt to lay her cheek against his bare chest. When, in response to his soft urging, she let her hands stray downward, she discovered that he was already huge, and she could feel his heat through the cloth that barely contained his eagerness. At this physical evidence of his desire for her, her own passionate needs overcame her.

They tore at each other's clothes until all their garments lay mingled together on the fir needles of the forest floor. Andrea reached down to spread out the discarded clothes. Then he lifted Rosalinda, holding her against his heart as he sank to his knees and laid her on the clothing.

"Rosalinda," he whispered, making poetry of her name, "I have dreamed of you every night. Rosalinda, my beautiful, blushing rose, why are your cheeks so red? Surely, you are not embarrassed? I have seen you unclothed before."

"That was by the light of one candle," she said. "Now I can see all of you very clearly, and you can see me."

"I see beauty, and the warmest, kindest heart I have ever known."

"And I see my own dear bear," she whispered with a tender smile. "But I am sure you have grown since that night. I do not remember *that* part of you as being quite so large."

"Perhaps," he said with a knowing look, "you do not remember because *that* part of me was buried deep in you for most of our time together, so you could not see it."

"I don't think you should say things like that." She was shocked and yet excited by the memory his words conjured.

"No? Then I will let my actions speak what you will not permit me to say."

His fingertips found her nipples and teased, gently pulling, circling, creating spirals of warmth that moved downward and deeper, into the very core of Rosalinda's being. She shifted her legs and moved her hips, squirming under his attentions, restless for more, and still more. Her awareness of the rest of the world began to slip away, leaving her enclosed in a stand of fir trees, their trunks long and straight, their fallen needles fragrant beneath her.

She heard the birds chirping, saw the fir branches swaying, and then the area within her comprehension contracted further still, including only the man who caressed her with eager hands, whose breath was ragged, whose manhood, as hard and straight as a tree trunk, pushed against her, filled her, sent her soaring among the highest green boughs. Andrea's lips fastened on hers and would not let go. He thrust his tongue into her mouth again and again, matching each thrust of that other part of him until Rosalinda cried out even as he did, becoming one with him, accepting the scalding offering of his passion and returning it to him with all the love she had to give.

They lay joined for a long time, Andrea still buried within her, Rosalinda wrapped around him with arms and legs and the twining hair he had loosened from her braid.

"I could not wait until later," he whispered in her ear.

"I did not want you to wait," she whispered back. "At the first moment I recognized you, this was what I wanted, too.

"There is so much I ought to tell you," she said when Andrea finally lay on his back staring up at the trees and she lay curled against him with her head on his chest.

"Tell me later," he murmured. "For this one peaceful hour, let me forget everything but you, and how happy I am to see you again."

"Will you visit Villa Serenita today?" she asked, unable to let all of her news wait.

"It's where I was going when I met you."

"There is a surprise awaiting you at the villa."

"I look forward to it, but meeting you here was the best surprise." He rolled over, pinning her beneath him.

"Actually, there are two surprises. And something important that I need to tell you."

"I tremble to imagine what your mother has in store for me," he teased, nibbling at her earlobe as he spoke.

"You are going to like the surprises very much." She wished she could be sure he would like what she had to tell him as much as he would enjoy seeing his brother and Francesco alive and well. Determined to be completely honest with him, she opened her lips to speak about the child she was certain she was carrying. Once again, he prevented her.

"Wench, will you be quiet?," he said, still teasing her. "For the next hour, I don't want to think about anything but Rosalinda and Andrea."

"You are going to be so excited," she said.

"Thanks to the way you are wiggling around beneath me, I am already excited." He demonstrated that he was speaking only the truth. "Stop talking and kiss me."

"You are a hard man, Andrea." Rosalinda choked back a giggle.

"And growing harder by the moment," he observed. "It has become obvious to me that the only way to keep you quiet is by torturing you into silence. Now, where shall I begin?"

"Do you actually expect me to assist you in this painful endeavor?" she demanded in mock resistance.

"I intend to extract your full cooperation," he threatened, placing himself at the entrance to her body. "Nor will I be satisfied until you scream for mercy."

"Cruel, lustful man," she gasped as he surged into her.

"Dangerous, seductive woman," he groaned, pushing deeper still.

A short time later Rosalinda did scream, but not for mercy and, to her delight, Andrea's cries were even louder than her own.

The shadows were growing long and purple across the little valley before Andrea tenderly picked the leaves and fir needles out of Rosalinda's hair and helped her to dress.

"I suppose we have no choice but to ride to the villa," he murmured, putting his arms around her as if he could not bear to let her go. "I do not think we will have much time alone together once your mother sees me and begins asking questions about how well I have followed her orders. Let us savor these last few moments of peace." He held her close for a long while, and Rosalinda did not protest.

They rode toward Villa Serenita side by side until the path became too narrow. Then Rosalinda rode behind him and Andrea turned in his saddle every few minutes to smile at her. Rosalinda always smiled back, but her mind was busy. There were so many questions she wanted to ask Andrea, yet she had asked none of them . . . any more than Bianca had asked the important questions of Vanni. Like her sister, Rosalinda had accepted her lover's attentions, had given herself to him, and had postponed all questions, all doubts, all explanations, until later. In light of what she had done on this sunny afternoon, Rosalinda began to think of Bianca's behavior with Vanni less as a betrayal and more as a foolish lapse brought on by passion.

When they came down into the lowlands and had space to ride together again, Rosalinda moved her horse to Andrea's side. He welcomed her presence with another of those warm smiles that delighted her heart. Then, seeing her face, he turned as serious as she was.

"I want you to be prepared," she said. "So much has happened since you left. There are things you ought to know before we reach the villa, including the nature of those surprises I mentioned earlier, and a few less pleasant events."

"Tell me," Andrea ordered, speaking in the brisk, clipped fashion of a military commander. In his voice and face Rosalinda saw again the new toughness she had noticed on first meeting him, before passion and tenderness had overtaken them both. The alteration only enhanced the attraction of this man who, in many ways, remained a mystery to her.

"The bad news first," she said, pulling her thoughts away from all the things she still did not know about Andrea. "Niccolò Stregone has been here." Matching her speech to his own brevity, she told him about her two meetings with Stregone. Andrea listened with a set face, saying nothing, but Rosalinda sensed the building anger in him.

"The other news is far happier, with only one discordant note to it," Rosalinda went on.

"After the last tidbit, I will be glad of good news," Andrea said, "but tell me about that discordant note first."

"I cannot tell you the one without revealing the other. Bianca and I are at odds because she betrayed me with your brother, thinking he was you."

"*What?*" Andrea reined in hard to stare at her. A joyous smile spread across his face. "The rumors I heard are true? Vanni is alive? Why didn't you tell me before this?"

"I did try," she reminded him. "You would not hear a word. You wanted to make love."

"So I did. Am I to assume from your shocking statement that Vanni and Bianca have also made love?"

"She says not—or, at least, not completely, whatever that means."

"I can imagine what it means. Vanni is a formidable seducer when he puts his mind to it. Poor Bianca was probably overwhelmed by his charm."

"Andrea, she did this thing thinking Vanni was you! And you never told me that you and your brother are twins," Rosalinda ended on an accusing note.

"When I mentioned him to you, I thought Vanni was dead. It was all I could do to speak of him. The grief was too deep for words." He grinned at her, that grief forgotten. "I trust Bianca has sorted us out, so she knows one brother from the other by now. I would rather be embraced by the sister with whom I am more familiar."

"This isn't funny," Rosalinda exclaimed.

"No, it isn't funny, it's miraculous!" he cried. "It is the most wonderful news I could hear. The world is set right again. Rosalinda, my brother is alive! Vanni is alive!"

"He was pleased to learn you are alive, too," Rosalinda said. "Andrea, there is more. Francesco Bastiani is with him. They are both staying at the villa."

"Thank God! Rosalinda, you could give me no happier surprise than this." Andrea threw back his head and let out a shout of joy followed by a burst of laughter. "Do you know what this means?"

"What does it mean, Andrea?" Rosalinda had never seen Andrea so exuberant and yet, for all his open delight in the news she had given him, still there was that new toughness about him. She knew she ought to tell him her other piece of important news, that she was becoming more convinced every day that she was carrying his child, but she decided to wait. She would give him a chance to adjust to having Vanni back again, and then she would tell him. His next words confirmed her in her decision.

"Vanni, Francesco, and I will conquer Aullia and Monteferro together," Andrea exaulted. "I shall have you, my wonderful Rosalinda, and if Vanni wants Bianca, your mother will not dare to refuse him. My brother and I will have all that we want, your mother's wildest ambitions will be realized, and, as for Stregone, I promise you, he will pay for putting you into danger to rescue him from the river, and he'll pay again for frightening you by the waterfall. Stregone will pay for every wicked crime he has ever committed."

"You leave me breathless," she said, startled by his manner as much as by his ambitious promises. "Andrea, I have never seen you like this."

"Because I have never been like this. Today I am the happiest of men. Just think, Rosalinda! For almost a year, I have believed my brother dead, but he is alive. He is here, just a few miles away, and I will see him before the sun sets. And my dear friend, Francesco, too. And you love me, my beautiful Rosalinda. You told me you do, not an hour ago, while you lay in my arms. What more could any man ask than one true woman to love him, a beloved brother by his side, and an honest friend?"

"What more, indeed?" Rosalinda murmured, unwilling to break into his joyful mood with her own concerns. "Except, perhaps, the answers to a few dozen nagging questions?"

Chapter Sixteen

At the villa, Bianca and Vanni were on the terrace. Bianca held a basket of flowers that Vanni had been helping her to gather. The looks they gave each other and the smiles and low words they exchanged openly proclaimed the tender affection between the two.

Rosalinda and Andrea entered the garden by the path from the stable. Andrea stopped at the sight of his brother, leaving Rosalinda to walk on for a few steps before she realized he was no longer with her. When she turned to him, the expression on Andrea's face brought tears to her eyes.

"Some part of me did not dare to believe your news until I saw him alive," Andrea whispered. He held his saddlebag slung over one arm. Setting it down and opening the flap, he began to grope inside until he located what he wanted and pulled it forth. Rosalinda saw a flash of blue enamel and gold and recognized Vanni's dagger. Andrea strode forward.

"Vanni, that is a puny knife you are using to cut those flowers," Andrea called. "I have a better one for you." He held out the dagger, hilt first.

"Andrea!" Vanni leapt off the terrace, jumping across all of the steps and falling into Andrea's arms. So impetuous was Vanni's embrace that Rosalinda grabbed the dagger out of Andrea's hand just in time to prevent an accident. Vanni did not notice. He was laughing and weeping at the same time and pounding Andrea on the back. Andrea's eyes were moist, his joy only slightly more restrained than his brother's.

The two of them made so much noise that Valeria looked out the sitting room door to see what was happening. She disappeared at once, only to reappear a short time later with Eleonora, Francesco, and Bartolomeo.

"Francesco!" Andrea left his brother and ran up the steps onto the terrace, where his condottiere friend enfolded him in a tight bear hug.

Rosalinda and Vanni followed Andrea to the terrace. While the three men embraced again and talked excitedly with Bartolomeo and Eleonora, Bianca approached Rosalinda.

"How happy they are," Bianca said. "I wish all brothers and sisters could live together in peace and take such pleasure in each other's company."

"So do I." Rosalinda slipped her arm around Bianca's waist in the old, familiar gesture, not minding the basket of flowers Bianca still held, wanting only to let her sister know of her abiding affection in spite of their recent differences. "Perhaps, in time, you and I will regain that pleasure."

At Valeria's suggestion, a long table was set up on the terrace so the evening meal could be served there. The cloth was of fine white linen, Bianca arranged some of the flowers she had gathered into a golden bowl for a centerpiece, and Rosalinda fixed wax tapers into a pair of five-armed gold candelabra so the diners would have light after the sun had set. Through the long, warm June twilight the eight of them sat about the table, their spirits high, eating, drinking Eleonora's best wine, talking, and laughing.

Andrea sat next to Rosalinda, his hand often touching hers, his nearness a source of pleasure to her in spite of the many questions and lingering doubts in her mind. She pushed both doubts and questions aside, refusing to consider them until another time. On this evening of reunion she would allow nothing to spoil Andrea's happiness, or her own. They were together again. For the moment, that was all that mattered.

All the others at the table seemed to feel the same way. Even Eleonora did not speak of the mission on which she had sent Andrea, instead spending much of her time conversing with Francesco, who sat at her right hand. Only after the meal was over and the servants had been sent away, when the cheerful company lingered beneath a star-strewn sky with a last bottle of wine and a dish of dried dates and figs for nibbling, only then did the conversation turn serious, and it was not Eleonora who began the discussion, but Francesco.

"After listening to Madonna Eleonora and Bartolomeo describe their plans and your involvement in them," Francesco said to Andrea, "I have decided to join you, if you will have me."

"I was hoping you would volunteer." Andrea responded at once, looking pleased at Francesco's offer.

"I want to be included, too," Vanni said. "You cannot keep me out of it."

"Of course you will be included." Andrea grinned at his brother.

"However," said Francesco, "I think a change in plan would be wise."

"What change?" exclaimed Eleonora. "Andrea understands exactly what I want him to do, and I expect him to carry out my orders as we agreed."

"With the alteration I am suggesting, the end result will be the same," Francesco told her, "but if we take Aullia first, it will then be easier to conquer Monteferro."

"How so?" Eleonora demanded with a frown.

"I still have friends in the Aullian army," Francesco said. "I am certain that many of them will be happy to join us against the Guidi. Their change of allegiance will reduce the number of men available to back the Guidi family. That desertion will make the conquest of Aullia easier. Those same men will also enlarge the army available to us when we do march on Monteferro."

"An interesting suggestion, Francesco," Andrea said. "I will consider it most seriously."

"You have no right to make such a decision without consulting me," Eleonora began.

"I am a soldier, madonna. You are not," Francesco said, cutting off her further protest. "Believe me, I too want revenge on Niccolò Stregone, for the personal reasons which I have explained to you. As for the Guidi family, I was aware of their depredations in Monteferro before you and Bartolomeo described the situation to me. The Guidi have all but ruined a once prosperous city-state during their years of control over it. While the people suffer, the Guidi have amassed a huge fortune for themselves. Now that they hold Aullia, they will soon impose on it the same high taxes and corrupt government under which Monteferro struggles."

"My informants tell me the process of draining the

treasury of Aullia is already well under way,'' Andrea said.

''A large part of the treasury is certainly draining into the pockets of that evil dwarf, Stregone,'' Vanni voiced his opinion. ''If ever there lived a treacherous councilor, Stregone is that man. Only let me get my hands around his throat and he will not survive to arrange any more assassinations.''

Bianca made a frightened sound at this declaration of violent intentions. When Vanni turned to her, to touch her hand and reassure her, Bianca pulled her fingers from his and moved her chair away by a few inches. Vanni looked puzzled but did not comment and soon returned his attention to the conversation, which was growing more intense.

''Stregone is a wily fox,'' said Francesco, ''but we will bring him to earth. I know how to do it.''

''How wily can he be,'' asked Rosalinda, ''if he was foolish enough to show himself here? He was almost drowned in the river, and almost died again when he fell at the waterfall.''

''He was following Vanni and me,'' said Francesco. ''He could not let us get away, and I suspect he did not trust his henchmen to carry out the task of finding and killing us.''

''But you did get away.''

''Thanks to you, Madonna Rosalinda.'' Francesco smiled at her from across the table.

Bianca made another soft sound of fear, making Rosalinda wish for her sister's sake that the conversation would change to a different topic. This was not to be. The very person who should have been most aware of Bianca's secret terrors now took up the subject.

''Why was it so important to Stregone that you and Vanni not get away from him?'' Eleonora asked. She had been listening with close attention to what the men were saying. With her eyes narrowed in awakening mistrust, she addressed Francesco. "Are you so dangerous to Stregone that he would try to kill you himself?"

"Not I," Francesco answered her. "Vanni. And Andrea. He would then want to eliminate me as a witness to his crimes."

"Why?" Eleonora asked again, her voice charged with a peculiar tension.

"To make himself secure," Vanni said. "He killed our father and tried to kill us, too. He would have succeeded were it not for Francesco's bravery in getting Andrea and me to safety. We had to fight our way out of the city, the three of us against Stregone and a dozen of his men. Then they pursued us into the mountains."

"I see." Eleonora spoke somewhat absently. She appeared to be deep in thought, but Rosalinda had no doubt her mother was listening to every word Vanni spoke and was drawing her own conclusions.

"I was wounded in the fight," Vanni said. "Stregone himself slashed my left arm, inflicting a deep wound. He would have killed me had Francesco not seen what was happening and hastened to my aid. That was when Francesco and I were separated from Andrea in the confusion. That's why Andrea and I believed each other dead for the better part of a year."

While Eleonora's calculating glance swept from Vanni to Francesco and then on to Andrea, Rosalinda put her hand over Andrea's. She had not known about the confrontation Vanni spoke of, the desperate attempt of three men to win through to a freedom that was scarcely less dangerous than the fight itself. Andrea had told her only of the loss of his brother and of his flight to the mountains, claiming that the rest of the details were too painful to recount. Now it seemed to Rosalinda that Andrea had never told Eleonora about that battle, either. Rosalinda saw her mother regarding Andrea with a fascinated, speculative gaze that suggested there were as many unanswered questions swirling through her mind as there were in her daughter's thoughts.

"There are few men important enough to be assassinated by Niccolò Stregone himself," Eleonora said, "and fewer still of those men also have twin sons whom Stregone would personally want to assassinate. I have asked this question of you before, Andrea, and always you have evaded an answer. I allowed the evasion because I needed you to work for me and because I believed you would carry out my orders as you were sworn to do. Now I must insist on an honest answer from you. What is your family name?"

"Vanni hasn't told you?" As he spoke, Andrea's fingers closed around Rosalinda's hand, holding her as if he feared she would be torn from him if he relaxed his grip.

"Vanni put me off, as you have done," Eleonora said. "So did your friend, Francesco, though he was quick enough to admit to his own family name when I guessed it. I should have guessed your name, too. I would have done so, had I not been distracted at that moment." She shot an accusing glance at Francesco.

"And what is your guess, madonna?" Andrea asked in the softest, most dangerous voice that Rosalinda had ever heard him use.

"Sotani." Eleonora's tone matched Andrea's for quietness and danger. "It is the name of a family of vipers."

"Not true, madonna!" Vanni cried. He would have said more, but Francesco silenced him with a motion of one hand.

"It is true." Eleonora answered Vanni's outburst

while keeping her eyes on Andrea. "The confirmation of my assumption lies in Francesco's insistence that you should use the army for which I am paying to conquer Aullia first. You young men are the twin sons of Federigo Sotani, the late Duke of Aullia."

"Yes, madonna, we are." Andrea squeezed Rosalinda's hand so tightly that she winced. He did not seem to notice.

"What a fool I have been!" Eleonora sprang to her feet. "I am financing the return to power of the sons of the man who arranged the assassination of my husband!"

"No!" Vanni shouted. He was on his feet, too, confronting Eleonora face to face. "Our father would never have condoned such a wicked deed."

"Vanni is right." Andrea had not moved. He still sat next to Rosalinda, with her hand clasped in his, and he spoke in measured tones. His voice was calmer than his brother's, and his face revealed nothing of his emotions. "Our father and Girolamo Farisi were on friendly terms."

"They were rivals!" Eleonora declared, her eyes flashing.

"Friendly rivals," Andrea insisted. "They admired and respected each other. You insult the memories of both men to suggest otherwise."

"And you insult my intelligence with your claim of an honest father!" Eleonora leaned forward, her palms flat, her fingers splayed on the tabletop. "Here you sit, at my table, having eaten my food and accepted my hospitality for the night, clutching my daughter's hand as if she could save you, while your brother follows Bianca around as if he were a lovelorn puppy. I tell you, Andrea Sotani, neither you nor your brother will ever have a daughter of mine to wife!"

"On the contrary, Madonna Eleonora," Andrea responded with perfect composure, "I intend to make Bianca Duchess of Monteferro just as you wanted and, in addition, to make Rosalinda Duchess of Aullia. Do not forget, you have already promised Rosalinda to me as my reward for carrying out your plans. I will not release you from that promise."

"Reward?" Shocked by this revelation, Rosalinda snatched her hand away from Andrea's grasp. "I am no man's war booty!" A white-hot fire was burning in her breast. She knew what it was. Her heart was breaking. Ignoring the pain, aware of where her duty lay, she got up from her seat to join her mother.

"There, you see?" Eleonora snarled at Andrea. "My loyal daughter will not have you."

"As for Bianca," Andrea went on as if neither Rosalinda nor Eleonora had spoken, "You yourself have said to me that she will need to marry a great nobleman who is strong enough to hold and rule Monteferro in her name, since a woman cannot rule on her own. What better nobleman than the brother of the neighboring duke?"

"Marry?" Vanni exclaimed at this speech. For a moment he looked stunned at the idea his brother had put forth. However, he recovered quickly and smiled at the equally astounded young woman sitting next to him. "Bianca, will you marry me?" He reached for her hand.

"Marry the son of the man who killed my father?" Bianca cried, scrambling out of her chair to get away from him. Quickly, she moved to stand on the other side of her mother from Rosalinda. "I would rather die!"

"Madonna Eleonora," Andrea said, maintaining his calm tones amid the passionate emotions being displayed by the women, "I advise you to agree to the arrangements Francesco has described to you. I can promise that Monteferro and Aullia will exist side by side in friendship and complete harmony for as long as Vanni and I live, and we will endeavor to see to it that our children, who will be first cousins, will also live peacefully together."

"Do not try to manipulate me with false promises," Eleonora cried. "I have believed too many of your lies to be trapped by them again. You are greedy for power."

"I did not entrap you, madonna," Andrea pointed out to her. "It was your own friend, your honest retainer, Bartolomeo, who first suggested this plan of capturing Monteferro to me. Please remember that the entire scheme was originally your idea."

"Madonna Eleonora," Bartolomeo broke into the quarrel, "you will recall that I have always insisted that the Duke of Aullia had nothing to do with your husband's death. Though they were often rivals, as you say, those two men were never true enemies. I continue to believe the culprit was Niccolò Stregone, acting on behalf of the Guidi family."

"If that is so, why did Stregone flee to Aullia as soon as my husband was dead?" Eleonora asked the men. "Why did the Duke of Aullia accept Stregone into his court so readily?"

"Stregone claimed to be fleeing from the vengeance of the Guidi against him because he had been your husband's chief councilor," Andrea said. "The claim seemed reasonable and so my father, who was no friend of the Guidi, made a place for Stregone at his court. It is my belief that Stregone's arrival at Aullia was part of a planned deception, that Stregone secretly remained in the pay of the Guidi family, in return for which he regularly passed information to them. I believe that information helped the Guidi to take over Aullia.''

''I agree with this theory, Andrea,'' Bartolomeo said. ''It fits with what I know of Stregone and of the devious methods of the Guidi.''

''Don't you turn against me, too, Bartolomeo,'' Eleonora cried.

''We are not against you,'' Francesco told her. ''We all want the same thing, the end of Niccolò Stregone, the restoration of the rightful rulers of Monteferro and Aullia, and peace between the two cities. It seems to me that we ought to be able to reach an agreement rather quickly.''

''You expect me to agree with the sons of Federigo Sotani?'' Eleonora cried, staring at Francesco. ''Are you mad?''

''Admit what is obvious to every man here, Madonna Eleonora,'' Andrea said. ''You are checkmated. While you used me as your weapon to take back Monteferro, I was using you to take back Aullia for myself. Since my father's death, I am the rightful duke.''

''I will admit no such thing,'' Eleonora said, drawing herself up with great dignity. ''Nor will I reach any agreement with men who manipulate me, who lie to me and cheat me. Andrea, Vanni, Francesco, all three of you are to leave Villa Serenita at dawn tomorrow. Bartolomeo, if you are in accord with these schemers, you may leave, too. You men may not believe a woman is capable of ruling a city in her own behalf, but I tell you, unreliable creatures that you are, that I was once a full partner with Girolamo Farisi in ruling Monteferro!''

''If that is so, madonna,'' said Vanni, most unwisely, ''then I am surprised you did not know that he and my father were never murderous enemies.''

Eleonora's only response to this remark was a look that should have scorched poor Vanni into cinders.

"I know how to manage my own lands here," Eleonora went on with no diminution in passion and as if Vanni had not spoken at all. "I will give the orders to the men-at-arms, I will see to the fields and the harvest. If need be, I will gird on a sword and fight Niccolò Stregone hand-to-hand if he threatens me or my daughters!

"As for you," Eleonora exclaimed, leaning forward again until she was almost nose to nose with the still sitting Andrea, "as for you, I rue the winter night when I admitted a bear to my house!

"You have not defeated me, Andrea." Eleonora straightened to put an arm around each of her daughters. "Do not underestimate me."

"That I would never do, madonna," Andrea said.

"You are to be gone by first light. If you are not, I will set the men-at-arms on you." With that threat, Eleonora swept from the terrace into the sitting room, taking her daughters with her.

After pausing only to exchange a few whispered words with her husband, Valeria followed the other women into the house, leaving the men alone.

"A woman of fire and passion," mused Francesco, looking after Eleonora.

"A woman of great determination," Bartolomeo said, "as my wife and I have cause to know."

"I do believe the late Duke of Monteferro must have been a happy man." Francesco's gray-blue eyes were twinkling.

"Happy for the most part," Bartolomeo agreed, adding with the hint of a smile, "but sometimes he was bedeviled."

"Well, Andrea, prince of schemers." Francesco turned to his young friend. "What say you, now that my military advice and the knowledge of your full name have together raised a storm of emotion among the ladies? Shall we take Aullia first as I suggested? Or is it to be Monteferro as Madonna Eleonora wants?''

''Both,'' said Andrea.

''What?'' Francesco gave a hearty laugh. ''Now, there's a fine madness for you. Though, knowing you as I do, I am sure you have good reasons for whatever you plan.''

''The army I have raised is large enough to divide into two parts,'' Andrea said. ''However, I believe a bit of trickery will win us more than the use of brute force. The people I have talked to, most of them friends of Luca Nardi, all claim Monteferro is ripe for revolt and that Aullia is in a state of perpetual unrest since the Guidi took it. Francesco, your contacts inside the Aullian army will be a great help to us if they make the situation in Aullia worse for the Guidi.''

''And is this reason enough to attack both cities at once?'' asked Bartolomeo, looking from Andrea to Francesco as if he found this new idea difficult to comprehend.

''If we attack one city,'' Andrea said, ''we will give Stregone warning of our intentions and thus provide a chance for him to escape. By taking both cities at the same time, we can trap him wherever he is and capture him.''

''Perhaps, after you have him, you can wring the truth of Girolamo Farisi's death out of the wicked creature,'' Bartolomeo suggested. ''That murder has haunted Madonna Eleonora and her daughters for too long.''

''A confession from Stregone that the Duke of Aullia had nothing to do with her husband's assassination would do much to soften Madonna Eleonora toward these two young men,'' Francesco agreed. ''Which, in turn, would facilitate their marriages with the ladies their hearts desire.''

''How I wish I could be a part of your campaign,'' Bartolomeo said with a sigh for the masculine, military pleasures he would be missing. ''But my place is here, where I have been for fifteen years. I cannot leave Madonna Eleonora.''

''From what I have seen of the women of Villa Serenita this evening,'' said Francesco with a chuckle, ''Madonna Eleonora and her daughters together would very likely have your head if you proposed to leave them, and your wife would sweep up your remains after they were finished.''

The men shared a laugh at the incomprehensible ways of women. Then they refilled the wine glasses before they drew together around the table to talk of military matters until the candles guttered out and left them in darkness.

Chapter Seventeen

"Liars! Wicked schemers!" Still furious with the men an hour after leaving them on the terrace, Eleonora paced back and forth in her private suite of rooms. "There must be a way for me to circumvent their plans."

"Why would you want to do so?" Valeria asked. "My dear friend, Andrea intends to carry out the very same scheme that you devised."

"Not my scheme." Eleonora halted, whirling to face Valeria. "His scheme, modified, changed against my wishes, into what Andrea wants. Don't you desert me, too, Valeria."

"You know I never would. Haven't I been with you for all these years? Nor will Bartolomeo leave you."

"Do not try to convince me of that, not when he is below, conferring with those two spawn of the Sotani line and their condottiere friend."

"When he has finished conferring with them, Bartolomeo will know everything the others are planning,'' Valeria said with serene reasonableness. ''You may be certain he will tell you what those plans are.''

''Bartolomeo will know only what Andrea and Francesco want him to know. Hah! Francesco! That man.'' Eleonora bit off the condottiere's name as if the very word hurt her mouth. She resumed her pacing. When she spoke again there was a distinct note of regret in her voice. ''After so many years, I had almost begun to believe that I might dare to care. . . . What are you girls doing, standing by the door?''

''Mother,'' Bianca said in a quavering voice, ''there will be violence done when Andrea and Vanni take Monteferro and Aullia. There will be bloodshed, and people hurting each other.''

''Of course there will,'' Eleonora said. ''Warfare cannot be conducted without violence.''

''I can't bear the thought of Vanni or Andrea being wounded or killed. Mother, can't you stop it now, before it starts?''

''Bianca, this plan was originally intended to restore your birthright to you,'' Eleonora declared. ''To achieve that goal, a certain amount of violence was acceptable to me. However, the plan has been taken out of my hands, and nothing I can do or say will deflect those men from their intentions. You heard them with your own ears.''

''I don't care about my birthright,'' Bianca cried. ''I don't want anyone killed for my sake, and I don't particularly want to be a duchess. I would be content to live here at Villa Serenita always, if only Vanni could be with me.''

''How long do you think an ambitious man like Vanni would be content with our reclusive way of life?'' Eleonora demanded.

"Mother, please." Rosalinda put a protective arm around her sister. "Can't you see how upset Bianca is? She has found a man she loves and now—"

"What has love to do with a noble marriage?" Eleonora interrupted, her voice rising in anger.

"You loved our father," Bianca cried.

"An affection which grew slowly, after we were married for a while, after I knew him well enough to appreciate the kind of man he was," Eleonora said. "My marriage was arranged by my father. I had nothing to say about the choice of my husband."

"Well, I do want something to say about whom I marry."

Bianca's defiance startled her mother, who stared at her for a moment before responding. When she spoke, it was plain that Eleonora was doing her best to control her feelings, but the undercurrent of rage over alterations in her plans that she was powerless to prevent, and her belief that she had been deliberately used and misled, were all there in her voice.

"My daughters will marry when, and whom, I decide they will marry," Eleonora said. "Do not think you can thwart my decision on this. I forbid you to see either of those young men, or Francesco, before they leave tomorrow morning. Nor will I allow you to receive letters from any of them. Valeria, I expect you and Bartolomeo to stand with me on this. See that my wishes are carried out."

"You know I will," Valeria said.

"Mother, you are being cruel!" Rosalinda cried. She was deeply disturbed by her parent's attitude, yet she understood why Eleonora was so angry and so adamant. Torn between wanting to calm her mother and wanting to soften Bianca's distress, she could not think about her own situation. Consideration of what she would do in the future would have to come later. "Perhaps if you would relent enough to let Bianca see Vanni, so she can say a final farewell to him, she would not be quite so unhappy."

"I thought both of you had renounced those wicked men," Eleonora said. "You did refuse to marry them. Have you changed your minds so quickly?"

"No," Bianca sobbed, "but I can't stop wanting Vanni."

"You will have to learn to stop," said her mother. "A woman can learn to do anything if she puts her mind to it. I have learned to accept events that, when I was your age, I could not believe it was possible to survive. Yet I did survive, just as I will find a way to use this evening's betrayal, to turn it around until I have achieved what I set out to do last winter when Bartolomeo first recruited Andrea to our purpose."

"Rosalinda," said Valeria, "why don't you take Bianca to her room and stay with her for a while, until she recovers from her distress?"

"I will never recover from this evening," Bianca said.

"Oh, do as Valeria says," Eleonora ordered. "I cannot think with you weeping and sighing, Bianca, nor with Rosalinda looking as if the world has collapsed around her. Just see that you do not attempt to rejoin your would-be lovers, for if you do, I will know of it and you will be severely punished."

"Go on, girls," Valeria urged in a gentler voice. "Your mother won't be alone. I will be here as long as she wants my company."

"Come, Bianca." Rosalinda led her sister out the door and down the corridor to her room. Bianca's bedroom was draped in rosy silk, with many cushions scattered about. It was very different from Rosalinda's simpler room, which was blue and white. After pushing aside the billowing folds of pink silk bed hangings, Rosalinda shoved several pillows out of the way so she and Bianca could sit together. Bianca collapsed on Rosalinda's shoulder, her tears drenching Rosalinda's gown.

"I was so happy today," Bianca sobbed.

"So was I," Rosalinda whispered, thinking of tall fir trees, a sunlit meadow, and Andrea's hot, stirring kisses. Regret for what she had lost stabbed through her.

"Until this quarrel erupted." Bianca gulped back another sob.

"It is far more than a quarrel, Bianca."

"I know it is. Rosalinda, my heart is breaking in two. How can I love a man whose father killed my father? How can I want to be in Vanni's arms, or fear for him when he goes into battle? But I do! I do! If Vanni dies at Monteferro, I will want to die, too. Oh, I am more wicked than I ever dreamed I could be! This love I feel for Vanni is far more reprehensible than embracing him when I thought he was Andrea."

"Our mother would say it is." Rosalinda held her sister tighter.

"What of you?" Bianca asked. "Now that we know everything, do you still want Andrea?"

"I don't know what I want," Rosalinda said. "I only know I am in great pain."

"But you are not crying. You are so brave." Bianca sighed. "I wish I had half your courage."

"Take off your dress and I'll put you to bed," Rosalinda offered, to prevent Bianca from asking any more questions.

"I am sure I won't sleep." Nevertheless, Bianca began to pull at the laces of her dress. Rosalinda helped her sister to remove her clothes and then tucked her beneath the rose-colored counterpane.

"You are so good to me." Bianca tried to smile through her continuing tears. "I do not know why you should be so kind to me when I am so wicked."

"You are not wicked, only foolish sometimes." Rosalinda sat on the bed and took her sister's hand. "If I am kind, it's because you are my sister and I love you in spite of any differences between us. And because I know we are all capable of great foolishness."

"Not you." Bianca drew a deep breath and shifted to a more comfortable position. "Not Mother. I do not think she has ever been foolish in her entire life."

"Oh, my dear, you have no idea how foolish I have been," Rosalinda whispered. "As for Mother, I suspect she was on the verge of a foolish act and regrets her weakness now, and that is why she is so angry with Andrea and Vanni. And with Francesco. Especially with Francesco."

Bianca sighed again, and her hand in Rosalinda's went limp. Rosalinda smoothed back her sister's golden hair and kissed her brow. Bianca did not respond. Sure that she was asleep, Rosalinda tiptoed out of the room.

In her own bedchamber she paced back and forth, not in anger as her mother had done, but in grief and loss. The tears came slowly, seeping out of her eyes and running down her face. She did not sob or rub at her eyes as Bianca did when she wept. Rosalinda just kept walking across her room, again and again, trying to think, to find a way out of her own problems, and Bianca's. As she paced, Bianca's question resounded in her mind.

Now that we know everything, do you still want Andrea?

Rosalinda did not know the answer to that question. Physically, she wanted him. Her body ached for his touch, but she was not sure that Andrea loved her. He had lied to her, by what he had said and by what he had deliberately left unsaid. He had admitted that he was using Eleonora to get what he wanted. Rosalinda thought he had been using her, too. He had not hesitated to make love to her while he was hiding in the attic room because, in Andrea's mind, Rosalinda already belonged to him. She had been promised to him, and he was merely taking possession of his gift a few months ahead of Eleonora's schedule. And no one had bothered to tell Rosalinda. After the revelations of that evening, Rosalinda doubted that she could ever trust Andrea again.

But she was carrying his child. She was certain of it now. If her mother was right in her accusations, the baby growing beneath Rosalinda's heart was the grandchild of the man who had plotted to kill that baby's other grandfather. She was glad now that she had postponed telling Andrea about the baby. He would go away on the morrow unaware that one passionate act had resulted in a new life. Rosalinda would see to it that he would never know.

She would not have to bear the baby alone. Her mother would soon become aware of Rosalinda's condition, for someone was bound to ask why she had no monthly linens to be washed. When that happened, Rosalinda would have to reveal her secret. Her mother would be disappointed in her, and more angry than ever with Andrea, but this would be one more of those unhappy events in her life that Eleonora would learn to survive.

"No, not unhappy." Rosalinda put a hand on her abdomen and spoke to the baby growing there. "I will never let anyone make you feel unwelcome. Your Aunt Bianca will love you almost as much as I do. She will dote on you, and so will Valeria and Bartolomeo. They both love children and regret that they were never able to have any of their own.

"Mother will forgive me the very first moment she sees you," Rosalinda went on, still speaking to the baby. "And as for me, I will give you all the love you deserve, in addition to the love I would have bestowed on Andrea, if our lives had been different. You will grow up here, at Villa Serenita, safe and happy. I'll teach you to ride. I'll show you all the mountain paths I know. If you are a girl, Bianca can teach you fine needlework, for I am not very clever at it, and Valeria will show you how to cook. If you are a boy, Bartolomeo and Lorenzo and the other men-at-arms can teach you manly skills. Boy or girl, Mother will surely want you to learn Latin. I warn you now, my little love, declensions are no fun."

"Rosalinda?" Unheard by her sister, Bianca had crept into the room. "I woke up and couldn't fall asleep again. Who were you talking to?"

"I'm sorry if I disturbed you," Rosalinda said, brushing at her wet cheeks.

"You didn't." Bianca drew nearer. "You're crying. You never cry. What's wrong?"

"The same thing that made you cry."

"No," Bianca said. "You aren't like me. What happened this evening might make you angry, or determined to do something to change an unhappy situation. It wouldn't make you cry."

"I can't tell you what's wrong," Rosalinda said. "Not yet."

"Why not, when you know all of my secrets? I won't tell anyone else if you don't want me to. Is it something to do with Andrea? Why do I even ask? Of course it is."

"I have to tell someone," Rosalinda whispered.

"I've been hiding this secret for more than a month, and every day I have grown more certain of what is happening to me. Bianca, will you swear not to speak a word of what I'm going to say until Mother knows of it?"

"I swear," Bianca said, coming closer still.

"I am with child by Andrea." It was a great relief to Rosalinda to say the words out loud. By doing so, she gave form and substance to what was happening within her body.

"You and Andrea—? That night when I saw you together in the servants' quarters?" Bianca gasped at the enormity of her sister's confession. "Oh, Rosalinda! Does he know?"

"I haven't told him. After what happened tonight, I don't think I can tell him."

"Oh, my poor dear." Bianca touched Rosalinda's arm, her eyes wide with surprise and sympathy. Then the sisters were holding on to each other, both of them in tears. All differences between them were forgotten. They were allies again, as they had been in childhood, and Bianca remembered that she was the elder. It was her turn to offer comfort.

"It could easily have been me," Bianca said. "I would have done nothing to stop Vanni, no matter what he wanted to do with me. I cannot blame you, Rosalinda, for I have given way to the same desires. Only tell me what I can do that will be of most help to you, and I will do it."

"At least we are so private here that no one outside the villa will know," Rosalinda said, trying to find a brighter side to her situation. "There will be no great scandal over this. Mother would hate a scandal. So would I. Not for myself, but because scandal would mark this innocent child before it is ever born."

"There is one possible solution, if you are willing," Bianca said. "Andrea does want to marry you."

"After what I learned about him tonight, I'm not sure I want to marry him. And you heard Mother. She would never allow it. And if I were to run away and marry him, what a huge scandal that would create! What would the people of Aullia say? Once they learn who my father was, what would my impetuous action do to Andrea's chance to become Duke of Aullia? There is nothing else for me, Bianca, but to stay here and tell Mother the truth and face her wrath. At least I won't have to tell her for a few weeks. She may be calmer by then. And I am glad it isn't you. I cannot imagine what Mother would do if the daughter she hopes to make Duchess of Monteferro were to announce that she is with child while still unwed," Rosalinda finished on an unsteady laugh.

"Don't joke about this," Bianca said. "Now, I want you to listen to me. Whatever happens, no matter what Mother says when she learns of your condition, or how angry she is, you and I will face this problem together. I will not be separated from you, and I will help you all I can. Nor will I allow Mother or Valeria to insist that an unmarried girl cannot attend a lying-in. I swear to you, Rosalinda, I will be with you, holding your hand, when your baby is born."

"Thank you," Rosalinda whispered. "I am so glad you are my sister."

"It's about time I showed some courage. You know, we could use the small room next to this one for a nursery." Leaving Rosalinda's side, Bianca went to the wall, to knock softly on it. "One of the men-at-arms is an acceptable carpenter in his spare hours. I heard Valeria say so after he made some extra pantry shelves for her. We'll have him cut a door just here, and put a nice frame around it. Then you will be able to get to the nursery without going into the corridor when you want to tend the baby. Isn't there a cradle in one of the storerooms upstairs?''

''Bianca!''

''There, I've made you laugh. I knew I could. Rosalinda, did you know that Ginevra, one of the women who helps Valeria in the kitchen, is expecting a baby?''

''So I have heard,'' Rosalinda said, remembering the useful information Ginevra had imparted to her.

''Well,'' Bianca went on, ''Valeria told Ginevra to rest as much as possible. Therefore, you must rest, too. You are not to walk back and forth all night in your bare feet. Get into bed right away.''

''Have you become a midwife?'' Rosalinda smiled at her sister's enthusiasm, but she was forced to admit that she was tired. It had been a long, eventful day, and her body craved rest. She got into bed as ordered, and Bianca joined her. They fell asleep curled up in each other's arms.

It was not quite dawn when Rosalinda was awakened by a soft knocking on her bedroom door. Bianca still slept beside her, undisturbed by the insistent sound. Sliding out of bed, Rosalinda went to the door. She had only opened it a crack when Andrea pushed his way into the room.

''You may not come in here,'' she protested. ''Mother has forbidden me to speak to you.''

''We are leaving shortly.'' Andrea reached for her, but Rosalinda moved away. With one finger on her lips, she pointed to Bianca's sleeping form.

''I won't wake her,'' Andrea said in a softer tone. ''I could not leave without saying good-bye to you. Rosalinda, in spite of the quarrel last evening, I beg you to trust me, and to believe in my honesty. I am sure that when I present Monteferro to your mother, she will forgive me for not telling her who I am. Then I will claim you for my own.''

''Claim me?'' Rosalinda repeated. She was hard put to keep her voice low and not shout at him. ''How dare you say such a thing? I told you last night that I am not a prize of war.''

''I didn't mean it that way,'' Andrea insisted with some impatience. ''How else can a penniless exile win the woman he wants, except by making his fortune in war? I agreed to your mother's plan because I knew it was the only way I could hope to regain the position and the wealth that would make her consider me as a suitor for your hand. That is why I insisted on her promise that I might marry you once Monteferro was conquered. It was because I want you, not because I think you are a piece of loot, to be taken by the victor.''

''If you were another man, with a different father, your scheme might have worked,'' Rosalinda said. ''You don't know my mother very well, Andrea. She will never forgive you for what you have done. If it's true that your father had my father killed, there can be no future happiness for you and me. Even if you could convince my mother to agree, I would still refuse, no matter how often you declare that you want me.''

He had not said he loved her, only that he wanted her. Tears of hurt and anger filled Rosalinda's eyes. Wanting was not the same as loving, and she knew the difference. She wondered if Andrea did.

''Andrea?'' Vanni pushed his way into the room. ''Francesco is looking for you. We have to leave now. Ah, Bianca, my dear love.''

Seeing Bianca, who was, amazingly, still asleep in spite of the two men in the room and their whispered conversation, Vanni stole toward the bed.

"If you waken her, you will answer to me," Rosalinda said. "She only fell asleep a short time ago. Leave her alone. Leave *me* alone. Neither of you should be here."

"There are tears on her face." Vanni bent to kiss Bianca's cheek. He spoke in a soft whisper, yet Rosalinda heard him clearly. "I have a treasure to recover, that has been stolen by a wicked dwarf. When it is mine, sweet Bianca, I will return to lay it at your feet.

"Until we meet again, Rosalinda." Vanni left the bed and came to Rosalinda, to place a soft kiss on her cheek, too. "When Bianca wakens, tell her that I love her. Are you coming, Andrea?"

"In just a moment." Andrea took Rosalinda's hand in his. When she tried to pull away, he would not let her go. "You are my dearest treasure, Rosalinda, and no one can steal you from me."

"I am not yours," she responded. "I do not think I can ever be yours."

"No matter what the future brings, I will always desire you. And I will come back to you." Lifting her hand, he pressed his lips to her fingers. Then he was gone, leaving Rosalinda to lean weakly against the door while she regretted the things she could not tell him and the life they would not have.

Now that we know everything, do you still want Andrea? Bianca's question came back to haunt Rosalinda. Yes, she wanted Andrea. And she loved him, whether he loved her or not. She felt as if her heart was torn out of her with his leaving. She wished she could run to him and tell him about the child they had made. She wished he had been honest about his identity from the beginning.

Now that we know everything... Did they know

everything? Was it possible that some valuable piece of information was still lacking, perhaps a clue that Andrea's father was not responsible for the assassination of the Duke of Monteferro? It was the only hope Rosalinda had, and she did not know where or how such information could be found. She did not even know what it might be.

"Not much of a hope," she whispered, moving to stand beside the bed where Bianca slept. "All I know for certain is that, if they live and if they are successful, those three men will return. When they do, perhaps we can think of a means to prove or disprove my mother's suspicions."

She fell silent, one hand on her still-flat abdomen. And then she heard the sounds of horses riding away from the villa.

Chapter Eighteen

"I cannot bear this waiting." Bianca pushed her hat down more firmly over her head, so her face was shaded. "Vanni and Andrea have been gone for weeks."

"Just over a month," said Rosalinda, sitting back on her heels to straighten her spine and shoulders before she attacked the next clump of unwanted green leaves.

The sisters were in the garden pulling out weeds, a task Rosalinda usually hated because it meant she had to stay in one place for a while. Lately she had found it relaxing to put her hands into the earth, to remove the weeds and thus assist the plants to grow and flourish. She supposed the change in her attitude had something to do with the new life growing within her.

"When are you going to tell Mother?" Bianca kept a close and loving watch on her sister these days and she had noticed Rosalinda's weary movements. She spoke softly, with an eye on Eleonora, who was working a short distance away, cutting herbs while the day was still cool.

"Not until I have to," Rosalinda said.

"The longer you wait, the more angry she will be when she learns the truth," Bianca warned. "Especially when she discovers that I have been mixing up our monthly linens to help you hide your condition."

"I keep hoping good news will come, that Andrea will appear in triumph with unassailable proof that his father was innocent of our father's death. I fear it is a foolish hope."

Rosalinda wrestled a particularly tenacious weed out of the ground. She held it up with its long root dangling. "I ought to know better than to rely on dreams and hopes as if they were facts. My hope has been like this root, deep and stubborn, clinging to my heart as this plant was clutching the soil until I pulled it out. Perhaps the time has come to uproot hope, too." Rosalinda opened her fingers, letting the weed drop into the wooden bucket that sat on the ground between her and her sister.

"This might be a good time to tell Mother. She has been remarkably quiet of late," Bianca said.

"She is sorry for scolding us so harshly after Andrea and Vanni left," Rosalinda responded. "I think she misses Francesco, too. Perhaps she even regrets her quarrel with him."

"How can she miss a man she knew for only a few days?" Bianca murmured.

"It only took you a day or so to love Vanni," Rosalinda said.

"That was different."

"Was it? Francesco is a healthy, vigorous man, and a rather attractive one, too."

"They did seem to have much in common." Bianca

frowned, considering Rosalinda's words. Then, in a disbelieving tone she said, "Our mother and a man?"

"Why not?" Rosalinda asked. "She has been alone for fifteen years."

"I am sure she has not acted on her feelings," Bianca said. "If, indeed, she has such feelings."

"Oh, of course she will not have such feelings." Rosalinda glanced at her parent and then at Bianca, and a slight smile tilted the corners of her mouth upward. "She is a *mother,* after all."

"You are teasing me," Bianca said.

"Am I? We both know Mother is used to hiding her emotions."

"Not when she is annoyed."

"Have you ever seen her weep for our father?" Rosalinda asked. "Or heard her bewail the ill fortune that sent her into exile at a young age, to live out fifteen years of her life in an isolated villa? She never displays jealousy of the happiness that Valeria and Bartolomeo have in each other, nor is she anything but pleased at joyous events in the lives of the men-at-arms and their families. We take her interest in all of us for granted, but I think she has been lonely beyond our knowing."

"She is thirty-eight years old." Bianca stared at the slim figure of Eleonora in her old blue dress, hat over her pale hair, basket on her arm, moving among the herbs.

"Not too old to love," Rosalinda said. "Or to be loved."

"I never thought of our mother in this way." Bianca's voice was filled with the wonder of a new discovery.

"Neither did I, until I loved Andrea," Rosalinda said. "Now I understand her better with every lonely day that passes for me."

"If what you say is true," Bianca observed, "she must be as worried as we are. And because she sent Francesco away with angry words, she must be desperately unhappy, regretting her anger now that he is in danger. I know that is the way I feel about Vanni."

"Now you know why I keep postponing my shocking revelation," Rosalinda said. "I don't want to add to her burdens. And, as I said, each morning I hope the new day will bring good news."

During the darkest part of the night, a gate in the wall surrounding the city-state of Aullia swung open to admit a small group of men. Other men awaited them inside, and together they made their way through the shadowed streets to the ducal palace. There, at a side entrance, secret words were exchanged and more men joined the group. Their footsteps were soft but unrelenting as they headed for the reception chamber where Antonio Guidi and Niccolò Stregone were. Any palace guards who opposed the group were swiftly silenced, though these were few in number, for the Guidi were not greatly loved, by either their subjects or their paid protectors.

Antonio Guidi was not the actual ruler of Aullia. He was merely the representative of his older brother, Marco, who was the head of the family and who made his residence in Monteferro. Antonio was a soft, lazy man who habitually overindulged in food and drink, and who saw no reason to place himself in unnecessary danger. When he saw the two dozen hardened mercenaries who filed into the reception room uninvited and who then took up positions around its walls, Antonio feared the worst. Seeking shelter from the swords and daggers that gleamed in the hands of the mercenaries, he at once placed himself between Niccolò Stregone and a wide table. Then he saw the two men who had come into the room on the heels of the mercenaries, and Antonio Guidi knew there was no place of safety for him.

"Bastiani!" Antonio Guidi's voice broke on a gasp of fear as he faced the helmeted condottiere.

"Good evening to you, Antonio," said Francesco Bastiani. In vivid contrast to the other man's well-fed, overdressed figure, Francesco stood tall and hard-muscled beneath his armor, ready for action and alert to any danger. He put out a hand to slow the forward progress of the younger man, also wearing armor, who had entered the room with him. "I urge caution, my lord. You do not want to chance losing all just at the moment of victory."

"Andrea Sotani!" Antonio Guidi's eyes bulged as he recognized the person with Francesco. "You are supposed to be dead. Stregone swore to me that you both were dead."

"Don't you know by now that you cannot believe this treacherous councilor of yours?" Andrea taunted softly. He sent a contemptuous glance toward Stregone.

"How dare you set foot in Aullia?" Niccolò Stregone demanded. "The Sotani family has been exiled from this city."

"Not exiled," Andrea said. "Murdered."

"Is your brother dead, then, like your father?" Antonio Guidi asked in a hopeful voice.

"I don't think I am going to answer that question," Andrea responded, grinning in a way that made Antonio Guidi shiver in spite of the heavy velvet robe he wore. "Instead, I will let you wonder if I plan to extract a painful vengeance from you for the death of more than one member of my family. I will tell you that I have a large army camped outside the city walls."

"Antonio, don't listen to him," Stregone said. "He

is lying and he's trying to make us distrust each other."

"If the Guidi were wise," Francesco remarked, "they would have distrusted you from the first, Stregone."

"Guards!" Antonio Guidi shouted to the armed men standing around the room. "Seize these men! Take them to the dungeon." Not a soul moved at his command.

"In the year since you murdered my father, you have ordered too many of their comrades to the dungeon. Your mercenaries won't follow you anymore," Andrea said. "Now it's your turn to visit the dungeon, Antonio. Guards, take him below."

"Yes, my lord." The guards stepped forward. "Shall we take Stregone below, too, my lord?"

"Well, Stregone?" Francesco moved toward the little man, who stood glaring at the guards as if daring them to lay a hand on him. "Will you stay here with us and provide the information we seek, or will you take the gamble that these men will let you live long enough to reach the dungeon? They do not view you with kindness, you know. Which is why they were so easily suborned to Andrea's side."

"Don't expect me to give you information that will help you to take Monteferro into your hands in addition to Aullia," Niccolò Stregone said, with a sneer for both Andrea and Francesco.

"That won't be necessary," Andrea told him. "We already have Monteferro in our hands. We had other subjects in mind for your interrogation."

"I will tell you nothing." Stregone's lips were drawn back in his feral version of a smile. "I don't believe for a moment that you hold Monteferro. Whatever information you want, I'll keep it to myself."

"You may change your mind after a bit of tender

coaxing on the rack,'' Francesco said. At his signal, the guards took Stregone by the arms and forced him out of the reception room behind Antonio Guidi. ''After a few days of torture, a double beheading in the piazza might be nice,'' Francesco remarked as prisoners and guards reached the door.

At these words, Antonio Guidi's knees gave way, a weakness that required the guards escorting him to carry him out of the room. Niccolò Stregone was braver than his master. He laughed, a bitter, harsh sound. Pulling his arms out of the grasp of his guards, he left the room on his own, his pointed chin high, his dark eyes hurling daggers at those surrounding him.

In Monteferro, a similar scene was being enacted. Vanni was already inside the city, hidden in Luca Nardi's house. Near midnight, Vanni and Luca appeared at the entrance to the ducal palace and were readily admitted by the guards, who knew Luca and knew he came often to the palace at odd times.

Marco Guidi was as astonished as his younger brother to discover how easily a hated despot could be overthrown. But he was not the soft weakling that Antonio was, and so he fought until Vanni brought him to a halt with a wicked thrust to his sword arm.

''I am sorry about this,'' Vanni said to him. ''*Madonna la duchessa* Eleonora Farisi begged us to shed as little blood as possible, but you were determined to resist.''

''Eleonora Farisi?'' Marco groaned as he spoke the name, but whether it was from the pain in his arm or from the realization that his rule was over, neither Vanni nor Luca could tell. ''There is no stopping a determined woman, is there? But Eleonora Farisi has no living male heir.''

"She has two healthy daughters," Vanni said, "the older of whom I intend to marry."

"I knew we should have killed the entire family when we assassinated the duke," Marco said.

"The same way you tried to kill my family?" Vanni asked. "I hope it makes you miserable to learn that in addition to me, my brother is very much alive and so is Francesco Bastiani, whom you also tried to kill. The two of them are presently at Aullia. I trust they are in control of the city by now."

"Give me a dagger and let me die," Marco Guidi said.

"We are going to do our best to keep you alive," Vanni told him. "For the present."

"If you want to be secure in your rule of Monteferro," Marco Guidi warned, "you will have to kill Niccolò Stregone. While he lives, your life is not safe—nor are the lives of Eleonora Farisi and her daughters."

"That," said Vanni, "is very likely the only subject in this world upon which you and I agree."

"In the name of heaven, Vanni, will you kindly get rid of all these servants?" Brushing past half a dozen bowing men, Andrea stalked into the reception room at Monteferro. He was followed by Francesco Bastiani, who looked no happier than Andrea at the escort that had accompanied them from the palace entrance.

"It has been like this for the past four days," Vanni said, waving the servants aside with a blithe gesture. "They are so delighted to be rid of the Guidi family that they are falling over themselves to anticipate my every wish.

"Besides, Andrea, you are the representative of our nearest neighboring city, the first head of state to visit since I took control of Monteferro. Thus, you must be greeted with the proper degree of magnificence. It would help if you were to dress the part,'' Vanni ended with a frown for his brother's serviceable green wool doublet, matching hose, and riding boots.

"Do your people know how high their taxes will be to pay for all of this?'' Andrea's searching glance took in the rich furnishings of the room and the retainers clustered in the doorway, hanging back at Vanni's gesture.

"That's another reason they love me,'' Vanni said. "I have promised to review the matter of taxes. For years the Guidi have been extorting every ducat they could from these wretched people. As a result, the treasury is full.''

"How nice for you.'' Andrea's tone was dry. "In Marco Guidi you have had the better brother to rule your city for you. Thanks to Antonio Guidi and his extravagances, Aullia is close to bankruptcy. My treasury is empty.''

"You'll find a way to turn things around. You always do.'' Vanni's confident grin lasted only as long as a single heartbeat. Noting that Francesco was dressed in the same simple manner as Andrea, Vanni asked his brother, "Am I correct in guessing that this is not a congratulatory visit? What's wrong? And who is ruling *your* city in your absence?''

"I left Domenico Ricci in charge,'' Andrea responded, naming one of the condottieri.

"I know him well,'' Francesco said, to reassure Vanni. "Of all the mercenary captains at Aullia, he's the best. We can trust him.''

"You haven't said what's wrong.'' All laughter gone from his face, Vanni met his twin's eyes. "It's serious, isn't it? If it weren't, you never would have left Aullia so soon after taking it.''

"I have the worst possible news for you," Andrea said. "Niccolò Stregone has escaped."

"Gesù!" Vanni swore. "How the devil did that happen?"

"In Stregone's usual way," Andrea said. "Flattery, bribery, a bit of treachery in turning two otherwise decent guards against each other. I have often wondered how Stregone is able to twist the minds of men so they will do what they know is wrong. He even got his own dagger back. Or so we think. It's missing. You remember it, don't you, Vanni? It's the same dagger that killed our father and wounded you."

"I am not likely to forget it," Vanni replied, rubbing at the arm once slashed by the weapon.

"I sent men out to search for him as soon as we discovered he was gone," Andrea continued. "We have learned that Stregone kept a horse and a packed saddlebag ready and waiting for him at a farm just outside the city—a fact which suggests he did not entirely trust his friends the Guidi brothers. But what really worries me is that, when Francesco and I questioned the guards who were watching Stregone and who were suborned into letting him escape, both claimed before they died that Stregone mentioned your interest in a certain fair-haired lady who lives quietly in the mountains."

"You had the guards tortured into making confessions?" Vanni spoke as if he found this impossible to believe, and he looked relieved at Andrea's response.

"You know how I feel about a confession wrung out of a man by torture," Andrea said. "It cannot be relied upon. Subjected to enough pain, a man will say anything to secure relief. No, it was not me, but Stregone who stabbed the guards who helped him. No doubt it was his idea of a fitting reward. He used that cursed dagger of his, and he did it in such a way that the men were sure to die, but would live long enough to impart the information to me. He was careful to tell the guards that his spies have discovered where Eleonora Farisi and her daughters are living. Stregone wanted me to know where he is going, and he was sure I would come to you and tell you what I know. This is his way of issuing a challenge to us.''

''If Stregone knows Bianca's true identity and where she is living, then she is in danger.'' Vanni was totally serious, the jesting, teasing young nobleman gone and in his place a hard-faced warrior.

''So is Rosalinda.'' Andrea's mouth was drawn into a grim line to match his brother's expression.

''And Madonna Eleonora.'' Francesco's blue-gray eyes were as cold as ice, and his hand rested on the hilt of his sword.

''I will leave Luca Nardi in charge here at Monteferro,'' Vanni decided with no hesitation. ''Francesco, how many men do you think we should take with us?''

''Just the three of us are going,'' said Francesco. ''The fewer we are, the faster we can travel. Stregone is most likely alone, so numbers aren't important.''

''He's right,'' Andrea said to Vanni. ''Speed is what matters. We have to reach Villa Serenita before Stregone does, and he has been on his way since midnight. Once we warn Bartolomeo, he will provide men-at-arms, and we will have all the help we need.''

''Vanni, you should change out of those fancy clothes you're wearing,'' Francesco said, eyeing the younger man's blue velvet and gold robes. ''I will see to the horses and provisions. We ride within the hour.''

Chapter Nineteen

"I don't know what is wrong with me today. I cannot sit still." Rosalinda left her lessons at the table in the sitting room and went to stare out the window. "Perhaps I have been good too long," she said on a sad, little laugh.

"It's not that." Bianca joined her sister, linking arms with her. "I am oddly restless, too. It's as if something is happening—or is going to happen soon—that deeply concerns me and I am only waiting to learn of it. I have no taste for lessons, either."

"If only I could ride," Rosalinda said, closing her eyes so she could imagine it, "just mount my horse and ride with the wind in my face, across the meadows and into the hills."

"I think it would be most unwise for you to get on a horse," Bianca said. After looking around to be sure no one had come into the room, she lowered her voice and said, "Think of the baby, my dear."

"The baby is all I have been thinking of," Rosalinda answered. "It's why I made so many mistakes in Latin today. I am going to have to tell Mother in the next few days."

"It will be for the best," Bianca said.

"I'm not sure of that, but it must be done. You and I know how cautious Mother always is. Once I tell her, she will insist I give up riding altogether. I will be confined to the villa all through the autumn, my favorite season. Then the snows will come, and she probably won't let me set one foot outside the door until after the baby is born. I will go mad from being confined."

Biting her lip to keep tears of frustration at bay, Rosalinda rubbed her hands over her abdomen. She was halfway through her pregnancy, and to her it seemed she was growing rounder by the hour. The high-waisted gowns she wore had hidden her condition until now, but soon it would be obvious to everyone. Rosalinda was certain that only Bianca's clever handling of their monthly linens and Eleonora's distraction about the affairs of Monteferro had so far prevented her observant mother from asking probing questions.

"You must not endanger the child," Bianca said.

"I wouldn't do that," Rosalinda promised. "But if I were to take a gentler horse than my usual mount, and if you were to go with me, I cannot think there would be any harm in a short ride."

"I'm not sure it's a good idea," Bianca said, hesitating.

"I feel perfectly well," Rosalinda insisted. "The slight sickness that formerly plagued me in the mornings has disappeared, apparently for good. If it were not necessary to keep this secret, and if I were not so worried about Andrea, I could honestly say that I have never been healthier or in better spirits. But I need to move! I want fresh air and sunshine.''

Rosalinda did not add that she also craved the exhilaration of following steep tracks to the high meadows where dainty flowers bloomed and icy little streams carried the sweetest, coldest water in the world. Bianca was a different kind of person and so, no matter how much she loved her sister, Bianca would never understand how important it was to Rosalinda to stand in an open alpine meadow and lift her face to the heavenly blue sky and the warm sun, to feel free and unfettered by the rules that bound young women even here, in this serene and remote location.

With her hand still on the roundness that contained her baby, Rosalinda accepted the truth that she would never be unfettered again. The child she carried bound her firmly to the lower altitudes. There was no sense of loss in the realization, only an acknowledgement on Rosalinda's part that she was soon to embark upon a new aspect of her life. Before she could do that, she wanted to say farewell to the freedom of her youth.

''If you promise to be very careful,'' Bianca said, ''I will go with you.''

''Thank you.'' Tears stung Rosalinda's eyelids. ''I need to make this one last trek into the hills.''

''I don't know why it's so,'' Bianca said, ''but I do understand that you feel a deep connection to those mountains. And it's I who should thank you for letting me go with you, when I'm sure you would rather go alone.''

Rosalinda nodded, unable to speak just then. Bianca noticed her slightly teary mood and tried to lighten it.

''I do wonder,'' Bianca whispered, ''whether you are going to be able to fasten that doublet you insist on wearing when you ride.''

''I admit, I hadn't thought about it.'' Rosalinda's

mood veered abruptly, as it often had in recent days. Tears forgotten, she chuckled at the image Bianca had suggested. "I will just have to start a dashing new style and wear my doublet unfastened."

On a burst of gentle laughter, the sisters put away their lessons and hurried to change into riding clothes.

Two hours after Rosalinda and Bianca had departed on their ride, Andrea, Vanni, and Francesco reached the boundary of Villa Serenita lands.

"Signores, you must leave at once." Lorenzo was the sentry on duty, and he held up a hand to stop the three who had come galloping along the path at breakneck speed. "I have specific orders from Madonna Eleonora not to admit any of you again, under any circumstances."

"Madonna Eleonora's life may be in danger," Francesco declared, "not to mention the lives of her daughters. We have come to warn them."

"I am sorry, signores, but I must obey my orders. You may not pass."

Andrea noticed Vanni setting his shoulders and gathering the reins more tightly into his hands. Knowing his brother as well as he knew his own heart, Andrea was sure Vanni intended to make a dash for it, to rush past Lorenzo, to ride the sentry down if he must, in order to reach the villa. Just as surely, Andrea knew the unfortunate effect such a precipitous action would have on Eleonora. The woman would refuse to listen to anything Vanni or his companions had to say, and she would scoff at their warnings, calling them an excuse the men were using to get to her daughters. Diplomacy was called for in this instance, not impetuous action.

Stifling his own desire to dig his spurs into his horse's sides and ride with Vanni, Andrea sent a stern glance his brother's way and shook his head. He was relieved to see Vanni sit back in his saddle, awaiting Andrea's next movement.

"Lorenzo." Andrea leaned forward over the neck of his horse. "You and I became friends last winter, while you helped me to recover my skills with weapons. Did we not?"

"So we did," Lorenzo said, "and I regret the necessity to refuse you entrance to the villa. I beg you to understand my position."

"I do understand," Andrea replied. "Were I to set a man as sentry for me, I would expect him to be as scrupulous about following my orders as you are about the orders you have been given."

"Thank you, signore." Lorenzo nodded his agreement with these sentiments, and Andrea was pleased to note that he relaxed his rigid stance to a small degree.

"However," Andrea continued, "there is a favor you could do for me that will not defy orders. I see you have a second guard nearby. Is that Giuseppe?" Andrea indicated a mounted man-at-arms a short distance away, who was watching them as if he were wondering if he ought to join Lorenzo. "You could send him to Bartolomeo with a message from me, and we could leave it to Bartolomeo to decide whether I and my companions are to be admitted."

"I could," Lorenzo said after taking a while to consider this proposal, "but only if all three of you give your word of honor not to attack me once I am alone with you."

"By heaven, I'll attack both of them if they keep us waiting here much longer," Vanni muttered. In a louder voice he said, "Bianca's life is in danger. Don't you care about that, Lorenzo?"

"No, Vanni, it's as I said." Andrea raised a cautionary hand to his brother. "If you or I give orders to the guards in our employ, we expect those orders to be followed. Lorenzo is only doing his duty. We don't want to get him into trouble, but we do want Bartolomeo to learn we are here, and as promptly as possible, because we have come on an urgent errand."

By this time the second guard, Giuseppe, had ridden over to join Lorenzo.

"We give you our word," Andrea said, speaking to both of the sentries, "that we will remain where we are until Bartolomeo is told that we are here, and we will abide by the decision he makes about admitting us."

"Very well, signore," Lorenzo agreed. "What you ask is reasonable and I will accept your word. Go, Giuseppe. You have heard him; you know what to say." At a jerk of Lorenzo's head, the second guard set off for the villa.

The three impatient travelers settled themselves to wait. After a little while, Lorenzo agreed to Andrea's request that they be allowed to walk their lathered horses and water them in a nearby stream. This meant they were actually upon Villa Serenita land, but when Vanni whispered a suggestion that they remount and ride as fast as they could to the villa, Andrea refused.

"Aside from the dishonor of breaking our word and the impossibility of convincing Eleonora to listen to us if we take such action," Andrea said, "Bartolomeo keeps the men-at-arms well trained and ready for combat. If we are wounded, or worse, we won't be much help to anyone."

"We have seen no sign of Stregone," Francesco noted, attempting to allay Vanni's concerns. Even though he had a horse available to him, he will have to take care to avoid the men Andrea sent to search for him, a problem that ought to delay him for some time.

My guess is that we are here well ahead of that villainous dwarf.''

''If Stregone thought we could get ahead of him,'' Vanni objected, ''he never would have let those guards he stabbed know where he was going. He intended to be here first, waiting for us when we arrive.''

''I'm afraid I agree with you, Vanni, but for the moment, there is nothing we can do except wait,'' Andrea said. He kicked at a clump of grass, finding it did nothing to relieve the strain of worry over Rosalinda's safety. He could only hope that Eleonora, in her role of strict mother, was keeping her daughters close to the villa. ''Where in the name of all the saints is Bartolomeo? Does he plan to let us stay here with no word from him until we grow weary and leave?''

''Here comes someone.'' Francesco squinted, looking across the expanse of farmed fields toward the villa in the distance. ''There are six riders.''

''Signores.'' Giuseppe arrived ahead of the other riders and drew up next to the three men who were waiting impatiently to hear what he would say. ''Bartolomeo wants you to come with us. Lorenzo, more sentries are on their way to assist you, in case you need them.''

''Bartolomeo sent an armed escort for us?'' Andrea frowned at the mounted men-at-arms, all of whom he knew from the previous winter. All of them were grim-faced and unfriendly at this meeting. Andrea's tone was dry when he said to Giuseppe, ''We are honored.''

''Signore,'' Giuseppe said, ''if you attempt to evade us, we are to cut you down.''

''I find it difficult to believe that Bartolomeo gave you that order,'' Francesco said as he swung back into his saddle. ''It's not like him.''

''Madonna Eleonora gave us the order,'' Giuseppe replied. ''She said she does not trust you.''

"What a woman!" Francesco's broad smile flashed. "I can't wait to see her again."

They did not meet Bartolomeo in his office as Andrea had expected. Instead, still under escort, they entered the villa through the garden, where plums ripened on one tree and apricots on another, while the bees busied themselves with the herbs and the brilliant flowers of early August.

It was a peaceful scene, with the mountains tall and stately in the distance. Andrea found it difficult to imagine that danger could lurk here, in Eleonora Farisi's domain, where order and reason, scholarly learning and good manners, were paramount. Yet he knew that where Niccolò Stregone was, there was always the chance of sudden violence and cruelty.

And Stregone *was* nearby. Andrea could amost feel the man's presence. From the way Vanni looked from the garden to the mountains, Andrea knew his twin was thinking about Stregone, too, and trying to calculate where and when that devious man would strike.

Then the guards ranged themselves along the terrace and Giuseppe pointed toward the sitting room door. Andrea, Vanni, and Francesco all entered without protest, for this was where they wanted to go. In the familiar room Eleonora, Bartolomeo, and Valeria awaited them. But not the sisters.

Glancing around, Andrea noticed Bianca's doves rustling about in their cage. He saw Rosalinda's Latin text and her handwritten lesson on the table next to a scrap of parchment bearing what he recognized as Bianca's fine, even handwriting with its graceful flourishes. Rosalinda's handwriting was not as elegant as Bianca's, but it was clear and easy to read. Diverted from his urgent purpose for a moment, Andrea smiled to see the evidence of Rosalinda's scholarly industry. The table looked as if Rosalinda and Bianca had just left it. Andrea could picture Eleonora sending her daughters from the room as he and his companions approached the villa.

Knowing Rosalinda as he did, Andrea thought it likely that she and her sister would not be far away. He wondered if Rosalinda, with her warm heart and her insistence on her personal freedom, would find a way to join them. Or had Eleonora ordered Rosalinda and Bianca confined to their rooms during this visit?

"Why have you come here?" Eleonora did not waste time on polite greetings or flowery inquiries about the health of her unbidden and most unwelcome guests.

"Madonna." Pulling off his hat with a flourish, Vanni went down on one knee before her. "We have much to tell you, but first and, I believe, dearest to your heart, we are here to announce to you that the Guidi no longer rule either Monteferro or Aullia. Andrea has been proclaimed Duke of Aullia. As for Monteferro, I have come as promised to lay the city at your feet and at the feet of your sweet daughter, Bianca. I am here to proclaim the restoration of the Farisi to Monteferro."

It was a bold speech, and one typical of Vanni. Eager though Andrea was to warn these people against Niccolò Stregone, still he noted with interest the play of conflicting emotions across Eleonora's face. In her reaction to Vanni's declaration, Andrea hoped to see some indication of what Eleonora would say when he asked for Rosalinda's hand.

"And what reward do you expect for your valorous deeds?" Eleonora asked, staring down the length of her high-bridged nose at Vanni on his knees. In her silver-gray brocade gown, with her hair dressed high and rubies dangling from her earlobes, she looked every inch the duchess.

"Madonna," Vanni said, "I hold Monteferro so securely in my control that I was able to leave the city without concern for what would happen during my absence. It is my honor to offer Monteferro to you."

"In payment for what?" Eleonora demanded in a voice like ice.

"I ask only the hand of your beautiful Bianca in marriage," Vanni answered. "I love her with all my heart, and I will endeavor to make her happy for the rest of her life."

"Keep Monteferro," Eleonora said, still in that same icy voice. "Keep it until I find a way to take it from you. As for my daughter, I told you when last you were here that I would never give either of my children to the sons of Federigo Sotani, and I have not changed my mind. At that time, my daughters told the two of you that they agreed with my decision. They have not changed their minds, either."

"Let us hear it from their own lips," Andrea said.

He had to see Rosalinda. Standing in the room where they had passed so many contented evenings during the previous winter, he knew he could not live another hour without sight of her. When Rosalinda and Bianca were in the sitting room, then he would warn all of them at once about Niccolò Stregone. Eleonora hated Stregone more than she hated Andrea or Vanni. She would heed his words. If, for some perverse reason of her own, she chose to ignore what he said, Andrea was sure Bartolomeo would listen. In the meantime, all he wanted was Rosalinda within his vision.

"Let Rosalinda look me in the eye, and Bianca look Vanni in the eye, and let each of them say of her own free will that she refuses to marry a man who has honestly won her,'' Andrea insisted.

''After you have heard a repetition of what you already know,'' Eleonora told him, ''you will be escorted off my land and never again will you be permitted to set foot on it. The next time we meet, you three will be prisoners and Monteferro will belong to the Farisi in truth, not offered as a bribe from the children of a murderer.

''Valeria,'' Eleonora turned to her friend, ''will you ask Bianca and Rosalinda to come to the sitting room?''

''They aren't at home,'' Valeria said. ''They went riding.''

''No!'' Andrea exclaimed, his thunderous tone causing Valeria to jump backward a step.

''How long ago did they leave?'' Vanni demanded.

''Did they say where they were going?'' Francesco asked.

''Bianca said only that Rosalinda wanted some exercise and that she was going, too,'' Valeria answered, looking from one grim masculine face to another as she spoke. ''It was, perhaps, three hours ago.''

''Andrea, we have to find them,'' Vanni exclaimed.

''You will do no such thing,'' Eleonora declared. ''Is that your scheme? To kidnap my daughters, to carry them away and marry them by force? Guards! Come in here!''

''Will you forget your stubborn, misdirected resentment long enough to listen to me?'' Andrea caught Eleonora by the wrists so quickly that she could not prevent what he did, and he held her facing him so he could look directly into her furious eyes as he spoke.

''Vanni and I mean no harm to your daughters. Niccolò Stregone has escaped from Aullia after making threats against Bianca. We believe he is on his way to Villa Serenita, if he is not here already.''

"Hold!" Bartolomeo shouted, stopping the guards who had rushed into the room at Eleonora's cry and who were now about to take Andrea and Vanni into custody. Giuseppe had his hand on Andrea's arm to pull him away from Eleonora, but he stepped back at Bartolomeo's order.

"Madonna Eleonora," Bartolomeo said, "I suggest we hear what Andrea has to say about Stregone. Andrea, if you will release the lady, I guarantee the guards will not touch you."

Andrea let go of Eleonora's wrists. She staggered and Francesco put an arm around her waist. When she pulled away from him, he removed his arm at once, but he did keep a hand at her elbow to steady her, and to that she did not object. She remained standing close to Francesco while Andrea revealed all they knew and what they had guessed of Stregone's intentions.

"Do you expect me to believe these fabrications?" Eleonora asked scornfully when Andrea was done. "This is an excuse you have invented to gain entrance to the villa."

"Are you willing to risk your daughters' lives on that unfounded accusation?" Andrea demanded. "Will you allow old bitterness and anger, and your own stubbornness, to rule your actions now?"

"No." On Eleonora's face, fear replaced anger and scorn. She went white and began to tremble. Swallowing hard, she leaned against Francesco for support, and when she spoke again her voice shook. "Of course not. Nothing matters more to me than Bianca and Rosalinda and their safety."

"We must begin a search at once," Vanni said. "We have to find Bianca and Rosalinda before Stregone does."

"Yes," Bartolomeo agreed. He then proceeded to

give concise orders to the guards, who left the room as soon as he was done.

"I'm going with them." Andrea headed for the door and the terrace.

"So am I." Vanni was right behind his twin.

"Not so fast." Bartolomeo blocked their way. "I can see you have ridden hard, and you probably haven't eaten recently."

"I don't care about that," Vanni exclaimed. "I am going to find Bianca."

"The guards who were here will begin the search and will inform their comrades to be on the watch for Stregone. Take half an hour," Bartolomeo advised. "Eat, drink, and catch your breath. Your minds will be the clearer for the respite and thus you may find the girls more easily."

"There's sense in what he says," Francesco spoke up. "I know I would search with greater energy after a chunk of bread and a wedge of Madonna Valeria's good cheese."

"You shall have it, and a pitcher of wine besides." Valeria left the sitting room, heading for the kitchen.

"The first thing to do," Francesco said, "is decide where Bianca and Rosalinda would be most likely to go. I suspect Rosalinda will be the leader."

"She is as bold as ever her father was. Always, she prefers to ride the higher trails," Bartolomeo said, "though whether Bianca will agree to accompany her on those paths, I cannot say. Let us hope they stay together. It will make our task easier."

"I know some of Rosalinda's favorite trails. I can show them to you," Andrea offered. He thought of a rockfall across a narrow path, and then of a sunlit meadow with a clump of tall fir trees where he and Rosalinda had spent a passionate afternoon. He grew warm at the memory of her kisses and of the sweet curves of her firm young body. If ever he held her in his arms again, it would take the devil himself to tear them apart. The devil or Niccolò Stregone.

Valeria arrived with a tray hastily piled with food and drink. In addition to the bread and cheese requested by Francesco and the promised pitcher of wine, she had included a platter of grapes and juicy plums.

"Leave that on the table," Eleonora instructed. "Let the men serve themselves. Come with me, Valeria. I will need your assistance."

After a quick look in Bartolomeo's direction, Valeria followed Eleonora from the room.

During the next half hour, while the men refreshed themselves, they discussed with Bartolomeo the arrangements for securing the borders around Villa Serenita so no one could enter.

"Of course, it is impossible to guard the paths into and out of the mountains as I would like," Bartolomeo said. "I have always relied on the river as a barrier to intrusion and have set men to guard the meadow and, most particularly, the old Roman bridge and the ford across the river at the other end of the valley." Bartolomeo broke off suddenly, staring as Eleonora and Valeria returned.

Eleonora had changed her clothes and was now wearing a dark blue woolen riding dress, with her hair tightly braided and confined beneath a net. With its loose lines and long sleeves that buttoned at the wrist, the gown was at least fifteen years out of style, yet it set off Eleonora's upright posture and still slender figure to perfection, and the color emphasized her pale complexion, giving her a curiously youthful appearance in spite of her worried expression and the hard set of her mouth.

She wore matching blue leather gloves and carried a small riding whip.

"I am going with you," Eleonora announced to the startled men.

"Madonna," Andrea protested, "there could be danger."

"If there is danger for me," she responded, speaking so readily that it was clear she had thought about her arguments before appearing in the sitting room, "then my daughters will face even greater dangers. How could I not join the search for them, so I can be with them when they need me? You cannot stop me, Andrea. Nor you, either," she snapped, her eyes on Francesco's face.

"Madonna, I admire your courage," Francesco told her. "But have you considered what you are risking?"

"I know exactly what the stakes are," Eleonora said. "Bartolomeo, tell the stable hands to saddle a horse for me.

"Valeria," Eleonora went on, "prepare a room in case there are injuries to be treated. You will need bandages, ointments, needles and thread—"

"I'll see to it," Valeria promised, interrupting her friend with a smile that said she understood Eleonora's desire to be sure all would be in readiness should her daughters require such help. "I will also have food available when you, and the men-at-arms, return."

"I am leaving three men to guard the villa and the outbuildings," Bartolomeo told his wife.

"We women who are left behind can defend ourselves. You have taught us well, my dear," Valeria said, smiling into Bartolomeo's eyes. She let her glance rest on each of the other men in turn and, finally, on Eleonora.

"Come back safely, all of you, and bring our girls home, too."

Chapter Twenty

Niccolò Stregone had decided he would go to France. There was still time to retrieve his treasure, to do the other deed he was determined to accomplish before leaving, and then to make his way through the mountains before snow fell in the highest passes. If he was clever, he could be safe in France while his pursuers were stopped by the Alpine winter.

Stregone hated cold and snow. He hated France, too. It was a dirty country, as he remembered all too well from the one visit he had made there years ago. The French did not bathe as often as Italians did, and their language was abominable. Still, life in France was preferable to a painful death in Italy. Stregone did not doubt that, if he remained south of the Alps, he would not live much longer. He would be recaptured. It was inevitable. Torture and a hideously painful public execution would follow.

He had enough loot stowed away in his secret hiding

place to buy himself a comfortable life in France. He would purchase a pleasant house and then make certain the servants he hired kept it clean. He would insist the servants bathe regularly, so they did not smell. He would burn only sweet-scented woods in the wintertime, to keep his house warm.

Then, when he was bored, which would certainly happen after he had been safe and at ease for a while with nothing to occupy his mind, then he would work a little intrigue, gain a bit of power, insinuate himself into the confidence of some dim-witted nobleman until Stregone himself was running the nobleman's affairs. If he could do it once in Aullia and twice in Monteferro and come away with his skin intact, he could do it in France, and more successfully, too, since the French were not as clever as the Italians.

He had returned to his native village with a purse tucked away in his saddlebag. Few folk in the village recognized him anymore, but they all knew the value of gold coins. By making a donation to the local church he had engaged the good will of the village priest, who in turn had chosen four sturdy, honest young men to act as bodyguards on the journey through the mountains. Assured of protection against the bandits who preyed upon travelers in the highest passes, Stregone had only to load his treasure onto the packhorses he had purchased and then lead the horses back to the village. On the morrow, he would be off for France.

There remained one other task. Before he left Italy forever, Stregone intended to kill the two stupid females who had almost found out his hiding place. Only recently had his spies discovered who they actually were. There was a certain delicious irony in knowing that the daughters of Girolamo Farisi had grasped his hand to rescue him from the river and that, later, they had been the ones to pull him out of the pool beneath that cursed waterfall.

Stregone felt no gratitude for what Bianca and Rosalinda had done for him. The wenches had to die. Though he had temporarily lost the high position and the ready access to powerful men that gave his life meaning, the deaths of Bianca and Rosalinda Farisi would round off his days in Monteferro and Aullia very nicely. Very neatly. Stregone always liked to tie up the loose ends of any intrigue he devised.

The Sotani brothers would be heartbroken. Stregone chuckled at that thought, then improved upon it. Nay, they would be more than heartbroken. Vanni might well find it difficult to hold power in Monteferro without Bianca Farisi by his side. Stregone laughed to himself, knowing just how that impetuous boy could be brought down and Marco Guidi restored. If Marco Guidi still lived.

But no. The great Stregone, manipulator of the lives of lesser men, would be far away in France, living a new life. Marco Guidi would have to fend for himself.

The day was perfectly clear, which meant there would be light until Niccolò Stregone, intriguer and proud villain, had done all he intended to do and had led the horses loaded with his treasure back across the Roman bridge and along the straight, ancient road, deep into the mountains, to the village where he had been born. He was certain that by the time the Sotani brothers discovered his absence from Aullia, gathered their men-at-arms, and made their way into the mountains to Villa Serenita, it would be too late for them to save the women they loved, or to prevent the departure of their enemy from Italy.

Feeling almost happy, Nicolo Stregone kicked the horse he rode, urging it to greater speed, certain that all he wanted awaited him in the next valley.

Chapter Twenty-one

"Let's stop at the waterfall before we go home," Rosalinda suggested.

"Aren't you tired?" Bianca asked. "I know I am weary. We have ridden to that terrible rockfall and to a lovely meadow and I have listened to your romantic stories about both places. I am sure if you knew where to find the cave in which Andrea once sheltered, you would insist upon visiting it, too."

"That is why we should go to the waterfall," Rosalinda answered. "All afternoon we have ridden where I wanted to go. The waterfall is your special place, where you first met Vanni."

"All the more reason to stay away from it," Bianca muttered. "I am embarrassed to think of what I did there with Vanni."

"Don't be embarrassed on my account. I have long ago forgiven you. Come on, I'll race you along the edge of the meadow." They were just moving out of the hills and entering the flatter land, where it was possible to ride faster than on the rocky mountain tracks. Rosalinda gave her horse a slight nudge with her heels. "Come on, Bianca!"

"Oh, do stop!" Bianca cried. "You know you should not ride so fast. What if you are thrown? Rosalinda, come back!"

But Rosalinda was well ahead of her. Bianca could see there was nothing for it but to follow her sister, and as quickly as possible, in case Rosalinda needed her help. They raced across the sloping ground, skirting the forest, keeping to the edge of the meadow, until Rosalinda drew up, laughing and breathless, at the place where the familiar narrow path wound its way into the trees.

"Rosalinda, how could you do something so dangerous?" Bianca cried. "Just think what might have happened!"

"I am more concerned with what did happen," Rosalinda said. Her cheeks were flushed, and her hair was coming undone from its braid. Moreover, her face was glowing with an inner joy. "This babe of mine must be a son, who will love riding as much as I do."

"How can you possibly know that?" Bianca asked, surprised by the tenderness and pride radiating from her sister.

"Because he just kicked me to tell me how much he enjoyed our ride," Rosalinda answered.

"More likely, the poor mite was terrified that his mother would be thrown and he would be lost," Bianca exclaimed. "Anyway, you can't tell whether it's a boy or a girl—Rosalinda, did you say the baby moved? You felt it?"

"He was digging his heels into me the same way I guide my horse." Rosalinda rubbed the spot. "There have been some slight flutterings before today, but I wasn't certain what I was feeling. These were his first hard kicks. Now I am sure he is real. There is a small person here." Looking down at herself, she rubbed more gently.

"How wonderful. What joy for you to know it's a vigorous child." Bianca's delighted smile disappeared almost immediately as a new thought took hold of her. "Once again, I envy you, Rosalinda. I will never experience what you are feeling right now."

"Don't be too sure. You know that old saying Mother repeats so often, about the way Dame Fortune plays tricks on us all, to upset the plans we make."

"A fine trick of Fortune, indeed, if I were to marry and become a mother," Bianca murmured wistfully.

"Or even become a mother without marrying," Rosalinda teased.

"Don't make jokes. Childbearing is serious business. Rosalinda, you must not ride anymore."

"You are right. I have thought too much of what I want, and not enough about what the baby needs. After today, I will remain peacefully at home. But for now," Rosalinda said, swinging a leg around and jumping to the ground, "since we are here, and since it will be our last chance until next summer at the very least, let's visit the waterfall. I'm thirsty after our long ride. Aren't you?"

"Yes, I am, but it will be painful for me to return to that spot." Bianca stayed on her horse.

"All the more reason for you to go there. Lay your grief to rest, Bianca. Say farewell to Vanni at the waterfall, as I have been saying farewell to Andrea all during this afternoon."

"Is that what you've been doing? Truly?" Bianca asked. Slowly, she dismounted, too.

"I know I will never see him again." Rosalinda's lower lip trembled.

"Nor will I ever see Vanni." Bianca's voice broke. Without another word, she took her sister's hand and together they started along the path.

The clearing was deserted, a quiet green haven after the bright sunshine of mountain and meadow. The amount of water gushing over the rocks and into the pool below was not as great now, in August, as it had been in spring, when the streams fed by melting snow had been in full spate. The moss on the stones around the pool looked dry and brown in the places where the spray no longer reached.

But the water in the pool was still cold and sweet when the sisters knelt to drink from it and to splash it onto their faces.

"What must it be like in winter, with the water frozen?" Bianca wondered. "Vanni could never climb on those rocks then."

"Vanni will not climb on those rocks again, at all," Rosalinda said. "He will not come here again. He would not dare, not after Mother sent him away and forbade him to return."

Bianca rose from her knees, her hand on Rosalinda's arm, dragging her sister up with her. She looked around the clearing, noting with painful resolve the very spot where she and Vanni had lain upon her cloak, where Vanni had touched her and done wonderful things to her. Bianca could not regret what she had allowed on that day, for it might well be the only taste of passion she was ever to enjoy, but she knew the time had come to root her inappropriate love for Vanni out of her heart. Only then could she return to the contented life she had known before that impulsive young man had disrupted her peace. Only after Vanni was completely gone from her thoughts could she be of true service to Rosalinda and her baby, both of whom were going to need Bianca's loving help for years to come.

"I do renounce Giovanni Sotani," Bianca said in a loud, ringing voice, speaking to trees and rocks, to the waterfall and the clear blue sky, as well as to Rosalinda. "From this hour onward, Vanni is no part of my life. I hereby dedicate myself to my beloved sister and to our mother, to good works and a circumspect life, until the day I die."

"I don't think you have to go quite that far, Bianca," Rosalinda said in a softer tone.

"I want to," Bianca replied. "I meant every word."

"I know you did. But you will discover, as I have, that it isn't so easy to tear love out of your heart and never think again of the one you love, especially in the middle of the night, when you are lonely and wakeful and he isn't there to comfort you. The best you can hope for is to put love aside during the daytime, so you are able to go on with the way of life you have chosen."

"And what of the night?" Bianca cried, looking frightened. "What shall I do then if, in spite of my honest efforts, I cannot rid myself of this love our mother has forbidden?"

"At night, pray for courage," Rosalinda said. "It's what I do."

They stood hand in hand, both close to tears, gazing at the clearing one last time until, on a mutual sigh, they turned to go.

"Rosalinda?" Bianca said, her eyes on the falling water.

"Yes, my dear." Rosalinda paused at the edge of the clearing, waiting for her sister.

"There is something behind the waterfall."

"What do you mean?" Rosalinda retraced a few

steps to stand beside Bianca.

"There isn't as much water coming over the edge of the rocks as there was in the spring," Bianca pointed out, "and so, if I stand just here, I can see through the falling water to the space behind it. Look, Rosalinda. Stand here and you will see it, too."

"See what?" Rosalinda's sharp eyes probed the area Bianca indicated. "Bianca, that's a cave. There is a cleft in the rock behind the water."

"Do you see that narrow ledge?" Bianca asked, pointing. "If someone were very careful, and were small enough, he could tiptoe along that ledge and get into the cave."

"Perhaps," Rosalinda said, considering the problem of reaching the cave. She shook her head. "There is no way to climb up to the ledge. It's a sheer drop."

"Not climb up," Bianca said. "Climb down. From the top of the rocks. See those cracks in the rock that are just big enough to poke your toe into? And the tree roots sticking out to make handholds? It looks possible to me."

"Well, I have no intention of discovering if it can be done," Rosalinda said, one hand over her abdomen. "I might have dared the climb down from the top last spring, but now I have more important matters on my mind."

"I didn't mean that you should try it," Bianca said, her eyes still on the rocks and the waterfall. Her voice was soft and wistful when she continued. "Up there is where I first saw Vanni. He was clambering around on the cliff, near the waterfall. I wonder if he was trying to get down to the cave?"

"How would he know of it?" Rosalinda asked. "He was unfamiliar with this area, and we have agreed that the cave cannot be seen in springtime, when there is more water."

"He was up on the cliff the second time I met him, too," Bianca went on as if Rosalinda had not spoken. "Now that I think about it, he appeared to be searching for something. Both times, when he saw me, he grabbed a tree branch so he could swing down to where I was. What could he have been looking for up there?"

"We will never know," Rosalinda said. "You did just renounce Vanni, didn't you?"

"Yes." Bianca sighed. "You are right. It's time to go. Time to put Vanni out of my mind."

Together they started toward the open meadowland and the sapling where they had tied their horses. Bianca glanced over her shoulder for one last glimpse of the waterfall. In the next moment, her hand came down on Rosalinda's wrist, with her fingernails digging in so hard that Rosalinda cried out and stopped where she was.

"Rosalinda!" Bianca hissed.

"Let me go, Bianca. You're hurting me."

"Someone is up there."

"Where?" Rosalinda managed to pull her arm away, but only because Bianca was so fascinated by what she was seeing that she relaxed her grip a little.

"In the cave." Bianca spoke softly, as if she were afraid she would be overheard. "Someone just looked out of the cave."

"That can't be," Rosalinda declared. Then she fell silent, staring openmouthed when a figure appeared on the ledge just outside the cleft in the rocks. Whoever was up there was carrying a cloth-covered bundle wrapped inside a coarse net. The corners of the net were drawn together and fastened to a heavy rope. As the sisters watched, half hidden as they were on the path toward their horses, the figure on the ledge grasped the rope and began to let down the bundle.

"What is he doing?" Bianca whispered.

"We can see what he's doing," Rosalinda whispered back, somewhat impatiently. "What I want to know is, what has he got in that bundle?"

"It's going to fall into the pool," Bianca exclaimed.

"No, it's not. Look, he's swinging the rope so the bundle will miss the water."

With a heavy thud, the bundle landed on dry ground just beside the pool. The man on the ledge let go of the rope and vanished back into the cave. The freed rope dropped onto the bundle and as it hit the cloth covering the bundle, one corner of the cloth flew open. Out of the opening tumbled a loop of large, creamy pearls.

"It's a necklace," Bianca whispered, seeing the pearls.

"Yes, but whose necklace?" asked Rosalinda.

Both girls fell silent then, for the little man had just reappeared on the ledge with a new length of rope, to let down a second bundle in the same way as the first. When the bundle was on the ground, he grabbed the rope, which at its upper end was fastened to something solid inside the cave. Holding on with both hands, he let himself over the edge and slid down the rope from ledge to ground.

"That is the most amazing thing I have ever seen," Bianca whispered.

"Bianca, do you recognize him?" Rosalinda asked. "I do. He is the little man we pulled out of the river last spring, and later out of that very pool at the bottom of the falls."

"Niccolò Stregone," Bianca breathed.

"The same. From what we have heard of him and what we have just observed, I would guess that he has been hiding stolen goods in that cave.''

''But how did he know of the cave?'' Bianca asked.

''Never mind that now,'' Rosalinda said. ''We need the men-at-arms. I'll stay here and watch him, so we'll know in which direction he has gone if he leaves before you return. Bianca, mount your horse and ride toward the villa. Surely, you will see one of the sentries along your way. Send whomever you meet here at once and then ride on and alert Bartolomeo.''

''I won't leave you here alone,'' Bianca said.

''Someone has to go, and you have been warning me all day about riding too fast,'' Rosalinda replied. ''I promise, I will stay hidden among the trees. I'll be perfectly safe. Please hurry, Bianca. That terrible man can be up to no good. Whatever he is doing, we have to stop him.''

''I do regret disappointing a lady, but you won't be able to stop me.'' An arm snaked around Rosalinda's neck and a dagger point pressed against the vein in her throat.

''Did you think I couldn't see you from up there, on the ledge?'' Niccolò Stregone asked. ''You imagined you were hidden among these bushes, but from that height I could see you with no difficulty. And while you stupid females argued about who should ride for help, I was able to creep up behind you.''

''Let my sister go,'' Bianca cried. ''Please, you mustn't hold her that way. You don't understand. She is—''

''No, Bianca!'' Rosalinda screamed, terrified that Bianca would reveal her pregnancy in hope of eliciting mercy from Stregone. Rosalinda was sure he was incapable of mercy. The information would only give him more power over her. ''Just be quiet, I beg you!''

''Always a good rule for a female,'' Stregone said

with a sneer. "Do be quiet, Bianca."

"What are you going to do to us?" Bianca asked him.

"I knew you would not fail me." Stregone's lips drew back over his teeth in a smile that was not a smile at all, but a threat of violence to come. "I had a feeling the three of us would meet here again, for the last time."

"What do you mean, the last time?" Bianca demanded.

"I suppose it is possible that we will meet yet once more," Stregone said. "In hell. If you believe in hell. You two will be there long before I am."

"H-hell?" Bianca was unable to voice more than a croak.

"I am going to kill you," Stregone told her, speaking as if he were making pleasant conversation.

Rosalinda had both hands on his arm, trying to pull it away from her throat so she could breathe. Stregone loosened his grip a little and she took a noisy gulp of air. She could see how frightened Bianca looked. But whether her sister was terrified or not, Rosalinda knew that Bianca was not going to leave her alone with Niccolò Stregone. Therefore, there was no hope of Bianca getting to her horse and riding to alert the guards. Nor, to be truthful, would Rosalinda be willing to leave Bianca to Stregone's nefarious intentions if she were the one able to get away.

Their only chance of rescue lay in making a disturbance loud enough that someone would hear them and come to investigate. Rosalinda decided she would make as much noise as she could, as soon as she could do so without being strangled into permanent silence. In the meantime, while she waited for a chance to scream as loudly as possible, she tried to think of a way to gain enough control over the situation to delay Stregone's bloody plans for her and her sister—and her baby.

"Let Rosalinda go." Bianca stood white-faced but remarkably defiant for a young woman who was usually timid and exceedingly cautious. "Kill me instead."

Rosalinda suppressed a cry. Bianca was willing to offer herself as a sacrifice in order that Rosalinda and her unborn child might live. There could be no greater proof of her sister's love. But even before he spoke, Rosalinda knew what Stregone's response would be.

"No, no," he said, as if he were reassuring Bianca. "I want both of you dead. First I slit this one's throat while I hold her. Then it will be easy to kill you. You are the weak sister, Bianca. You will stay to weep over Rosalinda's body and, while you do, I will plunge my dagger into your heart."

"Before you kill us," Rosalinda said, trying to put some authority into her voice, "tell us why. We have done no harm to you. In fact, we have saved your life on two occasions."

"You have repeatedly interfered with me and what I was trying to do," Stregone snarled. "Don't you know, you foolish girls, that it is a mistake to risk your own lives to save someone else unless there is an immediate benefit to be reaped for yourself from your action?"

"I think it is a noble thing to do, whether one is rewarded or not," Bianca stated in a surprisingly firm voice.

"Little you know," said Stregone with yet another sneer.

"What is in those bundles you dropped from the cave?" Rosalinda asked, to keep him talking.

"Gold," said Stregone. "Jewels. A bit of gold plate, but not much, since it is bulky and can be difficult to move expeditiously. Coins, strings of pearls, and unset jewels are always preferable to plate or other large pieces. Those two bundles contain my treasure.''

''How did you know about the cave?'' Bianca seemed to understand the need to play for time, to delay Stregone's murderous intentions in hope of circumventing them. ''I would be interested in knowing about that.''

''Would you?'' said Stregone, looking pleased at the question. ''Well, I will satisfy your female curiosity. You see, it was a clever scheme on my part.''

Each time he spoke, Stregone loosened his grip on Rosalinda's throat just a little bit. She kept both of her hands on his forearm, pulling steadily downward against his strength. It was possible that she might get free of him and, if she did, she would have no compunction about using on him the small knife she carried hidden in her skirt.

''For your information,'' Stregone said to Bianca, ''I was born in the village that lies along the old road, just through the mountain pass to the north of this valley. I do not boast of it, you understand. It was a squalid beginning, of which I am not proud.''

''That doesn't explain how you knew about the cave,'' Rosalinda said. She pulled a little harder on Stregone's arm, forcing it down by another inch or so.

''I was a scrawny youth, always small for my age and often tormented and laughed at by the other boys because I was so small,'' Stregone answered her. ''As a result, I spent a lot of time wandering alone through these hills and thinking of ways to revenge myself on those stupid village fools. I discovered the cave about this time of year, when the water was low, as it is now. I was just fourteen. Shortly thereafter my father died, and the local priest suggested I leave the village to make my way in the world by my wits, which are considerable."

"I am sure they are," Rosalinda said. "My sister and I have had ample evidence of your intelligence." Just a little more steady pressure on his arm and then a sudden jerk, and she ought to be free. She took a deep breath and tried to relax all of her muscles so Stregone would not guess what she was about to do.

"I never forgot the cave," Stregone said, looking toward it. "Often and often as the years passed, I have returned to deposit my hoarded wealth there, in those secret chambers behind the waterfall. That cave is safer than any bank. Never was I disturbed while I was about my business in this hidden glade, until you two appeared, interfering, upsetting my well-laid plans." He glared at Bianca, his full attention on her for the moment.

Rosalinda siezed the opportunity. Suddenly tightening her fingers on Stregone's forearm, she pulled downward as hard as she could. At the same time she stamped hard on the top of Stregone's foot. With a yell of pain and surprise, he let her go. Instantly, she whipped out her knife.

"Rosalinda, be careful!" Bianca screamed.

"Run, Bianca! Run for help! Call the sentries!"

Stregone slashed at Rosalinda with his dagger, ripping the sleeve of her doublet and drawing blood from her arm. Rosalinda knew she had to get the dagger away from him. She circled him, looking for a chance, copying the movements of the men-at-arms whom she had watched while they practiced this kind of hand-to-hand combat. But Stregone was experienced and swift, and he had no scruples about injuring a woman. He slashed at Rosalinda again, nicking her arm a second time, and blood spurted. Rosalinda was too intent on her opponent to feel any pain.

Bianca, however, was fully aware of what was happening to her sister. She shrieked, and shrieked again. Rosalinda's nerves jangled from the tension and the sudden, shrill noise. Stregone did not so much as flicker one eyelash. He just kept his dark, unblinking gaze on Rosalinda's face, watching her eyes to see what her next move would be.

Suddenly, the clearing was crowded with men. Francesco was standing beside Rosalinda, threatening Stregone with his own dagger. Quick as lightning, Stregone dove between Rosalinda and Francesco, and stabbed Francesco. Then Francesco was on the ground with Stregone's dagger in his ribs. Bianca rushed to Rosalinda's side, looked down at Francesco, and began to scream.

At first Rosalinda thought Bianca was screaming at her. It took a moment to realize that Bianca was looking at Niccolò Stregone, crying out an old, never-forgotten anguish as if it had only just happened.

"It was you!" Bianca yelled at Stregone. "You! You did it! I saw you there, in the reception room! And I saw your dagger planted in my father's chest, the same way it is buried in Francesco now. I remember that fancy hilt. I recall hearing you boast to my father that there is no other like it. You killed my father with your own hand!"

"Here, Bianca." With a groan, Francesco wrenched the dagger from his side and held it up for Bianca to take.

"Francesco!" Eleonora rushed into the clearing and dropped to her knees beside the fallen condottiere. "Don't you dare to die! We need you alive."

"I will do my best to obey your wishes, madonna," Francesco responded in a decidedly weak voice.

As Eleonora pressed her hand to his wounded side to stop the flow of blood, Bianca seized the dagger from Francesco's lax fingers. Holding it with the point aimed at Stregone, she moved toward him in so resolute a manner that no man among those in the glade attempted to prevent her.

"My father trusted you," Bianca told Stregone through set teeth. "I heard him say so. And you betrayed him."

As if in a dream, Rosalinda watched her sister approach Stregone. She was scarcely aware of her own trembling or of Andrea's arm around her, supporting her. She barely noticed the other men crowding into the clearing, witnesses all to the scene playing out before them. She did see Vanni rush to Bianca's side with his sword drawn and his own dagger in his left hand. However, Vanni did not attack with his weapons. Instead, he began to taunt Stregone.

"You had help in your betrayal of Girolamo Farisi, didn't you, Stregone?" Vanni said. "You couldn't manage it alone, so you were forced to enlist my father in your scheme."

"No!" Stregone's teeth were bared again in the wicked grimace that passed for a smile with him. "It was my scheme, my intrigue. All of it, mine alone! Federigo Sotani was too honest to wish for the removal of a man he regarded as a friendly rival. Marco Guidi was not so scrupulous when I approached him with the scheme. He was happy to take the credit, and the glory, but the overthrow of Girolamo Farisi, the planning, the execution, the actual blow that brought him down, all were my doing. Federigo Sotani had nothing to do with Farisi's death."

Eleonora was still kneeling beside Francesco. Upon hearing Stregone's bold confession of guilt, she made a sound that was part cry of horror, part shout of rage. Leaving Francesco in the care of a man-at-arms, Eleonora rose to advance on Stregone like an avenging angel.

"I call heaven and earth and all here present to witness your confession," Eleonora declared in a deadly voice. "Niccolò Stregone, you are condemned out of your own mouth."

Bianca was sobbing, with tears pouring across her face, but still she clutched the dagger Stregone had used to strike down her father. She struggled to speak clearly, so everyone could hear her.

"After murder, you resorted to looting," she said to Stregone, "and to still more looting before you murdered Federigo Sotani.

"Vanni, I believe that is the treasure he stole from your father, that you were searching for when I first met you," Bianca went on, pointing to the bundles on the ground as she spoke to Vanni. "I think some of it must have come from Monteferro, too. Stregone told us he has been accumulating it for years and hiding it in the cave behind the waterfall."

"Give up, Stregone," Andrea shouted. "You have confessed. Now answer for your crimes like a man."

"I know of no reason why I should answer to men of lesser wit than mine," Stregone responded. "I will never surrender, and you will not take me. I always leave myself an escape route."

So swiftly that no one could guess what he was going to do or try to stop him, Stregone snatched his dagger back from Bianca and sheathed it. He leapt to the rope, which was still attached by one end to the second heavy bundle of treasure he had let down from the ledge. By its other end the rope remained secured inside the cave. As agile as a monkey, Stregone began to climb up the tautly stretched rope toward the cave.

"There's no purpose in trying to escape that way," Vanni called after him.

Stregone's only response was a scornful laugh, as if he would defy human reason.

"I'll cut the rope," Andrea said. "If it loosens suddenly, he may fall off. Then we can pull him out of the water." He rushed to the bundle, to slash at the rope with his sword. He severed it from the bundle with one stroke and the lower end of the rope swung free.

"Too late," Vanni said. He squinted, looking upward against the bright sunshine. "He doesn't need the rope any longer. He has reached the ledge behind the waterfall."

From far above them Stregone laughed again, mocking Andrea's effort to stop his escape. Reaching for a sturdy tree root, Stregone left the ledge and began to climb along the rock face beside the waterfall, pulling himself upward with the sureness of long familiarity, toward the top of the cliff and freedom.

"Let's send some of the men-at-arms around the side of the hill and up to the top by the easier slope, to capture him there," Andrea suggested.

"It would be a waste of time," Vanni objected. "It will take too long. By the time they get to the top of the waterfall, Stregone will be gone."

"He must not escape!" Eleonora raised both her fists to the sky and shook them as if she would shake down Stregone from his high perch.

"He has already escaped," Bianca said, moving to stand next to her mother.

"Let all the saints in heaven render justice on this murderer of honest men," Eleonora shouted. "In the name of Girolamo Farisi, of Federigo Sotani, and of all the others whom he has killed, dear heaven, do not let this wicked creature escape to destroy still more lives!"

From the high rocks above there came a derisive laugh in response to Eleonora's pleas. With a shout of triumph, Stregone reached the top of the cliff and climbed over it. He stood there, a dark shape against the bright sky, legs apart, his fists planted on his hips. His scornful laughter at his opponents rang on the wind. Watching him, Eleonora groaned and sank to her knees, her hands clasped, her head bowed.

"I do not ask for vengeance's sake," Eleonora cried, "only for justice. For evil to be punished. Please! Please!"

An inhuman scream silenced everyone in the clearing. Slowly Eleonora came to her feet again, Bianca and Rosalinda flanking her, the eyes of all three fixed upon the sight of Niccolò Stregone capering along the rocks. It was not a dance of victory over his enemies, but a now desperate attempt at escape.

To one side of Stregone, the wall of rock continued upward for another hundred feet or so. From that higher elevation, an eagle had just swooped down upon him.

"The eagles have a nest up there," Vanni explained to those in the clearing, who drew closer together to stare at the drama. "When I was climbing around on those rocks, I took great care not to get too near to it. I stayed on the opposite side of the stream. An eagle will fight to the death to protect its nest and its young."

The eagle attacked Stregone again, its wings flaring backward, its beak open and its sharp claws extended. Stregone fought it with his dagger, the only weapon he carried. The screams of eagle and man mingled in a terrible howl. Under the bird's fierce onslaught, Stregone was driven to the very edge of the cliff. With another shriek, the eagle thrust its beak forward, pecking at the man's eyes. Stregone flung out an arm to protect himself, stumbled back a step, and fell off the cliff.

He landed beside the bundles of stolen treasure and lay there, unmoving. In the clearing absolute silence reigned, while in the sky an eagle screamed. Looking up, Rosalinda saw the bird, its wings spread, soaring high on the wind, wild and free. Eleonora saw it, too.

"Farewell, my dear protector," Eleonora whispered. "Your last duty to your daughters, and to me, is done."

Lorenzo was among the men-at-arms, and he went to Stregone to turn him over, face up. Into Stregone's chest his own dagger was plunged to the full length of the blade, with his hand still grasping the ornate hilt.

"There's heavenly justice for you," Lorenzo said. "He has been slain in the same way and by the same knife he used to kill so many better men. He must have fallen on it when he landed."

As if it had been waiting for this final sign that Niccolò Stregone was indeed dead, the eagle dipped lower over the clearing, made a graceful turn, and flew out of sight. Watching it, Eleonora smiled.

"What shall we do with him?" Lorenzo asked, indicating Stregone's body.

"Take him to the next village northward along the old road," Rosalinda answered when her mother hesitated. "He told Bianca and me that he was born there. Let him be buried there, well away from our lands."

"Send two men-at-arms with him." Eleonora had recovered from her momentary lack of words.

"At once, madonna." Lorenzo began to give orders to the men.

"Andrea, you are to go with them," Eleonora continued.

"I would prefer to return to Villa Serenita with the rest of you," Andrea responded, his eyes on Rosalinda.

"Do not argue with me," Eleonora warned him. "I have good reason for what I do. You are to tell the story to the village priest and let him decide on the disposition of Stregone's body. Then you are to bring the priest back to Villa Serenita with you, and as promptly as possible. If you make haste, you ought to rejoin us about midday tomorrow.

"Now, Vanni," Eleonora went on, turning to the other twin, "unhand my daughter and see to packing up that ill-gotten treasure for transport to the villa. We will decide later what is to be done with it."

"Mother, some of those plundered goods belong to our family," Bianca said.

"Your mother is right, my dearest," Vanni told her. "It's best if we are gone from this place as soon as possible. We can examine what's in those bundles and restore the goods to the rightful owners later. For the moment, I believe your sister would be glad of your attention."

"How pale she is." Bianca regarded Rosalinda, who was standing very still, keeping her back turned and not watching as the men-at-arms carried Niccolò Stregone's body out of the clearing to load it onto one of the horses. Andrea gripped Rosalinda's shoulder in passing. Then, under Eleonora's sharp eye, he hastened to follow her orders, striding off after the men-at-arms whom Lorenzo had just designated to accompany Stregone's body.

"Rosalinda," Bianca murmured. When she put her arm around Rosalinda's waist, her sister leaned heavily against her. "What a terrible thing for you to see. Do you feel faint? Or ill?"

"No, just sad and confused. This last encounter with that dreadful man must have been far worse for you," Rosalinda said. With a shudder, she laid her head on her sister's shoulder. "How brave you were, Bianca. You would have died for me."

"I am glad it wasn't necessary. Come along, I'll help you to your horse." Bianca led Rosalinda out of the clearing.

"Now it is time for you, Francesco." Brushing aside the man-at-arms who had been tending the condottiere, Eleonora bent toward him. She put out a hand as if to touch his face, but halted in mid-motion. "Can you ride, or shall I have the men carry you?"

"With so formidable a lady to sustain me, how could I do aught but ride?" Francesco lurched to his feet, then stumbled. "Perhaps just a bit of help to mount my horse. Then I should be fine."

"Giuseppe, help him," Eleonora commanded. "And stay close beside him. I don't want him to fall from his horse and break his neck before he can make his excuses to me."

Bartolomeo appeared just as Bianca and Rosalinda left the forest. It was he who lifted Rosalinda to her horse, and he who rode beside her on the homeward journey.

"Thank heaven you are safe," Bartolomeo said. "When Andrea and the others arrived to warn us that Stregone was coming here, we were all sorely worried about you. To cover as much ground as possible as quickly as possible, our party split into two groups. I led the men under my command toward that path into the mountains that you are so fond of traveling."

"Bianca and I were there earlier," Rosalinda said. "You probably just missed us."

"Tell me what happened. Your mother has given me only the barest explanation. I am glad to see she is greatly concerned with Francesco's well-being," Bartolomeo said with a smile.

As they rode along, Rosalinda recounted the tale of the fatal meeting with Niccolò Stregone, noting with considerable admiration the way in which Vanni had taunted Stregone into making his confession of murder.

"Just as I told your mother, that young man is remarkably clever," Bartolomeo said with satisfaction at having his judgment of Vanni confirmed. "She sent for a priest, did she?"

"I don't know why," Rosalinda said. "Mother didn't explain and I am too tired to try to reason it out." *And too upset by the way Andrea left me so easily to care about anything but his going,* she added silently to herself.

"You are unusually pale." Bartolomeo looked closely at her. As if he could read her thoughts and wanted to comfort her, he added, "Andrea will surely return on the morrow, and I do not think your mother will send either of those young men away in anger again."

Bartolomeo must have seen more in Rosalinda's set face and haunted eyes than he allowed her to know, for as soon as he lifted her down from her horse, he gave her over to Valeria with stern instructions for her care.

Under Valeria's supervision, Rosalinda was helped to her bedchamber, undressed by a sympathetic but unprying maidservant, and supplied with a tub of hot, scented water. She was so grateful for the opportunity to ease an assortment of bodily aches and twinges that she almost burst into tears as she sank into the tub.

Half an hour later, warmed internally after drinking one of Valeria's hot tisanes, and with the two shallow wounds on her arm smeared with Valeria's herbal salve and bound with clean linen by that competent lady, Rosalinda climbed into bed and pulled the covers up to her chin. Whether from the herbs in the tisane or because of her own sleepiness, a sense of peace and security began to steal over her.

Bianca was with Vanni. Through her open window Rosalinda could hear their voices from the terrace below and she could tell that they were not arguing. Bartolomeo had assured her that Andrea would return soon. Niccolò Stregone was dead and could never hurt any of them again.

Most important of all, her baby was kicking merrily, sure proof that the horrors of that day had not damaged the fragile life growing within her. With a tender smile, Rosalinda turned on her side and wrapped both arms around her belly.

Of course, there was still the question of how she was going to explain to her mother that she was carrying Andrea's child. And how she was going to tell Andrea, and what would happen then.

Before she could become caught up once more in the worries that had consumed too many of her recent hours, Rosalinda's healthy body asserted its need for rest. She sank into a deep slumber, where murder, treachery, and political intrigues ceased to matter, where even the question of Andrea's feelings for her seemed unimportant, and all that concerned her was gentle repose and the knowledge that her baby was safe.

Chapter Twenty-two

"You were fortunate, Francesco," Eleonora said as she finished wrapping his chest with clean linen strips. She had refused to allow Valeria to attend to Francesco's wound though, as always, that faithful friend stood by in case she could render some service. "Your chain-mail shirt and thick doublet deflected Stregone's blade. You have suffered only a flesh wound, and I think it is a clean one. It ought to heal quickly, unless you are foolish enough to attempt some manly action that tears open the stitches I have made."

"There is only one manly action that interests me at the moment," Francesco responded, catching Eleonora's hand and bringing her fingers to his lips, "and to it, I do not think you are yet willing to agree."

"To it, I do not believe you are yet equal," Eleonora snapped back at him.

"My recuperative powers may surprise you. Pleasantly.'' Francesco grinned when Eleonora pulled her fingers out of his grasp.

''You need to rest,'' she said, not looking at him, handling the unused bandage as if rolling it up neatly were the most important thing in the world to her. Only the flush on her cheeks indicated that her inner emotions were not as serene as her outward appearance.

Without protest, Francesco swallowed the entire contents of the goblet of spiced wine that Valeria offered to him. Shortly thereafter the herbs with which Valeria had infused the wine began to take effect and Francesco dozed off.

''I will call someone to sit with him,'' Valeria said.

Outside Francesco's room, Eleonora suddenly slumped, putting a hand on the wall to steady herself. At once, Valeria's hand was at her elbow.

''My knees are weak,'' Eleonora said with a self-deprecating laugh. ''How embarrassing.''

''Not at all.'' Valeria helped Eleonora toward her own suite of rooms. ''From what Bartolomeo has told me, you might have lost your daughters this day. Furthermore, by Stregone's confession you have learned a great and unexpected truth. It would be surprising if you were not feeling somewhat unsettled.''

''Unsettled?'' Eleonora repeated with a gasp. ''Valeria, for more than fifteen years I have been wrong about Federigo Sotani. I have maligned a decent man, repeatedly calling him a murderer. How could I have been so mistaken?''

''Your grief at the death of the husband you loved was too deep,'' Valeria said. ''In those days you were not thinking clearly. Once your mind fixed upon an idea, you could not let it go, so you continued to believe in Sotani's guilt.''

"I do repent that false belief now," Eleonora said.

"Your mind will be easier tomorrow, after you have had time to consider all that has happened," Valeria assured her friend. Releasing Eleonora to stand by herself, Valeria opened the door to Eleonora's private suite of rooms.

"Yes," Eleonora said, entering her dressing room. "Tomorrow. After the priest has come and I have made my confession. After I have torn that wrongful hatred toward Federigo Sotani out of my heart, where it has lain, corroding all my thoughts and actions, for so many years. Then, perhaps, I can begin anew. Do you think I am capable of change, Valeria? Or am I too old?"

"You are only one year older than I," Valeria replied, her eyes sparkling with delightful feminine secrets, "and Bartolomeo tells me with some regularity that I am still remarkably young. And attractive."

"Does he?" Eleonora sounded wistful.

"Eleonora, I am your oldest and dearest friend. I know you better than anyone else, even your daughters. And I tell you that you can do anything you want to do. Now, today, tomorrow, whenever you want. For the first time in your life, you are free."

"Not quite," Eleonora said. "There is still Monteferro. And Bianca's future. I must work out a plan . . ." She fell silent, lapsing into deep thought.

"And Rosalinda," Valeria added. "I have been meaning to talk to you about her. But not now, not after today's events. It is possible that Rosalinda's problem will resolve itself without our help."

"What did you say? What about Rosalinda? She's not ill and trying to hide it from me, is she? I have noticed how pale and quiet she has been of late, but I put it down to longing for Andrea and assumed she would get over it in time."

"Doubtless, she will, in time," Valeria said, and went away, leaving Eleonora alone with her thoughts.

On the terrace, Bianca and Vanni were still talking, Vanni having just completed a vivid description of the way in which he, with the help of Luca Nardi and a few other brave men, had seized Monteferro from the Guidi family.

"And so now you are Duke of Monteferro." Bianca's eyes were lowered, so Vanni could not see the look in them, nor could he guess at her feelings.

"My sweet Bianca," Vanni plunged on with what he meant to say, "your mother's chief objection to my proposal that you and I should marry has been her belief that my father was in some way responsible for the murder of your father. Now she has heard from Stregone's own lips that my father had nothing to do with that crime. Therefore, Madonna Eleonora's objection is removed and we are free to wed."

"Do you really want to marry me?" Bianca asked.

"Of course I do. How can you question my intentions?" Vanni exclaimed.

"Perhaps I am wondering if you want me because you love me," Bianca said, "or whether it is because marriage to me would legitimize your control over Monteferro."

"I hold Monteferro too firmly for it ever to be taken from my grasp," Vanni stated boldly. "If anyone dares to question my right to rule, Andrea will come to my aid at once, as I will go to his aid if his position in Aullia is threatened. I want you—and I do need you, Bianca—but for love, not for reasons of state."

"You love me?" Bianca raised questioning blue eyes to his face, not yet daring to believe, seeking in his expression confirmation of his claim.

"Can you doubt that I have wanted you since the first moment I beheld you?" he asked. "I have never disguised my desire for you, and when we met, I did not know who you were."

"That's true enough," she said. "At that time, you did not know me, or my family. To you, I was just a girl in a forest clearing."

"We were fortunate to meet and fall in love without the encumbrance of our family histories and your mother's very proper reservations. I think them proper now," Vanni said with a smile. "Now that those same reservations are of no consequence."

Bianca did not respond to these remarks. Vanni watched her pace across the terrace stones to the steps. She stopped with one hand resting on the urn while she looked at her mother's garden and then at the mountains. He heard her sigh, but he had no inkling of what she was thinking.

"Bianca? Will you marry me? I cannot imagine that your mother will refuse her permission now."

"Can't you?" Bianca asked. She fell silent for a moment, then went on. "How long it seems since the day, less than a year ago, when Rosalinda came home from a ride into those mountains, to tell me she had seen a bear on the path. Now the bearskin is gone, and in its place I see silk, gold, jewels. A famous title.

"I am greatly changed since that day." She faced him again. "Nor am I any longer the silly girl who was jealous of her sister, as I was when you first saw me. Be warned, Vanni, I will continue to grow and change so long as I live."

"I have changed, too," he said, "though not enough. I have no great skill in statecraft, Bianca. Andrea is the twin who was taught to rule, while I was permitted to live a freer life. But I suspect your mother has trained you well, and you could teach me what I will need to know. Together, you and I could repair the wrongs done to Monteferro during Marco Guidi's rule and make it a great city again. But I do not think I can accomplish all I want to do there without you at my side each day, and in my arms at night. And when our lives are done, I want our children to inherit a prosperous and secure Monteferro."

"Our children?"

"Your mother should approve the idea of Girolamo Farisi's grandchildren ruling the city that once was his," Vanni said. "Don't you agree?"

"I will not marry you for the sake of Monteferro, though I know my duty well enough," Bianca said. "I have been told about my duty since I was old enough to understand the word. You do not know me at all, Vanni, if you think I will be content with only a title and duty. I want passion! I want to give way to a desire that will never end. I want a man who will love me until death parts us, and who will be faithful to me as my father was to my mother. Why are you smiling at me like that? Have I said something you think is funny?" she asked in an offended tone.

"Sweet Bianca, you have just said what is in my heart, what I have been trying to tell you all this while. Obviously, I have not said it very well, or you would not doubt my love for you."

"Then say it again," she demanded. "Say it simply and clearly, with no mention of the duties and responsibilities that will await us in the future, should I decide to accept your proposal."

"Bianca Farisi, I love you with all my heart," Vanni said. "I will love you until the day I die. I will love you even after I die, when I hope we will meet again in the next world and spend eternity together there. I will never want another woman, and I will do everything in my power to make you happy. I ask you again, will you marry me? If, of course, your mother has no objection?'' He ended his passionate declaration with a boyish grin.

''I will see to my mother,'' she said with firm assurance.

''Then, you will marry me?''

''Yes, Vanni, I will.'' A tear of joy glinted in Bianca's eye. It was quickly blinked away, to be replaced by a mischievous twinkle. ''Now that you have asked me as I wanted to be asked, you may kiss me if you like.''

''If I like?'' His embrace lifted her off her feet. With Bianca's hands braced on his shoulders, Vanni whirled her around and around, while he grinned up at her and laughed for sheer happiness. Then he let her slide down along his body, so she would feel his hardness and know how urgently he desired their marriage.

''Oh,'' she said in reaction to his obvious eagerness.

''Yes,'' he whispered. ''Oh, indeed. But I will wait, Bianca, until we are properly wed and blessed by a priest. Then you and I will share a glorious marriage night.''

At last, with Bianca standing on her feet again, Vanni's lips touched hers in the kiss she had granted. Slowly they sank to the terrace steps, to sit there with their arms entwined while they shared the longest, sweetest kiss either had ever known.

When Vanni pulled Bianca closer still, his arm brushed against the white rosebush. Disturbed by the movement, a few of the late-blooming roses on Bianca's bush released their petals, which drifted over the lovers like fragrant snowflakes.

* * *

"Dukes?" Rosalinda exclaimed to her sister. She got off her bed to pace across her bedchamber to the window. "Both of them? They succeeded so well and so quickly?"

"I think Vanni could succeed at anything he wants," Bianca said, touching the gold ring set with a sapphire that Vanni had removed from his own hand and placed on her finger. It was too big; she had wound it with ribbon to make it fit, but she would not hide it. "I am going to marry Vanni. He asked me yesterday, and I agreed."

"What does Mother have to say about your decision?" Rosalinda asked.

"She doesn't know yet. She has decreed a household meeting in the sitting room this afternoon. We plan to tell her then. Rosalinda, if Mother objects, will you speak on our behalf? I love Vanni so much, and I know he loves me. I made sure of his affections before I agreed to marry him. But we are not certain what Mother's reaction will be to our announcement."

"Of course I will tell her I think you ought to marry," Rosalinda said, "though what weight my words will carry, I cannot guess. Why don't you tell her now, before this meeting she has called? She might be more likely to agree if you and Vanni speak to her in private. I'll go with you if you want."

"We can't. She is with the priest and has been for more than an hour. I cannot think what she has to confess that would take so long," Bianca said.

"The priest? He's here? Then Andrea is here, too? He hasn't left the villa since he returned with the priest, has he?"

"Vanni said Andrea wanted a hot bath after days of riding, and then a nap, but he will join us this afternoon," Bianca responded to her sister's questions.

"He didn't even come to see me." Rosalinda's voice betrayed all of her hurt and disappointment.

"Rosalinda, so much has happened in the last few days," Bianca said, trying to comfort her sister. "I am sure Andrea will speak to you soon, and you will have a chance to tell him your wonderful news."

"I'm not certain I should tell him," Rosalinda said. "I don't want him to feel an obligation he would prefer not to assume."

"What nonsense!" Bianca exclaimed. She was sorely tempted to shake her sister and might have done so if Rosalinda had not looked so dejected. For the present, Bianca decided, words alone would have to suffice. "I am sure Andrea is as true to you as Vanni is to me."

"But you have not lain with Vanni yet, have you? It makes a difference, Bianca. Mother has told us often enough about noblemen who toy with girls and then shirk their responsibilities after the girls are ruined."

"Andrea would never do that. Rosalinda, he does care for you. If he didn't, I couldn't have been jealous, could I?"

"That was last spring. So long ago." Rosalinda's voice caught on a sob. "Andrea has had what he wanted from me. Several times. Now, he doesn't care anymore."

"This is your condition speaking," Bianca said. "You have kept your secret for too long. Too much has happened to you in the last few days. At least those wounds Stregone inflicted on your arm were not serious, but I would not blame you if you took to your bed in tears after that terrible scene at the waterfall."

"What about you?" Rosalinda asked. "During that same scene you were made to recall the hour when our father died, in all its frightening detail."

"Well, it's a strange thing about that," Bianca responded, pleased to have Rosalinda thinking about something other than her own unhappiness. "Reliving every detail of what happened on the day Father was killed, and not just the selected bits and pieces that I repeatedly dreamed, seems to have banished my worst fears. I will always mourn our father's untimely death, but now I find that I can put aside my grief and remember how much Father loved me, and how much I loved him. In remembering, I have been freed of guilt and sorrow, so that I can go on with my life as I am sure Father would have wanted.

"Now, listen to me, my dearest," Bianca said, returning to her original subject. "I *am* going to marry Vanni. Nothing will prevent it. And, no matter what Mother says, no matter what she wants you to do when she learns of your pregnancy, you will always have a home with Vanni and me in Monteferro. We will not desert you."

Bianca did not think Andrea would desert Rosalinda, either, but she could see that her sister was in no state to believe in Andrea's love. Bianca seriously considered going to Andrea's room, to shake him into wakefulness and tell him to get himself to Rosalinda at once and declare his love for her. All that kept her from immediate action was the sure conviction that Rosalinda would soon discover her sister's hand in the affair and not only blame Bianca, but refuse to credit anything Andrea said as a result of Bianca's interference.

Nor could Bianca tell Vanni about Rosalinda's pregnancy. It was Rosalinda's secret to tell, not Bianca's. She could only hope that Andrea had good reasons for his reticence and would soon explain those reasons to Rosalinda.

At the present moment, all Bianca could do was help Rosalinda to dress in the gown in her wardrobe with the fullest skirt and the highest waistline. While she drew the laces as tight as possible without making her sister uncomfortable, Bianca reflected that Rosalinda's condition could not remain a secret much longer.

No one else ever learned exactly what passed between Eleonora and Father Tomaso, the elderly priest who had come to the villa with Andrea, but he was waiting with her in the sitting room when the other members of the household joined them in late afternoon. They were all there: Rosalinda and Bianca, Bartolomeo and Valeria, and Vanni with Andrea, who came in a bit after the others had assembled. Francesco was already seated in the most comfortable chair. He kept his left arm against his side in a protective way, but otherwise he showed no ill effects of the wound he had suffered on the previous day.

"Now, then," Eleonora began, looking from face to expectant face. "Before anything else, I must offer a profound apology to you, Andrea, and to you, Giovanni, for the hatred I have held against your father and for my stubborn belief that he, whom I knew to be a man of honor, would stoop to commit or to condone a treacherous assassination."

"Madonna Eleonora, please," Andrea interrupted, "there is no need for this apology."

"Allow me to continue, Andrea. This is part of my penance."

"Then, by all means, madonna, say what you must."

"I have in the past spoken unkind words to both of you young men, and I have made rash accusations against you. I am sorry." For all her professed regret, Eleonora's head was still held high and she did not tremble or reveal any other sign of deep distress as she spoke. She looked anything but penitent. She looked, in fact, like a duchess holding court, and Andrea and Vanni both smiled at her pride, for they understood that emotion, having a fair share of it themselves.

"Madonna Eleonora, I accept your apology in my father's name as well as for myself, and I thank you for it," Andrea said with formal gravity when she was done.

"And so do I," Vanni added. Then, before Eleonora could go on, Vanni said, "This seems an auspicious moment in which to renew my suit for Bianca's hand."

"Indeed?" Eleonora looked down her nose at him. Her eyebrows rose by an inch or so. "Francesco has told me several times that you are not as frivolous as you appear to be."

"No, I am not," Vanni said. "Madonna Eleonora, you of all people will understand when I say that in any court, even the respectable court my father maintained, there are always opposing factions struggling for power and for the friendship, or at least the confidence, of the ruler. In such a climate, twin sons are a danger.

"To prevent any group from using Andrea and me against each other or against our father, as soon as we were old enough to understand the situation, our father himself advised us to allow the world to believe that my only interests were elegant food, fine wines, pretty women, rich clothing, and grandiose displays of wealth. If I could appear to be frivolous enough, Father hoped no one would attempt to set me in power over Andrea's slain body. In truth, it was not a difficult masquerade for me. I only had to emphasize certain of my real interests, and besides, I never had any desire to rule Aullia."

"Yet you seized Monteferro, and you do rule there," Eleonora stated rather coolly.

"Monteferro I will rule for Bianca's sake only, and

with her help if you will permit us to marry, madonna, for I do perceive how well you have taught her to assume the role of duchess. You will find me ever loyal to your daughter. In fact, I love Bianca so well that I will never be capable of causing her any distress."

"You are a man," Eleonora responded to this passionate declaration. "Therefore, in one way or another, you *will* cause her distress."

"No, madonna, I assure you," Vanni cried. It was plain that he wanted to say more on the subject, but Eleonora cut him off, addressing herself to the priest.

"You see, Father Tomaso, the impetuosity with which I have been dealing of late," Eleonora said. A corner of her mouth turned upward as if she was fighting the urge to laugh. "Now that you have heard this young man's pleas, do you still agree with my decision?"

"Certainly, Madonna Eleonora, I see no other path for a responsible mother to take." Father Tomaso's face was grave, but his wise old eyes were dancing with a humor that more than matched Eleonora's own.

"Very well, then, since I have the approval of the Church," Eleonora said. "Bianca."

"Yes, Mother?"

"You are to wed the Duke of Monteferro. Do not object. It is your duty to obey the wishes of your elders."

"Yes, Mother." Bianca looked stunned to be so easily given the permission for which she had been prepared to fight. She recovered quickly, however, and smiled and put her hand into Vanni's.

"We will waive the banns," Eleonora informed the company. "The ceremony will take place as soon as the contract is signed. Rosalinda, take your sister upstairs and find her something suitable to wear. Valeria, make up Bianca's bed with clean sheets. Her room will do very nicely for a bridal chamber. We will forego a grand wedding feast in favor of a formal reception once we are in Monteferro.''

''Mother, what are you saying?'' Bianca cried.

''That you and Vanni will be married tonight,'' Eleonora replied.

''Madonna, the hour,'' Father Tomaso protested.

''I know it is already far advanced,'' Eleonora told him, ''but I believe we can have all in readiness by midnight. Bianca and Vanni will be married shortly after the new day begins. Then, Father Tomaso, you can return to your village, and the newlyweds will be on their way to Monteferro by dawn.''

Only a rather lewd laugh from Francesco halted Eleonora's fevered planning. She turned to the condottiere with a questioning look.

''Ah, madonna, I do admire you,'' Francesco said. ''How I wish I could order my soldiers as skillfully as you arrange the lives of those around you. Will you allow me to make a pertinent suggestion?''

''What is it?'' Eleonora regarded him with some indignation over his interruption.

''As you predicted, and thanks to your good care, my wound is healing quickly and cleanly,'' Francesco said. ''If you will postpone the journey to Monteferro for a day or two, I will be sufficiently recovered to accompany you. The delay will also give Vanni and Bianca at least a brief time to—er, become more intimately acquainted. Which is, if you will recall from your own history, an important aspect of a successful marriage.''

''A point well made, Francesco,'' Vanni said. He grinned his thanks at his friend, who winked back at him. ''Madonna Eleonora, we will not depart for Monteferro until the day after tomorrow, and we will leave then only if my sweet Bianca agrees to do so."

"But there are arrangements to be made for your formal entry into the city with your duchess," Eleonora protested.

"Since I am Duke of Monteferro, it is for me to make the arrangements," Vanni told her. "I shall do so with the help of my wife, and of my brother and ally, the Duke of Aullia," he finished with a firmness that made Eleonora look at him with new respect.

"Have you any objection to the wedding plans I have put forward?" Eleonora asked him in a gentler tone.

"None at all," Vanni said. "I do thank you, Madonna Eleonora, for understanding how eager I am to marry your daughter. Bianca, have you any objection to wedding me this night?"

"Oh, no." Bianca's face was aglow, and her blue eyes were shining. She looked at Vanni as if she wanted to throw her arms around him. Instead, she made a graceful curtsy to him. "Thank you for your consideration of me, my lord."

"Bianca, I will always consider your wishes," Vanni told her. "If you and Rosalinda will leave us now, your mother and I will settle the terms of our marriage contract. Then we will meet to start our lives together when the new day begins."

"Rosalinda, I must speak with you."

"Not now, Andrea. Bianca needs me." Rosalinda shook off Andrea's restraining hand on her arm and started across the hall. On the stairs, Bianca looked down at them, nodded, and continued on her way to her room.

"Rosalinda," Andrea said again, "you must know that I—"

"Rosalinda, what are you doing, dawdling here?"

Valeria cried, coming out of the sitting room in a rush. "We have so much to do that I am quite distracted. Andrea, I believe your brother would be glad of your presence while the terms of the marriage contract are decided."

"Francesco is there to back Vanni if he needs support," Andrea said, his eyes on Rosalinda, who seemed determined not to look directly at him.

"Andrea?" Vanni appeared in the sitting room doorway. "Would you mind joining us?"

"In a moment, Vanni." Andrea sounded distinctly frustrated. "Rosalinda, please."

From the sitting room came the sound of Eleonora's raised voice, followed by Francesco's deeper, but still agitated tones, and then Bartolomeo's more measured words.

"Rosalinda, your mother is a hard woman," Vanni said, running a hand through his dark, curly hair. "And Francesco is just as difficult. I am caught between them."

"Andrea," Rosalinda said, "your brother needs you, as my sister needs me. Whatever you have to say to me must wait." She headed for the stairs with Valeria at her side.

"Damnation." Andrea scowled and raked his hand through his hair in a gesture remarkably like the one his brother had just used. "What am I to do, Vanni? I cannot get a moment alone with her. I am beginning to believe she is avoiding me."

"Surely, she cannot doubt your affection for her," Vanni said.

"I don't know." Andrea looked up at Rosalinda, who had reached the top of the stairs. "She has changed. She has withdrawn from me and I don't know why. And the fates are conspiring against us; every time I try to talk to her, we are interrupted.''

''Wait until after the wedding,'' Vanni suggested. ''Then all the attention will be on Bianca and me and no one will notice if you take Rosalinda aside for a private conversation.''

''I suppose you are right. There is nothing I can do now, while she is with her sister and Valeria.''

''What you can do,'' said Vanni, ''is come and help me. I tell you, Andrea, I will not live with my mother-in-law! She will try to rule Monteferro for herself! Some other provision for Eleonora will have to be made, but anything I can think of will only antagonize her and make Bianca unhappy.''

''I have an idea that might work,'' Andrea said, and led the way back into the sitting room.

Chapter Twenty-three

For a ceremony prepared in such haste and conducted an hour after midnight, the wedding of Bianca and Vanni was surprisingly elegant. This was in large part thanks to Valeria's efforts. At her order, the small chapel on the second level of the villa was bedecked with late summer flowers from Eleonora's garden, and the tall gold candlesticks on either side of the altar bore the finest beeswax candles. Father Tomaso wore a set of white-and-gold vestments that Valeria had brought out of storage for the occasion.

Nor had the various participants slighted the occasion by their personal garb. Eleonora was resplendent in deep wine-colored brocade threaded with silver, and Valeria had taken time from her harried schedule of last-minute arrangments to change into her best gold silk gown. Bartolomeo was clothed in a rather old-fashioned long green robe.

Rosalinda wore a rose silk gown. Hoping to conceal

her rounded figure she had drawn over the dress a loose, deep green brocade tabard that was open down the front and trimmed with gold embroidery.

The twins and Francesco were simply clothed, each of them having brought only a single change of garments along on their hasty journey, but all were freshly bathed and brushed. Vanni was in blue wool doublet and hose, Andrea in red, and Francesco in russet brown. In the glow of candlelight, they all made a fine showing.

But it was Bianca who drew every eye when she stepped into the chapel on Bartolomeo's arm. Gowned in palest blue silk, she wore as her only jewelry the pearl earrings that had once belonged to her mother. She had given Vanni's gold-and-sapphire ring back to him temporarily, so he could use it as her wedding band. Bianca's straight blond hair cascaded down her back, unconfined by net or pins. Her face was lit by an intense inner joy. Her cheeks were pink, her eyes sparkled with happiness, and her lips curved in a sweet smile as soon as she saw Vanni waiting for her.

It was not customary for brides to carry flowers, but Rosalinda had slipped out to the terrace to pluck a few blossoms from the white rosebush. There were not many roses blooming so late in the season, so only three perfect, five-petaled flowers were wrapped with silver ribbon into a simple bouquet.

"One for you, one for Vanni, one for your love," Rosalinda had whispered, putting the flowers into Bianca's hands just before she started down the aisle.

The chapel was packed with the men-at-arms and their families, for Bianca was well loved. Several of the older women wiped their eyes at the sight of her, remembering when Bianca had been a little girl.

When Bianca stood before the altar holding Vanni's hand, the contract was read by Bartolomeo, who was acting as Eleonora's representative. Afterward, all the interested parties signed it as witnesses to its legality. Then Father Tomaso said the first mass of the day and blessed the marriage of the Duke and new Duchess of Monteferro.

In the dining room after the ceremony, Valeria produced a simple feast of cold meats, bread and cheese, wine, fruit, and small, sweet cakes drenched in honey and cinnamon syrup.

The bride and groom did not linger long after receiving the good wishes of family and friends. While Eleonora was engrossed in conversation with Andrea and Francesco, Vanni drew Bianca out of the dining room and into the hall.

"Do you think anyone will follow us to your bedchamber?" Vanni asked, glancing back into the room they had just left.

"I hope not," Bianca whispered. Vanni bent to kiss her, and she could feel herself blushing. She knew what she and Vanni would soon do together. She wanted him to make love to her. The memory of what he had done beside the waterfall earlier in the summer sent a flood of warmth coursing through her veins. There was more to be learned about lovemaking than she had experienced on that day, and she trusted Vanni to give her pleasure again, this time without guilt on her part.

But the reversal of her mother's opinion about Vanni and her agreement to the marriage had been so abrupt that Bianca's thoughts were spinning. She was still trying to comprehend the wonderful fact that she and Vanni were actually married when Bartolomeo joined them.

"Be happy always." Bartolomeo kissed Bianca on each cheek. "You and Rosalinda have been like the children Valeria and I never had."

"Oh, Bartolomeo." Bianca's throat tightened. "How can anyone say thank-you for loyalty such as yours? There are no adequate words." She threw her arms around Bartolomeo and kissed him.

"Treat her kindly, Vanni." Bartolomeo's voice was rough as he handed Bianca back to her new husband.

"I will," Vanni promised, his arm about Bianca's shoulders.

"I will remain here to prevent anyone from intruding on your privacy, as merrymakers sometimes do when the wine flows too freely." Bartolomeo planted himself firmly at the foot of the stairs. "Go to your bridal bed, and I wish you joy. Go quickly, before someone comes."

With more whispered thanks, they fled up the stairs and along the corridor to Bianca's room.

"As if we were culprits," Vanni whispered. "I feel slightly wicked, running away like this."

"So do I," Bianca agreed.

While Vanni bolted the bedchamber door, Bianca went to the open window, to stand there in the cool breeze with both hands pressed to her burning cheeks. There were candles lit in a triple-branched holder. That was Valeria's doing. Bianca had seen her leave the dining room just a short time before and return with a smiling glance at the newlyweds. Bianca saw that the bedcovers had been turned back in an inviting way. She stared at the clean white sheets and began to tremble.

"My sweet Bianca, you look absolutely terrified." Vanni approached her with a smile.

"It is one thing to kiss and caress each other spontaneously, in a forest glade," Bianca said. "It is quite another matter to lock ourselves into a bedroom with all the world knowing what we are going to do." Her glance slid nervously away from the waiting bed.

"Would it help if we spread your cloak on the floor and made love upon it?" Vanni asked. Deliberately, he laid one hand on her shoulder and let a fingertip slip beneath the edge of her gown. The neckline dipped low into a wide angle that was so deep it almost met the high waistband. Within that tantalizing angle only an inch or so of the thin linen of Bianca's chemise hid the gently swelling curves of her breasts.

"On the floor?" she gasped. "No. We—I—Vanni!"

His fingertip had traveled along the neckline of her dress to the top of her chemise. While she gazed down at his hand, Vanni tested the softness of Bianca's swelling flesh, the pressure eliciting a soft cry from her. Daring more, he reached under the linen. There he found her nipple already taut and puckered and began to stroke it.

"Oh, Vanni." Bianca bit off a moan of disappointment when he removed his hand. His nimble fingers were at the laces of her dress, loosening them. Then he was pushing dress and chemise off her shoulders, baring her to the waist. She resisted the maidenly urge to cover herself, instead allowing him to gaze at her for as long as he wanted. She saw that his cheeks were flushed, and she wondered if he knew how exciting she found it to be standing in her bedchamber, half undressed, alone with a man who looked at her as if she were the very embodiment of perfection. She cried out with pleasure when Vanni lowered his head to take her breast into his mouth. By the time he released her and began to tear away the rest of her clothing, Bianca could scarcely think.

He lifted her into his arms, the blue wool of his doublet scratching her tender skin. Bianca wrapped her arms around him and kissed him while Vanni carried her to the bed, pushed aside the rose hangings, and laid her upon the sheets.

"How beautiful you are. Lovelier than I dreamed, and I have dreamed of you beside me like this on many a lonely night since first we met." Vanni's hands caressed her shoulders, lingered on her breasts, moved slowly downward to hips and thighs. He lowered his head to kiss her inner thigh. Bianca gasped, writhing at his heated touch.

Vanni smiled and began to remove his doublet. Bianca watched him with avid eyes. His linen shirt was next, Bianca following his every movement, taking in his firmly muscled chest and strong arms as they were revealed.

"You have two scars." She stared at his left forearm.

"This one is from the wound Stregone inflicted, more than a year ago," he told her, touching the raised line of skin that crossed his upper arm. His fingers moved to the second scar. "This one is older. It is the souvenir of a youthful tavern brawl. My days of drinking, wenching, and brawling are over now. And not regretted. Not for an instant." He gazed at her thoughtfully for a moment, as if gauging her emotional state, before he turned his back and quickly stripped off his hose.

He was beautifully made, his back rippling with muscles, his buttocks tight and rounded. His legs were long and straight. It was all Bianca could do to keep herself from reaching out to run her hands up his legs from ankle to buttock and along his back to his shoulders. It was what she wanted to do, so she could feel his skin, with its contrasting textures of youthful smoothness, manly hardness, and crisp, curling hair and well-trained muscle. She saw his shoulders lift as he took a deep breath. He turned around to face her, letting her see his heavy arousal.

Bianca stared. Her jaw dropped. Vanni was the most intimidating sight she had ever encountered. And yet, even so, she was fully aware of the flaring warmth in her lower limbs that rushed upward as she continued to gaze at him. That heat melted her bones and touched the very core of her body. She still wanted to caress him, but she did not dare, for she could see the problem that faced them, and she felt like crying with the frustration of her romantic hopes.

"Vanni, I do not think we can possibly fit together," she said in a sad little voice. "You are a giant, and I am a small person. Oh, I am so sorry to disappoint you."

But Vanni did not appear to be at all disappointed, nor did he seem to recognize any problem. He lay down beside Bianca and gathered her into his embrace. The sensation of his bare skin against hers was enthralling. But that huge part of him prodded at her thigh when he drew her nearer, and Bianca shuddered at the heat and the stiffness of his manhood.

"Will you trust me?" he whispered, nibbling at her ear as he spoke. His breath was warm on her neck, and his lips traced a moist trail from her ear to the base of her throat.

"I do trust you," she responded, torn between heartbroken tears and the renewed longing that surged through her when he continued to caress her as if nothing was wrong. "But the problem must be as obvious to you as it is to me."

"Bianca, please believe that I will do no serious harm to you," Vanni said.

"I believe you will try not to hurt me," she replied. "But how can you help it if you persist in what you are supposed to do?"

"I'll show you how." He raised himself a little to

look into her eyes, catching and holding her gaze. "You know I love you. If you love me, Bianca, then give yourself into my care."

She could not take her eyes from his. Her lips parted on a sigh of regret for what could not be, just as Vanni's mouth descended. On his lips she tasted wine and the honey and spices from the sweet cakes he had eaten. She tasted his tongue, hot and smooth as velvet against her own tongue. His chest rubbed against her breasts, and the motion of rough hair on her sensitive nipples sent ripples of pleasure curling downward through her being to the place that was becoming uncomfortably warm despite her trepidation. So intense were these sensations that it was a moment or two before Bianca realized where Vanni's hand was, or felt the distinct tightness as her body closed around his probing finger.

He had touched her there before, the first time they had lain together, in the forest. The result of Vanni's intimate caresses then had been an amazing, unexpected pleasure. Perhaps he would be content merely to repeat what they had done then. With an eager cry, Bianca lifted her hips, pushing against Vanni's hand, pressing toward a repetition of that earlier release.

Through the blissful sensations that pulled her inevitably toward the end she so desired, Bianca became aware of Vanni separating her legs and of the texture of his hard masculine thighs between her own.

"Vanni?" Her eyes widened, her body tensed, and her fingers clenched around his upper arms as she realized what he was about to do.

She was afraid, but she was by now so thoroughly aroused that she could not stop herself from pushing against his hand. If only he would give her the release she craved and then stop. She knew instinctively that what she wished for would not be satisfying to Vanni.

Vanni desired more. He wanted everything Bianca had to give him. She was a coward to be so squeamish. Bianca looked down at the size and rigidity of her new husband. It struck her that an engorgement so huge must be horribly painful, and she realized that for Vanni's sake, she had to do what he so desperately needed of her.

"I love you." Vanni removed his hand from her, adjusted his position, and began to stroke smoothly into her. "Say you love me, too."

"I love you, Vanni." Her heart swelled with her love for him and with the fatal sweetness of the sacrifice she was about to make in the name of that love. At that moment, she did not care if Vanni's passion tore her to pieces. Even if it were so, she would give herself to him as he desired.

Vanni pressed more deeply into her body until he met a barrier. Bianca winced, gasped, and felt herself stretching until Vanni filled her completely. Amazingly, she was unhurt. Her soft cry of surprise brought a question from him.

"Am I hurting you?"

"No, but it is an extremely tight fit," she answered.

"Wonderfully tight." He withdrew a little, then came into her again.

Bianca sighed and caught at his buttocks, to pull him closer. All her innocent fear was gone, and in its place came a renewed and intensified desire. Every movement Vanni made, every kiss he bestowed on her filled Bianca with tenderness and a growing warmth until she was simmering with longing, bubbling with the need to have Vanni deeper, and deeper still inside her. She moved, wriggling closer, opening herself to him. Vanni laughed in triumph and stroked harder and faster. Bianca groaned with pleasure and met Vanni thrust for thrust, forgetting everything but the passion they were sharing.

An uncontrollable ecstacy burst upon Bianca with such force that she was torn out of herself and hurled into a new place, where she and Vanni were made one. Her heart overflowed with joy when she heard his wild cry and knew he was in that same place with her. Her happiness was complete when he held her against his heart and tenderly caressed her, whispering words of love until her breath ceased to come in strangled sobs and her heart no longer pounded at her ribs.

"I was silly to be so afraid," she said later, when they lay at peace.

"Not silly," Vanni told her, his lips on her brow. "Only inexperienced."

"I should have known you wouldn't hurt me."

"Never." He kissed her tenderly. "I would die before causing you pain."

"Vanni? How often can husbands and wives do what we have done?"

"Why do you ask?" Vanni teased. "Would you like to do it again?"

"If it would not be too much trouble for you," Bianca said, "I would very much like to do it again, now that I know everything about the act and thus I am no longer frightened at the thought of your great size filling me. Now I know you will fit most delightfully, if very tightly."

As she spoke, Bianca was pleased to note that Vanni's size had increased suddenly and that it appeared to be undiminished since his last effort at a husband's duty. Happy to know he was ready so promptly at her suggestion, she wondered if he would object if she were to touch him there, to test with her own fingers the strength and heat that had filled her body to their mutual pleasure. But before she could ask, Vanni spoke.

"Ah, so you think you now know everything about the act, do you?" His chuckle was a dark, dangerous sound that made Bianca look away from his manly attributes and into his eyes. The passion she saw burning there nearly stopped her heart with excitement.

"You have just begun to savor the possibilities," Vanni whispered. "Come closer, love, and let me show you a new way."

Rosalinda was happy to have all the attention directed to her sister and Vanni. She was not feeling well, perhaps because she had been forced to lace herself too tightly into her best gown in order to make it fit. Seeing her mother in close conversation with Andrea and Francesco, Rosalinda seized the opportunity to leave the dining room for the coolness of the garden. Once there, she reached under her tabard to loosen the laces of her gown. Taking a long, relieved breath, she moved to the far end of the garden, away from the lights of the house and into the shadows. It was some time later when she heard a footstep on the gravel path. With a startled sound she turned, expecting to see one of the men-at-arms heading for the stable.

"I didn't know you were here," Andrea said. "I didn't mean to disturb you."

"If you wish to walk in the garden, I will leave." Keeping her face averted from him, Rosalinda brushed tears off her cheeks. When she would have returned to the house, Andrea blocked her way.

"I am glad I found you. Rosalinda, you have been avoiding me since I returned to Villa Serenita." Andrea's voice was bleak with accusation.

"I? Avoiding you?" Rosalinda cried. "It's you who

left me, to take Niccolò Stregone's body home and to fetch Father Tomaso."

"At your mother's command."

"You could have refused."

"How often have you refused to obey your mother when she ordered you to do something?" Andrea demanded. "And now she is sending me away again, in early morning."

"Is she, indeed?" Rosalinda tried to speak coldly, to convince herself as well as Andrea that she did not care whether he left Villa Serenita or stayed. She told herself it was feminine weakness on her part to long for his arms around her and his mouth on hers.

"I am to ride to Monteferro," Andrea said, "to meet there with Luca Nardi. Together we are to make the arrangements for the formal entrance of Vanni and Bianca into Monteferro."

"Bianca and Vanni," she corrected. "Bianca is the rightful duchess; therefore, her name should come first."

"You sound just like your mother," Andrea said, adding, "Two months ago, when she sent me away from Villa Serenita with Vanni and Francesco, you agreed with your mother and rejected my proposal. I told you then that I would come back for you. Here I am, Rosalinda."

"To collect your booty?" Rosalinda asked.

"There is no further obstacle to our marriage," Andrea said in a perfectly reasonable tone.

"No obstacle whatsoever," Rosalinda said, speaking with as much sarcasm as she could manage when she felt like bursting into tears over Andrea's lack of romantic fervor, "except your prospective bride's distaste for a coldy arranged marriage made for political motives."

"Are you refusing me?" he asked.

She could hear the injured manly pride in his voice. But what of her own pride? If Andrea loved her, why didn't he take her into his arms and kiss her and tell her so? Why didn't he put all of her questions and doubts to rest with words of love instead of citing logical, masculine reasons why they should marry?

She wondered if she had been mistaken in him from the beginning. He had known all along who she was, for he had recognized her father's portrait in the sitting room almost as soon as he arrived at Villa Serenita. He had not hesitated to take her virginity when she had gone to his room late at night. And he had admitted to her mother during that infamous dinner party on the terrace that he had taken advantage of Eleonora's plan for Monteferro for his own reasons, to put himself into power in Aullia. These were the acts of an accomplished schemer, not a lover.

Rosalinda decided she could not tell Andrea she was carrying his child, not until she was certain what his true motives were. If, as she was beginning to suspect from his cool manner toward her, he did not feel any tenderness for her, then she could never tell him and she must continue to reject his proposal. She could imagine no sadder fate than to marry a man whom she loved deeply and passionately, who did not love her. Such men took mistresses and their wives were miserably unhappy. Rosalinda knew as much from her mother's descriptions of court life, and she also knew that she could never learn to live with such deception.

Rosalinda's unhappy ruminations were interrupted by a flood of candlelight onto the terrace. The sitting room door was wide open, and Eleonora stood silhouetted on the terrace.

"Andrea, I suggest that you begin preparations for

your ride to Monteferro,'' Eleonora called. ''Rosalinda, is that you? What are you doing outside at this hour? It is almost dawn. Come inside at once.''

''You haven't answered me, Rosalinda,'' Andrea said.

''Rosalinda!'' Eleonora exclaimed.

''Rosalinda, wait!'' Andrea reached for her hand, but Rosalinda eluded him and started toward the terrace.

''Answer me, Rosalinda,'' Andrea demanded. His handsome face showed hard and set in the light streaming from the sitting room door, and his eyes held a fiery gleam that could only be the anger of a man thwarted in what he wanted.

''You cannot command me, Andrea,'' Rosalinda said, pausing in her flight from him. ''I have not agreed to become your possession. If you want something of me, you must ask politely.'' With that, she ran up the steps to the terrace, where Eleonora awaited her.

Chapter Twenty-four

When the group of fifteen or so travelers from Villa Serenita was a short distance away from Monteferro, Andrea appeared, riding from the city with Luca Nardi. They were accompanied by a single retainer, who held aloft the banner of the Duke of Aullia, three gold stars arranged in a triangle on a red ground. Seeing Andrea, Rosalinda pulled hard on the reins of her horse, bringing the animal to a halt, while the rest of the party continued to move forward around her as if she were a rock in the middle of a steadily flowing stream.

Andrea was garbed in deep red doublet and hose. His matching, flat-brimmed hat sported a bright blue feather tucked into the band at the crown. Luca Nardi was more soberly clothed in his usual dark blue banker's robe.

Still concealed among her companions, who by now had also stopped, Rosalinda watched Andrea and Vanni laughing together. How handsome the brothers were, and how similar their features. Yet their personalities were clearly imprinted on their faces, and anyone who knew them could easily tell them apart. Vanni was the more lighthearted twin, while Andrea's serious nature showed not only in his face, but in the way he carried himself. Loving him, longing for him to declare that he loved her in return, Rosalinda waited, praying that Andrea would acknowledge her presence, hoping he would come to her.

Having greeted his brother and kissed Bianca, Andrea moved on to Eleonora and to Bartolomeo and Valeria, all of whom accepted his courtly salutations with a grave courtesy to match Andrea's own. Then it was on to Francesco for a warmer, more comradely handclasp. Turning from his old friend, Andrea looked around until his eyes met Rosalinda's. She held her breath. There were words he could say that would tell her what she wanted to hear without revealing to others what emotions lay within his heart.

"Madonna." With a cool politeness that bordered on complete indifference, Andrea inclined his head in lordly acceptance of her presence. "You look well."

"Thank you, my lord duke. I am in excellent health. As you also appear to be." Was this to be the extent of their conversation? After the way they had parted, Rosalinda did not expect him to pull her off her horse and into his embrace, but she had hoped for some sign of emotion in his first words to her. How could she love him so dearly, and he be unaware of what she was feeling? But was he really unaware of her? Impulsively, she decided to do something to reach him, to make him respond to her.

"Andrea." She put out her gloved hand to catch at his sleeve. "I am sorry for the quarrel we had at our last meeting. I wish you would listen to my explanation of why I was so difficult."

"I would be happy to hear anything you wish to say to me, Madonna Rosalinda, but at the moment my first duty is to my brother, and to your sister. This is their day, after all, and other concerns must wait. Perhaps later." The smile he gave her was, to Rosalinda's eyes, blatantly false.

"Of course, my lord." Aware of the way in which the others in their group were watching and listening to this exchange of words, Rosalinda tried to keep the disappointment out of her voice, tried to sound as calm and icy cold as she possibly could, to show all of them, as well as Andrea, that she did not care if he chose to be rude to her.

"I do understand. Don't let me detain you from your very important duties. Ah, Luca, how wonderful to see you again." Rosalinda extended her hand to Luca Nardi. Though she bestowed her brightest smile upon the banker and appeared to be giving him her full attention, she was aware of the long, hard stare Andrea sent her way before he turned his horse and rode back to the head of the procession.

"Here come the others. Andrea and I outdistanced them," Luca said to Rosalinda. He pointed along the road in the direction of Monteferro, to a troop of horsemen that was galloping toward Vanni's company.

"That," explained Luca, "is a delegation of city officials, coming to extend their formal greetings to Vanni and Bianca. The festivities are about to begin. Earlier today I feared it would rain, but it appears that heaven is blessing your family's return to Monteferro." Luca glanced upward, to the bright and cloudless sky.

The officials who had ridden out to meet them were all richly dressed and jeweled, as were the men and women from Villa Serenita. It was a dazzling cavalcade that formed an hour or so later under the direction of

Luca Nardi. At the head of this splendid procession, the Duke of Monteferro and his duchess entered their city, riding side by side through the main gate and along the broad thoroughfare to the piazza and the cathedral.

Every building along the way was hung with brilliant banners, their designs combining the gold Farisi eagle on a green background with the Sotani emblem of three stars on a red ground. Garlands of flowers stretched across the streets just above the riders' heads, and every citizen had turned out to cheer the handsome young duke and his beautiful lady. Befitting the great occasion, the service held in the cathedral was appropriately long and solemn, and the reception that followed at the ducal palace was longer still.

"How strange it is to return after so many years," Bianca whispered to Rosalinda shortly after they entered the great reception room. "It appears very different from the room I recall on the last occasion when I saw it."

"And different from the room our mother described to us," Rosalinda added. "I am sure it has been redecorated at least twice since you were last in it. Bianca, does it cause you pain to be here?"

"I expected to be disturbed, but I am not," Bianca said. "The memory of our father's death will always sadden me, but I do believe he would rejoice to see us all here today."

"Indeed, he would," said Eleonora, who had overheard this conversation. "This is the life for which I trained you, Bianca. Go now to stand beside your husband while you greet the dignitaries." She watched with a satisfied smile as Bianca crossed the room to where Vanni waited for her.

Eleonora, who had been welcomed back to Monteferro like a dowager queen returning to her kingdom in triumph, looked happier than Rosalinda could remember ever seeing her, and Bianca was moving through her tedious duties with grace and effortless tact. But Rosalinda was soon tired. The hall where the official banquet was held after the reception was hot, with no breeze to alleviate the effects of too many heavy perfumes. The food was over-rich and there was too much of it. Rosalinda began to fear the long parade of courses would never end.

Whenever she and Andrea had come face to face during the interminable day, he had spoken only the shortest, most formal words to her and he appeared to be distracted. Knowing from what Luca Nardi had told her that Andrea had taken the responsibility for the success of the day's ceremonies on his own shoulders, Rosalinda tried to be understanding. Still, she wished he would spare a few moments for her, to make her feel personally welcomed to the palace where she was now to live and to promise there would soon be time for them to hold a private conversation. That he did not only convinced her of his lack of any true interest in her.

The sight of Andrea engaged in laughing conversation with a lovely—and slender—young woman only increased Rosalinda's distress. By the time evening arrived, she was more convinced than ever that the fear she had once voiced to Bianca was true. Andrea had played with her affections and his only concern with her now lay in the advantage that a cold-hearted political alliance would bring him. That being so, if a more brilliant marriage was offered by a powerful family, Andrea would turn from Rosalinda without a second thought.

When, at last, well after midnight, the ladies assigned to attend Rosalinda had formally escorted her to her bedchamber, when she had sent all of them away, insisting to their scandalized shock that she wanted to be left alone, she still could find no peace from the worries that plagued her. She had ordered her ladies to open the windows before they left her. The noises of a busy city were jarring to one who was accustomed to the quiet country. When Rosalinda went to the window to look out, she could not see the mountains, but only the lights of Monteferro. Never in her life had she felt so lost, or so lonely.

Nor did the passing of time lessen Rosalinda's sense of isolation. The ensuing days brought more receptions and more long banquets, during which Andrea treated her with cool, formal respect but never spoke a word to her on any personal subject. It was Bianca who told her that Vanni and Andrea were spending many hours each day working on a treaty between Monteferro and Aullia, with Eleonora, Francesco, and Luca Nardi in attendance to offer advice.

While the men and Eleonora were thus occupied, Rosalinda and Bianca were often together, but they were always surrounded by retainers and would-be friends, and by so many people begging Bianca to use her influence with Vanni to convince him to agree to some favor, that the sisters were not free to engage in the private talks they had always taken for granted.

As the new duke's sister-in-law, who was known to be on excellent terms with him, Rosalinda was not overlooked by eager petitioners. On the afternoon when an overdressed courtier drew her aside and subjected her to a long, whining speech imploring her to talk to Vanni about giving him an office at court, Rosalinda had had enough. She broke away from the courtier, leaving him to stare after her in astonishment at her brusqueness.

Making her way through the press of people in the

duchess's reception room, Rosalinda caught Bianca by one hand, pulling her out of the group surrounding her. Rosalinda did not stop until she and Bianca were standing in a niche beside a window where, Rosalinda hoped, they could have a moment of privacy.

"Go away. Leave us!" she snapped at a lady who stuck by Bianca's side. "I want to talk to my sister alone.

"I am stifled here," Rosalinda said, turning to Bianca. "I can't breathe for all the people. It is too noisy. I cannot see the mountains." She paused, trying to control the trembling of her lower lip.

"It is a great change from our former life," Bianca agreed. "I am sure you will grow used to it, in time."

"Never! I'll die if I stay here. I am going home—to my real home, to Villa Serenita."

"You can't do that," Bianca protested.

"I am telling you so you won't worry about me or wonder where I am." Rosalinda was not going to argue about her decision. Her mind was made up and she would not change it. "I don't think anyone else will miss me. They are all so busy, they won't even notice I have gone. Even you are occupied every hour of the day. And at night you have Vanni to talk to, though even then you don't have any real privacy. Everyone at court gossips about the fact that Vanni spends every night with you."

"A duchess does live a remarkably public life," Bianca said. "And I do have more duties than I expected."

"That's just it," Rosalinda said. "I have nothing useful to do here. At Villa Serenita, I can oversee the harvest and direct the women in putting aside food for the winter. Since Bartolomeo and Valeria have come to Monteferro with Mother, I can take their places at home. As for Mother, she is so preoccupied with statecraft, and with Francesco, that she hasn't even noticed that I am—that I—'' Rosalinda bit back tears. While her sister watched her with worried eyes, Rosalinda lifted her head and tried to give the appearance of restored composure.

''Oh, my dearest, I did not realize just how unhappy you have been,'' Bianca whispered. ''Perhaps if you and Andrea could settle matters between you—''

''He does not love me,'' Rosalinda interrupted in a fierce whisper. ''If he did, he would not be so polite and distant when we meet. He would talk to me and listen to what I have to say. He would put his arms around me and kiss me and hold me close. And then, when he did caress me, he would *know* why I have been so difficult and unhappy.''

''I am not sure about that,'' said Bianca. ''I have only been married for a little more than three weeks, yet already I understand that men must be *told,* and then told again, the simplest truths that women understand by intuition. Vanni is the most considerate of husbands, and I love him with all my heart, but on several occasions I have been forced to a most unladylike directness in dealing with him. And to unflinching persistance when he does not understand at once. Of course, when he does comprehend my exact desire, he always gives me what I want,'' Bianca finished with a chuckle and a slight blush.

''I cannot simply walk up to Andrea and make an announcement,'' Rosalinda said. ''He is constantly surrounded by people. Just as you are. Here comes a man now, who looks eager to interrupt our conversation.''

''Madonna Bianca.'' The approaching courtier bowed low. ''The duke has asked me to inform you that the representatives of Venice are arriving at the palace gate. The duke requests your presence in the large audience chamber when he greets the delegation.''

''I will be there immediately. You may go, Vincenzo,'' Bianca said in a firm voice when the man did not move. ''I will first finish my conversation with my sister.''

''As you wish, madonna.'' With a frowning glance at Rosalinda, the man backed away.

''I am keeping you from your duties,'' Rosalinda said.

''Don't worry. It will do the Venetians good to have to wait for a while. Everyone else caters to their wishes. We will not, and thus we will gain their respect.''

''You make a remarkable duchess. Mother's stern training seems to be serving you well.'' Rosalinda smiled, then became serious again. ''Don't try to stop me from leaving, Bianca. I am going to take with me Lorenzo and Maria who, according to Maria, are both eager to go home, and one other man-at-arms who is also homesick. We will depart in early morning.''

''I don't think you should be alone at Villa Serenita,'' Bianca objected.

''I won't be alone. Most of our men-at-arms and their families are still living there. Like me, they have no desire for city life.''

''Vanni says the ducal palace at Aullia is set in a large and very beautiful garden,'' Bianca remarked with studied casualness.

''I don't care if it is set in Paradise!'' Rosalinda exclaimed. ''I have no intention of going to Aullia, nor will I marry a man who regards me as nothing more than the prize for his military accomplishments, and who thinks he can ignore me whenever he pleases. His actions prove that Andrea does not love me.''

''I think you are wrong, Rosalinda. I can see you are

overwrought, and I wish you would change your mind about leaving."

"I won't."

"My dearest, you are more like our mother than you realize," Bianca said. "You are every bit as stubborn as she is. Once an idea has fixed itself in your mind, you will not let it go. You may be as wrong about Andrea as Mother was about Andrea's father. What will you do if, like Mother, it takes fifteen long years for you to learn the truth? And consider this, Rosalinda: Andrea will want to produce an heir. Whether it is you or another lady, he will marry soon."

"Vanni's man is still waiting for you, Bianca. Your husband requires your presence." Rosalinda tried not to let Bianca see how that last verbal thrust had hurt her, and all the more because it was true. Andrea would have to marry before long. Rosalinda recalled the ache in her heart when she had observed him talking and laughing with a pretty woman. The thought of Andrea naked and clasped in another woman's embrace nearly brought Rosalinda to her knees. But she would not be deterred from the course she had set for herself. If Andrea did not love her as she wanted to be loved, then she would live the rest of her life at Villa Serenita and never see him again. Bianca had insisted on a declaration of passionate love from Vanni before agreeing to wed him. Rosalinda would settle for no less.

"Good-bye, Bianca," Rosalinda said. "Will you come to me when my baby is born?"

"Of course I will." Bianca's blue eyes were too bright, her smile too obviously forced as she fought against the tears she would not shed in public, before the courtiers. "I promised to be with you when your time comes, and I will keep my promise. The Duke and Duchess of Monteferro will spend Christmastide and

Epiphany at Villa Serenita, enjoying a private celebration with their families. And if you still wish it when that time comes, I will swear Vanni to secrecy."

"Thank you. I love you, dearest sister," Rosalinda whispered.

Bianca kissed Rosalinda lightly, as if they were parting for no more than the afternoon and evening, and then she went away with Vanni's waiting courtier.

"Where is she?" Andrea strode into Bianca's private reception room like a warrior charging into battle, scattering ladies in waiting, serving women, and astonished male courtiers to left and right.

"Where is who, my lord?" Bianca faced him calmly, hands folded in tranquil grace at the high waist of her dark blue silk gown. Pearls were wound through the braids piled high on her head, more pearls hung from her earlobes, and a heavy gold cross served as the pendant on her pearl necklace. With the composure of a woman secure in her position, Bianca regarded the angry man before her as if he were a peculiar but fascinating animal.

"Where is Rosalinda?" Andrea demanded.

"Can't you find her?" Bianca smiled at him, hoping to infuriate him still more. If Andrea became angry enough, he might begin to comprehend just how deeply he cared for Rosalinda, and how badly he had neglected her over the past few weeks. It was clear to Bianca that her brother-in-law needed to admit to himself that he loved her sister with all the fire and passion of which the Sotani brothers were capable. Only then would Andrea be able to convince Rosalinda of his love.

"You know I can't find her," Andrea said. "No one has seen her for three days."

"And you are only now discovering that she is missing?'' *Poor, foolish man,* Bianca thought with the wisdom of a new and well-loved wife. *I can see that I will have to take a hand in this affair, whether Rosalinda wants me to or not. I do believe she will thank me for it in the end.*

''What is this unseemly noise about?'' Eleonora had been standing near a long window, talking to a group of older women whom she knew from her own days as duchess. Now she left her friends to join Bianca and Andrea. Stopping next to her daughter, she took up a pose identical to Bianca's, hands folded at her waist, face calm and expressionless.

''Do either of you know where Rosalinda is?'' Andrea felt like strangling both Bianca and Eleonora out of sheer impatience with their undisturbed composure. They had not been so devoid of emotion while they lived at Villa Serenita. It occurred to him that they were deliberately hiding their feelings from him. He glared at Eleonora. ''You must know where your daughter is.''

''I do confess, I have been greatly preoccupied in recent days, and thus I have not paid much attention to Rosalinda. It is a lapse for which Bianca has rightly chided me. As I now chide you, Andrea.'' Eleonora assumed a sweet smile to match the one on her daughter's face. ''Bianca tells me that Rosalinda has decided to go into retirement.''

''Retirement?'' Andrea almost shouted the word. ''Do you mean, she has entered a convent?''

''Hardly,'' Bianca said, meeting the fury in Andrea's eyes with an expression of cold annoyance. Deliberately, she let Andrea wait through a few agonizing heartbeats before she divulged any more information. ''Rosalinda found court life tedious. She has returned to Villa Serenita.''

"What?" Andrea exclaimed. "Why would she do such a thing?"

"I have just told you why," Bianca said.

Andrea was bewildered by Bianca's manner toward him. This was not her usual gentle, yet slightly reserved way of treating those whom she met in a public setting. Bianca did not raise her voice to him, nor did her sweet, smiling expression change, yet to Andrea she conveyed the distinct impression that she did not approve of him. Bianca did not disapprove of Rosalinda for foolishly running away before Andrea could find an appropriate time to talk to her and insist on an answer to his proposal. No, Bianca's disapproval was directed at *him*.

"Thank you for the information, Madonna Bianca." With a bow so brief it was almost an insult, Andrea turned to leave.

"Andrea!" Bianca's voice was so commanding that for an instant Andrea imagined it was her mother who had spoken. But Eleonora remained silent and perfectly still at her daughter's side. It was Bianca whose brows were drawn together in a frown.

"Madonna?" Andrea paused in mid-step, marveling at the transformation in his formerly timid sister-in-law. Bianca was fully aware of her power and very beautiful in her newfound confidence. Andrea could understand why Vanni was half mad with love for her.

"I never thought you were a stupid man, Andrea," Bianca said. "Do not disappoint me by acting the fool now."

"What do you mean?" Keeping his eyes locked on hers, Andrea took a step back toward Bianca. "What is it I should know, that you haven't told me?"

"You will have to ask Rosalinda about that," Bianca said, "after you have told her everything that is in your heart."

"Rosalinda knows what is in my heart," Andrea said.

"Do you really think so?" Bianca said no more. She just looked at Andrea with that strange little smile on her lips until he bowed again, more properly this time, and left the room.

"How very difficult it is to remain here and do nothing," Eleonora said, looking after him.

"I pray that I have done the right thing," Bianca said. "And that Rosalinda will forgive me."

"I am glad you confided in me," Eleonora murmured. "If you had not, I would be even more concerned over Rosalinda's future than I am."

As he ran down the stairs leading to the palace courtyard, Andrea's mind was in turmoil. Just an hour before his appearance in Bianca's reception room, he and Vanni had agreed on the final details of the treaty between Monteferro and Aullia, which the brothers believed would ensure peaceful relations between their cities so long as the Sotani family ruled both places. On the advice of Luca Nardi, taxes were to be lowered as soon as the treaty was signed.

"This one paragraph," Luca had promised, "will result in the devotion to their respective dukes of businessmen, bankers, and ordinary folk alike. No one wants to pay taxes, though most men will pay them if they see some benefit to themselves in doing so. During the years of Marco Guidi's rule, the people of Monteferro were taxed into near bankruptcy and, during the year since your father's death, a similar process was begun in Aullia. Men who once feared what the future would bring will be pleased by a decrease in taxes. I need not remind you, my lords, that contented citizens do not plot to overthrow their governments."

"Unless there is a Niccolò Stregone lurking about to

drip venom into the thoughts of some too-willing man," Andrea had noted.

"We will take care that a creature like Stregone never again infests either city," Vanni had said with firm assurance.

With the terms agreed upon, the treaty was turned over to the secretaries, who would make several neat and careful copies of it. Until those copies were completed and ready for signing, Andrea had little to do. For the first time since leaving Villa Serenita, he was not concerned with arrangements for his brother's arrival at Monteferro or with matters of state. Now, at last, he was free to seek out Rosalinda, to overcome any lingering objections she might have and convince her to accept his proposal of marriage.

Because she was Eleonora's daughter, Andrea had expected Rosalinda to understand why he had been so busy of late, and why he had taken care not to single her out for special attention. Courts were veritable jungles of gossip and intrigue, and many of the retainers and officials at Vanni's court were folk who had once been loyal—or who had claimed to be loyal—to Marco Guidi. In such surroundings, it was best to walk carefully until true fidelity could be separated from devious intentions. Andrea had no wish to place Rosalinda in a difficult situation by subjecting her to gossip. He was sure she would realize all of this without an explanation from him.

He had not expected to discover that she was gone. Nor had he expected the cool disdain he encountered in Bianca's manner. Eleonora's coldness was easier for Andrea to comprehend. It would take Eleonora some time to forgive him for his initial deceit in not revealing his identity to her when he first arrived at Villa Serenita. But Bianca had always been friendly toward him, and her present attitude gave Andrea serious pause. The sisters had obviously discussed his reticent conduct toward Rosalinda. It seemed that Rosalinda was not as understanding as he had thought she would be, and she had told her sister so. The sooner he spoke with Rosalinda, the better.

Within an hour of his interview with Bianca and Eleonora, Andrea was on the road to Villa Serenita. He took with him only two men-at-arms, and he spared neither men nor horses in his eagerness to reach the villa.

Chapter Twenty-five

"My lord duke, wait." Lorenzo tried to prevent Andrea from leaving the stable yard. "Maria says that Rosalinda is very angry with you. I think you should let me announce your arrival at Villa Serenita and then allow Rosalinda to decide if she wants to see you."

"It is not your place to announce me," Andrea reminded his former comrade of the practice yard. "You are a man-at-arms, not a damned majordomo."

"Do not scoff at Bartolomeo's position, my lord. If he were here, he would tell you what I have just said. Andrea, stop!" Lorenzo shouted, forgetting the difference in their social positions in his agitation as Andrea pushed past him and headed for the garden. "Come back here!"

"I have ridden until I am sore and weary." Andrea flung the words over his shoulder. "Having finally reached the villa, I will not stop until I see Rosalinda."

''She may not want to see you. My lord duke, please wait.''

Rosalinda was in the garden, where she was cutting herbs to be hung in the stillroom to dry. Turning around in surprise at the sound of Lorenzo's raised voice, she looked toward the garden entrance, still holding a sprig of lavender in one hand and a pair of shears in the other. The handle of a flat basket filled with herbs was slung over her left arm, and her face was shaded by her mother's old, broad-brimmed hat. She went very still when she saw who was the object of Lorenzo's futile orders to halt.

''I am sorry, Rosalinda,'' Lorenzo called. ''He would not listen to me.''

''It's all right, Lorenzo. I will deal with this intruder.'' Rosalinda eyed Andrea warily as he approached her. When she spoke to him, her voice dripped icy scorn. ''How dare you come here to annoy me? And how dared Bianca tell you where I had gone? It was my sister who sent you after me, wasn't it?''

''Bianca understands, as you clearly do not, what the demands of high office are,'' Andrea said. He moved closer to her on the gravel path, until Rosalinda put up her right hand to stop him. Since she still held the shears in a tight grasp, Andrea came to a halt at arm's length from her. It was not the shears alone that gave him pause. There was something different about Rosalinda. Beneath the shadow cast by the brim of the straw hat, her eyes were hard and her mouth was pulled into a tight, angry line. Her gray gown flowed loosely around her, making her look as if she had gained weight, yet her face was gaunt. Andrea stared at her, puzzled by her altered appearance.

''If your duties are so onerous, my lord duke,'' Rosalinda said, ''then you ought to have stayed in Monteferro to fulfill them. Or, alternatively, you might go home to Aullia to see to your affairs there."

"I am not leaving Villa Serenita until you and I have settled this ridiculous dispute that you seem to think lies between us," Andrea said.

"Ridiculous?" Rosalinda took a menacing step toward him. "You colossal knave! You thick-witted, uncaring brute!"

"The last time we quarreled in this same spot," Andrea said, trying his best to remain calm in the face of Rosalinda's rising anger, "your complaint against me had something to do with our fathers. Since that night, I believe you have also felt that I have been neglecting you."

"You ignored me every day that I was in Monteferro," she cried. "You have made it clear that you want nothing more to do with me. Day after day, I watched you flirting with other women, laughing and talking, sitting with them at those interminable banquets. While I grow heavy and—"

"Flirting?" Andrea interrupted, laughing at her. "Rosalinda, I was trying to protect you from gossip. You have no experience of courtly life and, therefore, no idea just how nasty courtiers can be once their curiosity is aroused. If anyone at Monteferro thought that you and I—"

"There is no need for you to protect me." It was Rosalinda's turn to interrupt and she did so by brandishing the shears at him as if to prove her point. "I am well able to protect myself."

"Rosalinda, I came here to ask you again to marry me."

"No!" she yelled at him. "Leave me alone, Andrea. You bedded me, you had what you wanted from me, and now you no longer care about me. Go away, before

I call out the men-at-arms to throw you off this property.''

Andrea glanced from his furious love to Lorenzo, who had followed him into the garden and remained there, perhaps with the notion of coming to Rosalinda's aid if she should need a champion. Having overheard Rosalinda's last, loudly spoken words, Lorenzo was wearing a scandalized expression. A motion from Rosalinda brought Andrea's attention back to her. She had taken a step away from him and toward the house.

''I have not begun to have all I want from you,'' Andrea told her. ''Would it resolve your doubts on that subject if I bedded you again?'' With a swift movement that gave Rosalinda no hint of what he was planning to do, Andrea grabbed the shears from her and tossed them onto the ground. An instant later, he swooped Rosalinda into his arms. The basket of herbs landed beside the shears, scattering fragrant greenery across the garden path.

Rosalinda fought him, but Andrea was determined to prove to her how much he wanted her. He would take her to her bedchamber and make passionate love to her. When she lay quivering with passion beneath him, perhaps she would believe that he wanted to marry her because he loved her.

But when he reached the terrace steps, Lorenzo was there before him, blocking his way. Andrea hesitated for a moment. As if she sensed a chance to escape from his unwanted embrace, Rosalinda continued to fight, kicking and squirming while Andrea tried to deal with the man-at-arms.

''I will not hurt her,'' Andrea promised Lorenzo. ''But I do not think there is any other way to make this stubborn girl listen to me. I do assure you, my intentions are completely honorable.''

''Lorenzo, help me!'' Rosalinda hit out at Andrea with both fists at once. He almost dropped her, but then he tightened his hold, securing her against his chest.

''Surely, Lorenzo, you have quarreled with Maria from time to time,'' Andrea said.

''That I have.'' Lorenzo's searching gaze moved from Rosalinda's flailing fists and angry face to Andrea's calmer expression. He moved aside, letting Andrea proceed toward the terrace and the house.

''Lorenzo, you traitor!'' Rosalinda screamed over Andrea's shoulder.

''She will thank you for this tomorrow, Lorenzo.'' On those words, Andrea kicked open the sitting room door. Once inside, he set Rosalinda on her feet.

She was a remarkably lovely sight. During her struggles, the hat had slipped to the back of her neck, where it hung from the ribbons tied beneath her chin. Her glorious hair was loosened from its single braid, tiny curls forming a dark, shiny halo around her head. Rosalinda's lips trembled, and her eyes were filled with angry tears.

Andrea reached out to untie the hat ribbons. She slapped his hand away.

''Don't touch me!'' she cried.

''I can see in your eyes that you want me as much as I want you,'' he said. ''Why won't you admit what you are feeling?''

''Because you don't love me. You used me, Andrea. You did not tell me the truth about yourself until Vanni said too much and you were forced to admit who you are. Worst of all, you made a bargain with my mother that treated me like a piece of merchandise.''

''I have explained to you that at the time, I was a fortuneless exile.'' Andrea spoke with all the patience he could muster, given his rising passion. Holding Rosalinda in his arms had almost undone him. He was not sure how much longer he could restrain himself. "That bargain with your mother was the only hope I had of making you mine."

"It was the only hope you had of getting your dukedom back," she said with quiet certainty. "If you had made the bargain for my sake, you would have told me about it. But you didn't." On that, she walked out of the room.

"You foolish little—" Andrea took a deep breath, trying to control himself while knowing his self-control was near its end. He followed Rosalinda into the hall, catching up with her just as she reached the stairs that led upward to her bedchamber. Again he lifted her into his arms. This time, she did not fight him, not until they were safely away from the steps and he was shouldering open the door to her room.

Maria was there, putting away some clothing. With Rosalinda's old russet wool doublet in her hands, Maria gaped at Andrea, and at the woman who was once more pounding at his shoulders with clenched fists.

"Maria, do something!" Rosalinda cried. "This barbarian brute won't put me down."

"Maria," Andrea told the maid, "go and find Lorenzo. He will answer your questions."

"But my lord," Maria gasped, "what are you going to do to Rosalinda?"

"I am going to make love to her," Andrea responded, heading for the bed. "Right now. This instant. It's up to you whether you want to stay and watch us or not."

"Oh!" Rosalinda's screech of outrage was punctuated by the sound of her bedroom door closing as Maria fled the room. "Andrea, how could you?"

"Sometimes, bears are forced to resort to desperate measures," Andrea said.

Whatever Rosalinda might have said in response was stopped by Andrea's mouth on hers. She fought him, but not for long. Her lips softened under his, and the fists that had been pounding at his chest unclenched until her hands were flat against his shoulders.

"Sometimes," Andrea murmured a short time later, "bears themselves become desperate when their desire is thwarted for too long."

"I can't let you do this," Rosalinda wept. "I won't." But her head fell back, allowing him free access to her throat and to the tender area just above the neckline of her gown. Andrea's arms tightened around her. She shuddered in mounting pleasure.

"I knew you wanted me. I was sure you wouldn't resist for long." Andrea's voice was filled with the triumph he felt at her eager response to what he was doing.

"Yes, you are very sure of yourself, aren't you, Andrea? Your self-confidence may well be your greatest fault." Her mood swung from desire back to rage so swiftly that Andrea released her in surprise when she grabbed his hair and began to pull it. She was now standing in front of him, both hands wound into his thick hair, pulling hard. Her eyes were blazing with anger, and with another violent passion that Andrea fully understood because it matched his own need.

Reacting out of that need, he shoved her on both shoulders, not pushing hard, but just firmly enough to make her sit down on the foot of her bed. He caught her face between his hands and kissed her, letting her feel his desire, letting his tongue move slowly but forcefully into her mouth.

The fingers at his scalp relaxed. Her emotions already aroused, Rosalinda began to respond to his renewed kisses, as he had been sure she would. But Andrea was faced with a serious problem. His own desire had reached a crucial point. He simply could not wait any longer. With a trembling hand he reached down to pull her skirts up to her hips. Her thighs were soft and warm when he spread them so he could stand closer to her, and the place between them was moist and ready when Andrea touched her there. He groaned, suddenly frozen with uncontrollable need, afraid to move or to continue caressing her.

"Oh, Andrea." Rosalinda seemed to recognize how desperate his condition was. Her hands worked at his clothing, freeing him, pulling him toward her. "I don't care what happens later, or what your real feelings are. I'm tired of fighting what I want. I want *you.* I want you now. Come to me, Andrea."

Her legs still dangling over the edge, she fell backward on the bed. Immediately, Andrea answered her invitation. With an ecstatic moan, he plunged into her heated softness. Braced on rigid arms above her, he watched as rapture overtook Rosalinda. Her eyelids fluttered closed, her lips parted on a sigh, her cheeks were flushed, and her every feature was softened by sweet desire. Andrea barely had time to think how beautiful she was before his own rampant desire overcame him. In an uncontrolable response to the way her body was tightening around him in repeated ripples of fulfillment, Andrea moved, stroking into her just once. A gust of fierce heat shook him and he exploded, pouring himself into Rosalinda, filling her and completing himself in an act of possession and love.

It took a few minutes for him to realize that he was still on his feet, braced over Rosalinda, with her legs wrapped around him. She lay on the bed, watching him with an expression that was definitely softer and far more tender than the coldness with which she had first greeted him in the garden. It occurred to Andrea that there was much to be said for untrammeled sexual desire, especially when the woman was as eager as Rosalinda had been.

Her eagerness meant that, whatever she said on the subject, her tender feelings for him were unchanged. Rosalinda would never give herself to a man she did not love. Surely, the pleasure they had just shared would prove to her that he loved her, too. Certain that any remaining problems between them could easily be resolved, Andrea let himself collapse beside her on the bed.

"We never even removed our clothes," he said, running a gentle finger along her chin. With equal gentleness he turned her face toward his. "I love you, Rosalinda. How could you have doubted it?"

"I have told you why. And you have never said that you love me, until now." A lone tear trickled down her cheek. Andrea kissed it away.

"Did you really expect me to know what was in your mind?" she asked. "If you did, then you have been a bigger fool than I."

Stung by the accuracy of her words, Andrea did not bother to answer her. Instead, he put his mouth on hers. When she did not fight him, he slowly deepened the kiss. It had, after all, been more than three months since they had lain together in an alpine meadow, and Andrea was a young and vigorous man. Rolling over, he pinned her upper body beneath his while he began to inch her skirts upward. He would pull the loose dress off over her head so he could touch and caress her wherever he wanted. He would prove to her how much he loved her, prove it beyond any question. Before Rosalinda left her bedchamber, she would know that Andrea was hers completely. And she would know that she was his.

She caught at his hand as he tugged on her skirt and petticoat, stopping him for a long moment while she gazed into his eyes. Then, with a little sigh of surrender, she took her hand away. Andrea pushed her clothing to her waist . . . and stopped, staring at her exposed body in disbelief.

For a long time, he could say nothing. He could only gape at the rounded abdomen beneath which his child lay. He knew Rosalinda well enough to be absolutely certain the child she carried was his.

"When I saw you standing in the garden in this loose dress, you did look as if you had gained weight," he said when he was finally able to speak. "But your face is so thin that I thought it was an illusion, because the dress has no waistline. And just a few minutes ago, I imagined your bunched-up dress and petticoat caused the bulge I noticed." Passion forgotten for the moment, Andrea drew apart from her, watching her reaction to his growing rage at her deception.

"You weren't going to tell me about this miraculous secret, were you?" he said in an accusing tone. "Yet you were angry with me for not revealing my family name to strangers, at a time when I was in danger of my life? For shame, Rosalinda! What is fair for you ought to be fair for me, too! How dare you complain of my actions?"

"I had good reason for what I did," she declared. Seeing the outraged expression on his face, she added, "It seemed like a good reason to me."

"Did it?" Andrea's voice was dangerously smooth. "And what reason was that, Rosalinda?"

"I was determined not to be forced into marriage with a man who did not love me. Bianca and I once made a vow that we would insist upon love from our prospective husbands."

"I do love you."

"But you have never said it until today," she responded.

Andrea longed to scold her, to tell her how wrong she had been to doubt him. But, looking deep into Rosalinda's troubled, frightened eyes, he knew he would have to rein in his righteous anger over her actions or else chance losing her forever. Perhaps, from Rosalinda's point of view, she had just cause to wonder if he was using her for his own selfish ends. With that thought in mind, Andrea modulated his voice and tried to sound more sympathetic than he actually felt.

"This is why you ran away from Monteferro, isn't it? This is a secret that cannot remain hidden much longer, unless you disappear into these mountains, to this place where no one will reveal what you do not want known.

"Do you hate me so much that you would keep my own child from me?" he asked, some of his anger seeping through his rigid control. "How could you betray our love, and imperil our child's future, by not telling me about this?"

"I did it because I will not marry a man who does not love me," she said with a stubborn set to her mouth and chin.

"How many times do I have to say it? God in heaven, woman, when will you believe me?" Despite his good intentions, Andrea's patience slipped and his voice rose. "Since the first day I saw you on a mountain trail, while you still imagined I was a bear, you have been the only woman for me. You proved the truth of my belief when you alone were willing to help me out of a snowstorm and into the light and warmth of your home.

"Everything I have done since that winter night has

been done with the hope of proving my love for you and of making you my wife. I risked my life to make your mother's dream for Bianca a reality, in the belief that once Bianca was Duchess of Monteferro, Eleonora would permit our marriage.

"All of this I have done for you, Rosalinda, and still you do not believe I love you. So be it." Andrea withdrew his gaze from hers to look at the creamy mound of skin beneath his hand. His fingers moved on Rosalinda's abdomen in a tender caress.

"I have been wrong about you, haven't I?" Rosalinda whispered, sounding as frightened as the look in her eyes.

"Completely wrong," Andrea said, still caressing that lovely mound of flesh. "Bartolomeo claims that you greatly resemble your father, but I now have proof that deep in your soul you are every bit as stubborn as your mother. And sometimes every bit as wrong as she can be."

"Bianca said much the same thing," Rosalinda told him.

"I am sure your sister is right. She seems to be a surprisingly good judge of human nature. Which means that I shall have to reconcile myself to living with an impetuous, stubborn, difficult woman. Unless, of course, you intend to ruin the life of this babe who might one day be Duke of Aullia by refusing to marry his father before he is born. In Aullia," Andrea said sternly, "bastards cannot inherit."

"I did worry about that detail," Rosalinda said.

"Ah, I see. To add to all your other faults, you are now confessing a taste for gambling. Because you lacked faith in me, you put our child's future at risk." He kept his voice stern, but there was a growing warmth in Andrea's heart.

"I am sorry," she said. "I had to be certain of your love. I will marry you, Andrea."

"Will you?" He longed to take her into his arms again, but before he did, there were concessions he was determined to wring from this willful, fiercely independent, and altogether enchanting woman he loved. "You must understand, Rosalinda, that from time to time I will be preoccupied with matters of state, as I have been over the past few weeks. When I am thus occupied, I will not have the freedom in which to pay as much attention to you as you might wish. It is a great honor for me to rule the city my father once held. I intend to repair the damage the Guidi family has done to Aullia, and then to preserve the city in peace and prosperity for our children and grandchildren. More, I want the descendants of the ordinary citizens of Aullia to inherit peace and a chance for a decent life. My preoccupation with these concerns will not mean that I do not love you. I will require your understanding, Rosalinda. And your help, for I cannot do it alone."

"I will have to live in a city," Rosalinda said, sighing.

"Aullia is closer to the mountains than Monteferro is," Andrea said. "From the duke's private suite of rooms, there is a wide view of the same mountains you see from Villa Serenita. Of course, from Aullia, you will look at the other side of those mountains."

"That might be an interesting change," Rosalinda said. Then, more cheerfully, "Bianca told me there is a large garden surrounding the palace."

"It's more like a wild park, certainly not as carefully tended as the ducal gardens at Monteferro. But then, the entire court at Aullia is much less formal than the court at Monteferro. You may do as you like with the garden," he promised.

"I shall have to call on my mother for help," she murmured with a mischievous glance at him.

"I was afraid of that. Ah, well, perhaps if Eleonora visits us, so will Francesco."

"I wouldn't be at all surprised." Rosalinda sobered, thinking. "Our children," she said, very softly.

"Our *legal* children, my love. It does appear that you are compelled to marry me for their sake."

"I suppose so." Again she sighed.

"As soon as possible, Rosalinda." Andrea could not tell from her manner whether she was pleased or unhappy at his insistence. He decided to continue to be firm with her, while he instructed her in exactly what he would expect from his duchess. But before he could begin his lecture, she caught his hand and pressed it down hard on her abdomen.

"Do you feel it?" she asked. "There it is again. The baby is moving."

"I feel it." Stern intentions forgotten, Andrea stared, awe-stricken, at the place his hand was covering. Tears prickled at his eyelids. He did not care if he wept. The life beneath his hand was a miracle forged out of love. And suddenly it no longer mattered to him whether Rosalinda was a perfect duchess or not, so long as she was *his* Rosalinda, wild and tender and loving, the kind of woman who would rescue a bear from a snowstorm and give the frozen creature shelter. But he did harbor a new fear.

"Do you think I hurt him, before?" Andrea whispered.

"I cannot think love will ever hurt a child," Rosalinda answered. "Andrea, do you remember Ginevra, Giuseppe's wife? They have two children, and she is having another at Christmas, near to the same time when our child will be born. Well, Ginevra told me one day that Guiseppe makes love to her regularly until just a few weeks before their babies are born, and she claims to have the easiest births and the healthiest babies of any woman here at the villa.

"So you see, Andrea, you will have to make love to me again if you want a healthy son for your heir." Reaching out to him she touched him with a delicately searching fingertip. "I do wish you would remove your clothes."

"Rosalinda, promise me you will remain always at my side. I need you." As he spoke, Andrea hastened to obey her command.

"Only for this?" Having torn off her own clothing while Andrea was occupied with his garments, Rosalinda pressed herself against him, savoring his warmth.

"For this, yes." His hand slid downward, searching between their bodies. "For all you can teach me about love. And for your support and advice. I cannot rule alone, my love, and you are the one person I can trust completely."

"There is always Francesco." Rosalinda sighed in pleasure and arched her back. Andrea's questing fingers located the spot that ached to feel his touch.

"Francesco lacks your charms," Andrea murmured, letting his fingertips stray into heated, sensitive flesh. "And, at the moment, he has other interests to pursue. Forget Francesco."

"*Andrea.*" Rosalinda shivered and moaned, her whole body convulsing. Obeying her love, she forgot everything but the sweet sensation of Andrea's possession of her in a wild eruption of passion.

"What other interests does Francesco have?" Rosalinda asked much later, when she could think and speak again.

"Your mother," Andrea said. The setting sun beaming in the window showed her the twinkle in his dark eyes when he lifted his head from her breasts to see her reaction.

"Oh, that," she said, to tease him. "Bianca and I have known about Francesco's interest for months. I do hope Mother decides to marry him. I wouldn't want her involved in a scandal."

"Speaking of marrying," Andrea said, smothering the laughter that threatened to interfere with a serious statement, "first thing tomorrow I will send Lorenzo for Father Tomaso. While he is gone, you and I will write out our marriage contract together. As soon as the priest gets here to bless our arrangement, we will marry. I am certain your family will understand our haste."

"Poor Father Tomaso," Rosalinda said with an exaggerated sigh. "We will wear out that sweet old man with our frequent summons to Villa Serenita."

"Does that mocking comment indicate the end of your resistance to my proposal?" Andrea asked. "Have I finally succeeded in convincing you that I love you?"

"Well, as to that, my lord duke, you know how uncertain I have always been of your true feelings," Rosalinda said. With a sly smile, she added, "I fear the only way for you to prevent future doubts on my part is by telling me several times a day that you love me with a great passion, and then by proving it each night."

"It will be my pleasure, madonna." He nipped playfully at her ear. "So that you will never misunderstand me again, I do solemnly promise that, however busy I may be with affairs of state, I will find time to tell you every day and show you each night that I love you completely and forever."

"Even when you are old and decrepit, my lord duke?" she asked with great seriousness.

"Even then, I will find a way." His eyes gleamed in the golden late afternoon light. "I promise you, Rosalinda, I'll find a way to keep you happy. I am the Duke of Aullia. I can do anything."

"Do you think we will quarrel much?" she asked.

"Probably," he answered, gazing at her with love and rising warmth.

"I will never run away from you again," she said.

"And I will never again keep secrets from you," he whispered.

"I love you, Andrea."

"I know." His mouth touched hers lightly. "I've known it all along."

Epilogue

"Andrea, are you sure this is where you want the bearskin to stay?" Eleonora asked.

"I can think of no better place for it," Andrea said. "Have you any objection?"

"No, not really." Eleonora pursed her lips, studying the bearskin. "I am only surprised to learn you do not intend to take it to Aullia when you and Rosalinda return there."

They were in the sitting room at Villa Serenita and Bartolomeo had just spread out the bearskin in front of the hearth. Shortly after Andrea's first appearance at the villa, Bartolomeo had turned the bearskin over to one of the men-at-arms, whose favorite occupation was hunting. For lack of anyone else at the villa who was able to do such work, the man-at-arms had made himself an expert at curing and preparing animal skins. Thanks to his efforts, the once stiff and smelly pelt that

Andrea had worn while a fugitive was now a rug with soft, shiny fur.

"It was in this room, before this very hearth, that I first relinquished my disguise as a bear and became a man again," Andrea said. "Bartolomeo, I thank you for the gift of this rug." Andrea clasped hands with the faithful Bartolomeo, who then excused himself and departed the sitting room to find Valeria.

"With your permission, Madonna Eleonora, I will also ask you to excuse me," Andrea said. "Rosalinda should have young Federigo put to bed by now, and I find that I am also in need of a midday nap. Fatherhood can be tiring."

"A nap. How discreet you are." Noting that Andrea did not look the least bit tired, Eleonora repressed a smile. She had smiled a great deal in recent months, and had laughed more often than she could remember doing since she was a girl. It was lovely to be so lighthearted and free. She supposed some of her newfound joy had to do with the realization of all her hopes and dreams for her daughters, but there was also the unexpected delight she found in the infant grandson whom Rosalinda and Andrea had produced on the previous Christmas Eve, and in anticipation of a second grandchild from Bianca and Vanni in the coming autumn. There was a third, more intimate reason for Eleonora's happiness and it awaited her, rather impatiently, on the terrace.

"Do not let me keep you from your bed, Andrea," Eleonora said to her son-in-law. "You will want to be alert and rested when your brother arrives later today. Bianca did say they would be here before sunset."

"Ah, Madonna Eleonora, from the very first you have always understood me." Andrea kissed her on the cheek before he strode out of the sitting room.

He was scarcely gone before Francesco poked his head through the open doorway to the terrace and leered at Eleonora.

"Are we alone at last?" Francesco asked.

"For a little while." Eleonora left the sitting room to join her husband.

It was a warm and sunny mid-June day, and the rosebushes were in full bloom. Eleonora stood at the top of the steps to the garden, breathing in the soft, delicate fragrance of the white roses and the rich, sensual perfume of the red roses. It was a heady combination. When Francesco came up behind her and wrapped his arms around her waist, Eleonora felt positively dizzy with delight.

"Perhaps we should retire for a nap ourselves, before the ducal retinue from Monteferro appears," Francesco suggested.

"What a lecherous old man you have turned out to be." Eleonora leaned back against her husband's broad chest.

"Did no one warn you about aging condottieri before you married me?" Francesco teased. He turned Eleonora around to face him and his blue eyes were twinkling. "I must confess, madonna, that no one told me about the lecherous interests of dowager duchesses, either."

"You are a truly wicked man, Francesco." Eleonora caught her breath just as his mouth met hers.

"Bianca and Vanni won't stay long," Eleonora remarked when Francesco finally released her from a long and heated kiss. "The next heir to Monteferro must be born in the city, and Vanni won't want to subject Bianca to a homeward journey too near her time."

"I smell a plan in the air," Francesco said. "A plan

that will remove us from this peaceful villa and force us to Monteferro by early September.''

''Will you mind very much?''

''Not if we can return here before winter comes.'' Francesco lifted his gaze to the mountains and the blue, blue sky. A happy expression softened the craggy contours of his face. ''This place is home to me now, Eleonora. Every day I thank your father for building Villa Serenita and for giving it to you. However, there is one change I would like to make.''

''Oh?'' Eleonora's voice took on a slight edge at the suggestion that Villa Serenita was not perfect. ''What change is that, Francesco?''

''Just a small improvement to the garden.'' With an amused tilt to his mouth, Francesco considered the herbs and the flowers and the little pool with the Florentine iris growing at its edge.

''What is wrong with my garden?'' Eleonora demanded.

''Nothing is wrong. I merely wish to make an addition, in honor of you and of our most improbable, but altogether wonderful, love.'' Francesco pointed to a sunny corner. ''There, I think, would be the ideal spot. We will put a bench just in front of it, so we can sit while we enjoy the spicy fragrance and the view of villa and mountains.''

''A bench in front of what?'' Eleonora pushed herself out of Francesco's arms to stand facing him with fists planted on her hips. ''I will not allow you to alter my garden. I have worked long and hard on it—''

''This garden needs another rosebush,'' Francesco interrupted her. ''You have planted a white rose for Bianca, and a red rose for Rosalinda, but where is a bush for you?''

''For me?'' Eleonora said, looking thoroughly astonished. "I never thought of such a thing."

"Then, it's time you did. I envision a rose with flowers as pink as your cheeks when your anger is aroused—or your desire," he said, kissing one of those cheeks, which was glowing with a distinctly rosy tinge. "Furthermore, the bush planted in your honor will produce a bloom with petals as soft as your lips and a scent as tantalizing and spicy as your embrace. This lovely rose will, of course, be cursed with thorns, but they will only make the blossoms it bears seem all the sweeter once they are successfuly plucked."

"A soldier, and a poet, too," Eleonora murmured, returning to his embrace. "You are quite right, Francesco, my dear. We do need another rosebush."

"I am glad you approve of my plan, because Vanni and Bianca are bringing the very bush with them today."

Francesco kissed her quickly, before Eleonora could protest this announcement, which clearly indicated that he had made up his mind about the change to her garden before discussing it with her. After a moment, Eleonora ceased her efforts to get free of his embrace so she could argue the point with him. Instead, she gave herself up to the pleasure she always found in Francesco's kisses. It was some time before she could speak again.

"We will plant the new rosebush together," she said, "but I will tell you exactly where to place it, and I will decide where that bench you mentioned should be."

"Of course, my love. Whatever you want," Francesco murmured, and bent his head to kiss her again.

BESTSELLING AUTHOR OF *LONGER THAN FOREVER!*

FOUR WEDDINGS AND A FAIRY GODMOTHER

Only a storybook affair like the marriage of Cindy Ella Jones and Princeton Chalmers could lead to three such tangled romances—and happily ever after endings:

BELINDA

Kidnapped from the wedding party, the lonely beauty will learn how a little love can tame a wild beast—even one as intimidating as Cain Dezlin, the handsome recluse.

LILITH

Thrown together with Frank Henson, a seemingly soft-spoken security guard, self-absorbed Lilith will have to learn that with love and respect, there's a prince waiting behind every toad.

ROBERTA

The shy redhead's heart has been broken by a wicked wolf once before—and now that Maximilian Wolfe has shown up at the wedding she is determined to get to her grandmother's before the big bad Frenchman can hurt her again.

Connie Mason

"Each new Connie Mason book is a prize!"
—Heather Graham

Spirits can be so bloody unpredictable, and the specter of Lady Amelia is the worst of all. Just when one of her ne'er-do-well descendents thought he could go astray in peace, the phantom lady always appears to change his wicked ways.

A rogue without peer, Jackson Graystoke wants to make gaming and carousing in London society his life's work. And the penniless baronet would gladly curse himself with wine and women—if Lady Amelia would give him a ghost of a chance.

Fresh off the boat from Ireland, Moira O'Toole isn't fool enough to believe in legends or naive enough to trust a rake. Yet after an accident lands her in Graystoke Manor, she finds herself haunted, harried, and hopelessly charmed by Black Jack Graystoke and his exquisite promise of pure temptation.

_4041-7 $5.99 US/$6.99 CAN

Dorchester Publishing Co., Inc.
65 Commerce Road
Stamford, CT 06902

Please add $1.75 for shipping and handling for the first book and $.50 for each book thereafter. NY, NYC, PA and CT residents, please add appropriate sales tax. No cash, stamps, or C.O.D.s. All orders shipped within 6 weeks via postal service book rate. Canadian orders require $2.00 extra postage and must be paid in U.S. dollars through a U.S. banking facility.

Name____
Address______________________________________
City ________________________ State______ Zip______
I have enclosed $______ in payment for the checked book(s).
Payment <u>must</u> accompany all orders. ☐ Please send a free catalog.